THE WHITE OCEAN

THE GLACIAL ISLANDS

Heraldia

CRAKLAND

BRACH

BRUNTLAND

Umber

ROUGE

CRESCENCIA

VIOLINIA

SOLIDO

EXANICA

THE CEASELESS OCEAN

AQUARIA

ALSO BY DENNIS MAHONEY

Fellow Mortals

BELL
WEATHER

BELL
WEATHER

A Novel

DENNIS
MAHONEY

HENRY HOLT AND COMPANY   NEW YORK

Henry Holt and Company, LLC
Publishers since 1866
175 Fifth Avenue
New York, New York 10010
www.henryholt.com

Henry Holt® and ® are registered trademarks of
Henry Holt and Company, LLC.

Library of Congress Cataloging-in-Publication Data

Mahoney, Dennis, 1974–
    Bell weather : a novel / Dennis Mahoney.—First edition.
        pages cm
    ISBN 978-1-62779-267-7 (hardcover)—ISBN 978-1-62779-268-4 (electronic book)
    I. Title.
    PS3613.A3493355B46 2015
    813'.6—dc23

                                                                    2014030008

Henry Holt books are available for special promotions and premiums.
For details contact: Director, Special Markets.

First Edition 2015

Designed by Meryl Sussman Levavi

Maps by Melissa Batalin

Printed in the United States of America

3   5   7   9   10   8   6   4   2

For Coley, Jack, and Bones

BELL
WEATHER

Chapter One

Lush spring made amends for Root's monstrous winters and remoteness in the forest, but the snowmelt, mud, and early-season flux left the town unstable, prone to floods and violent storms.

It was daybreak. The heavy fog had just begun to brighten, and the blurry trees and hills cupped the narrow valley like a pair of giant hands enclosing something fragile. Tom Orange stood with his horse, two miles north of town, and saw a woman in the middle of the riotous Antler River. He was tired and he hadn't drunk his morning cup of smoak, so when the dull floral pattern of her gown caught his eye he disregarded it at first, assuming it was blossoms. Only blossoms on a huge, twisted branch—not a body. Not a thing worth saving in the wreckage of the flood.

Tom removed his tricorne, tightened up the ribbon in his ponytailed hair, and put his hat back on before the mist wet his scalp. Every spring the river surged with swirling flowers. White petals, black centers—they were minuscule and stemless and appeared in quick profusion, well before any known plants began to bloom. The river undulated white like a meadow made of foam. Some of the townspeople said they floated from the Wolf Mountains in the north. Others thought they blossomed at the bottom of the river and emerged when the potent spring current stirred them up.

Tom viewed the flowers as just another element of home, and yet this morning he had ridden down the length of Root's border, following the river and surveying its engorgement. Only once in old Nabby's antediluvian memory had the water risen high enough to overwhelm the town, but there was always that threat and nobody in Root, least of all Tom, dropped their vigilance with so much danger roaring past. Not to mention all the people who would question him in the tavern: Had the river drowned the wharf? Had it swamped Murk's Farm? It was easier to know when he was serving them a cider, easier to ride out and see it for himself.

Bones shifted hooves and snorted in the mist. He was a gangly, crooked horse who appeared malnourished, though he moved with graceful confidence and ate without reserve. Tom had found him last summer in the graveyard, standing with a crestfallen slouch beneath a tree, as if his owner had abandoned him but might reappear. It was said that people who perished in the wilderness, alone and far from home, walked as spirits to the town in search of others like themselves. There were numerous haunts in Root—the tavern had a child ghost, according to the cook—and Tom suspected Bones's owner had died in the forest, led the horse to the graveyard, and silently departed. That or providence, he thought. Either way, they'd quickly bonded.

Moments earlier, the two had shared a ripple of the flesh—a question in the fog, an instinctual anxiety—and Tom had dismounted Bones to see what he could find.

Dawn spread vermilion in the low-slung clouds. Looking harder at the branch he had earlier dismissed, he was puzzled by the different sort of flowers in the tangle. They were larger than the others, dark blue and dirty rose. Tom's boot began to slide very slowly in the mud. Not blossoms, he decided. They were flowers on a gown. Then he saw her all at once: a woman, maybe dead, her upper half held above the water by the branch.

He slipped and spun around, clutching at the grass and muddying his coat. The river nearly got him but he bellied up the bank. He mounted Bones, who cantered away before Tom was fully balanced on the saddle, and they raced along the riverside in something near to silence—just the hooves' boggy suction and the rumble of the flood.

They hurried south toward the town two miles off, where the ferry rope stretched bank to bank above the river. It was his only chance of catching her and holding her in place before the water swept her off to Dunderakwa Falls.

Every breath seemed to blow directly into his heart, billowing his chest and flushing through his veins. They were riding so fast, his hat blew away. The old bullet in his shoulder ground against bone. He squinted left and saw the branch still carrying the body. Then he lost it in the mist. They were barely keeping up.

Where the river met the mouth of Dampmill Creek, the flood spilled wide across an acre's worth of grassland. Tom, so preoccupied with following the woman, spurred Bones onward into the new-made marsh as if expecting that the flowers were indeed solid ground. Bones splashed in and waded to his chest. They struggled through the mire to the high, firmer ground, up a slope lined with birches to a thin, bare ridge. There the ground turned hard but they were suddenly befogged, suicidal as they galloped in their blindness on the path.

Now the river was invisible below them to the left. They would storm downhill and locate the wharf, where the fishing road began and they could ride along the bank again. Tom yanked the reins and Bones made his turn. Then the horse stopped short and Tom left the saddle. He was thrown along the horse's neck and landed on the ground near a tight stand of pines Bones had halted to avoid. His wrist folded back and streaked fire up his arm. He saw his own broken nose, weirdly crooked through his tears, and sniffed until the blood dribbled down his throat.

"Ruddy fucking trees!" he said, wiping off his eyes.

He was lacquered head to boot with slick black mud, but then he was up and riding Bones again, weaving downhill until the pines thinned away and he could finally see the wharf. They continued at a breakneck pitch, Bones rearing back to keep from tumbling over, Tom's straight legs rigid in the stirrups. The wharf was underwater but beside it, in the current, was a small rocky mound like a miniature island.

Silas Booker stood upon it, fishing with a gaff. He wore a smock and heavy boots and had a long, sturdy basket full of murkfins behind him. The river roared along, spewing up oceanlike and menacing around him. Petals from the spray were clinging to his hair, and he was so intent on balancing and managing his gaff that he didn't hear Bones approaching from behind.

Tom dismounted, jumping over the bank-side water to the mound. Rain came upon them. Giant drops began to fall and it was dismal, like a sinister undoing of the dawn. When Silas hooked a murkfin and turned to put it down, he yelped at the sight of Tom's figure in the gloom, still dirty from the fall, like a man made of mud. Silas backed away, slipping on the flowers till he very nearly fell and tumbled off the mound. Tom caught his belt.

"Silas, look at me. It's Tom!"

Just beyond them in the river went the woman on the branch. Silas took a breath and laughed through his beard.

"Hell's britches! I thought you was the Colorless Man—"

"I need your gaff," Tom said, snatching it away. He shook the murkfin loose but missed the open basket. It was a fish with poison hairs and short slimy legs, serpentine and bleeding and contorting round his heel. Tom kicked it into the water, where it vanished with a slap and left a clump of flower heads bloody in the foam.

"Damnation!" Silas said, more dismayed than angry, grabbing back the pole and holding on tight.

"Give me the gaff," Tom said, pulling it toward him.

Silas, though a coward, was prodigiously endowed. He was ripe and wetly grizzled, his hard-worked knuckles whitening and split, and he would sooner fight a friend than lose his precious gaff. He said, "You know they only surface half a week every spring—"

"There's a woman—" Tom began.

"—and that's a two-shilling fish you cost me," Silas said, too focused on his loss to heed Tom's words.

They wobbled back and forth with the pole between their chests. Murkfin blood dribbled to their hands. For a second through the rain, Tom could see the woman clearly—long black hair, raggedy and wet, contrasted with the spring-cold pallor of her skin. She was young, not a girl but scarcely into womanhood. Her eyes were closed. Her mouth hung ajar. She was beautiful and deathlike, elegant as silk, yet her grip upon the branch looked desperately alive.

Tom had never wanted to hold a woman more in all his life, and he considered diving in and swimming to her side. But he wouldn't get her out unless he had the hook, and she was vanishing again, speeding out of reach.

Tom released the pole and Silas staggered back, smiling with the prize until the rain made him blink. In the moment of distraction, Tom socked him in the gut. The pole clattered down and Tom picked it up, squinting from the pain—he had punched, like a dolt, with his newly sprained hand—and then he leapt off the mound and ran back to Bones, listening to Silas swearing in the spume.

"I owe you two shillings!" Tom yelled, racing off.

He galloped with the pole before him like a lance, trusting Bones to lead the way while he scanned the widening river, having lost her once again. He felt a tug upon his chest as if a rope, pulled taut, were knotted to his breastbone. His nose had swollen badly. It was difficult to breathe. Fog massed heavy just above the water but the sun had started burning off the layers in the east, leaving thin misty tendrils in the bright gold bloom.

Ahead stood the Orange, Tom's weatherworn tavern, cozy and reliable and glowing in the light. It was stout and double-chimneyed, on a hill near the river, safely distanced from the flood and higher than the ferry. To the right lay the town, a quarter-mile square of small, huddled houses that were bounded by the farms, and the forest, and the river. The meetinghouse steeple poked above the fog. There were lights in many dwellings—it was a town of early risers—but he couldn't see a single man or woman on the streets.

Tom halted Bones and ran toward the water, carrying the gaff and hollering for Ichabod, the ferryman and servingman who boarded at the tavern. He tugged off his boots and felt the chill through his stockings, but it was nothing to the shock of frigid water when he dove.

He broke through the flowers with a splash. Cold struck him like a great set of hammers tipped with needles, thudding but precise, bewildering his mind. The current was astonishingly strong below the surface and it tried to pull him under more than carry him along. He struggled with the gaff, swimming mostly with his legs, and fought to reach the middle of the river at an angle, gasping hard and stiffening up and looking for the woman.

From the shore, the flowers had seemed to form a smooth, gentle surface, but in fact they clumped and bobbed, often rising over his head. They made it hard to recognize the whirlpools and waves. He was battered more than once by unseen debris, and even floating backward with an unobstructed view, he couldn't spot the branch and worried it had passed.

He drifted to the ferry line: a thick twist of rope, suspended over the water, that extended bank to bank from columns on the docks. He floated underneath it, raised the gaff, and hooked the rope. The jerk was so strong, he almost lost his grip. The current forced him several extra feet beyond the line and there he dangled as the floodwaters surged up against him.

His breaths came in quick, light snatches at the air. His legs were numb, his wrist sprain a growing streak of flame. There were flowers in his eyes and petals in his mouth, sickly sweet and slippery when he tried to spit them out. Seven miles downriver lay the Dunderakwa Falls, and if he missed her—curse Silas and his God-rotting murkfins!—nothing but a miracle would pull her from her doom.

He finally saw the branch upriver, dead ahead. It was bigger than he'd realized, dangerously splayed like a wide black claw and coming fast, very fast. He hopped the hook along the line, half paralyzed with cold and moving to the side so as not to be impaled. There'd be one brief chance to get her off the branch. Here it came—he could see the little flowers on her gown, the whiteness of her scalp along the parting of her hair.

A limb beneath the surface cracked him in the ribs. The blow knocked him sideways, fully out of reach, and only fury at the pain allowed him to recover. With a wild bolt of energy, he grabbed her by the armpit, holding one-fisted to the handle of the gaff. The branch continued on, tearing at her gown. She was limp and almost naked when he pulled her free and clear.

The flowers swarmed around them, covering their heads, until his panic spiraled up to something like euphoria. Her body pressed against him, cold as any corpse. She was facing him and buoyant with her head lolling back, hair floating to his chin, breasts rising from her gown. Her slightly open mouth was her captivating feature—what a thing it would have been to see her take a breath.

The woman belched a lungful of water in his face.

She coughed herself awake and looked at him, amazed, as if confused to find the branch was suddenly a man. She squeezed him around the middle, murdering his ribs.

"Don't let go," he said.

She clutched him even harder in surprise, legs around his hips, hands fastened to his back. Her irises were dark—he couldn't see her pupils—and she seemed about to talk but coughed herself delirious. He realized only now, having caught her in his arms, that he didn't have the strength to get her to the bank. He would barely save himself if he tried swimming back and so they held each other close, stranded in the flood.

He couldn't hear a thing except the noise of rushing water, and he couldn't feel his hands or verify his grip. Any moment they'd be loose and headed for the falls. He looked at her with false reassurance to console her. Once he did—once she stared at him and seemed to understand—he knew for certain, falls be damned, he would hold her to the end.

A long wooden pole cracked him on the noggin. When he turned to see its source, it struck him on the nose. He bled again and blinked, smarting from the blows, and there was Ichabod the ferryman at last, right beside them.

He was balanced on the tethered raft, lanky and disheveled, reaching with his driving pole and almost falling in. The raft was broad and strong, railed on either side and stable enough for horses, made of planks atop a sturdy pair of dugout canoes. Ichabod was sweating from his fight against the current. He was a lifelong mute and now he spoke with his expressions, subtle changes in his close-set eyes and bony jaw that Tom interpreted to mean, "Grab the pole. Only choice. Any closer and I'll knock you underwater with the raft."

He was right. The raft was bobbing too erratically to trust. Tom dropped the gaff and lunged to get the ferry pole. He caught it but the woman's limp weight pulled him down. She was fading out of consciousness and dragging on his neck and Ichabod, though wiry strong, could barely keep his footing. Tom inched along, hand over hand. The woman started slipping underwater through his arms.

"Grab her hair," Tom yelled, finally at the raft.

Ichabod wove his bony fingers to her roots and kept her head above water, high enough to breathe. Tom hauled himself up and didn't let her go, aching from his injuries and growling like a winterbear. They pulled her up together to the safety of the deck. Ichabod removed his shirt and handed it to Tom, who wrapped her up and held her, cradling her head. They shuddered close together in the cold, misty breeze. She had flowers on her throat and petals in her ears.

He wrung the water from her hair and rubbed her shivery skin, summoning whatever faint warmth she had left, his swollen nose and broken ribs and reasonable questions overpowered by the wonder of beholding her alive.

Chapter Two

"Hours in the dark catching murkfins and you come along, steal my gaff, and catch a woman."

Silas Booker, smiling broadly at the curious passersby, stood in the mud of Center Street and blocked Tom's way. He wore the same fishy breeches he'd been wearing at the river—possibly the only pair of breeches Silas owned. The season's first horseflies twirled around his legs. Townspeople noticed Tom and Silas in the road; they were active with the business of a fair-weather morning—airing houses, running errands, trading for supplies—but they had all heard the story of the rescue in the flood.

"I'd gripe again about that bellywallop," Silas said loudly, "but there isn't any question that you went and took the brunt."

No, there wasn't, Tom agreed. He had a bandage on his wrist, a wrap around his rib cage, and grape-and-ash bruises underneath his eyes. The river chill had left him feeling feverish and brittle. His fatigue had only deepened from the necessary tavern work, especially now in spring when travelers braved the road again, no longer hindered by the valley's great snows.

They would soon arrive from Grayport, seventy miles southwest, or from Liberty, a hundred-odd miles northeast. Root was in the middle of the wilderness between—four hundred people in profound isolation with the river up the side and the forest all around them: a miniature town with a small, common green and farmland radiating outward from the center. If not for the road that linked the cities, they would likely be forgotten. As it was, they almost were. There were safer routes between Grayport and Liberty but none were so direct in the drier, warmer seasons. Swamps and gorges riddled the south; the northern passages were safer but a good deal longer. Several days could be recovered by the wilder way through Root, which made it a popular road for mail and urgent trips between the colony's two major settlements.

Soon the year's first travelers would emerge from the forest, and the Orange would be busy straight through to the frigid season of deadfall. With beer to brew, stores to fill, and countless daily chores, nothing would have prompted Tom to venture from the tavern but a summons to meet the woman he had rescued from the flood.

Her identity was fodder for a host of shifting rumors. She had been called a woman and a child, golden-haired and dark, destitute and wealthy. She was said to have floated from the distant northern mountains or emerged like the murkfins from underneath the river. There were rumors she might be a victim of the Kraw—a fierce tribe of women so bonded to the forest, they were said to be part of the flora, only semihuman—but the Kraw had not been seen around the valley since the war.

Her name was Mary, Martha, Dolly, Georgiana, or Elizabeth, and her death had been assumed with somber regularity as no additional news of her condition came to light. She had been kept in the care of Dr. Benjamin Knox and his wife, Abigail, since the hour of her rescue. After prohibiting visitors for the first two days, Benjamin had summoned his friend from the tavern that morning, and Tom had done his best to look respectable in polished buckle shoes, a fresh shirt and coat, and a tricorne as crisp as Silas's was limp. Tom never wore a wig— few in Root saw the need—and he kept his shoulder-length hair tied behind him with a ribbon. It was a perfect white ribbon from his younger cousin Bess, who had embarrassed him with smiles over the effort he was making.

"Now you're dandy as a jay," Silas said, and grinned. "Off to see her, I expect, and claim her as a prize."

"God damn it, no I ain't. You're as frivolous as Bess. I didn't save her life to warm my ruddy bed."

"She's better than a murkfin," Silas said sincerely. "People seem to think—"

His words were interrupted by a passing group of sawyers, one of whom complimented Tom's shiny buckles.

As owner of the tavern, Tom was wed to the community, and everyone in Root presumed to know his business. He was popular and didn't spurn the neighborly regard, but at the age of twenty-seven, he was tired of attention—for his valor in the war, for the scandal of his father—and now, in a year when public interest seemed finally on the wane, here was Silas spreading gossip that would set the town talking.

"He's off to see her now!" Silas hollered out, turning heads and sending Tom, hot as smoakwood, on his way.

He walked toward the Knoxes' house, avoiding people's faces to discourage any questions but intuiting—he felt it in their overlong stares—that they suspected he was going forth to meet his future wife. The sun at his back lit the houses he approached, but the unlit sides were shadowy and grim, caked with old snow the morning couldn't reach. Winter hung tough in spite of warmer air, yet the town's growing bustle had the energy of spring and the walk began to soften Tom's hard-packed spirit, which had seemed for many weeks impossible to thaw.

The Knoxes' modest house stood at the corner of the green. He had begun to cross the road when a sunshower fell, altering the hues of everything in sight. There were marmalade sheep grazing in the common, indigo trees, houses rippling blue. The air looked alive with shimmering gold and green, touched with spectral colors difficult to name. The colorwash was another of the town's native marvels. Tom felt as if a rainbow were pouring down around him, filling him with hopes he didn't quite believe.

The shower had ended by the time he reached the Knoxes' door, and it was only when he knocked and felt the water in his stockings that he realized just how bedraggled he'd become.

Abigail Knox opened up to let him in. She was a devout Lumenist whose faith coexisted with unembroidered fact, and she composed herself and dressed in rigorous accordance. Her frame was sharp and lean—the most Tom had ever seen her eat was half a dinner—and she covered herself completely in an ankle-length gown, bed jacket, ruffled cap, and, according to rumor, two layers of underclothes regardless of the season. Children ceased laughing in her presence, dogs cowered when they saw her in the street, and however much anyone disagreed with her in secret, no one saw the need to openly defy her.

"If you had come on time, you might have avoided the rain and kept yourself presentable."

"I didn't see a cloud."

"Or a clock," Abigail said. "At least you were invited. Do you know how many busybodies have come to the door in the last two days?"

"I'd imagine—"

"Twenty-nine, and those were only the ones who had the impudence to knock. Everywhere I go, they want to know the *news,* and everyone who comes receives the same answer: show me blood or broken bones or you have no Lumenous reason to be muddying the steps. My husband is a doctor, not a storyteller. There, they're looking now. Come inside before they think it's open house. And wipe your shoes. You should have worn boots." She pulled him inside, closed the door, and said, "Sheriff Pitt is here."

In any other household, Tom would have cursed.

"He thinks incessant questioning will finally win the day," she said. "Never mind that our enigma has yet to speak a word in self-defense."

"Defense of what?"

"Now you're talking like Pitt," Abigail replied, knowing the comparison would rankle Tom to silence.

She walked upstairs, expecting him to follow. Tom wiped his feet and wished he hadn't come, but by the time they reached the top and turned the corner into the hall, his curiosity was greater than his private reservations. They entered a small, bright room crowded with a bed, a night table, a chest of drawers, and one spindly chair that nobody was using. The bed faced the hall, but with the sunlight glaring after the darkness of the staircase, Benjamin leaning over his patient, and Abigail pausing just inside the door, all Tom could see was Sheriff James Pitt. He stood in his scarlet coat and yak-hair wig, skinny-legged but mutton-faced, as if whatever he ate and drank congealed above his neck. His wee protruding eyes were ardently suspicious but betrayed a constant panic that they might, at any moment, spot an actual offense.

"Out!" Pitt said.

He was a baritone who often tried speaking as a bass. Tom grinned wide and stepped inside the room. Before he knew it, Pitt's palm was firmly on his chest, pressing on his broken ribs and holding him at bay.

"Tom," Benjamin said, turning from the bed and smiling at his friend.

Pitt dropped his hand but didn't move aside.

Abigail inserted herself between them with a frown. She might have sighed if any part of her was ever less than rigid. "The two of you are worse than unbreeched children."

The Knoxes were childless after fifteen years of marriage, had never been known to kiss or embrace, and were generally viewed as siblings: sharply unalike but unmistakably related. Crueler whispers in the town called their childlessness proof of God's mercy, sparing unborn souls from such a bitter-apple mother. Benjamin, a popular man, was pitied for his lot, and yet he generally seemed content and wasn't given to complaint.

"I'm sorry, Abigail," Pitt said, "but I won't be interrupted in the middle of my questions."

"Saints support us, are you only at the middle?" she replied.

"Tom is always welcome," Benjamin said to Pitt, sounding as if the tension were a slight misunderstanding. He was a short and slender man of thirty-nine years, gentle as a fawn, gray in every hair, delicate of movement and possessing a voice best suited to a bedside. A calm exterior disguised his boundless energy and thought.

"Furthermore," Benjamin continued, "I invited Tom myself, and as the doctor of my patient and the head of the household"—Abigail raised her eyebrows—"I assure you that his presence is not primarily social, nor secondarily a matter of good form, given that he saved her, but rather tertiarily—or chiefly, I should say—a stroke of opportunity in both of our endeavors."

Pitt stood inert.

"What?" Tom said.

"Meet Molly," Benjamin told him, standing aside so Tom could see her.

She sat in bed with her legs beneath a quilt, supported by pillows, clean and alert and remarkably intact. Tom had a high opinion of his friend's abilities—Benjamin had treated nearly everyone in town at one time or another, and commonly saved his patients' lives in all but the most egregious cases—but Molly's good condition bordered on miraculous.

She was pretty in a weird, rather homely sort of way. Her hair was long and black, partly matted, partly tousled. She had slightly gapped teeth. Her eyes were out of alignment, one noticeably higher, and rounder, and darker than the other, so she looked half grieved, half luminous with wonder. Her expression, most engagingly, was volatile and ripe, as if she wanted to embrace him, fall to tears, or both at once.

It was strange to meet her again surrounded by the others, to be watched so intently while they shared a private look, one as wordless and profound as when he had held her in the water.

"Thank you," Molly said.

"It's good to see you dry."

She smiled with a twitch and rubbed her fingers on the quilt.

"You recognize Tom?" Abigail asked.

"Yes," Molly said.

"Excellent!" Benjamin cried without actually raising his voice. He turned to Tom and said, "I hoped if she remembered you, we might construct a memory bridge and cross the floodwaters, so to speak, to other recollections of her history and identity."

"You don't remember what happened?" Tom asked.

"She doesn't remember anything," Abigail said curtly, "aside from you and her name."

"Molly," Tom said, just to try it out.

She stared at him and froze as if afraid he didn't trust her.

"And what is your last name again?" Abigail asked. "It's hard to keep it pinned."

"Smith," Molly mumbled.

"Yes, *Smith.* And yet I'm sure you gave a different name the first time we asked."

"We've covered that," Pitt said, clinging to the fact, regardless of its truth, and glowering at Tom as if his visit were undoing even this one precarious clue.

The room was close and humid after the quick dose of rain. There was moisture on the window glass and sweat in Tom's clothes, and since it wasn't truly warm, it lingered like a fever chill, shallowing his breath and clouding up his thoughts. Molly touched a locket on a ribbon around her neck. He thought to ask her what it was—it might remind her of her past—but she hid it, growing flushed, when she saw what he was thinking.

"You don't remember anything at all?" Tom asked.

"Now and then," Abigail said, "she can't remember how to answer when she's spoken to."

"Enough, enough," Benjamin said, reassuring Molly with a light, avuncular pat. "I have been explaining to Abigail and Sheriff Pitt," he told Tom, "that certain traumas, such as drowning, knocks about the head, unconsciousness, exhaustion, and extremity of fear, to say nothing of certain phases of the moon, noxious plants, chronic malnutrition, and diseases of the brain—though I am confident in laying most of these aside—have been known to produce severe but often temporary amnesia. If we take into consideration—"

"Tom was knocked about the head," Abigail noted. "I believe he still remembers *his* last name."

Benjamin considered this but quickly disregarded it. "Now that Tom is here," he said, looking down at Molly, "does seeing him ignite a spark of recollection of the hours or the minutes that preceded your arrival? Perhaps by training your memory directly on the branch—"

Molly fidgeted discreetly, meeting Benjamin's look as if the memories might be there, written in the features of her doctor's kindly face.

"Describe your house," Pitt said, seeming to think authority was all they really needed. "Did you have your own room? A family or a husband?"

Molly sighed until she shrank and didn't breathe back in, looking down so her hair fell loose around her cheeks.

"Why don't you try something else?" Tom told Pitt.

"Like what?"

"Get on your horse and ask around. The Antler flows south, so chances are you ought to ride north. That's your left-hand side if you look toward the sun, but here's the complicated part: when the sun is going down—"

"I won't put up with this."

"You've already asked your questions," Tom said. "What are you still doing here?"

"What about you?" Pitt said, stepping forward. "All fopped up like a proper macaroni. Are you trying to impress the young lady, or puff your reputation so you sell more cider?"

"Mind your tongues," Abigail said, "or both of you can leave."

Tom unclenched his fists, aware, on loosening up, of how much pain he'd caused his sprained wrist. Pitt stood his ground, breathing boldly through his nose, as if he might arrest Tom for contempt of civic office.

"I apologize, Abigail," Tom said at last, feeling something like a rum burn rising in his chest. "But we ought to spread a net wider than the room."

Pitt crossed his arms. "Now apologize to me."

"I only want to help."

"Like your father?" Pitt replied.

It was all Tom could do not to throw him out the window.

"Root's hero has a deep black stain upon his name," Pitt said, speaking to Molly without the courtesy of facing her. "You might consider the facts of *his* storied past—"

"I don't care!" Molly said. "He saved my life. Let him be."

Pitt was startled to have pricked Molly's nerve instead of Tom's.

She shivered under the quilt and seemed about to swoon, lapsing forward on the bed and covering her face. She cried into her hands, surprising them anew.

Benjamin consoled her with a hand upon her back and looked to Abigail, speaking with the courteous authority of doctors. "Please show them out."

Neither man objected. Pitt left first, neither frowning at nor bumping into Tom when he passed. After Pitt and Abigail were gone, Tom took a final look at Molly—the poor thing had crumpled into sobs—and Benjamin said, "Wait for me downstairs."

Tom nodded and turned to go, relieved to hear the front door close behind Pitt but hollow, almost glum, to leave Molly there in tears. He met Abigail in the foyer. She gave him an unspoken censure for his part in the commotion and retired to the kitchen. Tom refused to pace but his thoughts roamed far, first to Pitt as a child, then to both their dead fathers, then to Molly's rush of color when she spoke in Tom's defense.

Benjamin joined him downstairs and led him outside. Abigail's hearing was alarmingly acute, and even on the street they kept their voices lowered.

"What do you know?" Tom asked.

"The brain is a fabulous organ," Benjamin said, "as capable of silence as of melody and storm. Oftentimes the lulls are more dramatic than the notes."

Tom paused as if to demonstrate his own dramatic lull, and after waiting a respectable length of time he asked again, "What do you know?"

Benjamin blinked behind his glasses, returning from abstraction to the muddy terra firma. "More than Pitt," he said. "Abigail is right: Molly remembers more than she admits, and I have gleaned several facts she believes are safely hidden. First and foremost—"

Benjamin's eyes were drawn away with an illuminated thrill.

"An upfall!" he said.

Tom looked to see the tall, swirling columns in the east. They were droplets being drawn from the river to the sky—upside-down rain resulting in a cloud that would swell until it drifted off, pregnant as a storm.

"There was a colorwash right before I got here," Tom said.

"I saw, I saw, but those are common. This is something else, something wonderful and rare. The flood," Benjamin said, grasping Tom's arm. "Is it rising or receding?"

"Going down," Tom said. "It was minor this year, barely crested—"

"The last recorded upfall was 1756, when the Antler swamped the creek and took the millwheel away. And now the Planter's Moon is Saturday night, and feel the eastern wind! Every weathercock turned! I dare say the river hasn't finished with its swell."

Benjamin checked his pocketwatch and memorized the time. Later he would note it in a thick black ledger, along with the temperature, barometric pressure, angle of the grass, and numerous other observations he was certain would lead to his ultimate deciphering of Root's climatological marvels. Tom was skeptical but smiled at his friend's high excitement. Before they could speak of it further, a red-haired boy sprinted up the road, splashing puddles on the way with devilish abandon.

It was Peter Ames, the youngest son of William the cabinetmaker, and he ran so fast toward Benjamin and Tom they had to catch him by the elbows before he skidded past.

"Easy," Tom said.

Peter slipped and fell. He stood without embarrassment and said with gleeful fear, "The Maimers is back! Another victim's just come; they took him to the Orange."

Benjamin slumped but steeled himself, sad and resolute. Tom hardened with a scowl, putting a hand too firmly on Peter's shoulder and frightening the boy with his expression.

"You're sure it's Maimers?"

Peter sniffed and nodded, scared of saying more.

Abigail appeared at the door with Benjamin's medical bag, her preternatural hearing having caught the brief exchange. She gave it to her husband, cast a disapproving look at Peter's clothes, and said to Tom, "You were right."

He took no more pleasure from her words than Abigail took in speaking them, and said again to Peter, "Are you sure—"

"Robbed and naked as the rest," the boy said. "He just come out of the woods and Fanny Buckman set to screaming. Mr. Ichabod and Bess took him inside, and Nabby said run to the doctor's, find Tom, bring 'em back straightaway. He's bleeding awful bad. The Maimers took his tongue!"

Chapter Three

Tom entered the Orange and bounded up the stairs between the taproom and the parlor, both of which looked empty at a glance, and squinted in the darkness after so much sun. He pressed past his ancient cook, Nabby, who knelt below the landing with a bucket and rags, wiping blood off the steps and angry with him now, not only for his pell-mell approach but for sloshing her water, bumping her head, and tracking mud where she had cleaned the minute before he came.

"And break my neck while you're at it," Nabby said, "and then you'll have a broke-neck cook and a poor tongueless wretch and I should like to see you keep an orderly tavern after that."

Nabby hated leaving the kitchen in the rear of the tavern without serious reason, but Tom knew her well enough to sense her irritation came from more than her abandonment of vittles at the hearth. She was shaken by the Maimers, and the victim, and the blood, and she was angry at herself for being so affected.

"The child is vexed. You know she fears blood," Nabby said, referring to the tavern ghost, a girl who remembered little of her earthly life except for a mother who had loved her, killed her, or possibly both. Nameless and invisible, she had lived in the Orange for a decade, and Nabby alone claimed to understand the knocks, creaks, and ethereal odors with which the ghost communicated. Tom could feel her now: a troubling air more like memory than ordinary sense, a fragrance in his thoughts that reminded him of loss.

Benjamin walked up behind them, stepping gracefully around Nabby and her bucket. He and Tom entered an upstairs room at the side of the tavern—dark and unfurnished but for a bed—that was usually reserved for vagabonds or prisoners. It was dim and low-ceilinged, and the window had bars. Tom's cousin Bess rushed to meet them at the door. She was twenty and petite, her honey-brown hair stuffed inside a cap, and he tensed to see her apron and her hands smeared with blood. Her eyes were wide and teary but she held herself straight.

"Excuse me, Bess," Benjamin said, passing through directly to the victim on the bed.

"Are you all right?" Tom asked his cousin.

Bess nodded unconvincingly. The smell of blood and herbs mingled with her warmth. "What are we going to do?" she asked.

"I don't know," Tom said. "Go and clean yourself up."

She set her feet and wiped her fingers on her apron. "I can stay."

"There's nothing you can do now that Benjamin's here. I need you downstairs—"

Contradicting him at once, Benjamin said from the back of the room, "Bess, my dear—I need a fresh pair of rags, absolutely clean. Boil them first, lift them with a clean-boiled fork, and hold them out to cool in the breeze. Do not touch them with your hands." It was a point he always stressed—cleanliness, cleanliness—and although he was often mocked for such a curious insistence, people humored him, encouraged by his regular success. "Also ice," Benjamin said, "and a bowl of moistened raspberry leaves, softly crushed."

She ran downstairs and Tom entered the room, just as Ichabod—unnoticed until that moment—opened the shutters to illuminate the victim on the bed.

The man looked drained of all his fluids, his complexion gray-green from the blood he must have swallowed. Bess had cleaned his chin but his neck was sticky dark. He had arrived completely naked and been dressed in a set of Tom's old clothes, which were long and ill-fitting. Ichabod held a basin under his mouth, allowing him to murmur out another pitiful flow. He looked from Benjamin to Tom with large blue eyes and seemed aghast that he could neither apologize for the mess nor offer a description of his terrible ordeal.

"It's all right," Tom said quietly. He touched the man's trembling shoulder and added, "You're in excellent hands. Dr. Knox is the best physician I know. I've seen him save a man who lost a portion of his skull. You're welcome to stay as long as you need, and if there's anything I can do—"

He stopped before the words "go ahead and ask," regretting how ridiculously formal he had sounded.

The victim answered with a blink, drooled into the basin, and looked at Benjamin with tears running to his jowls. Ichabod rubbed the man's back, and the sight of them together, the lifelong mute and the one just created, was as torturously sweet as treacle-berry seeds.

After a long, close inspection of the man's severed tongue, Benjamin said, "The worst of the bleeding is over. The cut is very neat, exceedingly so. Your assailants, it would seem, used a well-honed blade. You will still be able to speak, at least in altered fashion. Consonants will be difficult and flavors may be lost. But all in all—"

The man wept in earnest, sounding like a ewe. Benjamin propped him up, regretful but exhibiting a doctor's firm support.

"First you need fluids to restore what you have lost, blended with a tincture that will moderate the pain. Bring me a long-necked funnel," Benjamin said to Tom, "and a mixture of cider and smoak, one cup each, a measure of powdered cranch root, a pinch of salt, a quarter cup of sugar, and a half pint of rum. Mull it with a red-hot poker. I will add my own draft once the mixture has cooled."

Tom nodded and winced—the cranch root alone was enough to turn his stomach—but Benjamin was quick to add, "Even without the funnel, he would not be able to taste it."

The patient cried anew. Ichabod consoled him.

Tom went to the stairs and Pitt was coming up. Nabby had already left. The stairs were free of blood but Pitt had tracked another round of mud from outside, having failed to wipe his feet, let alone knock.

"You here to question him, too?" Tom asked.

Pitt stopped and squinted. There were eight steps between them in the stairway's gloom.

Tom refused to move and said, "I knew it wasn't done. I told you they'd attack again as soon as winter was over."

"It isn't your concern," Pitt said.

"The hell it ain't. It's scaring travelers, hurting business. There's a man upstairs bleeding in my clothes. This is everyone's concern, especially here in Root where we have to pay a sheriff who's afraid to earn his coin."

Pitt took a step and seemed to painfully restrain himself. "I've ridden out a dozen times."

"And ridden home with nothing. If I kept the tavern the way you keep the law—"

Tom hesitated, thinking he had made Pitt hiss. Rather it was Scratch, the cat who stalked the Orange. He'd been hiding on a step between the men without a sound and now he crouched, fierce and mangy, and defended his position. He was missing half an ear and had a milky left eye, and his decrepit coat was battle scarred and stank of rotting offal. Scratch vanished and appeared several times a week and threatened man, woman, and child with bites, sprays, scratches, and underfoot tangles that occurred too often not to be intentional. Tom had known the cat since time out of mind. According to Nabby, the oldest woman in Root, Scratch had been around since *she* was a girl. The sole explanation for the cat's longevity—excluding the assumption that the creature was demonic—was that every ten or fifteen years for nearly a century, Scratch had spawned an identical heir, who presumably killed his parents and returned, by feral instinct, to terrorize the Orange.

"Someone ought to shoot that cat," Pitt said.

"People have tried."

A drunk militiaman had done so once and everyone present had sworn he hit the mark. Four weeks later, Scratch reappeared, spry as ever, and stole a sausage before Nabby could impale him with her toasting fork.

"I'm coming up," Pitt said, seemingly to Scratch, who occupied the center of the stairs and wouldn't budge.

Much as Tom would have savored seeing Pitt maneuver past, he took a breath and said, "The man can't speak. Benjamin is with him. Do your job and check the road and come back later."

"You know damn well the Maimers will be gone." Pitt said it with a strain of genuine frustration, like a hunter with a quarry that he can't begin to track. "I won't keep riding out blind. I need the eyes and ears of people who have met them. You have to let me up."

"I won't."

"This is a public tavern," Pitt said.

"This is my private house."

Before Pitt could answer, Scratch attacked his leg, bloodying his stocking and raking his hands whenever he tried to wrest the creature off. The sheriff drew his gun and swung it like a hammer. Scratch jumped away; Pitt struck his own shin. He groaned and cocked the pistol, aiming at the cat, who retreated to the step where he'd originally been.

"Put it down," Tom said, "before you terrify a man who's already lost his tongue. Go and catch a Maimer, if it's truly your concern."

Pitt lowered the gun. He was too dignified to spit at the cat but openly considered it, sucking in his cheeks and staring at Tom as if he, and not Scratch, had torn his favorite stocking. "I'm coming back," he said. "And I will shoot this cat and anyone else who comes between me and the fellow upstairs."

Then he drew himself tall, like a pillar of the town, and strode out of the tavern to organize another futile sortie into the forest.

"Good cat," Tom said.

Scratch slashed the air and made Tom flinch before scrambling downstairs and darting out of sight.

"Tom," Benjamin said, suddenly behind him. "I need a quill and paper. Our man would like to tell us who he is and how it happened."

⚘

His name was John Pale, he was a lawyer out of Grayport, and he had written his story down before exhaustion overcame him. The ink was smudged and the sheet was dotted with blood, but his handwriting was beautifully refined and his account, however hasty, exhibited candor and clarity. Now the paper lay on a table near the front window of the Orange's taproom, where Benjamin sat looking thoughtfully into the night, while Tom prepared them each a hot cup of smoak.

Fire rippled in the great stone hearth, providing the room's only light aside from a candle at Benjamin's table. Nabby had retired to her bedroom off the kitchen, Ichabod was in his room upstairs overlooking the river, and Bess had forgone her own bed to sleep in a chair beside John Pale. Benjamin had used the raspberry leaves as an astringent and largely stopped the bleeding. They had poured the hideous draft directly into the patient's stomach with the funnel, and once the added medicine had dulled the worst of the pain, he had finally fallen asleep. The day had passed with few additional travelers, but many townspeople had come to the tavern for news of the latest attack. Sheriff Pitt and a band of armed companions had ridden into the forest and returned empty-handed, Tom had gone about his usual work, and Benjamin, having done all he could for John Pale, had seen to other patients and returned to the Orange after dark to sit with his friend and talk, at last, of Molly and the Maimers.

Tom stirred the boiling water into the freshly ground smoaknuts and set a pair of cups upon the table. He snipped tobacco from a twist, stuffed two pipes, and handed one to Benjamin. They lit them from the candle and puffed until a cloud swirled above their heads, where it mingled with the rosemary hanging from the rafters. Instead of speaking right away, they settled back and savored the quiet of the taproom with its dark wooden walls, its deeply scarred tables, and its permanent smell of woodsmoke, cinnamon, and bacon.

Tom picked the paper up and read it once more. John Pale had left Grayport on horseback the previous morning. The road remained in poor condition—passable, but slow—and he had made such terrible time that he'd been forced to spend the night at Shepherd's Inn, a small but honest house ten leagues away from Root. Just after sunrise, he reembarked and was stopped by a group of riders halfway between the inn and the Orange. They were five in number—one more than last year's reports of the Maimers—and wore identical black cloaks, tricornes, and masks. The masks were plain and hid their faces from their noses to their hats.

One of the five, the only one who spoke, barred the way with two of his companions while the other pair of riders blocked the road behind. The speaker asked John his name and destination. The lawyer had heard of last year's attacks and answered at length, offering not only his name but also the reason for his journey, his occupational history, how much money he was carrying—barely worth the trouble, they were welcome to it all—the name and pedigree of his horse, and everything else he could think of to make himself agreeable.

One of the riders took his reins and guided him onto the ground. He was told to remove his clothes, which he did without objection, trying to smile in his nakedness and hoping, through his talk, to sensibly dissuade them from their infamous finale.

The speaker raised his hand—it was gloved, holding tongs—and said, "It seems to me your tongue is worth its weight in silver."

The man behind Pale forced him to his knees. They held his arms, opened his mouth, and extracted the prize with the tongs. The speaker made quick work with a knife before depositing Pale's most worthy possession in a bag and galloping away, with the stolen horse and the other four riders, off the road and into the forest.

Pale staggered on, trying to stop the bleeding with his hands and fainting, more than once, on the long walk to Root.

The Maimers had first appeared last year and quickly grown to legendary status—mysterious men who appeared and disappeared, like figures in Nabby's most supernatural tales, after stealing everything a person owned and then, worst of all, the most valuable part of his or her self. In a single summer, they had taken an old man's majestic beard, a lady's golden hair, a scholar's eye, and a nursemaid's nipples. They had crippled a farmer's leg, slashed a dandy's face, and broken a blacksmith's elbows. Their attacks had finally ended with the onset of cold, and it had been hoped throughout the winter they would not begin again. But now a lawyer had lost his tongue, and even though Molly had emerged from the river with no apparent mutilation, Tom and Benjamin had spent the day wondering whether she, and not John Pale, had really been the Maimers' first victim of the year.

"Molly and I discussed Mr. Pale when I returned to the house at midday," Benjamin said, considering his pipe more often than he smoked it. "She inquired about the blood on my shirt, which I had neglected to change before entering her room. I explained what had happened and it left her quite amazed—as amazed, I would say, as anyone had been upon learning of the Maimers."

"Could the Maimers," Tom said, "be something else she forgot?"

Benjamin shook his head. "As I said to you this morning, she appears more frightened than legitimately fogged. My true purpose in inviting you this morning was not to jog her thoughts but to test another theory. I observed her when you came and saw what I expected."

"What?"

"Trust," Benjamin said. "I believe she may confide in you. Perhaps in you alone."

Tom leaned back with a quizzical expression. He drew upon his pipe until it crackled; he exhaled. "Why me?"

"You saved her life."

"So did you."

Benjamin sipped his smoak, taking time to think. "She was not in mortal danger once you pulled her from the river. I can scarcely claim credit for the speed of her recovery. The cold should have killed her, yet she bore it and survived, clinging unconscious to a branch, and had an appetite—a radiance!—by suppertime the very same day. Remarkable, remarkable . . . "

Tom leaned back, studying the wishbones dangling overhead. There was one from every Lumen Night since before Tom's family had acquired the tavern, and the oldest had furs of accumulated dust. Thirty-eight bones, every one of them intact. Nabby said the wishes remained within the marrow, that the bones protected anyone who boarded at the tavern.

"Her locket," Tom said.

"Contains a tooth," Benjamin answered. "I examined it while she slept. It is a partial tooth: the fragment, I believe, of an incisor. The reverse of the locket bears the maker's mark—twenty-two-karat gold, made in Umber—which makes her either a wealthy girl from here in Floria"—Benjamin puffed his pipe—"or a wealthy girl from Bruntland."

Three thousand miles overseas, Tom thought. A child of the mother country, floating here alone without a memory of anything but drifting into Root. Wealthy or a thief. Either way, far from home, be it Grayport or Liberty or weeks across the ocean.

"I have saved the most dramatic fact for last," Benjamin told him. "When I stooped to unclasp the locket, I had greater leave to examine her breasts."

Tom raised his eyebrows. Benjamin frowned, embarrassed and irked, from a strictly professional standpoint, by the misinterpretation.

"Molly gave birth," Benjamin said. "I would guess within a fortnight."

Tom bit down and cracked the end of his pipe stem. He lowered it and said, "You don't think the Maimers took . . . "

Despite the amber light pulsing from the hearth, Benjamin visibly paled as he considered, lost for words, a possibility that neither of them wanted to admit.

Chapter Four

CITY OF UMBER IN BRUNTLAND, CONTINENT OF HERALDIA
SEVENTEEN YEARS EARLIER

Lord Bell stormed the birthing room, having listened to the cries as long as he could tolerate and now, after battering the door into the wall, feeling staggered by the sight of so much blood. The gunmetal smell of it, the sheen upon the bed. How it glistened in the oil-light, appearing to have carried out a thick, violet clot—a baby, wet and wriggling in the governess's hands. The muggy air that damped his waistcoat and weighed down his lungs seemed a visceral extension of his young wife's blood.

The governess, Frances, almost slipped when she turned. She was slender as a heron, though without a heron's grace, and said, "M'lord!" at the violence of his unexpected entrance.

The room was broad and richly furnished with the four-poster bed against the pheasant-papered wall. Lord Bell strode across the floor, gazing at his wife between her wide-spread knees as she lay upon her back, staring up toward the ceiling. Frances stepped in front of him and held out the child, showing how its neck was strangled by the cord. Bell drew his penknife and cut it with a scowl, careful not to slit the miniature throat, and only then did Frances sob, overcome in her relief, quivering and fumbling with the newborn's limbs.

"Go," Bell said.

Frances hurried to a softly lit corner of the room where a table stood with swaddling cloths, a pitcher, and a bowl.

Catherine Bell had stopped crying. Finally it was done. She was white, as if her color might be draining with the afterbirth. Lord Bell adjusted her position on the bed—gently, very gently—when her head began to tip.

He shouted at the hall, where the household servants huddled out of sight.

"Bring the doctor!"

"On his way, m'lord," the butler said without coming in, mumbling something vague about a carriage in the storm.

Rain beat the roof. Bell knelt beside the bed.

"Cat," he said gently, leaning in close.

She seemed not to recognize his face in her fatigue. He held her hand upon her bosom—there was scarcely any breath—and used his other hand to smooth the ragged hair off her forehead. He still clutched the penknife he'd used to cut the cord, and the blade lay cold just above her eye. He kissed her lips and tasted her and knew that she was dying, and he cried for the first time in years, very plainly, dripping tears on her cheeks where they blended with her sweat.

"Catherine," Bell said, incapable of more, just the clarity and cleanliness of "Catherine, oh, Catherine."

Quieter and quieter, he whispered it and stared, fearing that she truly might vanish if he blinked.

"She isn't breathing," Frances said, muffled by the rain.

"Catherine," Bell said.

"M'lord, she isn't breathing."

"She is!" he yelled. "She is!"

He could feel it on his face, every tiny exhalation that was passing from her lips.

"Please!" Frances said, much closer, right beside him.

Bell squeezed the knife until the handle seemed to bend. He turned to her and shouted for the doctor once again; Frances didn't move but held the infant up to show him.

"Please, she isn't breathing, oh I've tried—she's going cold!"

Bell registered the deep, leaden blueness of its skin. He threw the knife against the wall and took the child by the ankles.

"Softly!" Frances moaned, as if she hadn't begged for help.

He dangled it aloft and slapped the baby on the bottom, half a dozen times until his palm began to sting.

"It isn't helping," Frances said. "Please, it isn't help—"

Bell slapped *her*, hard across the jaw. Frances backed away and finally held her tongue. He turned his hand upon the babe again, slapping at its back, at its thighs, at its chest, at its weakness and its breathlessness. He stopped and let it hang, wearied by his failure.

With a gurgle and a cough, the girl began to cry.

She cried as he had never heard a baby cry before, so fiery and red he almost dropped her in alarm.

"You've done it!" Frances said, laughing through her tears. She took the baby back again, admiring the sound. "Bless her, little thing, listen to her now! Breathe, let it out. There you are, m'love, go on!"

Bell returned to the bed and saw the umbilical blood smudged above his wife's left eye. He licked his thumb to clean it off, tasting it and wondering whether it was Catherine's or the child's, unsure if there was really any difference. Now her eyes were on his face, midday blue. He touched her hair along her collarbone and held her feeble hand. Rain pounded overhead, bearing down as if to crush them, and the sconces on the walls weakened in the gloom. On and on the infant cried, fabulously loud, neither slowing nor diminishing but growing every moment. He didn't dare turn and take his eyes off his wife— her watery expression and the flicker of her consciousness dissolving as if the rain were rinsing her away.

Yet the wails were all he heard, all he felt, all he knew. He looked and there was Frances with the child in her arms, crying out and reddening and breathing as she cried.

"Quiet!" Bell said. "Soothe her! Make her stop!"

He clawed his head until his wig fell sullied to the floor, and then he turned to see his wife had closed her weary eyes. Her body had the same bleached pallor as her gown, and both the blood and Catherine's hair looked darker through his tears. Bell slumped until his forehead pressed against her own.

For an instant all the world vanished in her stillness. A silence fell around them and he might have spent the night there, stupefied and calm, just the two of them alone. But the baby called him back, and with the cries he heard the rain again, and Frances crying, too, and all the servants' hissing whispers in the darkness of the hall.

He studied Catherine's face as if it might have been a portrait, worth his admiration but inanimate and flat. Not the woman he had married. Not a woman he could hold. He wiped his palms and tucked his handkerchief neatly in his pocket. His knife was on the floor, he suddenly recalled. He picked it up, snapped it shut, and walked toward Frances.

"Did Catherine choose a name?" he asked above the cries.

Frances stared across the room with a dawning look of fear, only starting to acknowledge that her mistress wasn't moving.

Bell repeated the question.

"Molly," Frances said, holding up his daughter.

"Quiet her," he said. "I need to speak with Nicholas."

He exited the room. Servants met him in the hall. Their expressions were composed, almost chiseled on their heads, and none of them was fool enough to offer a condolence. Bell strode past them to the stairs and started down. The doctor had arrived and was coming up to meet him, puny in a greatcoat and trembling from the wet. He craned to look at Bell, neck flaccid as a turkey's as he paused upon the landing with an educated smile.

"Please excuse my delay, Lord Bell!" the doctor said. "I had thought to come sooner . . . fought to come at all! I was far across the city, halfway to Woodchapel Gate, when I received your summons, and the rain overwhelmed me. The carriages were slow, my horse was nearly drowned," he said, wringing out his wig upon the clean white floor. "But judging by the sound, my worries were unfounded. Healthy lungs. A sonorous child! Best congratulations. Does the child have a name?"

"Molly," Bell said.

"Ah, a daughter! And the lady—"

"Dead," Bell said. "God damn your drowning horse."

He left the doctor thunderstruck, fumbling with his bag, and continued downstairs to the darkened study of the mansion's first floor, where he poured himself a tumblerful of rum and gulped it down. Catherine's shawl was on the lounge, near a book that she'd been reading. Bell dropped the tumbler. It didn't break but bounced along the rug, and when he bent to pick it up he stumbled to the floor, fighting nausea and a wild swirl of dizziness and heat.

He heard a servant in the hallway outside the door and struggled to a chair. They shouldn't see him on his knees; they were terrified already. They would look to him as Frances had, desperate for instruction. They had loved Catherine. She had coddled them and oh, how he'd chastised her and criticized her kindness. Catherine's ordinary kindness!

He placed the tumbler on the highboy and straightened out his waistcoat. Even downstairs with a hundred feet between them, he could hear the baby's cries as if the child were inside him. He imagined they could hear it from the stables, from the street. His son would hear it, too, and wonder what had happened. He would need an explanation. He would need to be consoled. That was *his* responsibility, Bell quietly remembered, having foolishly considered that his wife would offer solace.

Nicholas was drawing at a table in the library. He sat alone, a boy of six with black hair, black eyes, and skin the color of his dead mother's body. Frail from birth and perpetually ill, he had worried Catherine and disappointed Lord Bell until his fortitude, his will, and most of all his intellect had overshadowed any of his physical deficiencies. Nicholas had walked late but talked early. He struggled to eat but voraciously read, and wrote, and worked at mathematics far beyond his peers. He played with difficult books the way ordinary boys played war, showed a keen fascination with anatomy and guns, and practiced harpsichord simply but precisely as a clock.

Affectionate with Catherine and convivial with servants, Nicholas was stoic and at times even icy with his father, who often sensed rebellion in the boy's unwavering expression.

The library was bright with a pair of brass lamps and heavy with the smell of ink and moldy books. Catherine's shadowplants, carefully selected for a room without windows, had grown beyond their pots and sent their creepers, vines, and leaves crawling up the shelves. Even here the baby's cries were easily discerned, penetrating cherry and mahogany and oak, shearing through the million-page buffer of the cases.

Bell stood before his son, bloody and composed.

Nicholas sat and watched him with his quill above a sketch. Kidneys, it appeared, and their connecting apparatus.

"You have a sister," Bell intoned. "Her name is Molly."

"Mother—"

"Your mother is dead."

Bell could not recall the last time he had seen his son cry. Had he ever? Nicholas stared without a glimmer of surprise. He supposed the boy had sensed it—he had always been remarkably perceptive—or deduced it from the blood upon Bell's own clothes. Shock or fear might have tamped down obvious emotion, yet his young son's eyes had the clarity of scholarship, of someone who was carefully observing and recording.

"Come," Bell said, pulling Nicholas toward him in a violent embrace.

The boy did not resist but pricked his father with the quill, quickly on the shoulder, accidentally it seemed. Bell pushed him off and grimaced at the stain. "Sit," Bell said, loosening his collar. He was woozy from the strain again, and Nicholas had blurred. He wiped his eyes and said, "Your mother died of blood loss. It happens now and then, a complication of the birth. You mustn't think it all a frightful mystery. She bled and didn't stop and there is nothing further to explain."

"Her uterus tore," Nicholas said, so quietly that Bell leaned forward, trying to reconstruct the word—surely not "uterus"!—by picturing the movement of the boy's thin lips.

The sketch upon the table wasn't kidneys after all. They were ovaries, clinically precise and deftly drawn. Bell read the words "cervix" and "vagina," copied from the volume Nicholas had opened.

"You oughtn't . . . You're a child. I forbid—"

"I'm sorry," Nicholas said.

"Damn the doctor and his horse!" Bell shouted at the ceiling, pounding on the table and at last, with the outburst, startling his son.

"Catherine, o my Catherine. What am I to do?" he said, feeling like the room was moving in a spiral. He clenched his eyes and calmed himself. "You mustn't be afraid. We have suffered a terrible loss, a terrible loss. But people are depending on us now. Frances and the others. They will look to us—yes, even to you. Only six and yet a Bell. You must be brave and show them strength. You were crying for a moment. Were you crying? It is natural, of course, as natural as bleeding. But what are we to do with injuries that bleed? Stem the flow. Clamp the wound. So we will. So we must! But no: your eyes are dry. Look at me," he said, holding Nicholas's chin. "Have you heard me? Have you listened? Have you not a single tear for your own lost mother? She is looking at you now, looking down. Aye, she knows! The rain could be her tears, falling out of grief because she knows you do not care, not a whit, that she has died!"

Nicholas's brows tightened in perplexity, not about the rain—that was obvious to Bell—but from his father having posited a notion so absurd.

"Get up!" Bell said.

He crumpled the drawings and seized the boy firmly by the arm. The baby's wails steadily worsened as he dragged Nicholas out of the library, down the hall, and up the three flights of the rear staircase, and it was there, at the heavy dark door of Nicholas's room, that the boy began to sob.

"No," Bell said. "You are crying for yourself," and locked him in alone to think about his mother.

Bell retreated downstairs to the study once more. He downed another rum, hugged himself tight, and trembled in a deep velvet chair, unable to think because of the baby's noise, and Nicholas's silence, and the rain that fell and fell and did, after all, seem a judgment that was falling from above. Once the drink had taken hold and he was confident he wouldn't vomit, Bell returned upstairs, groaning as he climbed, to govern as he must before the home came to ruin.

Most of the servants hadn't left the third-floor hall. He directed them in turn and off they hurried, comforted as children with clear-cut tasks, to resecure the house against the storm, carry his wife's body to an adjoining room, prepare a late meal, burn the mattress and the linens, and go about their business as they would have done on any other evening. He spoke with the doctor, who had spent the last twenty minutes confirming Catherine's death but hadn't done a thing to ease the baby's cries, which had grown, like Nicholas's cool black stare, to seem a challenge—an affront—to Lord Bell's authority.

Frances sat apart and rocked the child gently, whispering and making little noises to console her. The girl was black of hair, wrinkled and misshapen, and the earlier blue of her skin had turned incendiary red.

"Has she suffered—"

"She is perfect head to foot," Frances said, speaking with a tone as soothing as her coos.

"A wet nurse—"

"Newton," Frances said, referring to the footman, "is bringing back two in case the first doesn't satisfy."

"Good. Very good," Bell said. "The child's cries—"

"Aren't they wonderful," she said. "And see the way her mouth is like m'lady's—"

"Why is she crying?"

Frances gawked at him, amazed. "Her mother gone and strangers all about," she began. "The strangling and the slaps . . . she is only now alive!"

"Give her to me," Bell said.

Frances leaned away and held the baby closer. Bell forced his hands under the bundle and she was forced to let go, much to her distress. He held the baby awkwardly and Frances stood to follow, but he ordered her to stay and meet the nurses when they came. She looked as if he'd kidnapped her own precious daughter.

He carried the baby through the house, away from everyone until they seemed the only two people in the home, her cries and his rigidity the only two forces in the world. He came to Nicholas's room, balanced the baby in the crook of his elbow, and opened the door without knocking.

The boy stood in the dark, silhouetted at the window, and didn't move until his father beckoned him to come.

"Hold out your arms," Bell said.

He placed the girl firmly into Nicholas's hands. Right away the boy's hold seemed entirely assured and Bell stepped back, confident his daughter wouldn't fall but anxious—he could not have said why—to see them there together, son and daughter, as a pair.

"Your sister," he declared.

"Molly," Nicholas said, and suddenly the baby fell silent and relaxed, her color flowing out and into her brother's cheeks, until they both looked healthy—she less inflamed, he less anemic—and Lord Bell observed them from the door, disregarded, thinking of his wife and powerfully alone.

Chapter Five

"*M*olly," Frances said, pausing in the garden with her tusk-handled pruning knife. "If you cannot leave that spider alone, I will serve it up for supper."

For six years, Frances had attempted all manner of correction with Molly, who thought of her governess's reprimands, exasperations, and emotional entreaties not only as variations on a game, but as constant reassurances of Frances's devotion. They were together in the courtyard behind the house, a thickly gardened refuge with high stone walls that almost made the bustle of the world disappear.

Umber was a compact, overpeopled city. Most of its central buildings were constructed of ghostly pale lunarite, a native stone of Bruntland, which gave the capital both the beauty and echoing hardness of an open-air cathedral. From the garden, Molly could see the neighboring mansions of Worthington Square and the tower of Elmcross Church, the latter's white belfry glaring in the sun, but with the burstwoods and roses clustering around her, it was easy to imagine they were deep within the countryside.

Molly put the ripe purple spider in her mouth.

Frances shrieked and rushed forward, only to snag her skirts upon the rosebush thorns. The spider struggled in Molly's mouth, dancing on her tongue and almost scrambling down her throat. She puffed her cheeks to give it room, surprised a thing so colorful had no distinguishing flavor. But neither did a grape, Molly thought, until you chewed it . . .

"Spit it out, spit it out!" Frances said, tearing free of the bush and opening Molly's mouth. Out the spider came, tumbling off her lip and landing in the moss—a vibrant combination to behold: violet-green. The lingering tickle on her tongue left her giggling uncontrollably.

"Oh, you wicked thing." Frances glowered but her eyes grew teary with affection. "Don't you know how poisonous they are? It might have bit you!"

"Those are safe," Molly said, relishing the pinkness of her governess's cheeks. "That's a sugarplum weaver. Nicholas told me. It would take a hundred of them biting all at once to make me sick."

"You mustn't do such things," Frances said, unconvinced. She saw the spider at her toe and leapt away. Molly laughed. The governess continued: "Is it any wonder that your cousins and the children in the park prefer each other's company?"

"Some of the children like me," Molly said. "I make them laugh."

"Their parents don't laugh, nor their governesses neither. You would have more friends if you would play with better manners."

Molly sulked and watched the spider crawl across the moss until it hid beneath a rock and left her feeling lonely. It was true: other children didn't actively avoid her, but they didn't seek her out as often as she hoped, and she received dirty glances from their guardians and mothers when she dug in public flower beds, and yelled, and swallowed bugs. Molly's father rarely socialized—"He gave it up after your mother died," Frances had once told her—and her truest young companion was her own friendless brother. Nicholas was generally too ill, or too bored by children his age, to set aside his studies for more than a hasty walk in the park. Their governess was all Molly had, most days.

Frances was thirty years old but dressed, and spoke, and acted much older—more like her father's musty great-aunts—yet oftentimes, especially when Molly drew her on, Frances ran and even laughed like the youngest of the household maids. She was pretty when her hair fell loose, and she had wonderful breasts for a woman so angular and thin. Molly noticed how they bobbed when Frances hopped away; she loved to nap upon her governess's bosom in the sun. As an infant, she had breast-fed emphatically—several wet nurses had been urgently retained—and how she loved to suck, even now, on everything from berries to the cream inside a pastry.

Having nothing else at hand, Molly settled for her pinky.

"Such a habit for a girl of nearly seven," Frances said. "You will never be a lady, sucking your finger and swallowing spiders."

"I'll sail to Floria and do whatever I like," Molly said.

"The savages will skin you."

"I'm not afraid of savages."

"The winterbears will eat you."

"I can outrun bears!"

Molly kicked her shoes away and darted off barefoot, running through the sumptuous abundance of the garden with the soft fronds palming at her skin, the mossy stones, and all the warm, wet ferns—oh!—moistening her ankles. What a joy it was to run. What a bother wearing clothes! Frances chased her, getting close, but Molly darted through a very tight gap between bushes, and she quickly left her governess behind and hurried on.

She ran toward the entrance at the kitchen, through the door and over the cold stone floor, through the pantry and the gilt room with all its sullen portraits—noblemen and ladies who had *never* sucked a pinky—which she hurried past, blowing raspberries, till she crossed the central hall and reached the library door.

She tugged it wide and panted at her brother, who was seated at a table in the middle of the room, moon-white and watching her, expressionless and calm. Molly's heartbeat punched. Lord Bell was there, too—it should have been a tutor, Father never taught on Wednesdays!—and the moment he turned to see her at the door, Nicholas smiled. Molly smiled back and flushed to her earlobes.

Lord Bell didn't chastise—household rules went without saying—but he stared to see if Molly would depart without reminder. Frances hurried up behind her, huffing from the chase. Molly looked at Nicholas—he seemed so lonely and dispirited without her, stuck inside with Father on a fine bright day—and she decided that her only means of staying was to climb. She scaled the nearest bookcase and hoped to reach the top. It was easy as a ladder, multicolored as a tree.

"Ignore her," said her father, turning back to Nicholas and forcing him to focus his attention on his studies.

Frances stood below and tried to whisper Molly down. The quiet of the room, the manners and composure tickled Molly to a laugh that made her brother chew his lip. She watched him as she climbed, hoping to impress him, and she didn't see the ceiling till she bumped it with her head. The knock surprised her and she reached up, rubbing where it hurt, and then her foot slipped free and she was dangling one-handed, fifteen feet above the hardwood floor.

Frances yelped. Lord Bell jerked around and banged his fist upon the table. One of the table leaves jumped and hit Nicholas's jaw, and Molly weakened at the sound, losing her purchase on the shelves. Nicholas stood and clasped his mouth, bloody at the chin, and Molly fell from the bookcase, her petticoats and hair fluffing up around her.

Lord Bell tried to catch her but she crashed through his arms and hit the floor hard, knocking out her wind and battering her hip. Frances, in her fright, had fallen backward in the doorway, ghastly white with vivid red hives around her neck. Molly scrambled to her side. Frances held her close until she finally got her breath, and she was just about to cry when she remembered Nicholas and pushed away, running across the room to see his wounded mouth.

Lord Bell caught her elbow.

"I'm sorry, m'lord," Frances said, wobbling to her feet. "It was all my fault. We were running in the garden."

"You were not to go running in the garden," Bell said. "You were to keep her calmly occupied while Nicholas was studying."

"Yes, m'lord, I'm sorry, sir. As I said, it wasn't her. I allowed it and I chased her. She was frightened of the chase. She didn't mean to climb—"

"I did!" Molly shouted. "Let me go!"

"Return to the garden," Bell said to Frances. "I will summon you when Nicholas's lessons are complete."

"M'lord—"

"Now," he said, squeezing Molly tight enough to bruise. "Close the door behind you."

Frances nodded with a curtsy that was virtually a swoon. Tears clung like little bubbles to the governess's eyes, and then she left and shut the door with the gentlest of clicks.

"Nicholas is bleeding!" Molly said.

Her father cocked an eyebrow and looked toward her brother. He was startled by the sight, glancing back and forth as if the siblings were deceiving him, but Nicholas's mouth was genuinely bloody.

"How—"

"It was you!" Molly said. "You struck the table and it jumped!"

Nicholas confirmed it with a quick, sharp nod.

"I would not have struck the table if you hadn't climbed the shelves," Bell said.

"I didn't mean to hurt him!" Molly yelled and tried to free herself.

Bell gripped harder. "Show me your mouth," he said to her brother.

Nicholas approached him.

"Take away your hand—a split lip, nothing more. Let me see your teeth. Ah," Bell said.

Molly wilted at the sight. Her brother had lost a fragment of his upper left incisor. Molly pinched herself as fiercely as she could and started crying.

Bell turned to her and said, "See what your unruliness has wrought."

"Nicholas, I'm sorry!"

"No," Bell said, looking at her brother, who for one bright second had regarded her with sympathy. "She mustn't be forgiven. She has injured you and injury requires proper justice. Think upon your lessons. *Lex talionis.* You have seen it in the Book of Light, as well as in the histories of clans and ancient kings. Even our own common law demands equality of recompense for certain types of crime."

Molly sobbed and shook her head, knees buckling underneath her.

Nicholas faced their father with a grave, princely dignity. "A thief would lose his hand."

"Yes," Bell said.

"A man who killed his neighbor's ox would have to pay an ox."

"He would."

"And if a rider dropped his reins, distracted by a bellman, and trampled a child in the street," Nicholas said, "should the bellman himself be trampled, or the bellman's own child?"

Bell hesitated briefly with a flicker of his eyes. "One should never drop the reins. The rider is to blame."

"Then you should lose a tooth," Nicholas told his father. "It was you who lost control in a moment of distraction."

Bell straightened up and answered with a grin: half a dozen of his pale beige teeth, neatly ordered. "I have told you more than once you have a future at the bar." He offered Nicholas a handkerchief, immaculately white and monogrammed *B*. "Still, she must be punished," he continued, looking down at her. "Tell me, Molly: did Frances start the chase or was it you?"

"It was me."

"Then Frances lied."

"No."

"She either chased you or she lied. Which is it now? The truth."

"That isn't fair!" Molly said, twisting free with her heart beating quicker than a bird's.

"Very well," Bell said. "I will hold you and Frances equally responsible. Unless you choose to bear the total punishment yourself."

Molly nodded in defiance.

"Twice the count or twice the force?"

"Twice the force," Molly said, bravely as she could.

"Nicholas, your shoe."

Her brother paused just long enough to register objection, but then he raised a leg without unbalancing his stance and popped the left shoe off his heel. It was stiff, silver buckled, with a black leather heel. Lord Bell lifted Molly by the armpits—he held her so infrequently, it came as a surprise how powerful he was—and took her to a chair, where he sat and bent her over, belly down, upon his thigh. She focused on the highly polished floor and held her breath, unable to see her brother with her hair fallen wild in her eyes.

Her father raised her skirts, exposing her to view, and said, "You are no stranger to discipline, Nicholas. You have learned to bear the blows. It is time you learn to deal them. Twenty for her and twenty for Frances. Land them flush and keep them firm, straight across the buttocks."

No! Molly thought. *Oh, he wouldn't ever hurt me!*

Her horror was assuaged when Nicholas refused.

"You must," Bell said, "or I will give her eighty."

Make it eighty or a thousand, only never one from Nicholas! Molly shut her eyes, dizzy from the blood swirling through her head. The first smack upon her bottom blew the air from her lungs.

"Very good," her father said.

Another smack, even cleaner, made her squirm and kick her feet.

"Hold her legs if she obstructs you."

Molly dropped her legs. She wouldn't cry or make a sound. She'd imagine it was Father, and she wouldn't raise her heels and force her brother to restrain her. The next several blows struck tears from her eyes. Ten. Eleven. Twelve. The sting had risen to a fire. Another and another, steady as a drum, until the pauses seemed to hurt as badly as the whacks. The twentieth was red, the thirtieth was white, and then the colors bled together and she shut her eyes and wept. She drooled upon the floor, contorting her expression till her face ached, too. When it finished, she was stupefied.

Abruptly she was upright and facing them again, her bottom so inflamed it seemed impossible it wasn't still exposed and being beaten. Nicholas stared at her with no apparent sign of recognition, not a glimmer of apology or violence or pity. His complexion hadn't warmed. He seemed as delicate as ever, breathing faintly as if he hadn't raised a finger in exertion.

"Return to your work," Bell told him.

Nicholas obeyed. Even when he sat and it was safe to steal a glance, he neither looked at her nor paused before resuming with his quill.

Molly's father led her out and shut the door behind them. They stood in the entrance hall, its skylight shining high above. The fresher air was like another day, a whole different season.

"You bore it well," Bell said, bending at the waist to see her up close. His eyes were soft, even timid, and his skin looked weathered in the strong illumination. She focused on the wire-stiff bristles in his nose. "You needn't ask forgiveness now. If Nicholas wishes, we will fit him with an artificial tooth."

"I didn't want to hurt him," Molly whimpered.

"Nor I you," her father replied. "My duty as a parent calls for discipline at times. Do not think I relish it. But punishment can edify, if only you allow it. Every lash can be a lesson, every weal a tiny scripture." He touched her on the ear and said, "I know that with maturity and governance—self-governance, Molly, and fewer of these incidents and trials—I will one day count myself proud to be your father." He kissed her on the head and sent her to her room, watching her ascend all thirty of the stairs.

As soon as she was free, Molly hid beneath the covers of her bed, lying on her stomach and imagining herself inside a cave made of snow. Every throb reinforced that Nicholas had struck her. Nicholas, her brother and her best and only friend. How he hated her—he must!— for costing him a tooth. How his aim had never faltered, how his strength had never waned! She heard the birds beyond the window and considered leaping out. Would the fall truly kill her? She would have to hit her head. They would grieve her then, and Nicholas would love her once again.

She stayed within her cave until the door creaked open. It was Nicholas. She knew because he sounded like a ghost.

"You can give me forty more!" she said, throwing off the sheet and turning round to meet him. The agony redoubled when she sat upon her heels.

Her brother smiled more than usual, perhaps to show the gap. The blood looked ferocious on his white silk shirt. His hand was in a fist. She noticed right away because his hands were always delicate, with fingers made for instruments, calligraphy, and scalpels.

"I have something else to give you," Nicholas said.

He opened his hand. Molly crawled along the bed until her nose was at his palm. In the center, so it seemed, was a tiny shard of porcelain.

"Your tooth," she said.

"Take it."

Molly held it with her fingertips.

He kissed her on the crown and said, "Keep it to remember it is *he* who tries to hurt us—as a promise that he won't have control of us forever."

"I thought you hated me!" she said.

"Don't be stupid," Nicholas told her. "But he will make me punish you again."

"I'll be good. I'll behave."

He smirked and said, "You won't."

Molly sat back, wincing at the pain.

He continued with a look much colder than his words: "Never forget how much I love you, even when I hurt you."

Molly squeezed the tooth so it bit against her hand.

"I'll never hurt you again," she said.

"You will."

"I won't!"

"You'll have to."

"Why?"

"We're the strongest people in the world," Nicholas said, and though his answer seemed ridiculous considering their wounds, she brightened from the inside out and tried to smile.

"We're stronger than everyone," she said.

"Except each other."

"But together—"

"Together," he said, imbuing the word with confidence and hope, even while his strength kept burning in her welts.

Chapter Six

Molly shut her eyes and sped her horse across the meadow, finally alone and racing from the family's grand country manor. She rode astride—there was nothing so foolish as a sidesaddle; Lord Bell himself disdained the convention—and felt the power of the beast's strong charge between her legs. Warm green wind billowed through her hair. The thoroughbred's musk blended with her sweat and what a glorious stink arose, what a riotous aroma, drenching out the rose-water fragrance of the day. She felt the muscles and the rolling undulations in her body and she might have been a runaway. She might have been a centaur.

Molly rode as often as she could, regardless of the weather, especially in summer when the family left the city for their sprawling country estate. She had taken her first lessons as a child and now, at the age of fourteen, could jump an energetic horse over any sort of obstacle. Her discipline and daring won approval from her father and he encouraged her to ride, especially today with the general paying a visit.

Lord Bell had talked of little else throughout the week. General Graves will be arriving, General Graves will be expecting, we must all of us prepare to be our best before the general.

"Your father's to be a colonel," Frances told her several nights ago, when she joined Molly and Nicholas for their customary after-dinner hour.

"He bought a regimental contract," Nicholas explained. "Now he'll buy a regiment and lead it overseas."

"To Floria?" Molly asked. "Are we all going with him?"

"Heavens, no." Frances laughed. "Unless you wish to fight a war."

"Against the Rouge?"

"And half the naturals," Nicholas said.

Dominion over Floria had been contested since the continent's discovery a hundred years prior. It was a land of fertile mystery, largely unexplored and rife with natural wonders—harbors cloaked in salt; ten-foot snows; native people called the Kraw, who were said to grow from the earth. It was also a land of riches, bursting with timber and marvelous crops. Some believed a panacea might be growing in the forests. Others believed that Floria, undiscovered during John Lumen's lifetime, was where the resurrected prophet went upon leaving Bruntland.

Three Heraldic countries had established permanent footholds. Solido had claimed an island portion in the south, but the Florian mainland had been split between Bruntland and Rouge, whose centuries-old hostility had flared, in recent years, between the countries' rival colonies in the distant New World. Floria's native tribes had chosen sides—the Elkinaki with the Bruntish and the Kraw with the Rouge—and now the fates of all involved would ride upon the outcome.

"Could we lose?" Molly asked.

"Your mother," Frances said, "is the only thing your father ever lost in all his life."

And so the general had arrived to speak about the war. Nicholas would meet him, as he always met the barons, earls, admirals, and other dignitaries in their father's constellation of acquaintances, and Molly—who was rather "too excitable" a spirit—was encouraged, quite emphatically, to ride about the grounds. She had gladly chosen a mount, a stallion named Tremendous, and ridden off the instant the general arrived.

Shadows cooled her face and she finally opened her eyes, slowing to a canter as she turned before the tree line. She had crossed the whole expanse of half a mile fully blind; far across the meadow she could see the distant manor with its barricade of hedges and the sunlight glinting off the glass.

Molly shook her hair and resettled her feet in the stirrups. Tremendous reared and whinnied. Several hundred birds flocked together overhead and made a cloud, ever shifting, like a picture of her life. She closed her eyes once more and galloped back toward the manor. Soon her father would be leaving. He had gone away before, even gone abroad, but never with an army, never to a war. She and Nicholas and Frances would be masters of the home, both here and in the city, for the next few seasons—maybe for a year. Or so she told herself, believing that the war would lumber on. Was it wicked to imagine her father a captive of the Rouge? Anything could happen in a real live war.

Tremendous galloped on. Molly kept her eyes shut and reveled in the dark. The heat had grown thick and they were slicing it apart. She felt the pollen in her mouth and summer spreading wide, the explosion of a million bright blossoms all around her. The meadow went forever—it was better than a dream, how they flew without restraint and hovered off the grass.

She sensed panic in Tremendous, opened her eyes, and saw the hedges. They were thirty feet away and coming up fast and she remembered that they weren't merely hedges but a wall, five feet of stone with a covering of ivy.

Just beyond stood the manor. Molly held her breath. It was too late to stop and she imagined floating up. Tremendous read her mind and they were perfectly in sync; they were lighter than a lark and sailing off the ground.

⚘

Born to wealth and bred to power, Lord Bell was an only child whose parents had been murdered in the peasant uprising of 1730. His father had been a rapacious landlord and had paid the ultimate price for oppressing the tenant farmers on the family's vast estate.

Lord Bell was more pragmatic. He collected the rents, kept the peace, and earned the farmers' goodwill despite contempt for their existence. As one of the wealthiest landowners in Bruntland, he commanded more respect than many of the country's true nobility, and after dabbling in politics and establishing himself within the higher spheres of power, he craved an opportunity for military glory.

This morning he stood in the manor's sunstruck conservatory, a glass-paneled room with marble floors and luxurious ferns, discussing the war with General Graves.

The general's regal posture hid the quiver in his jowls, his liver spots, and the frailty that had disappointed Lord Bell on first impression. Now, as the general spoke with the wisdom of experience, fiery of voice and solid as a statue, it was rather like standing in the presence of the king.

"Fort Divine was cowardice," General Graves said. "An absolute disaster, inexcusable and rash. Food and arms to last a month, and Chesterson surrenders to a hundred savages and half as many Rouge. He claims he had no choice, that Smith abandoned him by staying put in Haverdown, that he preferred to lose a fort rather than see it pounded by artillery. Artillery the Rouge *did not possess.* Their cannons had been mired twenty miles west. By all accounts, the fort was barely nicked, yet Chesterson surrendered our last and best defense of the Switchback and now the Rouge can sail their battleships and bloody fucking pleasure boats halfway to Bloom completely unopposed. He's been ransomed and relieved of his command and now he's back in Umber, charming women and children with tales of his adventures. The Kraw should have scalped him," General Graves declared. "He could have doffed his hair and been the toast of every drawing room in Bruntland."

He faced the tall, open doors and looked toward the sky, as if the ivied wall alone divided the conservatory from the field of battle three thousand miles away in Floria.

"Though what does it matter?" he continued, so softly that the question might have been rhetorical. He turned to look at Bell with the sun upon his back, like a veteran philosopher exhausted by the light. "I have seventeen grandchildren. The youngest is a fortnight old. His name is Adam—he has his mother's hair. Yet here I stand despairing of a fort half a world away."

"The empire—"

"Yes, the empire." Graves smiled, as if Bell were one of his newly minted progeny: adorably naïve. "And what if all of Floria becomes New Rouge? I have seen our empire triple in size, and every time it's grown, so has our expense in life and coin and bloody obligation. I have a manse with fifty servants and a county with a hundred working families, but do I occupy the manse to gather up the rents, or do I gather up the rents to occupy the manse?"

"Every child brings expense," Bell said.

"Parenting and warring are for younger generations. I leave the diapers to my daughters and the regiments to men like you. But you need to understand we may have lost Floria already."

"I have studied the maps," Bell said. "If Fort Élan were captured, we would sever—"

"Maps." Graves sighed. "They never show you swamps and clouds of stinging flies. They never show you war parties, or cowardly sons of whores like Chesterson. And yet for all I know anymore, you may be just the man to save our precious Floria. We need a stroke of will. We need some bloody *spirit*."

A shadow rose behind him as he said it, gargantuan and filling up the high open doorway.

Bell seized Graves and yanked him to the side; the general's bony elbow cracked a pane of glass. A horse thundered down, fracturing the tiles, and they cowered from the snorting and the huge rippling flank. Molly sat above them, with her head near the ceiling, and her wild hair and wide dark eyes were so outrageously alive that Bell might have shot her if his pistol were at hand.

"What the devil!" Graves shouted.

Molly dropped the reins. The stallion quieted and clacked more gently on the floor. She rubbed his mane and gracefully dismounted, staring fearfully at Bell until he jostled her aside and reached toward the horse.

The creature pinned its ears and bumped him into Molly. They were trapped against the wall and Bell expected any moment to be kicked, to be bloodied in an avalanche of glass. Molly squeezed free, threw her arms around the horse's neck, and softened its aggression with a word he couldn't hear.

"My God," Graves stammered from the corner of the room. "You might have been killed."

"I'm fine," Bell said with barely checked fury.

"*You*, young miss," Graves corrected, glancing warily at Bell as if his disregard for Molly were an omen of his newly bought command.

Molly answered the general in a tone best described as cavalier, but once again Bell failed to hear what she was saying, distracted as he was by the riot in his mind, and by the time he straightened his coat and calmed the tremor in his limbs, his daughter and General Graves had fallen into rapt conversation.

"This is Tremendous," Molly said.

"I dare say it is!" Graves answered.

Bell approached him to apologize—and drag away his daughter—but he couldn't find a way around the great wall of horse.

"I was riding with my eyes closed," Molly told the general.

"With your *eyes* closed. Remarkable," Graves said. "That has to be a four-foot wall."

"Five," Molly said. "He didn't even clip it!"

The two of them continued this way for several minutes, even when the horse urinated freely, splattering the tiles with his great black penis. The smell was overpowering, the flow a minor river. Bell stood bristling through the whole conversation, staring at his daughter as his blood pressure rose but failing to communicate his violent displeasure.

"The question now is how to get him out," Graves said, openly delighted by the strangeness of the problem.

"If we get a running start from the far end of the room," Molly said, "or better still the hall—"

"The staff will handle the horse," Bell said.

"Ah, there you are, Bell," Graves said, acting like he truly had misplaced him. "Your daughter here is quite the flash of fire," he continued, winking at Molly as if he had just met his eighteenth grandchild.

"General Graves," Bell said, going so far as to seize the man's arm and lead him to the door. "I must insist that we continue in the study."

"I sincerely hope you'll join us," Graves said to Molly.

"She will not—"

"Of course she will," Graves decided, chuckling now at Bell's apparent temper. "I should like to hear your feelings on the troubles in Floria," he said to Molly, who at least had the sense to look at her father for permission. It was not directly granted.

"But we can't leave Tremendous here alone," Molly said.

"Perhaps you would escort me to the study," Graves said, "while your father and the staff see about your horse."

⌘

"Father sat and listened for an hour," Nicholas said, "while the two of you talked about horses?"

"General Graves asked him questions now and then," Molly said. "We also talked about Floria and ocean travel."

"And then the general left?"

"It wasn't that abrupt."

"It must have seemed so to Father. He's been waiting all week to chew the general's ear."

"It's true," Frances said, sitting in a rocking chair and sewing silver buttons onto a shirt. "I found him in the night, quarter past three, poring over maps and planning what to say. 'I have it,' he said as I was bringing him a sherry. Said the whole war was plain as day, plain as day. He acted right certain that the general would agree."

"Instead he spent an hour listening to Molly," Nicholas said, bottling his mirth until his eyes began to pool. He had color in his cheeks, a flush that even the sun, searing every day throughout the hot Bruntish summer, had failed to raise as fully as his sister's wondrous story. "What happened to Tremendous?"

"Burke and Stevens led him out."

"How?" Frances asked. "The conservatory leads—"

"Directly to the hall," Nicholas said. "And from the hall they must have led him—"

"Through the study." Molly laughed. "The three of us were sitting there, talking over biscuits, when they opened up the door and walked him past the table."

Frances clapped her mouth, rigid at the thought. Nicholas erupted and his laughter—boyish and ebullient, so at odds with his cadaverous demeanor—tickled Frances's nerves and set her laughing just as fully. It was worth every penalty their father would decree to hear them both laughing like a pair of giddy children.

"Your poor father," Frances finally said, sweating from the unaccustomed fun at his expense.

"Bah," Nicholas said. "He hoped to make an impression. What more could he ask?"

The trio laughed again, louder than before, with the humid little drawing room cushioning the sound. Molly knelt to lay her head upon her governess's lap.

"Mind the needle," Frances said.

Nicholas grew preoccupied, losing all his jollity. Molly wondered at her brother's studious expression.

"Will he still go abroad?" she asked.

"Yes," Nicholas said.

"And we'll be rulers of the house."

"*I* will be the ruler of the house," Frances answered. "I hope you treat me kinder than you treat your father."

"We'll treat you like our mother," Nicholas said.

Frances held her breath and put the needle in her cushion. Molly looked at her, assuming she was basking in the sentiment, but Frances and her brother turned their heads toward the door. There were footsteps steadily approaching in the hall, the claps so sharp Molly wondered if Tremendous might have somehow found his way back inside the house.

Her father opened the door.

"Get off the floor," he said to Molly. "Frances, you may go."

Molly wobbled when she stood; the sudden rise swirled her head. She had hurried from the study when her father walked outside to see the general into his carriage, and she had done her best—successfully till now—to drive away the fear of what would happen to her horse.

"It wasn't Tremendous's fault," she said, wishing that her voice were not so childishly high. "You always say the rider is to blame if there's an accident. I was reckless, it was me. I will write to General Graves, apologizing—"

"No," Bell said, with something like a smirk. He smiled so rarely, the expression was difficult to read and so it scared her, as thoroughly as Nicholas's laughter had enchanted her.

Bell stepped aside to let Frances out. She slipped around him with a nod. He was curiously blank, refusing to acknowledge the governess but almost, with a lowering of his chin, seeming drained when she was gone and he had shut the door behind her.

Nicholas stood without a sound, eyes fixed upon their father.

"As it happens," Bell began, "General Graves thinks highly of my powers of authority. Give us a thousand soldiers like your daughter, he said, and the continent is ours. He was jesting, of course, and yet he trusts in my ability to lead, to build a regiment as spirited and strong as I have built our little family. If your intention was to drive him off and keep me safe at home, I am afraid that you have failed."

"You have your command," Nicholas said.

"I do," Bell replied. "But here I am, preparing to go, and how can I leave you here alone, leaping horses into rooms and God knows what?"

Molly breathed deeply, trying to enlarge herself. "I promise to behave as long as you're away. You can trust me."

"I most certainly cannot." Bell laughed but it sounded more contemptuous than mirthful. "You would turn the whole house into a wild gypsy carnival."

"I will govern Molly," Nicholas said.

Bell regarded him and sighed with wary, chilled respect. "You have always had a will and I have always had to guide it. I have half a mind to take you overseas when I embark."

Nicholas blanched even whiter than his ordinary pallor.

Bell rubbed his jaw and seemed to honestly consider it. At last he shook his head and said, "Your health is unreliable. The trip alone would kill you. I am forced to leave you here, not quite a man and not quite a boy. You lack the sure-footed wisdom to run a household, and your lenience with Molly is a long-abiding weakness. The two of you together . . . no, it simply won't do."

"Frances . . . ," Molly said, as if her father had forgotten.

Nicholas, however, saw the danger in an instant. "No," he said, stepping up firmly to their father, one hand limp, the other fisted at his side.

"In recent weeks," Bell said, "as I anticipated my departure, I thought a great deal of Frances's ensconcement, shall we say, and of the virtues of her character. Devotion. Predictability. Familiarity. She is popular with the staff, respected and obeyed."

"Loved," Molly said.

"Yes, loved," Bell agreed. "But like a child on a stallion, she is far too apt to let the reins slip away. I have hired a new governess, Mrs. Wickware, who brings a sterling reputation and extensive experience—"

"You can't," Molly said, gasping through her tears.

"It is done," her father answered. "I will speak to Frances now, before we travel back to the city, giving her time to make arrangements and—"

"You're sending her away?" Nicholas said.

"I must."

Molly marveled at her brother's instantaneous composure.

"You require someone stronger," Nicholas conceded. "With Mrs. Wickware in charge, Frances might remain and fill another position."

"Impossible," their father said. "She is, as you have noted, much beloved by the staff. In matters of debate, they would defer to her rather than to Mrs. Wickware. A house cannot be governed in a state of ambiguity, any more than Floria can bow to two crowns. But you need not worry over Frances. I have found her an excellent position in Crookbury. As I said, I am not unappreciative—"

"You are a fiend," Nicholas said.

"How dare you!"

"No, you can't!" Molly yelled. "You can't, it isn't fair!"

"It is necessary," Bell declared, ignoring Molly's sobs and staring with ferocity at Nicholas, father and son nose to nose and locked as if their gazes were hypnotic, even fatal.

"She's like our mother," Molly said.

"But she is not!" Bell erupted. "Your mother died fourteen years ago."

"So did you," Nicholas said.

Bell struck him backhand, cutting his cheek with a ring and knocking him down with fearful ease. Molly ran to hold him, Nicholas hugged her back, and they protected each other in a knot of hands and elbows. Bell loomed above them, his gleaming boot tainted with the horse's stale urine and his nostrils flaring open, audible and vulgar.

"I hate you," Molly said. "You're awful, I despise you."

Bell was startled by her vehemence and backed toward the door. The frame boxed him in, both confining and enlarging him. "If your defiance has resulted from an overwarm attachment to your governess," he said with overwrought composure, "I am required to warn Frances's new employers, who have children of their own and may object—"

"No," Molly said, clenching up tight. "No, it's us. Only us."

"Very well," Bell said.

Nicholas remained silent, his face so immobile as to resemble the plaster death masks he'd studied as a child, causing Bell to shiver as he pivoted, exited the room, and left his son and daughter huddled on the floor.

֍

Molly appealed to her father incessantly. She waylaid him on the stairs, and in the stables, and at the end of each day in his private room where he was bound to return, exhausted and irritable, to face yet another of her heartfelt pleas. His usual response being silence or avoidance, she resorted to flagrant disobedience—refusing to pack for their journey back to the city, failing to change her clothes or tidy her hair, and most of all knocking, and calling, and singing childish songs whenever she encountered a locked room and knew that he was just beyond the door.

It was no use. Lord Bell put her off without acknowledgment or rage, ordering servants to pack her bags as she pursued him through the house, until she finally despaired and ceased to badger him completely, spending all the time she could in the company of Frances.

Nicholas appealed to the staff, taking his time with each and wringing their hearts with recollections of Frances's qualities—her kindness, her reliability, and her advocacy, at one time or another, on every servant's behalf—to rally their support. Lord Bell was unaccustomed to revolt; perhaps great dissent would force him to reconsider, if only to ensure law and order in the home. But Nicholas's words had the opposite effect, reminding everyone from the grooms to the maids that even a woman as peerless as Frances wasn't guaranteed the favor of their master. The servants doubled their efforts to appease Lord Bell and keep themselves secure, leaving Nicholas and Molly unsupported in rebellion.

Frances took the news with remarkable aplomb. According to Newton the footman, who overheard the conversation, she remained completely silent as Bell explained the reason for her dismissal. Instead of panicking or pleading, Frances overcame her shock and then replied, softly balanced, that of course she understood: whatever was best for the family. Newton watched her leave the study, dry-eyed and poised, but she kept to her room for much of the following day, refusing meals and denying access even to Molly and Nicholas when they knocked. She revealed herself after dinner the next night, sitting in the drawing room for her customary hour with the siblings. She slumped as if a structure in her body had collapsed. Her skin was wan from hunger, her eyes were dark and raw, and although she smiled and insisted she would weather the ordeal, the draining of her spirit seemed to indicate a fate much graver than dismissal, like an illness that would steadily disintegrate her bones.

She held herself together until the morning of her departure, when the siblings carried her bags to meet the carriage that would take her out of their lives. Lord Bell had said goodbye inside the manor and had given her a gift—a silver brooch once belonging to his wife—and after the carriage had been loaded and Frances faced the siblings in her drab ruffled cap, she crumpled into tears and they were quick to hold her up.

"You can't leave!" Molly cried, burying her face in Frances's armpit and squeezing around her ribs.

Nicholas stood on the opposite side, appearing to hug them both but insinuating his arm, like a pry bar, to loosen his sister's too-tight embrace.

"Molly, look at me," he said when she had finally raised her head. He was calm but not unfeeling, clamping his emotions.

"I won't be calm, I won't accept it," Molly said. "I'll run away!"

"No," Frances told her, speaking with such severity that Molly felt slapped. "The thought of you alone—"

"But together," Nicholas said, and then to Molly, "Still together. You will not run away, because you wouldn't have me. And you won't worry Frances. And we haven't seen the end of this."

Frances nodded in approval, though the end had clearly come.

Molly hated her brother's voice and rational control, and she almost hated Frances for the brooch she'd accepted—such a trifle, after years of mothering and work. The carriage driver, Stevens, sat above them on the box and him alone Molly loved, for his patience in the heat, for how his thick black beard indicated strength. Stevens, at least, wouldn't hurry Frances off.

"You have been my whole life," Frances said to them at last, dabbing her eyes with a handkerchief and folding it again with heartbreaking care. "I loved your mother dearly and have tried my best to honor her."

"You did," they said together.

"I'll think of you and pray for you and *oh*," Frances moaned, her words bubbling over into fresh red sobs. "I will love you till I die!"

They hugged her once more and glued together in the sun.

When Frances pulled away, Molly felt as if her lungs had been extracted through her chest. She wobbled with the smudgy glare of August all around her, hyperventilating awfully in the swelter, and the dust, and the evaporating safety of her governess's care. Frances climbed into the carriage, took her seat, and closed the door. She faced straight ahead and didn't acknowledge them again.

Stevens cleared his throat and snapped the horses into action, giving the siblings a look of reassurance and apology. Molly and Nicholas watched until the carriage turned a bend. It disappeared behind meringue trees that quivered in the heat, and then they walked arm in arm, up the white stone steps, to where the hall beyond the door looked impenetrably black.

⚜

The Bells left the country manor and traveled home to the baked grime of Umber, where in spite of the smoke and dust, the lunarite buildings looked unnaturally pristine. It was white upon white from the towers to the monuments, each grand home as solid as a courthouse. The haze combined with the sun to make everything both blearier and brighter, and the flowers in the green at Worthington Square were as vivid as the paints of a semi-swirled palette. The family had scarcely arrived and settled back in the mansion when Molly and Nicholas, still reeling from the sudden loss of Frances, were made to see their father off, too. He had business to conclude that required several days' travel outside the city and, as he had already sent his luggage to Umber Harbor, he could finish his rounds directly at the ship and embark for Floria without the inconvenience of returning home to make his farewell.

The city air afflicted Nicholas's lungs—he rarely left the house in late summer and spent an hour each day breathing camphorated vapor—so, instead of seeing Lord Bell into his post chaise, the siblings met him in the study to say their goodbyes. Dust motes floated like the residue of smoke, constricting Molly's chest and all but suffocating her brother.

Lord Bell stood in his violet coat, scabbard at his hip and tricorne squarely on his wig. A portrait of their mother smiled gently from the wall behind his head. She was beautiful, their mother, softened by the oil paint with plump cheeks and ringlets in her hair. It was the truest likeness that remained, and every year the resemblance between mother and daughter had grown until today, when Molly entered the room, it might have been a mirror rather than a painting. Nicholas, too, resembled their mother more than he did Lord Bell, who examined his children now as if they could have been the offspring of some other man.

"I am sorry," Bell said with martial hardness, "truly sorry to be leaving with hostility between us. I have done what I believe is best, not only for the household, but for you and for my own peace of mind. You question my devotion and my love. They are real. I leave for war more concerned for your welfare than for my own, more concerned about your safety than for that of the men within my regiment. And so I leave you in the very best care that I am able, in the hope that I will find you well kept when I return."

Molly watched the handle of his saber while he spoke. The steel in his voice had forced her eyes down, and now that he was done, his words seemed to ring through the quiet of the room. Bell himself seemed muted by the speech he had given, by the silence and paralysis that followed in its wake. They might have stood forever if he hadn't looked at Nicholas and offered him his hand, rigid but emphatic.

"Goodbye," Bell said, sounding hoarse, even choked.

Nicholas neither moved nor spoke. He did however stare—fiercely, imperturbably—until their father's hand sank to his side and his scalp crept back, smoothing out his forehead. It made Bell's face more boyish than his son's, open where the latter's was determinedly locked.

Molly struggled not to wilt when the focus turned to her. Heat brought fine bright needles to her skin. Bell kissed her head, just above the hairline, and though he must have said goodbye she didn't register the word. By the time she cleared her thoughts and realized he had moved, her father had stridden across the room and almost reached the door. He looked smaller from the distance—a pint-sized figure in his ornamented coat, off to win a war, packaged like a present. He would soon face the ocean and the tumult of the colonies, the naturals and the Rouge and violence and death. How his uniform would shear beneath a hatchet or a knife! How a musket ball would perforate his fine white shirt.

"Father," Molly said.

He faced her from the door. She ran to him and hugged him and he staggered from the blow. He found his footing, mumbled a sound, and squeezed her back as if to crush her with the handle of his saber grinding on her thigh. She listened to his stomach roiling through his vest, felt his breath begin to shudder and his heartbeat rise. When she unlocked her grip and leaned back to see his face, he had an aura, faint pink, from a sconce behind his head.

"Be good," he said.

"I will," Molly whispered.

He touched her on the cheek and left her at the door. Molly turned around and Nicholas seemed a hundred feet off beside the mantel. He coughed harshly into his sleeve. Molly crossed the room and rubbed him on the back. He took a stabilizing breath and looked at her intently.

"You surprised him."

"I'm sorry," Molly said. "I should have been more like you."

"No," Nicholas said. "Loving him is strong."

"Then why did you—"

"I have other kinds of strength."

"But you still love—"

"You. You're my only—" he began, but he was racked by another round of coughs and didn't finish.

She wondered if he meant to say sister, hope, or weakness.

Chapter Seven

"Sit up," Mrs. Wickware instructed Molly again, "and spread your butter more gently."

Their new governess was a middle-aged beauty with blond hair, pale green eyes, and a single piece of jewelry: a white-gold ring in memory of her husband. The siblings were eating breakfast at the long mahogany table in the sky-blue dining room. Molly and Mrs. Wickware sat at either end, and Nicholas sat in the middle, on the side near the windows. A band of morning sun cut the tabletop in two.

Molly was ravenously hungry. Mrs. Wickware fed them far less than they were accustomed to eating, and most of their meals included foods that spoiled Molly's appetite. This morning it was tea and toast, a boiled egg, and a kipper. The kipper was beautifully prepared but Molly loathed the taste of fish: an aversion Mrs. Wickware considered both unnatural and curable.

This morning the governess spoke to Nicholas at length about his health.

"I wonder that your father failed to recognize the problem," Mrs. Wickware said. "Excessive hours in the library, a musty room without windows, lacking sun and open air, have been the *cause* of your infirmities, rather than relief from their effects. The remedy is exercise. Exercise and work."

Nicholas sipped his tea with an unsteady hand, looking grayer and weaker than the time, seven years ago, when he had nearly died of an undiagnosed ailment of the blood. In the weeks since Mrs. Wickware's arrival, he had endured a daily regimen of work and strenuous movement that Molly believed was threatening to kill him. He dusted, swept, hauled firewood, boiled linen, emptied chamberpots, and mucked the horses' stalls, beginning at sunrise and finishing at dusk, his only rest coming at meals and thirty minutes of reading before he slept. It was enough to grind a healthy man down, but Nicholas had struggled through—gasping, coughing, often collapsing—not only without complaint but with the zeal of a happy convert. Still, the strain had left him wan.

"If you cannot sit up straight, you will stand," Mrs. Wickware said to Molly.

The governess motioned to her manservant, Jeremy, a swarthy clod whose jaw accounted for nearly half of his enormous, square head. He seemed perpetually uneasy in a fine set of clothes and frequently adjusted his collar and his cuffs. Jeremy rarely spoke, appeared to think even less, and was content to stand aside and wait for clear instructions.

He grabbed Molly's chair and tipped her off the seat before returning to his place several steps behind her. Nicholas focused on Mrs. Wickware throughout, having pondered and agreed with her assessment of his health. Molly stood and cracked her egg on the corner of the table. She meant to eat it whole—how she loved a boiled egg!—but Mrs. Wickware laid her silverware down and stared at the broken shell that Molly had strewn around her setting.

"Delicate foods for delicate manners," the governess said. Her skin looked as lovely as the egg in Molly's hand, and at the subtlest smile on her dainty pink lips, Jeremy took the egg away before it could be eaten. "Nicholas may have it," Mrs. Wickware said. "Molly may have Nicholas's kipper."

"I already have a bloody kipper!" Molly said, close to tears.

Her objection was ignored as if she hadn't really spoken. Jeremy delivered her egg to Nicholas, who accepted it with a nod, and then he took the second kipper from Nicholas's plate and placed it next to Molly's. He licked his fingers clean and waited for further instruction.

"Eat," Mrs. Wickware said.

"No," Molly answered.

"If you refuse to eat them now, you will see them again at midday. You will have nothing but kippers until you have learned to accept what you are given."

So it went with all of Mrs. Wickware's punishments—repetition, multiplication, more and more of the same. Molly longed to sit in her chair and finish her toast and tea.

"I'd rather starve," she said.

"They say a starving man will eat his own boot before he dies," Mrs. Wickware replied. "You will surely eat fish before the day is done."

Molly tossed her kipper to the middle of the table, but before she could throw the second, Jeremy caught her arms and pinned her wrists behind her back. His grip was so strong she couldn't free herself or turn. Nevertheless she tried, flinging her hair about and stomping.

"Enough," Mrs. Wickware said to Jeremy, who gave himself an extra few seconds to comply.

Molly rubbed her wrists and backed away from the table.

"In my busy years as governess," Mrs. Wickware said, "I have come to know a great many young women and men. Your strengths are not unique. Neither are your failings. You no doubt think yourself extraordinary, for it is a trait that young people share: the conviction that their youth is startling and new. But I cannot be surprised, Molly. I have seen it all before, and I intend to lead you firmly to predictable maturity."

Molly looked to Nicholas and watched him finish his egg. Instead of acknowledging the argument, he said to Mrs. Wickware, "May I please be excused? I need to tidy my room before dusting the frames in the garret."

"The frames in the *gilt room*. There aren't any portraits in the garret," Mrs. Wickware corrected, disappointed he would make such a ludicrous mistake.

"Yes," Nicholas said, bowing his head and smiling at his foolishness. "I'm sorry, yes. The gilt room."

Mrs. Wickware excused him. He folded his napkin next to his plate, straightened his chair, and left the dining room.

Molly watched him go, picturing the garret.

⚭

Molly sat alone in her room, where she was supposed to be writing copies of the household schedules and rules. She had been told to copy them once on the first day of Wickware's reign, and the number had doubled with each refusal—two, four, eight, sixteen, and now the ridiculous thirty-two, which may as well have been thirty-two hundred as far as Molly was concerned. The sole reason she remained in the room was that to be caught elsewhere in the house would lead to Jeremy hauling her back, locking her in, and staying at her side the rest of the afternoon. So she sat at the window overlooking the street, jealous of the midday action there below: gentlemen in hats, ladies riding carriages, children unfettered in the late summer air.

Then she spotted Mrs. Wickware and Nicholas leaving the house to purchase leeches at the market. They would be gone for more than an hour, and as her hunger had grown unbearable, she decided to risk escape and crept downstairs, moving furtively and listening for Jeremy's plodding footfalls.

She entered the kitchen with its cool stone floor. Vegetables and herbs were strewn across the tables, cheese and feathered foul dangled from the rafters, and a glorious wholesome stew burbled in a cauldron. Two fresh pies—crushberry and apple—puffed aroma from the knife-slit X's in their crusts.

"You mustn't be here!" said the kitchen maid, Emmy, a girl of Molly's age who happened to be the cook's own daughter. The two of them looked at Molly with startled expressions and identical snub noses, the younger holding a broom, the elder with a cleaver.

"We have instructions," said the cook, "not to slip you any food."

"I'm given kippers," Molly said. "You know I hate kippers."

"And who do you think prepares 'em?" asked the cook, looking wry. "I use the very best butter I can find to make 'em flavorful, and all of it to waste, all of it returned."

She resumed cutting mutton to avoid Molly's face, sorry that she couldn't cook the siblings what they wanted.

"Mrs. Wickware told us you was copying the rules," Emmy said.

"Which we're waiting for to read," the cook snapped, redder than the mutton she was carving on the block. "Though we know the rules already and we don't intend to flout 'em."

"What if Jeremy finds you here?" Emmy asked, sweeping a circle at her feet and listening, like her mother and Molly, for heavy-footed steps.

"We'll be sacked, same as Stevens," said the cook, cutting both Molly and the mutton simultaneously.

A week earlier, Molly had visited the stables without Mrs. Wickware's permission. Stevens, the kindly coachman who had driven Frances to her new home, threatened Jeremy with a riding crop when he dragged Molly away. Jeremy reported the incident to Mrs. Wickware, and Stevens was immediately fired after six years of unimpeachable service. It had been the first of very few rebellions, since Mrs. Wickware's severity—combined with the scarcity of alternative employment in Umber's strained economy—had shaken the servants even more than Frances's dismissal.

"Are we to spend the next year as pitiful as dogs?" Molly asked, stomping forward.

Emmy backed away, trembly as her broom.

"Dogs have homes," the cook replied with bloody hands. "Those that don't starve in gutters. You must be more—"

"Like Nicholas, I know." Molly picked a napkin off a table and said, "Just a quarter loaf of bread."

"A quarter will be missed."

"The heel," Molly said. "I'll hide it in the napkin."

The cook chopped a bone and put down the cleaver, wiping her hands across her apron and turning her back to the room. She pulled Emmy close and showed her where to sweep. Once the pair had averted their eyes, she said, "I meant to throw it out or crumble it into the stew, and you had best scurry off before the lot of us is caught."

Molly laid the napkin down and covered it with her hands.

"I'm sorry to have worried you," she said. "Thank you for the very best butter on the kippers."

"Which is wasted if the kippers aren't eaten!" yelled the cook, turning to find that Molly was already gone, the heel of bread remained, and the crushberry pie was missing from the table.

Molly carried her prize halfway up the stairs and froze before the landing. Jeremy was coming just above her to the left. Before he turned the corner, she slid down the railing with a flowery poof of skirts. The quick descent and the sumptuous aroma of the pie made her dizzy and she almost dropped the dish, but she escaped through the parlor and reached the stairs on the opposite side of the house.

There was Newton, the liveried footman, trimming lamps and pleased to see her. He snipped a wick and said, "Nicholas desired you to know that he and Mrs. Wickware will return at three in the morning. I suggested that he may have meant three this afternoon, but he was most adamant, repeating it distinctly. Perhaps it was confusion from his terrible exhaustion."

"I'm sure you're right," Molly said, hearing footsteps behind her. "If Jeremy inquires where I am, please inform him I have hastened to my room after a necessary trip to fetch more ink."

"I will indeed," Newton said, widening his nostrils to appreciate the pie.

He stepped aside to let her pass and trimmed another wick.

Molly reached the upstairs hall just as the parlor door banged open, and the last thing she heard before she padded away, silent in her stockings, was the placid voice of Newton saying, "Yes, Mr. Jeremy. She has hastened to her room . . . "

⚓

Molly behaved during dinner, neither arguing nor slouching, and ate two whole kippers of the three that she was served. After days of sour looks and worsening petulance, her placidity seemed all the more angelic, like the hush when a newborn finally stops wailing. Molly sensed Jeremy's animal frustration as he stood behind her chair, unable to manhandle her without Mrs. Wickware's say-so, and Mrs. Wickware herself was nervously attentive, wondering why her troublesome

charge was suddenly a model of decorum. It was as though a spark-
ing fuse had fizzled at the bomb; the explosion didn't come and yet
the fear of it increased. Molly pleased and thank-you'd, curtsied and
apologized, and the tension of her manners persisted after the meal
to the weekly bloodletting.

The leeches Mrs. Wickware had purchased with Nicholas's help
were six inches long, greenish-brown with a fine red stripe along their
dorsals, and were kept in an earthenware jar. They had suckers fore
and aft, one for leverage and the other, triple-jawed with a hundred
minuscule teeth, to open a wound and feed. Mrs. Wickware believed
them to remedy fatigue, aches, fever, infection, tired blood, melancholy,
sanguinity, and countless other ailments, and so had ordered weekly
bleedings for the entire household, including Jeremy and herself.

Nicholas's health called for three weekly bleedings.

The first and only time Molly had been bled, she'd fought until
Jeremy had tied her arms to the chair. He had used the wrong knots,
however, and Molly had shaken free so dramatically that most of the
leeches had flown from her arms and landed, with viscous plops, along
the edges of the room.

Tonight, Mrs. Wickware again brought the leeches into Molly's
bedroom, where she placed the jar on a nightstand and set aside the
lid. Jeremy had been practicing knots all week and stood behind a chair
in the center of the rug. He had a length of dirty rope and looked eager
to employ it, but Molly took a seat and rolled up her sleeves unbidden. The room seemed to shrink with all of them together. Mrs. Wickware plunged her hand into the jar; leeches could be heard writhing
at her fingers.

She turned and asked Molly, "Will you need to be restrained
again?"

"No, ma'am," Molly said, turning up her forearms to better show
the veins. Her sweat thickened when the first slippery leech was
brought toward her. It was hungry and had already drawn blood from
Mrs. Wickware's wrist, but Molly stared at it directly and refused to
flinch away.

"Do you hope to be exempted on the grounds of good behavior?
This is not the proper attitude," Mrs. Wickware said. "Leeching,

though unpleasant, should not be viewed as punishment, you see, but as a beneficial practice we must all of us accept."

"I understand," Molly said. "I think it's humbug and hideous like everything you do. But I will patiently submit because I know I cannot win."

Mrs. Wickware flushed and looked at her triumphantly, her countenance enlivened, her rigidity dissolving. "I am satisfied to hear it. We learn by rote and force what later we believe through wisdom and experience. You cannot see the benefit but bow to my authority. I ask for nothing else. You needn't love me to obey me."

Jeremy loomed close, twisting on his rope. Molly balled her fists and didn't shrink away as Mrs. Wickware attached the first leech below her elbow. There was a momentary sting. She waited and it passed. "Leech saliva dulls the pain," Nicholas had told them over dinner, "allowing them to feed undetected on their hosts."

Undetected, Molly thought, if she were swimming in a pond—not sitting in a chair and witnessing the meal.

And yet she sat and let it happen, even when Jeremy leaned down to watch the leeches suck, and Molly imagined they were each a little Wickware at dinner, comfortable and swelling up full enough to pop.

༆

Molly lay in bed, waiting for the Elmcross Church bells to toll three o'clock. She worried she had missed it, having heard the bells at two so very long ago—what if she had dozed and missed the long-awaited cue?

Her bed had been moved to the room immediately adjacent to Mrs. Wickware's chamber, the better to ensure that she behaved after dark. On most nights, Jeremy forced her to the room and locked her inside. If Molly thumped or shouted, trying to disrupt Mrs. Wickware's sleep, Jeremy would lock himself in Molly's room and watch her sleeping from a chair all night long.

Tonight, however, Molly had climbed into her bed without being asked. Her door was locked as always but Jeremy had departed, and thanks to Molly's docility in the latter half of the day, Mrs. Wickware's suspicions fell away and soon her purring snores could be heard in the neighboring room. Molly passed the hours reading, and when Elm-cross Church finally tolled three, she blew her candle out, crept to the third-story window in her shift, and quietly opened the sash.

A thick warm fog had drifted over Umber from the sea, and all she could discern, thirty feet below, were the wrought-iron spikes of the fence surrounding the house. The rest of the street was pillowy mist, seeming substantial enough to catch her if she fell. She stepped out onto the narrow ledge and closed the sash behind her, fearing a draft under the door would rouse Mrs. Wickware. The only light came from the moon, which was gauzy in the fog and illuminated the haze rather than anything within it.

She had climbed throughout her life and had rarely fallen, thanks to her natural balance and an absolute, delusional belief in her abilities. The day in the library when Nicholas cracked his tooth had been the closest she had ever come to serious harm, but now, creeping farther and farther away from the safety of her window, she thought of the iron spikes and lost her purchase on the wall. She flailed her arm in circles, grabbed the corner of a shutter, and pivoted on her toes until her body swung outward like a door upon a hinge.

Her shift flapped. Her hair swung darkly in her eyes. A second later, she was back against the wall, clinging tight, panting against the shutter wood and doubting her resolve. Then a long knotted rope tumbled to her side, dangling from a window of the garret overhead, where Nicholas, invisible, was waiting in the shadows.

She safely reached the rope, and then she climbed and shut her eyes, still reeling from her slip, and didn't look again until her hands were on the sill. Nicholas pulled her in; his feeble grip was actually more a hindrance than a help. She clambered into the garret and sighed against the wall. The effort had exhausted her, but her weariness was nothing compared to that of Nicholas, who sat on the floor and shivered in the damp night air. When she hugged him, he was cold and smelled of chemicals and sickness. He had long been known to dose himself in secret when he needed. Yet his eyes were ghostly bright, reflecting the moon but seeming to glow much stronger from an indwelling light.

He opened a basket at his side and handed her a fat buttered roll, a small flask of wine, and a cold piece of mutton he had somehow procured without detection. Molly kissed his cheek and fell immediately to eating, greasing her lips and buttering her fingers.

"How were your leeches?" Nicholas asked, pleased to see her eat.

"I don't know how you bear it three times a week."

"I remember they are creatures feeding to survive. I cannot loathe a leech for following its nature."

Molly held his wrist, examining the veins, and said with a mouthful of roll, "I'm astonished you have any more blood left to suck."

Once her eyes adjusted to the dimness of the garret, she saw its cobwebbed corners and unadorned walls, along with a rocking chair, covered by a sheet, that Mrs. Wickware had stored after rearranging the house. It had been Frances's chair in her bedroom, a room now occupied by Jeremy, whose burliness and weight had called for stouter furniture.

"Has she written?" Molly asked.

"Possibly," Nicholas said. "The mail is taken to Mrs. Wickware directly from the door. I have hit upon a way to send letters out. Receiving them, however—"

"Have you told her how we're treated?"

"The news would make her suffer. I have told her we are well and miss her every hour."

Molly flumped backward onto her heels, sitting apart from Nicholas and lowering her head. The roll that she'd been chewing turned doughy in her mouth.

"She'd be here if not for me. It's all my fault! Frances, Mr. Stevens . . . Most of the servants try to avoid me. And you," she said, looking up to glower. "I know you play a role when Mrs. Wickware is watching, but you play it so well it almost breaks my heart. Even here alone, I would swear that you were angry."

"I am," Nicholas said, speaking so calmly, and with so little movement, that it seemed as if the words had issued from his mind. "I am angry at Father and at my own futility. And yes, I am angry at you—irrationally so, I openly admit. You are no more to blame for acting as you did than the leeches are to blame for feeding on our arms. Mrs. Wickware herself is merely who she is. I admire her extremity."

"Admire!" Molly yelled, standing up and stomping around the garret. "She has all of us in misery and buckled to her will!"

"She does it perfectly," he said. "Do you not find it wondrous that in so little time, she has screwed down the house tighter than our father? The servants are rewarded for exemplary performance. They are handsomely rewarded for informing on each other. Have you heard about Emmy?" Nicholas asked. "This very afternoon, she informed against her mother for giving you the pie."

"I stole it!" Molly said, spinning around to face him.

"But the pie was hers to guard. The woman's own child turned her in within the hour and received half a crown."

"It's horrible."

"It's masterful. With nothing but her will and a well-trained brute, Mrs. Wickware has silenced all dissent and shaped the home as she desires. You and I could do the same, instead of suffering and quailing. I have learned a great deal that we will use to our advantage. Please come and sit before your pacing wakes Jeremy."

Molly hesitated, furious but aware of just how noisy she had been. Her heart was like a cricket captured in a hand, frantic in the dark and struggling to spring. She tiptoed back and sat before Nicholas on the floor, feeling wretchedly alone and pushing the uneaten food out of sight. He held her hand, his touch so feathery she might not have noticed it but for the coldness of his fingers.

"We know her methods now," he said. "We know the servants fear dismissal and crave reward, yet most of them are willing to support us in revolt. I have spoken to each of them—"

"What revolt?"

"More of the same," Nicholas said. "A great deal more. Mrs. Wickware trusts me thanks to my dutiful compliance. I will carry on complying, as will all the servants."

"What of me?" Molly asked.

"Be yourself, far more than you have been. You must laugh at every stricture and defy every rule. You must shoulder all the blame and suffer all the penalties. I need you to be strong, but you will not be alone." He smiled and his chipped tooth glinted in the dark. Then his grip turned firm. "Many Mollys will assist you."

Chapter Eight

Mrs. Wickware had instituted a shut-door policy with the coming of autumn's cold. There were few greater threats to health than icy drafts, a fact she had expected Molly to appreciate given her constant, vocal worry over Nicholas's well-being. And yet the girl had flouted the rule from the day it was announced, not only refusing to close doors behind her but opening doors wherever she encountered them, and it was this—the long chain of household doors hanging wide—that Mrs. Wickware followed in pursuit of her devilish quarry.

Nary an hour passed anymore without Jeremy, the servants, or Nicholas coming to Mrs. Wickware with a fresh report of Molly's misbehavior, which had unexpectedly worsened after a single, promising day of near capitulation. Mrs. Wickware had never seen the like. One evening Molly had been leeched without struggle, admitting to defeat and seeming to submit, and then the very next day she had seemed possessed. She routinely rejected her meals, fled the dining room, and hid for much of the day, emerging just long enough to steal a piece of cake or a bottle of milk from the kitchen. One day Jeremy had locked her in her room, and Molly had emptied her wardrobe onto the busy street below. As punishment for this, Mrs. Wickware had taken the clothes Molly was wearing, certain it would teach her to respect her own belongings. Instead the girl escaped and sprinted through the house, entirely naked, astonishing the staff before returning, pink and laughing, to the safety of her bed.

There had been weeks of such behavior. Mrs. Wickware had attempted all manner of common punishment, from depriving Molly of comforts to locking her in closets, and although these efforts failed at every turn, she told herself that discipline would finally win the day, as when a long-standing illness yields to steady treatment.

Yet to make matters worse, the girl was unpredictable. Some days Molly would appear at breakfast, eat whatever was placed before her, and outshine the queen in ladylike comportment. She would follow every rule for half a morning and then, just as Mrs. Wickware's guard began to lower, she would abruptly reignite the flames of misbehavior.

This morning had been similar. Weeks of battle had left Mrs. Wickware prone to overreaction, and when Molly passed her in the third-floor hallway and failed to step aside, she was ordered to kneel and face the wall until such time as Mrs. Wickware returned. Molly had complied, saying, "Yes, ma'am," curtsying, and kneeling like a penitent, and had remained there—or so it was believed—for more than an hour, until Jeremy reported she had vanished.

Newton the footman had seen Molly running through the downstairs study not two minutes ago. Sure enough, Mrs. Wickware discovered, the study doors were open and fresh-cut flowers had been scattered on the floor. The study led to a narrow hall, where the chambermaid, blackened in a cloud of settling ash, explained that she had just emptied one of the hearth grates when Molly grabbed the pan and threw it into the air. Mrs. Wickware stepped around the ash, ignoring the maid's apologies, and followed the next open door into the gilt room, where the largest portrait—that of Lord Bell's father, high above the floor—was hanging upside down. She continued to the library, where Nicholas stood amazed before a castle made of books. It was six feet tall with battlements and towers, a marvelous construction he had found moments ago, he claimed, after hearing Molly's laugh and chasing her into the library.

"I saw her place the final book," he said, pointing to a leatherbound copy of *The Rise and Fall of the Lost Volcanic Islands*. "I said I would report her and she answered . . . "

Nicholas hesitated, seemingly reluctant to repeat what Molly had said. Mrs. Wickware's legs quivered when he paused. Her skin began to blotch and she was breathless, having walked much faster in the chase than she had realized.

"What did she say?" Mrs. Wickware asked.

"That I could tell the chicken-breasted harpy anything I liked."

She struck him on the cheek, sudden as a reflex.

He accepted the blow and said, "I'll take it down straightaway," beginning at once to reshelve the books, and Mrs. Wickware could not decide whether it was Nicholas's poise or Molly's pandemonium that made her want to knock the castle over, or—if only it were possible—to climb inside, close her eyes, and hide behind its walls.

She pursued Molly throughout the house, encountering finger-pointing servants and flagrant mischief at every turn. She visited the stables outside, found the groom trying desperately to calm the frantic horses, and followed a trail of dirty footprints back inside the house. They led her through the kitchen, up the rear stairs, and straight to the third-floor hall, where Molly knelt—neither breathless nor disheveled, the bottoms of her shoes immaculate—on the very spot of the floor where Mrs. Wickware originally told her to remain.

⚓

"You actually *saw* her enter the library?" Mrs. Wickware asked Nicholas at dinner.

She had questioned—repeatedly—everyone who had witnessed any part of Molly's escapade. How could anyone traverse the entire house, including the stables, and accomplish so many things in so little time unopposed and unassisted? It had taken two grown men with a ladder to reposition the inverted portrait in the gilt room, and Nicholas had spent hours returning the nearly five hundred books of Molly's castle to the shelves. And yet the servants' accounts harmonized down to the minute. Molly herself refused to speak a word in self-defense but rather smiled, seeming tickled by the story, until Mrs. Wickware locked her in a closet and stationed Jeremy at the door.

"It was just as I have told you," Nicholas said, lowering his fork and speaking very slowly. "I followed the sound of her laugh and saw her place the final book. When I threatened to report her, she said—"

"Yes, I understand, but did you see her running in? Surely she had been working in the room for quite some time?"

"I had passed the library ten minutes earlier," Nicholas said, "and nothing looked amiss."

"But don't you see that it's impossible?" Mrs. Wickware cried.

Before attempting to explain the obvious again, she picked up the lavender teapot and poured herself a cup, hoping to soothe her throat after hours of fruitless questioning. A long fat leech issued from the spout and overflowed the cup with a quick, dramatic plop. Mrs. Wickware shrieked and swatted it away. The cup exploded on the floor, the pot was overturned, and somehow the leech remained upon the table. She leapt from her chair and backed away, tugging the bell rope so emphatically its tassel tore free in her hand.

Newton and Emmy promptly appeared, but they could hardly make sense of Mrs. Wickware's incoherent fury. Once Nicholas explained the commotion, Newton collected the leech and swept the breakage from the floor. When Mrs. Wickware upbraided Emmy for delivering the pot, the kitchen maid grew incensed and said, with a fiery glow, that she had seen Miss Molly creeping round the pot and had chased her off, assuming at the time that she had come to steal the tea.

"She bedevils us!" Emmy said. "Always sneaking about, snatching food and sullying floors and interfering with our work! I am sorry, Mr. Nicholas, to speak against your sister, but I have never known a girl so bold in all my days!"

Nicholas bowed his head in woeful resignation.

"You can't have seen her in the kitchen!" Mrs. Wickware said. "She is locked inside a closet and has been for many hours!"

"Then it must have been her ghost, beg pardon," Emmy said, "or the girl's spitting image, with the same unruly hair."

"Excuse me," Newton said, gathering teapot shards. "I myself found Molly drawing pictures on the wall. I have only just finished painting over what she drew."

"What wall? When? What did she draw?" Mrs. Wickware asked, her voice trailing off due to shallowness of breath.

"In your own bedchamber, within the hour," Newton replied. "I would rather not communicate the nature of the drawings."

Mrs. Wickware ordered them all to abandon the mess and leave the dining room single file. They followed her up the stairs and down the hall until the four of them stood before a wide-eyed Jeremy, who rose from his stool in front of the closet and handed Mrs. Wickware the key.

She opened the door and there was Molly, roseate and calm. The closet was large enough to sit in, but the girl had apparently stood; the dust upon the floor and on the trunks was undisturbed.

Jeremy insisted he had not left his station.

"I was here upon the stool and didn't hear a sound."

He repeated himself verbatim when Mrs. Wickware informed him of the leech and of the drawings, and when she asked him yet again how Molly might have escaped, he flexed his jaw, smoothed his ill-fitting waistcoat, and refused to speak again.

Mrs. Wickware knew better than to interrogate Molly herself, and rather than satisfy the girl with fury and frustration, she pretended not to care, sent Molly off without additional punishment, and retired to her chamber with its newly painted wall, where she calmed her ruined nerves with half a bottle of wine.

⁂

Throughout autumn and deep into winter, Molly did as Nicholas had instructed, flouting rules and causing trouble at every opportunity. She shouted, laughed, kicked, overturned drinks, vandalized rooms, insulted Mrs. Wickware, bit and spat at Jeremy, stole whatever she could and broke whatever she couldn't. She kept refusing meals she didn't want to eat, and the cook, still peeved about the crushberry pie, initially refused to sneak her any food.

At the dinner table Molly fainted with hunger, only to be revived with spirit of hartshorn and placed, once again, before a loathsome plate of fish. One night when she refused to stay in bed, Jeremy tied her to the bedposts with knots that left bruises on her ankles and wrists.

She spent a long, panicked night gagged with a handkerchief, fearing she would suffocate and trying not to cry. She cried on most nights, and sometimes during the day when nobody would see.

She wondered how much longer she could actively persist, because although her brother's plan was seemingly in motion, Molly went days without a kind look from anyone in the house, and in the course of her rebellion she began to glimpse herself, reflected in the punishments and faults and accusations, as a creature unworthy of forgiveness or redemption.

Nicholas encouraged the servants to blame her for everything, including their own mistakes. Some with hearty consciences initially refused, but Nicholas convinced them by explaining the design. Others played along because they welcomed a permanent scapegoat, and because Nicholas rewarded them—using Lord Bell's money, secretly obtained—far more lavishly than Mrs. Wickware did.

In their grandest orchestration, Newton had scattered the flowers in the study, the chambermaid had dumped her own ashes, the gardener and coachman had inverted the portrait, Nicholas and three maids had constructed the book castle, and the groom had tracked manure into the house. Molly, who had knelt before the wall as she'd been told, left the spot just long enough for Jeremy to find her missing and returned before Wickware discovered she'd been gone.

The house was full of Mollys every moment of the day, and not an hour passed that one of the staff did not report a shocking new offense, genuine or faked, and trouble Mrs. Wickware with straight-faced deception.

As the governess and Jeremy were constantly distracted, Nicholas and the servants were trusted to go about their days largely unsupervised. With the exception of the choreographed disruptions, the household ran superbly and the liberated staff—no longer punished even for their own mistakes—was inspired to harry Mrs. Wickware further. They hatched their own plans, perfected their alibis, and collected their rewards without a pinprick of guilt.

They began to sneak Molly food when she was deprived of meals, loosen her bonds when they were overly tight, and buoy her with gentleness whenever they were able. Her vigor grew. Her spirits rose. She heightened her attack. Mrs. Wickware, frazzled and increasingly prone to drink, dispensed with punishment entirely and started to bribe and plead.

"If you finish your dinner," for instance, "you will be given an extra custard."

Or, "Girls who wash their feet deserve a finer pair of shoes."

Or, "You may do whatever you like, so long as you leave me in peace this afternoon."

To these and other inducements, Molly answered with defiance, until at last she swept through the house like an unchecked fire, and all that Mrs. Wickware could do was treat her own burns.

Leeches kept appearing in the unlikeliest places: baked into Mrs. Wickware's puddings, folded into her towels, writhing in her bed-sheets. One slithered from a bookshelf and landed in her hair. The weekly bleedings were abandoned and the earthenware jar was taken from the house, and yet the leeches not only persisted but increased in size and number.

Nicholas stole Mrs. Wickware's personal belongings. At first he merely moved them into adjoining drawers or rooms; she assumed that she herself, scatterbrained and often tipsy, was responsible. Later he kept whatever he took and encouraged the staff to follow his lead, pro-vided every item was delivered straight to him.

By midwinter, Mrs. Wickware was starting her days with wine and ending them with peach brandy. She continued to wake at day-break, but Molly woke earlier to dress herself, eat a secret breakfast in her room, and spy on her governess's movements through the keyhole.

One morning she heard the clink of the decanter on a glass once, twice, three times before a glow filled the hearth and Mrs. Wickware could finally be seen, disheveled in her nightgown. The governess lifted her personal lockbox onto a table and opened it using a key she wore at all times around her neck. Her firelit face immediately shadowed. She clawed through the box and finally overturned it, scattering the contents on the table and still not finding what she wanted. Then she ran toward the keyhole, fumbled for the bedroom key, and opened the door to find Molly, prettily dressed, standing there before her with a curious expression.

"Where is it?" Mrs. Wickware said, leaning close to Molly's face. "What have you done with it? You have to give it back!"

"What?" Molly asked.

Mrs. Wickware shook her by the arms, repeating herself and panting with a sweet-sour breath. But since Nicholas or one of the servants must have stolen the item in question, Molly's puzzlement was wholly unfeigned and Mrs. Wickware could spot no glimmer of deceit. She released Molly's arms and backed away, seeming about to fall and supporting herself in the doorframe.

"It was my husband's," Mrs. Wickware said. "My husband, dead and gone . . . I keep it to remind me of him. Please, Molly, please. It is worthless, but to me— Oh, you must give it back! You won't be punished, not a whit. You don't believe me. No, of course! You're worried I'll be angry. Leave it out where I will find it, anywhere at all, and we will never have to speak of it again. You have my promise!"

Molly watched without a word—even with the firelight behind her, Mrs. Wickware's tears were easily discerned—and took a small step forward, reaching out to hold the governess's hand.

Mrs. Wickware flinched like a child from a wasp. She retreated into her own room, inhaled sharply through her nose, and tried to conceal her trembling limbs by hugging herself and narrowing her stance.

"I'm sorry," Molly said. "I don't know what you've lost."

Mrs. Wickware staggered from the warmth in Molly's voice, unsure if it was innocence or masterful dissembling. Either way it meant despair—her treasure had been taken—so Mrs. Wickware returned to her table in a slump, where she locked the rest of her possessions into the box and raised her glass of sherry.

She had poured the drink in the dark, but now that the fire had brightened the room, she was able to see the dead, tumid leech in her decanter. She shoved it away with a spasm of her arm, overturning the decanter and spilling the sherry upon the rug, but after staring at the leech where it lay inside the crystal, she turned to the glass she had already poured and drank anyway, moaning as she gulped.

☙

Before the dawn of a late winter day, Mrs. Wickware awoke from a dream in which she and her husband rode together in a hansom. He was younger than she had known him in life, ruddy with success—he had just cured a government minister's daughter of dropsy—and was wearing a splendid blue ribbon on the tail of his wig. He squeezed her knee and said, "I am always at your side." He kissed her earlobe. She pushed him off and smiled out the window.

Now she opened her eyes in bed, and her attempts to reenter the dream were thwarted by a headache, a marrow-deep chill, and the curious markings, unfamiliar in the gloom, that she glimpsed on the wall beside her mirror. She pulled her covers off, wrapped herself in a robe, and lit a candle from the embers in the hearth. As soon as she raised the light, a single word leapt forth. It appeared to have been written by a finger dipped in ink.

ALONE

The room was nearly cold enough to see her own breath, but her skin began to moisten and the wallpaper rippled, like air above a strong source of heat. The shutters were locked. So were the doors. Mrs. Wickware checked them all, including those in the adjoining chamber, which had been empty ever since she had allowed Molly to return to her own private room. The girl's nightly proximity had finally unnerved her, and yet as soon as Molly had gone, Mrs. Wickware had missed her, feeling gravely alone in the dark and often summoning servants, at ungodly hours, for the sole purpose of seeing another human being.

She examined the word on the wall. The ink was wet—glistening and fresh enough to smell—and she rang the bell and swigged from a bottle of rum before the chambermaid appeared and was sent to fetch the others, everyone in the house.

Once the staff had gathered and seen the word upon the wall, she was amazed that none of them could offer an explanation. It was the first offense in months that hadn't been blamed immediately on Molly, whose hands—like those of the servants—were free of any stain. Nicholas alone had ink upon his fingers, but only from his quill and not enough to warrant Mrs. Wickware's suspicion. Yet her nerves were disarrayed and she seized both of his hands, holding them up and fixing him with a look more of lunacy than anger.

Nicholas, a full head taller, straightened up and stared at her with dark, contemptuous eyes.

"Don't be absurd," he said. "If I were to threaten you with words, I would do it to your face."

She sickened from his voice, unprepared for his defiance and releasing him at once. But Molly's pitying expression troubled Mrs. Wickware more. The world was in reverse, with Nicholas, once so frail, now suddenly reptilian, and the girl, so defiant, now angelically serene.

"Where is Jeremy?" Nicholas asked.

As if responding to the question, footsteps were heard upon the stairs beyond the room and seconds later he appeared, parting the servants with his bulk and scowling about with heavy-lidded eyes.

"Where have you been?" Mrs. Wickware asked.

"Someone blacked me hands."

"What do you mean, blacked your hands?" she said, her voice an octave higher.

"Soot," Jeremy said, looking about and settling on Molly. "I woke and there was greasy black soot upon me hands."

His hands were red and clean.

"You washed them in your basin," Mrs. Wickware said.

"Aye."

"Bring the basin."

Jeremy slouched forward, broadening his back. "I dumped it in the chamberpot. You're welcome to a look."

"How dare you!" Mrs. Wickware said, emboldened by her fear. "What of this? What of this?" she cried, pointing at the wall.

He saw the word and grunted as if her purpose was to shame him.

"You know I can't read," he said.

A fact she had forgotten. Jeremy's well-scrubbed fingers couldn't be ignored, but she was not yet prepared to openly accuse him, not without proof.

After she dismissed the staff and calmed herself with rum, Mrs. Wickware stared at the mysterious word for many minutes, thinking obsessively of Jeremy and his demeanor over the past few weeks. She had known the man for years, ever since her husband engaged him—a destitute gravedigger—to carry their belongings to a newly rented flat. He had proved so reliable, so willing to do the most menial chores, that he had been permanently added to their staff. Upon her husband's early death, Mrs. Wickware had brought Jeremy to her first governessing position, where his brutishness was useful in the care of wild children. He had always been trustworthy, if only for being stupid, pliable, and thankful of better employment after a decade of cold, muddy graveyards.

Molly's misbehavior had altered him, however. Because of his failure to constrain or intimidate Molly during the months of her rebellion, Mrs. Wickware chastised him often, in her drunken irritability, both for things that he had done and things that he had not. Jeremy had grown surly. Over the last fortnight, he had greeted Mrs. Wickware with evident displeasure, and although he continued to follow instructions, she feared that he was losing all respect for her authority.

She kept a very close watch over Jeremy throughout the rest of the day. Indeed, she followed his movements and questioned the servants about his activities with so much single-minded fervor that Molly's usual mischief went entirely unnoticed. Each of Jeremy's actions—"He is cleaning his shoes, ma'am," or "He was walking toward the library"—filled her with suspicion. How had he sullied his shoes? What business had an illiterate man in a room full of books?

It took a full pint of rum for Mrs. Wickware to sleep. When she woke the following morning and lit a candle, she discovered on the wall:

I CAN WACH YOU TO

Mrs. Wickware bolted from her room and rushed downstairs. She lost her footing near the landing, banged her hip against the newel post, and hurried on with tears streaming from her eyes. When she knocked on Newton's door—the first that she encountered—he answered her summons directly from his sleep, wearing a sleeping gown and robe and entirely bald, much to her surprise, without his customary wig. But it was he who looked amazed to see her there, wild-eyed and pale in nothing but her shift.

She seized his arm and dragged him along, shouting at every door, "Wake up! Come out at once!" and by the time they had crossed the house and reached the door of Jeremy's room, a mass of dazed and underdressed servants was assembled in the hall.

Molly and Nicholas moved to the front, standing on either side of Mrs. Wickware as she knocked, received no answer from within, and opened the door with a trembling hand. Jeremy lay in his bed like someone heavily drugged. The room was hot and smoky from a poorly vented fire, and now with the entire household trying to cram inside, the meaty stink of the chamberpot and of Jeremy's own rarely washed body made the atmosphere intolerably dense. Newton raised a candle.

At the moment when Mrs. Wickware spotted the ink on Jeremy's fingers, Nicholas stumbled into her shoulder, righted himself, and turned with curiosity to examine the floor. He knelt and found a plank that was loosened from the rest, and when he lifted it away and Newton lowered the light, they saw that Mrs. Wickware's belongings—everything she'd lost—were piled there together in the gap between the joists.

She fell to her hands and knees and rummaged through the items, picking them up and throwing them aside until the floor was strewn with them, while the staff, backing up, shuffled their feet so as not to be struck by a hairbrush, a pincushion, a hand mirror. Dozens of items emerged, some of which she hadn't even known had disappeared, and yet the one she wanted most was nowhere to be found: her husband's glass eye, which she had treasured since his death, often staring at the iris and pretending he could see her. It was the only fantastical thing that Ms. Wickware believed and therefore the strongest. She was lost without the eye.

Jeremy had come sluggishly awake in the commotion, knuckling into his face before he finally looked around and leapt to his feet, startled by the crowd. His legs had yet to wake. He fell against the wall, dashing his head upon the wainscot and dazing himself anew.

"What have you done with it?" Mrs. Wickware said from the floor, her face so distorted it appeared about to melt. "Tell me where you've hidden it!"

Jeremy hunched and scowled. "I haven't took a thing, you mad fucking wench."

"Call the constable!" she yelled, rising to her feet. "Call the constable at once!"

Newton handed off the candle and hurried up the hall, and were it not for so many others standing in the room, Jeremy might have closed his inky hands around Mrs. Wickware's throat. Nevertheless he clearly imagined doing it, staring dumbly at her neck and flexing his fingers as he struggled, in his strange lethargic rage, to shake confusion from his mind and grasp the situation.

Eventually he knew that staying put was not in his interest, and since none of the staff was willing to restrain him, he dressed and packed a trunk and hauled it to the door with Mrs. Wickware shadowing his heels, yelling, "Stop! I'll see you jailed for this!"

He left the house and lumbered off, wobbly on his feet but fast enough to vanish into the predawn gloom. Mrs. Wickware stood at the front door for some time, scarcely covered in her shift and needled by a very fine, windblown snow. At last she went inside and dressed to meet the constable, who promised to inform her as soon as Jeremy was apprehended. She spent the greater part of the day cloistered in her room, leaving only to reexamine the floor of Jeremy's chamber—the eye could not be found—until at nightfall she locked her shutters and door and fell asleep, with a bottle of rum hugged tightly to her bosom.

In the late morning of the following day, having overslept the sunrise and been insensible of the servants' tentative knocks upon her door, she woke in the frigid room with a headache and sickening pangs of hunger. But though her symptoms were appalling and she grieved the loss of her husband's eye, she lit the candle at her bedside and felt a glimmer of hope. Jeremy was gone, the worst was done, and there was something almost soothing in the thought of facing Molly, whose behavior, though appalling, rarely seemed malevolent.

But when the candle brightened the room, she saw the shutters were ajar, and there were large, muddy footprints leading from the window to her bed.

She found a wound upon her forearm, a mutilated leech lying on her table, and—written on the wall with her own sucked blood—a single word:

HELL

She covered her face and wept.

Chapter Nine

Molly aimed the gun and tightened her finger on the trigger. It was a flintlock pistol made of hardwood and nickel, and her arm began to shake until she worried the gun would fire accidentally as she paused. Mrs. Wickware's former chamber was bright and sultry from the late-August sun, and although her skin itched maddeningly beneath her garters and her stays, Molly squinted her eyes and refused to be distracted.

"Wait!" Nicholas said.

She smiled puckishly at this and thought of firing at once, but the tension of the music, sparkling as he played, enchanted her and charmed away her frivolous temptation. Nicholas finished the larghetto—it was "The Cuckoo and the Mockingbird," a favorite of theirs and one of his finer harpsichord transcriptions—and held his fingers over the keys.

"Wait a full measure. On the beat," Nicholas said.

He opened the allegro with a high glittery flourish. On the first determined beat, Molly fired the gun.

Smoke blossomed with the bang. The sound was deafening; she sensed her brother playing just beside her, but the harpsichord's notes were silenced by the after-ring. Her hand tingled sweetly from the powerful vibration, and the smell of burnt powder filled her with euphoria. The target—a human skull that Nicholas had purchased last spring—grinned back at her unharmed. The gun had not been loaded with a ball, only powder.

When the movement came to a close three minutes later, she could hear the delicate notes again and felt, as she so often did at the end of Brondel's works, a comfort that could turn upon a breath to woeful longing. The cure was more Brondel, more shots, more indulgence. But they all led to yearning and a color of despair.

Mrs. Wickware had retreated to the garret to drink, sleep, and fret. The menacing words and torments had continued after the departure of Jeremy, who had presumably fled Umber under threat of arrest but was believed by Mrs. Wickware to be watching the house and planning revenge. The stolen items had of course been planted under the floorboard by Nicholas, who had slipped a sedative into Jeremy's nightly drink and smeared the telltale ink upon the sleeping brute's fingers.

At Molly's urging, the glass eye had been "discovered" in Jeremy's pillow and returned to a tearful Mrs. Wickware, who kept it on her person at all times and was known to spend hours gazing at its deep blue iris. But whether the woman had truly gone mad or simply fallen into profound, constant drunkenness was undetermined and, frankly speaking, immaterial. Either way, she had abdicated all authority and felt safest in the garret, high above the street and away from the rest of the house. Servants delivered her meals and bottles of rum at regular hours. They tidied her things and replenished her laundry and gave her no reason to venture around the house, providing instead continual reports, both real and invented, of local break-ins, murders, and supernatural phenomena, which encouraged Mrs. Wickware to lock the door and cower, day after day, with the talismanic comfort of her husband's glass eye.

The servants catered to the siblings' every whim, not only because they were generously paid and enjoyed unprecedented liberty, but also because of the awe with which they viewed Nicholas, whose cunning had toppled Wickware. Meals were lavish and expensive, shared by everyone alike. Newton performed his basic duties but spent vast stretches of the day educating himself—he wished to become a lawyer— and modeling the latest fashions in the full-length mirror in his chamber. The maids did the minimum of necessary work, sending laundry out and leaving rooms, and even themselves, in luxurious disarray until the house, strewn with empty glasses and half-dressed servants, resembled the home of a libertine rather than that of a lord.

For all the apparent profligacy, Nicholas kept impeccable records of the household's finances. No expense or line of credit went unpaid, and by selling valuable items—mostly Lord Bell's—and lending money at interest to prodigal young gentlemen of Umber, he had actually increased the available funds while the rest of the city, including the gentry, felt the worsening pinch of an economy strained by a year of failing crops and the spectacular expense of the protracted overseas conflict.

Bruntland had finally won the war in Floria, thanks in large degree to their father's pivotal victories over the Rouge at Godshorn and Fort Pine. The swiftly promoted General Bell had written a letter—delivered by packet ship the previous week—informing Molly and Nicholas that much remained to be done before his return to Umber, and that given the peril of ocean travel in autumn, they were unlikely to see him home before the New Year. "What will you tell him when he learns that most of his best possessions have been sold?" Molly had asked Nicholas one day, as he was locking up the proceeds from several pounds of silverware.

"I have sold only a fraction of his things," Nicholas told her. "Most of them are pawned in Mrs. Wickware's name. The servants will corroborate our story that she acted out of drunkenness. The rest of the missing items will be hung upon Jeremy, who is already wanted for theft. We have the constable's report to verify the facts. When Father finds us as we are, he will admit his own folly in trusting us to Mrs. Wickware's care and will, I suspect, summon Frances home directly. I would summon her myself, but it must be Father's choice."

Molly didn't miss the discipline and bleedings, but she couldn't make peace, as Nicholas had done, with Mrs. Wickware's terror and debasement. She had visited the garret a number of times, hoping to alleviate the governess's loneliness, but Molly's appearance at the door had the opposite effect, convincing Mrs. Wickware that even the garret wasn't sacrosanct and might, at any time, be threatened.

"We have treated her abominably," Molly said as she cleared the barrel of the gun.

Nicholas sat before the harpsichord, its open lid exquisitely painted with a twilit sky. He had a thin dark beard and looked reasonably strong, having restored himself to something like his normal state of illness. He improvised a fugue, playing gently as he spoke.

"We claimed our natural right."

"Home," Molly sighed.

"Advantage," Nicholas said. "All my life, I have thought myself strong but feared myself weak. Illness, doubt, our father's and Mrs. Wickware's tyrannical rule—I have suffered and survived them, and have vowed not to suffer disadvantage again. Strength isn't granted. It is seized by the horns."

Molly faced him with the gun, inadvertently aiming at his thigh, wrist, and neck as the barrel bobbed around and signaled her annoyance.

"You sound like Father."

"Father lacks conviction," Nicholas said. "He acts but then he hesitates, preoccupied with rightness. He beat the Rouge in Floria because, for once in his life, he shuffled right and wrong aside and trusted in his strength. Please lower the gun. Waving it about is gravely impolite."

Molly kept it raised a moment longer in response.

Nicholas rounded out the fugue, its closing notes as chilly as a knife touching crystal. When the harpsichord was silent and the heat felt thick, Molly laid the pistol in front of Mrs. Wickware's former mirror, where the gun and its reflection leveled up as if to duel.

She studied herself in the glass. More than ever, her resemblance to her mother was remarkable, and yet the contrasts were every bit as striking. They had the same small nose and asymmetrical eyes, the same black hair and clear white skin. But her mother in the old portrait looked demure, with a very faint smile, almost sad in its serenity. Molly, on the other hand, was tousled in and out. She looked forever like a girl who'd been rolling in a bed, or a woman blown to laughter by a great rush of wind.

Her growing breasts were less pronounced because her hips and derrière had filled out, too. Yet they still looked surprising, buoyed by her stays, and felt delightful to her palms when she caressed them in the night. She thought it strange the way her baby fat had subtly returned, how she softened while her brother grew sinewy and sharp. She had her monthly blood now; the first time had alarmed her, but the chambermaid Elise had quickly eased her mind.

It was Elise that Molly had spied on throughout the summer when the maid, grown bold in Mrs. Wickware's absence, spent most of her nights with a chimney sweep who climbed through her window after dark. They lit a small tin lantern on the table near the bed and Molly watched them from the hall, peering through the keyhole, curious at first when she passed and heard the sounds, then compulsive, having stayed and grown obsessed with what she saw.

The chimney sweep was filthy and could not be called attractive. He was gangly, to begin, with a tall narrow face, and showed a great many ribs through his winter-white skin. Yet his muscles and his tendons were intriguingly distinct, and Molly gasped to see his manhood rising and engorging.

She was shocked to see Elise take the length of it inside her—how delirious she seemed, how at ease with his ferocity! The way his skinny buttocks clenched together when he thrust, how his balls slapped against her like a loose sack of coins. It was altogether vulgar. It was violent and wet. Her body opened and enveloped him, absorbing all his force the way a pillow takes a punch, and what astonished Molly most was how Elise appeared to strengthen, and the chimney sweep to weaken till at last it seemed to kill him. Molly envied her immensely. What a gorgeous ruddy sweatiness and languor in her limbs! How adoringly the chimney sweep embraced her in relief.

"I'm bored," Molly said.

"You're free," Nicholas answered. "You may do whatever you choose."

He was right, in spite of the fact that he was constantly directing her. He'd taught her what her father hadn't thought to teach a girl— politics, anatomy, and weaponry included—but as much as she appreciated all that she had learned, she chafed against his tutelage and yearned to get away.

Molly crossed the room and opened a sash. The street was lively far below, sunstruck and colorful with active passersby. There was a lady with a parasol and wide floral skirts. A tinker clinking spoons. A fiddler and a gypsy. Children sprinted by and Molly craned to see them, tipping dangerously forward on the sill.

"I want to go out," she said. "I haven't ridden in months, haven't swum, haven't—"

"We cannot travel as long as Mrs. Wickware is here," Nicholas said. "She must be kept—"

"As I am kept, bottled here in Umber."

"You could walk to view the sea."

"And look at ships I cannot board."

"Soon," Nicholas said. "The world will open its doors and you will choose whichever you please. Come. Reload the gun."

She twirled and clutched her hair. Another day, another week of stultifying lessons: kidneys, torts, firearms, sonatas and partitas. She walked toward the gun and said, "I want to use a ball."

"It is needless," Nicholas said, although the notion seemed to please him.

"Then I won't practice shooting anymore."

"You must."

"Why?"

"Because—"

"I know," she said, "I know," having asked the question strictly out of petulance.

The truth was that Mrs. Wickware's fear of home invasion was not entirely unfounded. There had, of late, been an upsurge of mutinous incidents throughout the city. Thefts, assaults, and murders; violent threats, both idle and enacted; speeches, strikes, and frequent calls to riot and revolt. The hungry lower class, unable to afford the barest of necessities, was demanding fixed prices in the marketplace, menacing vendors, railing against the government, and turning with alarming rapidity to crimes against the wealthy. With the cold season bearing down, there was no telling how severe the situation would become, and Nicholas insisted Molly learn to use a gun.

She thought of the people she had seen below her on the street and tried to imagine shooting someone dead—the tinker, perhaps, or one of the children's downtrodden parents.

"Will you practice once more if I allow you to fire a ball?" Nicholas asked.

"Yes."

"To Mercerón?"

"To Hark," she said, measuring the powder.

She poured it into the upturned barrel. Nicholas watched and played an F-major prelude—the faster one she liked, the one that worked her up.

"The balls are kept—"

"I know where they are," Molly said, hair falling around her cheeks as she opened the cherrywood box on the table under the mirror, picking out the truest, roundest ball that she could find.

She half-cocked the gun.

"Wadding fore and aft," he said.

She tore scraps from one of Mrs. Wickware's monogrammed handkerchiefs, added the wad, ball, and second wad, and tamped them down firmly with the ramrod.

"Note the depth of the rod," Nicholas said, completing the prelude and starting up the fugue. "You can tell whether a gun is loaded without placing your eye before the muzzle."

She felt the difference in the rod and then replaced it under the barrel. She primed the pan, closed the frizzen, fully cocked the gun, and waited for Nicholas to finish the fugue and start the prelude again.

"I suggest the northern wall," he said—the only one of the four that led to an empty room.

Molly raised the gun and held it at arm's length, warier than before, as if the pistol were a bomb, and trembled from the quickening excitement of her heart. The fugue's complexity advanced and rose to frantic heights. She tried to pick a target on the pheasant-patterned wall—the blue with the beady eye, or the gray with the angular wing?—until the music neared its end and the pheasants looked afraid.

She fired the gun with the closing note, jolting with the shot. When the billow cleared away, she saw the hole beside the birds, many inches distant from the spot where she had aimed. Her ears were cottony again, her blood exuberantly thrilled. She went to the wall and stuck her finger in the hole before turning around to Nicholas, who looked toward the door, oddly disconcerted.

Molly felt a tremor and thought, "There's someone on the stairs."

The door banged open, bouncing off the wall. Molly dropped the gun. Nicholas rose and stumbled on the harpsichord stool.

All was silent, all was ringing in the presence of their father, who was standing in his uniform, glorious and violet, saber drawn and cold blue fire in his eyes.

"What the hell!" said General Bell.

He stalked into the room, saber raised as if he still expected ambush. He was shorter than Molly remembered, weathered from the war and from the journey overseas. His skin was darker and his wrinkles had become more severe, and yet in spite of looking older he exuded youthful vigor. Molly backed against the wall, leaving the pistol on the floor and honestly believing that he might attempt to slash her.

Nicholas stood beside his overturned stool, and there was fear—Molly felt it—in his silence and rigidity.

General Bell stopped and put his boot upon the pistol. He was speechless, too flustered by the shot, the lingering smoke, the catastrophe of the room, and his thunderstruck children to do more than look, and huff, and stand until the blade began to quiver in his hand.

"You're home!" Molly said, stumbling forward as she spoke.

The movement startled General Bell. He tensed and widened his eyes.

"The shot . . . "

"It was me!" Molly said, involuntarily shouting. "Nicholas was teaching me in case . . . How can you be home?!"

She sidestepped his blade and forcefully embraced him, almost crying in her fright, almost laughing in her panic. Bell staggered back and pushed her off one-handed. He fixed her with a look so intense she couldn't speak, and then he spun around to Nicholas and said, "Outrageous! *Outrageous!*"

Without waiting for his son to hazard a reply, he strode to the door as if intending to board the first ship back to Floria, but then he stopped, clapped his heels together military-style, and asked without turning around, "Where is Mrs. Wickware?"

"Drunk," Nicholas said.

Bell's perfect wig crept backward on his scalp.

"Stay in this room," he said. "Do nothing until I return. If either of you leaves, if either of you moves—"

Molly trembled when he left without finishing his threat.

✢

The mystery of General Bell's early reappearance was no great mystery at all. Shortly after composing his last letter to Molly and Nicholas, in which he had written of returning no sooner than the New Year, he had received a summons to Umber from the Secretary of the Homeland, who had grown concerned about the popular unrest within the city and felt that Bell, who had so efficiently crushed the Rouge, was just the man they needed in the event of a serious uprising. Bell had sailed immediately and arrived this morning, having beaten the onset of autumn storms and enjoyed fair winds for the duration of his six-week voyage. He had hired a post chaise and ridden home directly from the harbor, and he had just entered the house and seen the disarray when the pistol shot rang out above him and he sprinted upstairs, fearing bloody murder and finding a scene nearly as atrocious.

Only a year of wartime command could have prepared him to master his emotions as he stalked through the house, hardening like diamond, and the full extent of the chaos rapidly revealed itself. After marching downstairs and slipping on a platter of half-eaten cake, he opened the first door he came upon and found Elise sprawled naked on her stomach. The chimney sweep, also naked, sprang from the bed, took one incisive look at the general in the doorway, and leapt out the window without a stitch of clothing. Elise jumped up and stood behind her bed, scarlet from her cheeks to her well-shaped thighs, having failed to grasp a sheet and concealing herself, as well as she could, with small fumbling hands. She fainted to the floor, spectacularly nude.

The cook and her daughter, tipsy on one of the cellar's finest vintages, were preparing a molded meringue in a lovely sea of custard when Bell walked into the kitchen. The daughter shrieked, the cook spilled wine across the custard, and Bell continued on his way, seeking Mrs. Wickware and getting one shock after another. The laundry maid, wearing a ball gown and surrounded by feral cats she had taken to feeding, was caught reading a scandalous novel in the library. The groom, who had learned to scrape a fiddle over the past year, sat in the stables playing an allemande to entertain the horses. So it went, room after room and servant after servant, until the majority of the house had been searched and the frantic staff hastened to bury evidence, tidying whatever they could before their master doubled back to question them at length.

Only Newton, who happened to be found in the act of polishing silver, escaped Bell's fury. That he was polishing the silver for his own refined pleasure was moot. He seemed to be the well-dressed epitome of duty. Bell eagerly enlisted him to search for Mrs. Wickware.

"She stays in the garret, m'lord," Newton said, betraying not the least surprise at seeing his master home.

The garret was locked. No one answered when they pounded on the door. Newton fetched a key and the two of them stepped inside. The garret had once been tidy but had fallen into neglect. Bats dangled from the rafters, furniture and crates had been arranged as a childish wall of protection around the bed, and all four corners were packed with empty bottles. The only bottle still containing rum was clutched to Mrs. Wickware's bosom, like a long-treasured doll that someone had threatened to snatch. She sat on the bed in her night-clothes. Her hair had not been cut or even combed in many weeks. She had grown both flabbier and flimsier from drinking, and she stared at them—her eyeballs filmy and enormous—barely comprehending their appearance in the gloom.

General Bell ordered Newton to summon the constable and a dozen reliable men, and then he locked himself and Mrs. Wickware into the garret and didn't emerge for more than an hour, not even when the officers had gathered in the foyer.

When they finally walked downstairs, Mrs. Wickware—according to those who glimpsed her as she left—appeared to have wept during her private time with Bell and bore a look of such utter desolation that the constable, a man of hard repute, draped her shoulders with a cloak and led her out with tender care.

The servants had done miraculous work in the hour while General Bell was cloistered in the garret. But however much they had managed to set right, there was no expunging the sights he had seen on his initial tour of the rooms, and everyone, with the exception of Newton, was taken by the constable's men to be questioned and held in jail until a detailed account of the year's derelictions was established.

Molly and Nicholas waited alone for more than two hours. From the window overlooking the street, they watched Mrs. Wickware and the rest of the staff being led away like common criminals, some of them in tears—including the groom, torn forever from his horses—and it was then that Molly's trust in her brother's design fell to pieces, and her guilt over the treatment of Mrs. Wickware multiplied with each of the fallen servants.

Nicholas himself seemed aghast at what was happening. He had meant to prepare the staff for this inevitable day, but he had banked on several more months to finalize arrangements. If all had gone to plan, their father would have returned to orchestrated chaos, a carefully wrought confusion with the servants at their best: loyal to a fault, overwhelmed but hard at work, struggling from the lack of Mrs. Wickware's direction.

"There is nothing we can do," he said now, leaving the window and straightening his collar in the mirror. "Our one remaining course is self-preservation."

"Or admitting this was our doing," Molly said.

He loosened his cravat to tie it more precisely, focusing on the knot as if perfecting it would neutralize the bedlam all around them.

"Do you believe," he asked, "that Father will reinstate the staff if he discovers they were acting on the license of his children? That Mrs. Wickware will suffer any less in her defeat? We must appear the victims of a drunk, thieving tyrant. We will meet him not in fear but in the joy of his return."

"What of the gun?" Molly asked.

Nicholas finished at the mirror. "Our initiative was strictly for protection of the home."

Molly chewed her fingernail and smelled the burnt powder on her knuckles. Pheasants watched her from the wall: *You might have shot us, wicked girl.* And what were the servants saying now? They would curse her and accuse her, her and Nicholas together. Every cruel look she had suffered in her life swarmed around her, thick as bees, and crowded out her thoughts.

Nicholas held her by the shoulders. His grip was so gentle that at first she didn't feel it.

"You are a woman of pluck and spirit," he said. "Not the girl he left. We will weather this together."

"Together," Molly said.

"I suggest you pin your hair and tidy your appearance."

Molly did as she was told, feeling plucky and, yes, more spirited than before. She brushed her hair, clenching her jaw until the knots and tangles came free, but just as she was about to pin it up, she heard their father's steps approaching on the stairs and went to Nicholas's side, still in disarray.

General Bell entered the room and strode directly forward, as if he meant to knock them down. Nicholas and Molly held their ground, forcing him to stop. He was close enough that Molly smelled the ocean on his clothes. They stood as they had been on the morning of his departure—their father in his uniform and tightly curled wig, the siblings arm to arm and facing him together—with the same dusty heat and overlong silence that had seemed, last summer, to have suffocated hope.

"You played a game at my expense and stained my reputation," Bell began. "Word of this will spread: the man who led an army but could not command his children."

"We are no longer children," Nicholas said.

"You are worse than little children!"

"Mrs. Wickware . . . ," Molly said, faltering at once.

Bell's expression of disdain was very close to hate.

"Are you saying you were victims?" he replied. "Children after all, once your governess abandoned you?"

"We did our best," Molly said.

"Your best is wrack and ruin. And regardless, you are lying. I have talked to Mrs. Wickware and deduced the true state of affairs. What a thorough revolution! What pride you must have felt."

"She misused us," Nicholas said. "We were strong enough to beat her."

"Strength." Bell sneered.

"Hector all you like. We won't be daunted anymore."

As soon as Nicholas said it, Bell was at his neck, gripping the cravat he'd so elegantly tied. Molly had seen her father strong-arm Nicholas before but this was something different, like a pistol truly loaded. Bell tightened the cravat until her brother couldn't breathe.

She shoved herself between them and was clouted on the ear. Nicholas freed himself and fell, clutching at his throat, and just as rapidly their father grabbed hold of Molly's hair. He forced her down, dragged her sideways, and dumped her in the corner. Then he stormed again to Nicholas, who covered up his head, and Bell began to kick him in the stomach and the ribs.

Molly reached toward the handle of the saber on his belt.

Bell detected her and spun away, sensing her intent. He put his hand upon the guard to keep the blade sheathed and then he stared at her, astounded by her outstretched arm. Molly knelt before him, equally amazed. For a moment she had really meant to hurt him. Even now.

She crawled to Nicholas. The sight of him extinguished all her fire. He was motionless and fetal with his arms around his face, and the pale blue rug was spattered with his blood. She heard him faintly moaning and was hesitant to touch him. Proof of their rebellion lay scattered all around—unwashed clothes, dirty cups and plates—as if exploded from the spot where the three of them had struggled.

General Bell stood tall with the sun upon his coat, and his long, lean shadow stretched behind him on the floor.

"You have brought it on yourselves. I hoped that you would change. I hoped to find you grown. Your bravado was enough to shake a drunken widow but your strength is only show. I am still your lord and father. There is God and there is me," he said, "and God cannot protect you."

Chapter Ten

In three frenetic days, General Bell hired replacement servants; restored the house to its original splendor; brought formal charges against Mrs. Wickware, the former staff, and the chimney sweep; confined a broken Nicholas to his chamber; and abandoned Molly to her own devices, rightly confident that he had cowed her, at least for the time being, into submission. The siblings were not to communicate without his express permission, for the present time denied, and he also raised the specter of separating them on a permanent basis: if Molly so much as attempted to slip a note under her brother's locked door, Nicholas would be enlisted in the navy, which given his chronic weakness was all but a sentence of death. The threat was not a bluff, nor was the prospect of sending Molly to St. Agatha's Refining School for Young Women, an institution so infamously harsh that it was unfavorably compared to convents and workhouses.

Molly woke especially early on the fourth day, determined to speak with her father at length before he set about the business of the morning. She followed Newton upstairs when he delivered a pot of tea; the footman neither talked to Molly nor acknowledged her presence when he entered Bell's room and left her in the darkness of the hall. Several minutes later, Newton emerged from the dimly lit chamber, halted at the door, and said to General Bell, as if he had nearly forgotten, "Nicholas's appetite has revived. He asked for eggs and coffee."

"Very good," her father said from deep within the room.

It was the first piece of news Molly had heard about her brother since the beating, and she almost thanked Newton with a hug before he left. Instead she waited for him to go and stood at the open door. Her father was already uniformed but hadn't donned his wig. His wool-gray hair hung loose around his neck. He stood before a carved mahogany table, which was strewn with letters and documents, and drank his boiling tea with grim preoccupation.

"You may not see him," he said before she asked.

Molly raised her chin and stepped more boldly to the center of the room.

"Is he recovering?" she asked.

"You already know," Bell said, "thanks to Newton's carefully timed report."

"Newton didn't—"

"Of course he did. You needn't worry," Bell assured her, putting down his tea and organizing papers. "The man has proved himself invaluable. Allowances are made in the case of exemplary service."

"But not for your children," Molly said.

"Is that a joke? You had the liberty of royals and infinite allowances, and look at what you did."

"You can't keep us apart!"

"Go," Bell said. "I haven't time for this today."

"No time for your own son and daughter?"

He snatched a letter off the table and thrust it into her hands. "Read," he said. "Newton found it nailed to the front door."

It was a ratty piece of foolscap, greasy and torn but inked with words that showed, in spirit if not in spelling, a strong determined hand.

To General Bell—
  We poor of Umber heerby give you notice of our solem oath to stand and fight together, and vow to hang to death before we see our children starve from want of bread and common sustinance, while you and yours grow fat, and do not force the markits to comply with laws of fair and honest prices, for we are Bruntlanders and good as you and the King, and as deserving of our bread

*and natural born rights, and if you do not use the power given to
you to make them execute those laws against this vilonas abuse
and put a stop amediately to the shipment of necesary grains out
of Umber, we will murder you and burn down your house and
leave your children fatherless and poor so they may know what
we and ours suffer each day in rechid destitushun.*

Take Care.

Molly stepped back against the black brick hearth. She could see,
as though the author's hand were hovering before her, every dip of
the quill and scratch upon the paper. The word "murder" seemed to
glisten in its freshness, very like the words Nicholas had scrawled on
Mrs. Wickware's wall. Her father took the paper back and slapped it
on the table. He opened a porcelain box and took a pinch of snuff.

"That is why I haven't any time to nurse my children. Every wretch
in Umber thinks himself a statesman. This is the third such letter fastened to our door. Their cries against the King are villainy and trea-
son. They mean to march tomorrow, here upon the square, and I will
meet them with a regiment of soldiers."

The thought of the army in Worthington Square was so outrageous
Molly laughed, but then her fear leapt up and choked the laughter in
her throat.

"Is there no other way?" she asked.

"Can I resurrect the crops or un-fight the Rouge? The war has gutted the treasury, the harvest was abominable, and whatever grain is
left must be sold to those who can afford it."

"The price of bread is lawfully fixed," Molly said, having learned
about the markets, to her boredom, from her brother.

"Laws are bent in desperate times," Bell said. "Are we to beggar
the market vendors for turning a profit and providing for their own
dependent families? Or shall we allow the blackguards who wrote this
letter, who storm the mills and threaten our lives, to take whatever
they please?"

"All they ask is fair prices," Molly said, sounding sulkier than she
wished.

"Fair?" Bell replied. "They threaten my life and children, call for fire and revolt and speak the word 'fair'? It wasn't I who made them hungry."

"But you will make them starve."

Bell smiled. It was a mirthless smile—the kind that people used to physically restrain themselves, a smile shown for insults to honor and intelligence.

"You think it simple," he said. "Rich and poor, sharing bread. Use my influence and wealth to blow away their sufferings. What would you yourself be willing to contribute? Shall I sell your favorite horse? He would fetch a goodly sum. A horse to buy them bread because they menace you with violence. Go to them and try."

He swiped the letter from the table, strode toward the hearth, and crunched the paper into her hands again, holding it in place—and Molly, too—and standing so close she couldn't focus on his face.

"You have always been selfish and shortsighted," he said. "No better than the mob, demanding what you want, smashing everything and everyone you find along the way. The Rouge felt the need to swallow up Floria. My children felt the need to overturn the home. And yet if everyone has rights, unlimited and free . . . "

He could find no language for the fate that he envisioned.

Molly squeezed the letter, hardening her knuckles underneath his grip.

Bell released her, stepping back and looking foreign in his uniform—a person whom she knew as if she'd seen him in a dream, too at odds with his reality to truly be familiar.

⚜

Overnight the city roiled. Bands of men with soot-blacked faces broke the wheel of a local gristmill, ransacked a boat loaded with wheat, destroyed a turnpike, and pummeled a pair of watchmen. Most of the affluent families in the vicinity of Worthington Square had already fled to the countryside, taking what valuables they could and leaving their houses to the mercy of the mob.

Molly spent the night hopelessly awake, drawn to the window time and again by distant shouts in the fog-drowned city. She washed and dressed long before dawn, eschewing her stays and feeling unsupported in their absence, and then she waited on the stairs and saw her father going out, his medals, boots, and buckles appearing to shine innately in the shadows near the door. He wore a tricorne and gloves and had a pistol at his hip, and when he sensed her there, he stopped and looked up.

"Stay in your room and lock the door."

"Shouldn't we leave?" Molly asked.

"No one drives us from our home."

"What if the mob attacks?"

"Your brother taught you to shoot," he said. "You have my leave to do so."

And then without so much as glimpsing his eyes a final time, she watched him leave the house, off to meet his troops. Molly waited to hear the sound of his horse, and once the hoofbeats had faded up the street, the quiet of the home and of the predawn city had an ominous weight, a rumble of things to come that seemed to vibrate the floor. She ran up the hall to her brother's locked door.

"Nicholas!" she said, rattling the knob and pressing her ear against the oak. He neither opened the door nor spoke, and she was stabbed with the possibility that Nicholas had died, his condition having worsened unexpectedly during the night.

"Oh, Nicholas, please!" she cried. "Speak to me, at least!"

But after many such attempts there was nothing else to do, so she convinced herself that Nicholas was merely fast asleep, having languished for days in injury and hunger.

She returned to her room and lit a candle. The air was damp and windless, and although her second-floor window opened above the street, she could see very little of the city through the gloom. The pistol lay beside her, fully loaded, on a table. She touched the handle now and then, hoping its presence alone would ward off danger, just as dressing for the rain seemed to guarantee sun.

She continued hearing voices, ever closer to the house. When day began to break, the voices overlapped. The mob was massing in the east and marching up the streets. Clanks and bangs echoed in the unprotected square, and the sun burned the mist into thinner sheets and tendrils. She discerned the men and women coming nearer with their weapons. Passing glimpses—a cluster here, a party there—made the crowd seem infinitely large, moving like a mudslide darkening the ground.

She half-cocked the gun and held it under the sill. The front of the mob appeared in a line, filling up the street between a pair of stately houses. Smocks and gowns, leather and wool; faces hard as bone. Hundreds more surged in behind them from the cross streets. A window broke. The voices coalesced, rising in a chant—"Old prices! Old prices!"—as the mob moved forward into the empty, elegant green.

They halted at the garden in the middle of the square—men and women, young and old, carrying sticks and signs and hayforks and tools of their professions. There was a blacksmith with hammer and tongs, a butcher with his knives, a woman with a torch, a beggar with a rock. Children stood among them, laughing out and shouting, glad as if the riot were a holiday fair.

They parted up the center to allow a small procession: four somber men wearing charcoal coats, following a tall, thin matron in a shawl. She had a bundle wrapped in funeral crepe nestled to her chest. At the sight of her, the mob fell quiet with its chant.

An unseen fiddle played "My Darlin' Dead an' Gone."

Molly leaned out and strained her eyes in dread. The church bell tolled. The matron bowed her head. The mourners stood aside like parentheses around her, and she stood for half a minute till the bell died away. A pale wreath of fog drifted through the green.

The matron raised the bundle: it was a small loaf of bread.

Molly's deep relief was jolted by the roar. Every implement and picket sign waved in fury as the mob rallied up around the woman with the loaf.

They stormed beneath the window in a sea of fists and boards. Dirty, angry faces spotted her at the window and Molly leapt away. She banged her head against a bedpost, moaned, and dropped the gun. Windows shattered downstairs. They were beating on the house and hollering for Bell, and as she fell to her knees and fumbled for the gun, footsteps pounded upstairs and reached the hall.

She aimed the pistol at her door and half-squeezed the trigger, and she almost didn't notice when the knob began to turn. The door opened smoothly on its oiled brass hinges.

Molly fired.

She saw her brother for an instant in the smoke.

"Nicholas!" she cried.

He fell against the doorframe and looked at her, amazed.

She ran to him and crouched, patting him down and searching for the blood upon his clothes. He smiled archly with his broken tooth and plum-colored bruises. Molly propped him up but he was stable on his feet. Maybe the ball had fallen out when Molly dropped the gun. That or she had missed. Either way, he was fine.

"Thank God!" she said and kissed him. "I went to your room, I tried to rouse you!"

"I was out before dawn, finishing arrangements. Bring the pistol," Nicholas said. "We haven't time to load it but the sight of it may help us."

Molly crossed the room, retrieved the gun, and followed him down to the rear of the house, where a small wooden trunk waited in the kitchen. Nicholas took the pistol and said, "You'll have to carry our luggage."

He had not yet recovered from the beating and he hunched, temples fluttering, his swollen face glistening with sweat. Molly lugged the trunk by its thick leather handle. Nicholas checked out back, saw that it was safe—the mob was still in front, battering the door—and led her into the courtyard. They hurried through the garden, where the roses' scent reminded her of summertime with Frances, and her heart bubbled up to think of seeing her again. Where else would they be going, but to Frances in the country? Then she wondered: *What of Father? What of Newton and the others?*

Nicholas urged her on. They exited the courtyard and stood in the narrow alley, where an offshoot of rioters discovered them and glared. Nicholas raised the gun and shouted, "Old prices! Old prices!"

A bearded man with a rag around his head barged toward them. They were wearing finer clothes than any of the rabble and the man flared his nose, smelling something rich.

He grinned at Nicholas's bruises and said, "Met the ugly stick!"

"So did you," Nicholas answered, pointing—with the pistol—at the rag around his head.

"Aye!" the man said. "Knot the size o' Parliament. Got it from the whoreson constable himself!"

He waved a poker as he spoke and almost hit Molly. Soon the rabble he was leading hemmed them in tight.

Nicholas gestured to his bruises. "From the hand of General Bell. I'm stealing his daughter here as recompense"—he squeezed her like a lover—"while the rest of you barbarians tussle over trinkets."

The bearded man guffawed, showing five brown teeth. He looked at Molly with lascivious delight and pinched her cheek. "What will Daddy say to that?"

"He'll read the riot act," she said. "Especially when he hears I'm three months with child."

Everyone around them howled out with laughter.

The man doffed his rag and showed his veiny knot. "May your children be a plague upon your bugger of a father!"

"Plague upon Bell!" Nicholas agreed.

The cry was taken up and spread around the crowd. Molly and Nicholas were jostled, pulled, and welcomed as companions, forced to go along until they reached the heart of the square. The boiling-onion odor of a thousand fevered bodies roused something deep in Molly's soul—was it hope?—that she recognized but hadn't fully felt in many months. The mob, however violent, was primarily exultant, surging shoulder to shoulder and gorgeously alive.

"Old prices!" Molly yelled, lugging the trunk.

"Burn it all!" Nicholas said. "Damn the King! Damn Bell!"

They moved with the crowd, across the street and over the walkway that ringed the circular green, trampling down flowerbeds and ornamental shrubs. The newly risen sun fell sideways upon them, but they always seemed to stand in someone else's shadow and the morning felt dark, even in the light. They reached the center of the green and were surrounded by the pale, regal homes.

The mob began to slow and partially retreat, gathering together like a muscle contracting. Molly wondered what had stopped them. She was too short to see above the acreage of heads, so she stood on the trunk, holding Nicholas's hand. She gasped and would have fallen, but the crowd propped her up.

"What do you see there, girl?" someone hollered at her back.

There was a hundred-foot gap before the mob's front line: a span of empty grass, a white stone path, and then the broad street beyond packed tight with ordered soldiers. They were perfectly arranged in rows of twenty men, endless violet uniforms and shining bayonets. At the head of the major force, two wider rows of soldiers had detached themselves and faced the mob in firing formation: front line genuflecting, second line standing, muskets at the ready, fully primed and loaded.

General Bell, just behind them on his huge speckled gray, sat boldly in the saddle with his saber to the sky.

Word rippled through the crowd. A busy hush fell upon them.

"Disperse!" Bell called, clear above the murmur.

Molly saw the matron with her bundled loaf of bread. She walked alone into the gap, dignified and small. The vanguard of soldiers cocked and aimed their muskets, and the matron raised the loaf as if it truly were an infant. She approached General Bell without a trace of hesitation—spine erect, chin raised, her own long shadow stretching out before her. She was fifteen paces from the bayonets when the mob, drawing courage, shuffled up behind her.

Molly's heartbeat stuck. She wrung her brother's hand.

General Bell raised his gun and fired at the bread.

The shot pierced the loaf and hit the matron in the chest. She staggered to her knees, still offering the loaf. The troops fired next, a forty-gun volley, bright fire like lightning from a thick white cloud. Half the mob charged. The rest began to flee, running every which way until the threat of being trampled vastly outweighed the chance of being shot.

Molly tumbled off the trunk and landed on the grass. Children scrambled over her. A woman kicked her ear. A ragged group of sailors almost stomped her underfoot but Nicholas wrenched her up and said, "The trunk! Take the trunk!"

They zigzagged away, following paths through the crowd that seemed to magically appear, random as the gaps in windblown rain.

There were screams and clashing blades, a thudding second volley from another line of soldiers. Molly crashed against a half-bald woman with a boning knife. The blade cut her arm just above the wrist. Molly felt the sting but didn't stop to look, and it was all that she could do to drag the trunk amid the tumult, watching Nicholas's coat and fearing she would lose him.

When they finally cleared the square, the mob began to thin. Molly paused for lack of breath before a grand, silent house, wishing she could enter it. The foggy dawn had sharpened to a crisp white morning and the cobblestoned street looked miraculously neat.

"Quickly," Nicholas said, running back to pull her on.

His nearness jolted her and energized her legs, and they were off again, fleeing with the other panicked rioters. One of them, a brawny man, was bleeding from his neck. A yellow-haired woman sobbed against a hay cart. A very young soldier cowered in a doorway, clinging to his musket. The crackling gunfire faded with the distance from the green and yet persisted, clear and simple in the oddly vacant neighborhood. Footsteps echoed off the elegant façades.

They came at last to the harbor, where news of the massacre had just begun to spread. Many of the laborers, fishmongers, and rope makers had come from Worthington Square and stood about the docks, mortally subdued, but there were sailors hard at work: nothing stopped the tide.

The air was briny cool and spiced with smoke and herring. Molly's lungs took the wind as fully as the sails. Sun struck brass and sparkled off the waves, a million glints of light that dazzled and dismayed her. Nicholas guided her down a flight of warped stairs, and it wasn't until they reached the end of a pier before she finally snapped alert and said, "What are we doing? Why are we here?"

A man below her in a skiff, turning when she spoke, balanced calmly with a pipe and winked his wrinkly eye.

"My name is Jacob Smith," Nicholas said. "You are my wife, Mary Smith. We are going to live with relatives in Floria."

"Floria!" she said, looking past him to the water, an infinity of silver-blue mystery and depth.

"I have arranged our passage on the *Cleaver*," Nicholas said, pointing to a merchant ship anchored offshore. It was long and double-masted with a grimy spread of sails, and the shadows made the hull look badly decomposed. "We have money enough to go. Means enough to live."

"Father will know you've stolen—"

"What does it matter?" Nicholas asked. "Assuming he survives"—Molly wobbled with the trunk—"we will be hours out to sea before he notices our absence. He will first search the city. He will think we fled to Frances. If he inquires here at the harbor, he'll be spoonfed a tale of newlyweds eloping."

"He will know," Molly said.

"We will need to keep our false identities in Floria, assuming he will hire men to follow and retrieve us. On the other hand, he may consider it good riddance," Nicholas said, "and go about his business, unencumbered by our lives."

"You cannot mean that!" she said, fearing it was true—fearing that the new world would openly embrace them.

She had dreamed of escape but not of the vastness of the sea, not of the chance, darkly dawning, that their father might be dead. She turned to look at Umber, cupping her hand against the sun. The roofs looked shorter and the buildings more provincial, more in keeping with a village than with the capital of Bruntland. Inns and taverns seemed to beckon, welcoming and snug, and carriages in motion had a fixity about them. They were landlocked, slow, could be halted, could be turned.

The boatman clapped his pipe out, eager to be off.

Nicholas handed down the trunk and said, "They'll soon be raising anchor."

Molly searched the streets, expecting to see their father race forth at any moment. There was little that would indicate the fury of the morning—no smoke beyond the buildings, no shots that she could hear. Even the cut above her wrist had already ceased to bleed.

She turned to face the sea and felt the city, home, Frances, all she knew and trusted glowing at her back with the warm, familiar sun. The prospect of Floria erupted into color like a painting of a fruit bowl tumbling into life—the flesh of it, the fragrances, the juices in her mouth.

"Father said the trip would kill you."

"He believed it," Nicholas said.

"We have money."

"Yes."

"You'll keep me safe?"

"Come. The ship is leaving."

Molly looked toward the *Cleaver*, almost laughed, almost fell. Had the pier begun to move? Was the ocean changing hues? She thought of running home and crawling into bed but then the sparkles on the water raised prickles on her skin. She would love to see a whale. She imagined being new.

"My name is Molly."

"Mary Smith," he said.

"Molly."

"Molly *Smith*."

She clenched her teeth and nodded, still Molly, still herself. Then before she weighed the danger, trusting Nicholas had done so, she climbed into the skiff, spread her arms to gain her sea legs, and marveled at the gut-deep loss of all stability.

Chapter Eleven

From the first night at sea, Nicholas was sick. His skin was yellow, green, or gray depending on the hour. Molly remained at his side in the cramped, moldy cabin, which was windowless and dim and stank of murky water. A pair of narrow cots dangled from the ceiling, so close they would have crashed if they didn't swing in tune. Molly cried and wrung her hands, scared to shut her eyes. Between the third and fourth bells—empty clangs, tolling lonesomely forever across the water—she thought of how the land would grow increasingly remote until the continents were equally beyond them, out of reach. How the dark swirled around her while her brother moaned and slept! She listened to the creaking boards and unfamiliar voices, swaying in her cot and slowly growing tired till the night overcame her and the world disappeared.

Next morning she was bored. Nicholas vomited and dozed, occasionally mumbling. When she tried to feed him bread, he cursed and pushed her off. The stifling cabin soon reminded her of closets back at home and so she went above deck, craving open air.

The seas had risen overnight. Great waves spread around them, a landscape of broad, fluid hills. The *Cleaver* lurched forward from a trough to a peak. The bowsprit lifted and the stern swooped low, tilting Molly's innards like water in a glass. She planted her back foot firmly on the deck and looked ahead, past the sailors watching her to see if she would fall. The sails bulged fuller, coming closer to the sky until the ship crested a wave and all the ocean lay below her. Clean spume, boiled tar, sweaty men—she breathed in the rich, foreign liveliness around her.

"Is it always so dramatic?" she asked a wall-eyed sailor trimming the mainsail.

"This is nothing," he said, speaking, Molly thought, with an overdone snarl.

She clapped her hands and smiled.

"We're like to see swells twice or thrice as big," the sailor said, squinting now with menace. "They will break upon the deck with terrifying force!"

"Will they, really?" Molly asked, turning to see if any of *that* day's waves held the promise of assault. "I assumed that many ocean tales were heightened for effect."

"Tales!" the sailor yelled. He gripped a knot and glared at her. His wide-set eyes and broad, flattened nose gave him the appearance of a hammerhead shark. "The terrors of the deep can't be found in tales!"

"Will we see them up close? The terrors of the deep? I've read of the leviathan and octopi and serpents. I would love to see the lightning or a great dirty blow."

He blinked at her, apparently confounded by her zeal, and followed her when she walked to the rear of the ship and leaned over the taffrail.

"Careful, now!" he said.

"Have you ever seen anyone drown?"

"Aye, too many to count."

"That's horrible!" she said, showing enough bright excitement that the sailor seemed proud, even privileged to have witnessed such a quantity of drownings.

His name was Mr. Knacker. He'd been sailing all his life. "Born at sea," he insisted, and she took him at his word. They continued this way for many minutes, Molly asking questions and delighting in the answers, Mr. Knacker—clearly basking in her lubberly attention—speaking, very sagely, like the saltiest of mariners. He neglected the mainsail for so long that the captain himself strode from the bow, brought Mr. Knacker to his wits again with nothing but a scowl, and looked at Molly as if he'd caught her drilling holes through the ship.

Captain Veer was rangy but immensely broad shouldered. His hair was long and black, and though his clothes were drab and functional—the same as those of the crew—he projected his command with tense contradiction: he was furious but calm, casual but grave.

"Stay in the cabin with your husband till the seas quiet down."

She pulled the windblown hair out of her mouth and said, "I'm not afraid, sir. I'd rather stay and watch."

Captain Veer stepped toward her as if he meant to shove her over.

"You imperil us all when you interfere with discipline," he said. "I'll have you carried like a sack unless you get yourself below."

And yet he said it with respect, not at all like Mrs. Wickware threatening her with Jeremy, and she decided not to rankle him, at least not on purpose.

"Thank you for talking to me!" she called to Mr. Knacker at the mainmast.

His eyes looked to Molly and the captain simultaneously, divergent in their motions till they locked on her alone. "You're welcome, ma'am," he shouted with an unchecked smile. "The pleasure was mine entire!"

It was difficult to tell which of the men was more surprised: Mr. Knacker, who had praised her for distracting him from duty, or Captain Veer, who seemed to view Molly as a worker of bewitchment.

And so it went for several weeks as Molly charmed the crew and vexed Captain Veer. She was an hourly distraction with her neverending questions, an obstacle to work as she explored the *Cleaver*'s deck, and the only pair of breasts for several hundred miles. The men were impressed with Molly's fearlessness and balance—at least a quarter of the crew had complimented her sea legs—and they enjoyed her constant awe at things they took for granted. Reef knots. Holystones. Meteors and moon dogs. The privy hole that fed directly into the sea.

This morning they had called her up to see a flock of bird crabs. These were delicacies at sea and difficult to catch, but they were drawn to passing ships and often tangled in the rigging. They were pearly gray and small, the size of Molly's palm, with membranous wings that folded into their shells beneath the water. In flight they had the quality of pale, peculiar bats, fluttery and quick and comically erratic. Without being asked, she joined several sailors who were climbing up to catch them.

When she reached the top of the mainmast, she paused to view the ship a hundred feet below. There was no trace of land. Everything was water and the sky, with its wavy streaks of herringbone cloud, was a white-capped mirror of the ocean far below. It was blue upon blue and she was floating in the middle. There were even two suns, one real and one reflected, and the ship seemed to hover in a universal sphere.

The *Cleaver* softly rolled, the deck slipped away, and she was straight above the water, higher than the bell of Elmcross Church. Molly stretched and pulled a crab off the uppermost stay, careful of its thin but razor-sharp pincers.

"Break its wings and drop it down!" a brawny midshipman hollered from below.

"I'm sorry," Molly said to the first, averting her eyes as she wounded it, but soon she was snapping their wings and dropping them down as if she'd done it all her life. She easily outpaced the sailor on the foremast, much to the amusement of the men upon the deck.

A crab fluttered past her hair, plucking several strands before clinging to the yardarm far to the left where Molly couldn't reach it from the mast. It was the plumpest she had seen and couldn't be ignored. She lay out lengthwise, straddling the yard, pretending it was nothing but a branch above a pond.

"Leave it be!" yelled a sailor underneath her at the rail, and yet he sounded halfhearted, as if he hoped to see her try.

Bellying along was awkward in her skirts. She would have hiked them up if not for all the men.

"Kraken's balls, get down from there!" Captain Veer yelled, having emerged from his cabin to discover her aloft.

In her startlement, she snatched the crab without really looking. Its pincer caught her thumb, slicing through the nail. Molly yelped and shook it off, the crab fluttered down, and then she tumbled off the yard and dangled by her hands. Blood made her grip dangerously slick. A fat gust of wind pressed the canvas to her body, threatening to bump her through the air like a ball.

Men shouted from below with contradictory advice. Molly scowled at her hands, commanding them to hold. Her bloody palm was slipping, so she swung herself hard toward the rope that ran between the mainsail and the foremast, high to low.

For a moment she was airborne, loose above the deck—a body in the wind between the broad white sails. She hooked the tether with her elbow and clamped on tight. Once she had a grip, she crossed her ankles over the stay and shimmied down, moving backward, hanging under like a sloth until she finally reached the foremast top and landed on the platform. From there the climb was simple, little harder than a ladder, and she snatched a final crab before she jumped on deck, bloody but intact, in front of Captain Veer.

She offered him the crab. He was tauter than the rigging and refused to take the gift. His eyes were black. He stared at her with murderous composure.

"Good morning, sir," she said.

The crew turned to wood. Captain Veer didn't speak, didn't blink, didn't breathe. The only part of him that moved was his scraggly dark hair.

"I'll go down to the cabin where I belong," Molly said.

Was it guilt that made her say it, or the captain's angry silence? Either way, she felt a mutinous desire to retract it, to climb another mast and see if he would shout.

Instead she dropped the crab and watched it flutter, briefly free, before it whirled toward the sails and tangled in the lines again. She looked at every sailor as she walked to the companionway but none of them, not even Mr. Knacker, raised his face to acknowledge her in front of Captain Veer. She sucked her thumb going down—it was bleeding unabated—and the gloom below deck was dungeonlike and heavy.

There was one other paying passenger aside from Molly and her brother: a chandler, who had spent the early days of the trip nearly as seasick as Nicholas. His name was Mr. Fen and he was taking his candle-making business to Floria, where materials were cheaper and demand was on the rise. Molly guessed that he was fifty. He had a suety complexion with a faintly moistened sheen, and he paid the captain handsomely for fresh-laid eggs, which he liked to suck raw by puncturing the shells. He was not so much shy as purposefully withdrawn, keeping to his books and rarely leaving his own private cabin.

Molly had engaged him with her usual tenacity. He humored her but asked more questions than he answered. This morning he lay in a hammock with a lantern overhead. The hammock and the lantern swayed together with the ship so that the light was always falling on his favorite book of ballads.

"I've done it again," she told him now, sitting on his traveling chest, and gave him an account of her adventure with the crabs.

Mr. Fen didn't speak until she finished. He stepped out of the hammock, leaving his book behind him, and approached her with an outstretched hand.

"Let me see your thumb," he said.

Mr. Fen examined it, holding at the joint and squinting at the crab-cut nail. He guided her off the chest, opened the lid, and pulled out a tiny bottle of spirits.

"Be brave and this will cleanse it," he said, addressing her, she felt, the way he might address a toddler. Molly looked away, determined not to wince. He popped the cork and poured. It felt like boiling water. Mr. Fen watched her face instead of her injured thumb. She ground her other hand's knuckles on the corner of the chest, diverting her attention till the sting began to fade. He corked the bottle, blew gently on her thumb to dry it off, and wrapped the wound neatly with a small strip of cloth.

"Thank you," Molly said.

Mr. Fen smiled. He put the bottle away and said, "You must be more careful. Other pains are far more difficult to soothe."

"So is the captain's temper."

"You always have a friend here below," he assured her.

"I'm glad of your companionship with Jacob so terribly ill."

Mr. Fen returned to his hammock, opening his book but keeping his attention courteously on Molly. "Is he improving?"

"No," she said, trying not to twitch or look away. "I fear he won't recover for the duration of the trip. He has always been prone to sickness."

"It was kind of you to marry him," Mr. Fen said, glancing at her hand, which was bare of any ring.

"We were destitute in Umber," Molly said, as if confessing. "But Jacob has excellent prospects in Grayport. Please forgive me—I should go to him now. Thank you for your care."

Mr. Fen nodded and reclined to read his book. The lantern just above him, momentarily erratic, bleached his face while the rest of him was darkened by the shadow.

She left him there and continued back to her own cabin, telling herself she needed more rehearsal for her lies.

Nicholas lay in his cot. His hair was slicked against his brow and he was dressed, beneath a blanket, in a badly ripened shift. The sea had worn him out and brought on the grippe, and now his fevers left him damp. Nicholas had packed in haste and traveled very light; aside from a pair of cloaks, extra stockings, and two spare shifts, they had only what they'd worn the day of their escape. The trunk contained little else—a medical book; the pistol; gold and silver coins—so she washed and dried his shifts as quickly as she could, barely keeping up with Nicholas's sweats.

Other than this and begging him to eat, there was nothing to do but wipe his forehead, straighten his blanket, and keep him company when he was conscious enough to notice. She did so now, cleaning his face with a rag and meeting his filmy eyes. He recognized her still— she felt relief at this whenever he awoke—but he lacked the strength and will to speak above a whisper.

She stood and held his hand—it felt as pitiful and flimsy as a bird crab's wing—and talked about her derring-do high above the deck. The stories of her day were all that seemed to cheer him, and it was this, more than boredom, that encouraged her to venture on deck every morning.

Whenever she was finished and had nothing left to tell, she talked about the life that lay ahead of them in Grayport.

"We'll have a house in the city, and every day I'll walk to the market and buy something new," she said, imagining a continent of unfamiliar foods. "We'll explore every street and visit every shop, and in the afternoons and evenings we can entertain our friends. We'll have very many friends, a whole second family. When we tire of the city, we'll go to a house in the country."

"It is wilderness," he murmured, "outside the city."

"We'll meet the Elkinaki—they've been friendly to the Florians— and after visiting their village, we'll return to the city and tell our friends of our adventures. Won't they be amazed! They'll beg to hear it all."

He fluttered forth a smile but the effort wore him out, and then he sighed and shut his eyes, falling heavily asleep. Molly checked his pulse to see that it was moving and her own strong pulse nearly drowned it out. She thought again of Grayport, imagining their house—a drawing room with rosy friends and curious liqueurs—but the vision felt puerile. What if Nicholas died? She might find herself in Floria alone, and what then? How would she survive without her brother to rely on?

⚓

Mr. Fen accompanied Molly on deck the following day. She had invited him out of habit, having done so daily the entire previous week, but she regretted it at once when he happily accepted. Disinviting him would only serve to deepen his suspicion, so she walked with him at length and answered all his questions.

"What are your husband's prospects?" he asked her near the bow. A dense bank of fog was approaching from the west and Molly paused to view it, sweating in the breeze. The warmth that pressed around them seemed to issue from the fog but she feared her perspiration would be misconstrued as stress. "Forgive me," he continued, "if I overstep my bounds."

"Not at all," Molly said. "I must admit, Jacob's prospects are vague. His education is extraordinary—I have never known a man more thoroughly developed—but he has yet to choose a path from the many at his feet."

"An autodidact," Mr. Fen said.

"Excuse me?"

"He has educated himself."

"Why do you think—"

"I apologize," he said, "if I assumed too much. A graceless tendency of mine. I remembered that you told me you were destitute in Umber and assumed he lacked for proper schooling."

"Oh, I see," Molly said, dripping more profusely. A smell of vegetation thickened in the air as if the fog, ever closer, were the steam of heated plants. "He was born amid wealth and lacked for nothing in his youth, but his father ruined himself in business and—I am ashamed to say it—took his own life when Jacob was fifteen. He and his mother lived as well as they could, but they were forced to sell most of their belongings to escape a growing avalanche of debt. She died last year."

Molly bowed her head, pausing in memoriam.

"I'm an autodidact," she said with extra levity, as if the previous subject had depressed her and she meant to perk herself up. "You may have noticed I am often posing questions to the crew."

"That I have," said Mr. Fen, pivoting to face her, close enough to give their talk an intimate appearance. "You are wonderfully precocious."

"Mr. Knacker," Molly said, relieved to find the wall-eyed sailor walking by. "What is the curious fogbank coming at the ship?"

Mr. Knacker walked up and bobbed with nervous pleasure. He and the crew had grown enamored of Molly's high jinks and chatter, but Mr. Fen had put a damper on her spirits that morning, acting like a chaperone and hogging her attention. She had felt the men's resentment when he led her by the arm. Even worse, Mr. Fen had seemed offended by their squalor, steering her away whenever they were near.

Mr. Knacker looked affectionately at Molly while keeping his colder, squintier eye directed at Mr. Fen. "That is waterbreath," he said. "Proof that we have reached the Serpentine Current."

He had described the current before: a potent flow of water streaming from the south, dividing the Eccentric Ocean halfway from Bruntland to Floria. Its vigor slowed ships, sometimes sending them a week off course. The current teemed with sea life pulled from the equator and its tropical heat was infamous for breeding vivid weather.

Molly turned to look and said, "The river in the sea."

"Aye," said Mr. Knacker. "Soon the water will be greener and the ship will start to drift. Our only way through is spreading sail and touching wood."

"Waterbreath," she said, enchanted by the novelty.

"A sailor's word for fog," mumbled Mr. Fen, who started walking off as if expecting her to follow.

"That it ain't," Mr. Knacker said exclusively to Molly. "It is breezes made of water, difficult to breathe. You might be scared of it at first because it feels like you're drowning, but it rarely lasts a day and few of us succumb."

Mr. Fen returned to her side. He put his hand behind her waist and said, "He's trying to impress you with his tales and superstitions. There is no cause for worry."

Molly felt a quiver of revulsion up her spine.

"It wasn't my aim to worry you, Mrs. Smith," said Mr. Knacker.

"I'm not afraid of waterbreath, however thick it comes!" she said, consoled by Mr. Knacker's friendly reassurance.

"Molly Smith is scared of nothing," said the grim second mate, descending from the foremast and landing with a thud. He had scars instead of wrinkles, and a beard like dirty snow. "It's Mr. Fen you've worried," he assured Mr. Knacker. "Took the man weeks to poke his head above deck."

"I beg your pardon," Mr. Fen began.

"Acts as if he owns her now," the second mate continued. "Mrs. Smith is one of *us*. Go pour a fucking candle."

"Come," said Mr. Fen, and squeezed Molly's arm.

"I'll stay and watch the fog," she said, pulling from his grip.

Mr. Fen squared his jaw as much as he was able, but his softness and his petulance were rather too effete.

"I'll see you below," he said to Molly, marching off with resolute strides.

"You won't see a thing," the second mate called, "once the *ghost fog* surrounds us!"

Much of the crew began to laugh. Molly couldn't help but join them.

⚘

But she did grow alarmed when the waterbreath arrived. She stood with Mr. Knacker at the bow to watch it come. The fog approached the *Cleaver* like a tidal wave, as wide as she could see from starboard to port—pale, faintly blue, and ominously silent.

They had encountered fog before and even the denser banks thinned once the ship was moving through, but the waterbreath intensified and utterly engulfed them. Molly felt as if a saturated bag were on her head. She gasped and couldn't breathe, which made her heart begin to race, which made her pant and hyperventilate and panic even more. Mr. Knacker and the second mate were hazy at her side. The sails disappeared. She couldn't see her feet. Captain Veer shouted orders from behind her on the forecastle but his voice was oddly muted in the hissing of the mist.

"Worse than I expected," Mr. Knacker said beside her, choking on the words until he coughed, and coughed again.

"Cup your hands around your mouth," the second mate instructed.

Molly did so. It kept away the thickest of the vapor, and she finally got a breath and felt her heart begin to calm. The temperature had risen ten degrees in half a minute and the air smelled of gardens after heavy summer rain.

"It'll be clearer in your cabin," Mr. Knacker said, "at least until it settles. Can I help you find your way?"

Molly clasped his elbow and breathed through her hand. He had bragged to her once that he could walk the deck blind, and now he proved it: she could see only an arm's length away. They shuffled to the hatch, where he guided her below. Before he wished her well and shut the door above her, Molly saw the waterbreath pouring down the stairs, where it spread upon the floor and pooled ankle deep.

Hurrying to her cabin, she passed Mr. Fen. He was lying in his hammock, dozing it would seem, but she felt as if his eyes opened slightly in the dark.

The atmosphere was thickening; the walls began to sweat. All the moisture would be ruinous to Nicholas's lungs. She entered the cabin, went to her brother's side, and tucked his blanket more securely, hoping to keep the air from dampening his clothes.

"The most extraordinary fog is filling up the ship," she said, smoothing down his cowlick and kissing him over the eye.

Nicholas looked at her and frowned, seeming puzzled by her face, as if she might have been a figment of an ongoing dream. He dropped his head and closed his eyes, possibly asleep. She cupped her hands above his mouth but couldn't feel him breathe and took them off again, fearing she would stifle him completely.

Molly's skirts hung heavy and her lungs felt full. She crawled beneath the blanket in her own swinging cot. Waterbreath slipped through every crack and filled the cabin. It was only midday but dark had come upon them, and despite her fascination and her fear, she fell asleep, terribly fatigued from drowning in the air.

☙

She woke beneath a solid weight, unable to open her mouth and thinking, in the gloom, that her head had gotten tangled in her own sodden blanket. When she tried to throw it off, her arms refused to move. Every part of her was pressed down tight against the cot. There was just enough light to see the waterbreath around her, like a dark foggy night with an inkling of the moon. Hot, putrid air pulsed around her throat. She heard a moan and thought it was Nicholas, but no—the moan was *with* her, and the pressure on her chest was someone else's body.

The shock made her struggle and she almost freed her face. Mr. Fen's palm tightened on her mouth.

"Quiet," came his whisper, "or I'll suffocate your brother."

Molly wheezed through her nose. Had he really said "brother"?

Mr. Fen's lips were just below her ear, but he had forced her head sideways and Molly couldn't see him. He groped her breast and squeezed his legs, slippery bare, around her stocking. She could tell that he was dressed in nothing but a shift. His nether part was firm and slid above her knee, up and down, back and forth against the muscles of her thigh.

She saw it clearly in her mind and longed to shrink away, but a deeper sort of weight had paralyzed her limbs. He ground against her leg. She struggled not to cry.

She thought of Elise in bed with the chimney sweep, remembering their joy, and then she prayed, small and wordless, that he wouldn't push inside her. Mr. Fen's balding pate rubbed softly on her cheek.

She looked for Nicholas but couldn't see his cot through the mist. He was safe in his oblivion. She hoped he wouldn't stir.

Between the sweat and the oppressive saturation of the air, she and Mr. Fen were tangled in a sticky mess of limbs, and once he spasmed, growing rigid when he flexed upon her thigh, she felt his body soften like a jellyfish around her.

After a long spell of silence, Mr. Fen raised his head and whispered in her ear. His voice was too sibilant and close to understand. All she heard was "secret." Then he peeled himself away. He tipped the cot climbing out and righted it with care, steadying its movement like a father with a cradle.

Molly watched him go. He vanished in the fog. When she finally reached down to pull the blanket over her legs, she felt the fluid on her thigh and rubbed it with her fingers. It was slippery as an egg white, copious and smooth. The darkness didn't cover her but held her there, exposed. She wished the waterbreath were rain, never-ending rain.

Chapter Twelve

Molly woke and couldn't remember falling asleep. She tried to convince herself that Mr. Fen's assault hadn't happened, that his body weight had simply been her own heavy limbs, his whispers mere delirium induced by the fog. But the smell of him had lingered, sulfurous and sweaty, and the cloth with which she'd cleaned her leg was crumpled on the floor. The waterbreath had thinned and it was easier to breathe. She could now see Nicholas distinctly in his cot. She changed her clothes before he woke, but even her extra shift had dampened in the night and every inch of her was sticky, every part of her was fouled.

She went to Nicholas's side, rubbed his arm, and woke him up. He looked at her and sighed but the sigh became a cough, so phlegmy that it choked him for a moment till he swallowed. He regarded her with no apparent knowledge of the night, as if she'd only just arrived to tell him it was foggy and he hadn't spent the intervening hours in oblivion.

"Good morning," Molly said, grateful he was sick; in health, he would have recognized the falseness of her smile.

"G'morning," Nicholas wheezed, and gestured for a drink.

She gave him sips of wine and talked about the waterbreath, worried Mr. Fen was listening at the door. What if he could hear the muffled conversation? What if he suspected she was saying something more? Molly raised her voice, enunciating her words, speaking of the fog and of the Serpentine Current. Nicholas chewed a biscuit and appeared to pay attention, but the air in the windowless cabin remained oppressive and he dozed again, his face slightly pinker from the wine.

She took his spare clothes to dry on deck. Mr. Fen's door was closed when she passed it and she hesitated, worried he would hear her creeping past. She thought of returning to her cabin for Nicholas's safety but, desperate for a walk among the crew, told herself that Mr. Fen had only meant to frighten her into silence.

The waterbreath was gone, the day was clear and bright, and a rich, warm wind fluffed the sails to sunny life. The vessel raced along the waves and all the seamen were delighted, calling out and laughing, and the morning air revived her as she hung her brother's clothes to freshen on the shrouds.

Mr. Fen appeared thirty feet away, partially concealed by the cross-hatched rigging. He looked at her intently, didn't waver, didn't blink. His stare was like a candle flame pausing in its flicker, turning for a moment into a sharp blade of light. Molly's vision swam. She felt as if the fog were in her lungs again. He didn't speak or gesture but she understood him fully: *I am watching every moment. Not a word or I will kill him.*

Nicholas's death would hardly be suspicious after weeks of constant illness. She could tell the crew directly and the sailors would believe her: she was popular and Mr. Fen was generally disliked. They would flog him and confine him all the way to Floria. But Captain Veer distrusted her and might dismiss her claim. Lacking any proof, Mr. Fen could walk away.

Refusing to cry or look afraid, she turned from his unwavering stare and walked to the stern of the ship, wobbly as a lubber who had just come aboard.

"Good morning, Mrs. Smith!" said Mr. Knacker, doffing his hat. "The *Cleaver*'s grown wings and we are flying 'cross the Serpentine!"

"Good morning," Molly said without her customary cheer, continuing ahead as though he were a stranger. She registered the hurt in Mr. Knacker's falling features but she longed to be alone and couldn't risk conversation, not with Mr. Fen assuming she'd accuse him.

The gleaming sea, luscious green with rippling sun and white-capped waves, was too alive and colorful to look upon today. Molly sat below the rail against a weatherworn barrel, found a short length of rope, and practiced a knot she had learned from one of the midshipmen. It was an octopus knot, named for its appearance and extraordinary hold, and she tied and untied it dozens of times as various members of the crew discovered her there, and greeted her, and asked whether she was well.

"Yes," she said to each without looking up.

The wizened second mate approached her and said, "Beg pardon, Mrs. Smith, but there's a large pod of mourningfish racing off the bow. They're marvelous quick and sad. It's said their great intelligence causes them to grieve."

He invited her to watch. Molly sullenly declined, and when the second mate returned to the crew with news of her indifference, the sailors were so concerned—she could see them in a huddle, speaking lowly, glancing over—they themselves lost interest in the mourningfish and went about their work, serious and quiet.

She had been sitting alone for an hour when a shadow moved beside her. Molly recognized his boots and how they planted on the deck, but she didn't acknowledge his presence when he loomed there above her, studying the ocean with his customary glower.

"You've done it wrong," Captain Veer eventually said without looking down, as though he sensed a faulty knot just by standing in its presence.

He was right. She had been tying it incorrectly every time, but when she double-checked her loops and turns, she couldn't spot her error. She loosened the rope and tried again, concentrating fiercely. He followed her attempt out of the corner of his eye. She failed and tried again, fumbling and annoyed, until he turned and said, "There. Pull the bight through the *left*."

"Yes, of course," Molly said, admiring the difference.

"The other way appeared to be correct," the captain said, "but would tighten up demonically as soon as it was wet."

She finished the knot, felt its strength, and loosened it with ease. It seemed a miracle, the way its whole complexity unraveled. She remembered how severely Jeremy used to bind her, and how completely they had caught him in their own tight snare.

Captain Veer walked away before she realized he was leaving. Molly stood and said, "Sir."

He stopped and turned around. The wind blew his shirt against his chest and showed his ribs, as well as a scar like a cutlass wound just below his throat. His breeches flapped. He'd grown an inch of beard during the voyage and reminded her of a pirate, dangerous but gallant.

She noticed Mr. Fen watching from afar.

"Thank you," Molly said.

The captain answered with a bow.

"At your service, Mrs. Smith," Captain Veer replied.

He paused as if intuiting she needed something more.

Molly took her knot and went below to sit with Nicholas.

⚓

She lay awake in her cot that night, dressed in all she owned, including her cloak and double stockings, underneath a blanket tucked tightly at her sides. She was attuned to every sound, down to the faintest creak of timbers. Shortly after two bells, she heard Mr. Fen creeping through the door and looked to Nicholas beside her, too far to reach and sleeping on his side, and hoped he wouldn't wake until the worst of it was done. Mr. Fen stepped between them in his dull gray shift. He checked on Nicholas himself and lifted Molly's blanket, smiling at the extra clothes she'd worn to keep him out.

"Hush," he said.

He opened her cloak and laid himself upon her. Every inch of her contracted when he hiked up his shift, letting the blanket fall so Molly saw his plump, hairless buttocks.

"No," Molly whispered.

"Then I'll smother him," he said.

He forced his hand between their bellies to the middle of her legs. Next he peeled her stocking down and rubbed against her thigh, presumably afraid of getting her with child and content to find his pleasure in a less invasive manner.

"Wait," Molly said, taking hold of his erection.

It was softer than expected, given its rigidity, and tacky with his sweat when she gripped it in her fist. Mr. Fen did not object but repositioned himself at once, allowing her to cup her other hand around his balls.

"Move it up and down," he said. "Nicely, up and down."

She did as she was told until he shut his eyes and moaned. Molly worked faster. He relaxed in his distraction. She was amazed that such a motion—little effort, little grace—could render him as helpless as a child in her power.

Molly reached beneath her back, still stroking with her fist, and found the octopus knot she had hidden in the cot. It was warm. It was wet. She had tied it incorrectly. Mr. Fen didn't notice when it looped around his scrotum.

Molly let him go, seized the dangling ends, and cinched the knot tight enough to hold a rolling cannon.

Mr. Fen constricted and he looked at her, aghast. The whiteness of his face turned furiously red and his sounds were otherworldly, like a corpse made to groan. He clapped his hands around the knot and tried to roll away. Molly felt the sway, held the cot, and stayed within it when he tumbled off and thudded to the floor.

He struck his elbow and his head and wobbled to his knees, as astonished by the mass of wet rope between his legs as by the fact that she had done it—by the fact that she had *dared*.

She'd expected him to flee; she panicked when he stayed.

He turned to Nicholas, enraged, to carry out his threat.

Nicholas had woken up and knelt beside his cot. He aimed the pistol from the trunk at Mr. Fen's chest. His eyes were clear and bright, his arm an iron bar. Only a dead man risen would have bettered the effect and Mr. Fen shrank, buckling over in his fear. He didn't move until Nicholas fully cocked the gun, and then he lurched toward the door and hobbled to his cabin for a long, hard night of wrestling with the knot.

Nicholas collapsed. In her haste to help him up, Molly tumbled from her cot. She banged her knee, got a splinter in her thumb, and crawled to reach him. Once she had him on his feet, she tried to take the pistol but he wouldn't let it go until she'd eased him into his cot again. The effort had fatigued him and he struggled to raise his head.

"I have to tell the captain straightaway," Molly said. "I couldn't prove myself before, but now the knot—"

"Proves nothing"—Nicholas winced and coughed—"but that you had him at your side."

"He knows we're brother and sister."

Nicholas revived. "How?"

"He guessed. I tried to lie. I didn't tell him! But we have to tell the captain what he did. Don't you see? He'll follow us in Floria and ruin all our secrecy. He has to be arrested."

"He'd be punished and released."

Molly groaned in agitation, flopped down, and bumped her tail-bone. She prodded at the sliver in her thumb. "What can we do?"

"Keep the pistol in your cot."

"And then?"

"Let me think," he said.

"No." Molly stood. "I'm going to the captain."

"Stay," Nicholas told her. "We have time enough to answer this. Tomorrow you will see it in the clear light of day."

<p>

Early next morning, something was amiss. Molly's ears popped. She blew her nose and yawned to work the pressure out. The *Cleaver*'s rises and falls were longer, more profound, and urgent shouts and footsteps sounded overhead. She'd grown accustomed to the sea but now her stomach felt the plunges, and the air had a cold, gray smell of greasy metal.

Nicholas hadn't moved since returning to his cot. After convincing her not to speak to Captain Veer about their trouble, he had given her the pistol, lain awake thinking, and eventually fallen asleep without another word. She'd tucked the pistol under his arm—she hadn't trusted herself to use it—and had slept until the strange new atmosphere awoke her.

Now she had to get them food and learn the state of Mr. Fen, and so she left her brother alone and crept through the hold as subtly as she could.

The door of Mr. Fen's cabin stood open and she paused to peek inside. Mr. Fen was gone. His book was in the hammock and his lantern hung above it, throwing just enough light to clarify the room. She entered warily and double-checked the shadows in the corners. The octopus knot lay severed on the floor, slightly bloody near the cut as if he'd nicked himself slicing through the fibers with a razor.

Molly hurried on deck where the day was scarcely brighter than the heavy dark below. The sea astonished her. The waves were vastly taller than she had expected. She'd have felt the motion more except that the *Cleaver*, taking longer to traverse the broader swells, rose and fell at wider intervals and seemed more controlled. In truth the sturdy ship was little better than a cork. It bobbed along, largely at the mercy of the ocean, and amazement took her breath when the bow began to crest.

They'd been sheltered from the gale by the great surrounding waves. Now the wind filled the sails and Molly felt the lurch. The humming of the rigging sounded like a choir, one of long-dead women keening for their lives. There were gray-black valleys. There were mountains spewing foam. The sky bulged low, swirling and contorting, ironclad with scraps of brighter mist whipping by. The bow began to dip and Molly tilted with the pitch. Down they went, falling smoothly, till the waves were all around them, taller than the mainmast and quieting the wind.

She heard the sailors then—she hadn't even noticed they were with her—shouting from their stations, swearing at the clouds.

Mr. Fen was not in sight. Molly walked the deck with concentrated effort, asking everyone she passed if anyone had seen him.

"No," they said in turn, focused on their duties.

Each of them impressed her with a warning, gravely spoken: "Get yourself below." "Use the privy, now or never." "Ask McGiverns for a rope and tie yourself down."

The second mate frowned at Mr. Fen's name, preoccupied with several men shortening the mainsail. "Hell on earth is tiddlywinks to hell upon the sea," he said, speaking less to Molly than to his own recollections. "Never worry, Mrs. Smith," he hastily continued. "Captain Veer will see us through. Go and ask him there afore."

The captain stood alone, regarding sea and sky. She was relieved to see him drinking from a small cup of coffee, as confidently balanced as a man upon land. When she wobbled up beside him, his expression changed her mind. Neither angry nor afraid, he stared with resignation, like the matron who had carried her loaf of bread to face the guns.

"Morning, Mrs. Smith," he said, dispensing with the "good." "I suggest you take a meal and tie yourself securely into your cot."

"Mr. Blake said the same. Is it really so dire?"

"Aye," the captain said.

They climbed another wave, much higher than the others, and the wind flung droplets from the corners of her eyes. She waited for the quiet of the next deep trough.

"Have you seen Mr. Fen? He wasn't in his room."

"Ask the cook if he has gone to get his eggs," the captain said. He drank his coffee in a gulp and turned to meet her eye. "Keep yourself below. We're in for evil weather. I have never seen the pressure fall as quickly or as far."

Molly's spirit fell as swiftly. She worried for the sailors who were bound to stay on deck—friends of hers and kindly men, minnows in the storm.

"Be safe," she said to Captain Veer.

She kissed him on the cheek. He softened like chocolate held briefly in her hand. Molly left before he spoke and saw the crew stifling laughs. It warmed her for a moment—Mr. Knacker winked hello—but then the spume smelled icy and the ship sank low and she imagined being drowned in the everlasting cold.

She collected two coils of rope from Mr. McGiverns and started below to get some food, but then a thought rippled up, causing her to stop: Mr. Fen unaccounted for and Nicholas alone. The pistol wasn't loaded. She'd been gone too long.

She hurried back and Mr. Fen was reading in his hammock. He looked at her and smiled with malevolent success. Molly felt her stomach falling through her bladder when she left him there and rushed down the passage to her cabin. A wave struck the ship and rocked it far to starboard. Molly hit the wall and landed on the floor.

She crawled toward her brother's cot, unable to see his face until she kneeled up beside him. Nicholas was sleeping with the pistol at his side. She laughed and kissed his hand, tied him down with half the rope, and made herself secure within her own swaying cot. The ship's chaotic motion steadily intensified and Molly lay awake, and listened to the storm, and worriedly obsessed over Mr. Fen's smile.

꒜

There were times she felt the ship had rolled upon its side, or underneath the water like a small wooden bubble. Lightning cracked, terrible as fractures in the hull—she couldn't see it but she smelled it, caustic and electric—and now and then her arm hairs tingled at the tips. Waves boomed from all directions. Molly gripped the rope that held her in the cot and tried to pray, using prayers she invented on the spot. Closing her eyes made the nauseating movement more pronounced, and the unrelenting storm began to wear her out. Eventually she slept. She dreamed of swirling darkness.

When she woke and looked around, Nicholas was gone. His safety rope dangled from the cot. She fought her own wet rope; the knot was tied correctly but refused to come loose. She tried to see if Nicholas was lying on the floor; half a foot of water sloshed against the wall.

Finally the rope came free and Molly stood. The water chilled her feet, cold as winter rain, and then a wave hit the *Cleaver* and the ship fell aslant. Molly slipped back, grabbing at the air, and struck herself senseless on a beam of solid oak.

Later, coming to, she remembered having fallen. She could not remember getting up and climbing into her cot. She was shivering and soaked but safe beneath her blanket with the rope she had loosened re-secured around her body.

Had the storm begun to weaken? She was swaying less dramatically. Her skull ached dully and her thoughts wouldn't stick, and looking around the room left her dizzy and depleted. There was Nicholas, however, safe within his cot again, motionless and quiet but observing her attentively.

"How?" Molly wondered, but she couldn't form the word and went to sleep again, falling into fathomless relief.

꒜

"Mrs. Smith," came a voice.

Someone shook her arm—Mr. Knacker at her side. He wore a cloth around his forehead, pink with rainy blood, and held a lantern up to see her.

"There you are. Up and at 'em."

"Nicholas," she murmured.

"Beg pardon?" Mr. Knacker asked.

She realized she had used her brother's real name, but before she had a chance to remedy the slip, Nicholas himself answered from the corner. He was sitting on the trunk, leg crossed above his knee, more alert than she had seen him since they left Umber Harbor.

"Nicholas was her childhood friend," he said to Mr. Knacker. "You were dreaming, my dear," he told her with a smile.

"Jacob," Molly said, straining at her rope.

Mr. Knacker freed the knot and helped her sit forward. Her vertigo returned and the cabin seemed to warp. Blood pounded in her temples and her stomach felt wrung, but after several slow breaths, the symptoms went away and Molly focused on her brother, comforted but dazed.

He looked like a boy freshly risen from a nap. His head was high. His eyes were warm. His face was calm and supple. Only now did Molly recognize the quiet of the cabin. Gone were the shrieking winds and urgent hollers of the crew. The ship, still ascending and descending with the waves, had a trustworthy rhythm and a balance in its rolls.

"The storm . . . ," she began.

"Did its worst," said Mr. Knacker. "We were beat to pulp and splinters but the captain fought us through."

"Your head," she said.

"'Twas nothing but free-swinging tackle." With the rag around the wound and his eyes so askew, he seemed to be a man long familiar with concussions. "Quite a few of us was battered, though. Mr. Darn has a bone jutting from his thigh, Mr. Shivers got his foot crushed flatter than a sheet, and poor McGiverns slipped off the mainmast and landed on his noggin. He's been knocked out solid with a dent ever since."

"How awful!" Molly said. Only yesterday McGiverns had

provided her with rope and he had smiled at her and told her not to worry, not a jot.

"What's more," said Mr. Knacker, lowering the lantern, "Mr. Fen has disappeared."

Molly gasped and looked at Nicholas. The lantern swung light over his face and made him younger, swung away and left him shadowy and old, unfamiliar.

"We've searched from top to bottom, stem to stern," said Mr. Knacker. "He must have ventured up and fallen overboard. The captain's all a fury, raging to and fro. The two of you was right to stay in your cots." He slumped and shook his head, bulging out his eyes. "What on earth possessed him? God be with him in the deep."

He pondered so long, Molly worried that he was addled, that the tackle had perhaps hurt him more than he believed. She refused to let him leave until he showed Nicholas his head.

"My husband studied medicine, enough to be a doctor."

Nicholas examined him. The lump was not severe. Molly tore a strip from the bottom of her blanket to replace the sodden bandage. Mr. Knacker grew teary—from the pain or Molly's care?—and didn't go until he had thanked her twice and sung her praise to Nicholas, declaring her a wife to make any husband proud.

"I see that you have made your usual impression," Nicholas said when he was gone.

"But what of Mr. Fen?"

Molly stood and crossed the room, closing up her cloak against the cold northern air.

"Perhaps he felt shame," Nicholas suggested. "Shame for what he was and fear of being caught. It's possible he threw himself over in despair."

"No," Molly said. She could almost see her breath. "He wasn't afraid. He was smiling when I saw him."

"When?" Nicholas asked.

"Just before the storm. He was smiling in his hammock as if he knew something wicked. I was scared he might have smothered you. What else could he have done?"

Nicholas considered this, at first as if to humor her but crystallizing, slowly, like a window growing ice. He stood abruptly. Molly's heart jumped backward in her chest. He turned toward the trunk, opened the lid, and dumped it out, and then he sifted through the extra clothes, shaking every article.

"The money bag," he said, and hurried out the door.

Molly followed up the passageway to Mr. Fen's cabin, where he ransacked the travel chest and blankets in the hammock. He examined every corner, every nook and board until he finally slumped down, grimly stunned, against the wall.

"He took it," Molly said. "Everything we had!"

"To the bottom of the sea," Nicholas replied.

"Maybe he's alive and hiding in the hold."

Her brother shook his head with dreadful resignation, losing his complexion like a man spilling blood. Molly clutched the hammock for support and almost fell.

"Nicholas," she said. "Oh, Nicholas, what have you done?"

The ship carried on, pitching forward down a wave. In the air, she could feel their destination fast approaching—the sting of autumn, even winter, in a land full of strangers.

"Nicholas," she said, but he was distant. He was gone.

Chapter Thirteen

Town of Root, Continent of Floria, 1763

Root burgeoned with fertility, surging back to life far more emphatically than other parts of Floria. Spring greened the town and brought better air—cool and minty in the shade, wholesome in the light—and the forest grew thicker after every burst of rain. The Antler River had receded, the flowers of the flood had drifted southward over the falls, and all around town people tidied up their homes, painting and repairing after winter's abuse.

Tom Orange swung his ax and split a log behind the tavern, where the garden was erupting with its pumpkin vines, bean sprouts, and panoply of herbs. His ribs had mostly healed and his bruises had diminished after the rescue in the river. He was active dawn to midnight, spirited and strong, busy as the song bees that looped around his head. These were bees that buzzed in melody to harmonize the hive. The songs were quick and simple like the music of the birds, but though a single bee was charming, and the hive all together made a gorgeous humming choir, three or four around his ears buzzing different tunes—in and out, in and out—were maddeningly noisy.

Tom swung his ax again, trying to ignore them. He was boiling wort for beer and needed more wood, but as so often happened at the critical stage of brewing, multiple distractions endangered his efforts. A song bee dove and crawled inside his hair, just as Ichabod gangled out to summon him inside and the ax blade jammed in a hard black knot. The bee was under his ponytail, tickling Tom's neck. He freed the ax, looked up, and said, "What?"

The voiceless Ichabod had lived in the Orange for so many years that his expressions and hand signs were comprehensible to Tom, except in certain instances of odd specificity. He gestured, "Come inside, someone is here," with perfect clarity but indicated trouble with his tall, knitted brow.

From the road around front came the sound of cheerful voices.

"Travelers," Tom said, surprised he hadn't noticed sooner.

But Ichabod responded yes, and no, and both together till his head began to swivel. Tom swatted at his ponytail but couldn't find the bee. He second-guessed how much sassafras and withered monk he'd already added to the hops, and he was about to check the angle of the sun—he kept track of the boiling time by instinct and slow-moving shadow—when Ichabod loped across the garden, picked a berry from a bush, and dotted it repeatedly on his forehead and cheeks.

He stood before Tom with his red-speckled face.

"Lem," Tom said.

Ichabod nodded.

Steam billowed from the pot and almost scalded Tom's chin. He backed away, clapped his neck, and caught the bee beneath his hair. It stung his palm twice but he didn't let go; if only he had hands big enough for Lem. Other bees surrounded him, apparently aware their compatriot was trapped, and buzzing something different now: a choral song of battle.

"Where's Bess?" Tom asked.

Ichabod pointed up, his finger ringed with bees, wincing as he did so and eager to escape.

Tom gauged the simmer of the wort by its burble. He had fifteen minutes, maybe less, till he strained it. Too soon or too late and it was hardly worth keeping. Ichabod was dutiful but couldn't read the boil. There was no good choice but to hurry inside and so he strode toward the door, letting go of the bee and leaving half his mind swirling in the belly of the copper.

He entered through the kitchen. Nabby chopped chickens, setting aside the beaks for talismanic garlands. She was short and had the spongy-firm skin of dried apples. No one knew her age; she'd been old when Tom was young. She spent every day of the year baking bread and pies, cooking meat, tending the hearth, and speaking of ghosts and omens as matter-of-factly as other people gossiped. Now she chewed a slice of liver, her infallible means of testing a bird's acceptability, and frowned as if to say, "I *know* a group has come."

Tom picked a stinger from his palm and fixed his hair. "Lem's here again."

"I have a nose," Nabby said.

Indeed, the nourishing smell of the kitchen had succumbed to Lem's stink, one of carcasses and flesh and foul, bubbling dyes. A smoaknut of tension grew in Tom's chest, very like the bullet lodged in his shoulder. He left Nabby with her beaks and walked up front.

The taproom was cozy-dim even in the daylight, its furniture and floor weathered smooth by decades of visitors, browned by dirt and polish, spill and wipe, smoke and time. Tom could almost stand straight inside the unlit hearth; one of its stones was like a face, another like a wolf. Windows at the front overlooked the road, with the town down left and the river down right. The room was big enough for fourscore people, tightly packed, and smelled of fire and tobacco, travelers' sweat and rum—an odor so familiar it was virtually his own. He knew the table nicks, the rafter cracks, the stains and warps and creaky chairs as thoroughly as any of the marks upon his body. However full of strangers, it would always be his home.

What to make of Uncle Lem: relative or stranger? He was muscular and tall, with receding, stringy hair. He stood in the middle of the taproom, blood-browned apron tied around his waist, bearing so little resemblance to his sister—Tom's diminutive mother, now deceased— that an unknowing eye would never have spotted their relation.

Tom approached him as a small group of travelers entered in the front. Before a word was spoken, Lem crossed the room and clomped aggressively to Ichabod, who'd followed through the kitchen with the berry-juice dots still covering his face. Ichabod flinched and cracked his elbow on the doorframe.

Tom caught his uncle by the arm, using all his strength just to slow him down. Lem turned and the window light clearly showed his face. His cheeks and forehead were mottled, like most of his skin, with small crimson freckles: the permanent marks of bloodpox. The marks were exceedingly rare—few people who caught the sickness during the last serious outbreak had lived; it had killed Lem's wife and nearly killed him—and they were generally less pronounced even among survivors.

"We were slapping song bees and Ichabod had berries in his hands," Tom said.

It was an explanation so unlikely, Lem paused to doubt it, giving Ichabod time to clean his face with a handkerchief and hurry outside to tend to the travelers' horses. Lem watched him go, grimacing and flexing. He was a lifelong tanner with an air of rotten skins. His tannery was failing due to his drunkenness and sloth. He was sober now, or seemed to be, and although Tom intended to keep him that way, he led his uncle to the gated bar in the corner, away from the entering travelers, and said, "Bess isn't here. I sent her up to Mapple's farm to get a brace of rabbits."

"She's upstairs. I seen her at the window."

Tom sighed and wished his cousin knew better how to hide. He said, "You can't keep doing this. She's here of her own accord."

"It ain't right."

"It wasn't right abusing her for years and driving her off midwinter, when you were laid up drunk and she had nothing to eat but horsemeat and old black bread."

Tom advanced when he said it, berating himself again for failing to help Bess sooner and physically inclined to hammer out his conscience.

"I'm turning a new leaf," Lem said. "But it's a hard thing when my own nephew treats me like an enemy. I won't hurt her anymore."

"Anymore," Tom said, to mark the underlying fact.

Lem narrowed his eyes, which were tiny to begin with, and said, "I'll fetch her down myself."

Tom opened the bar and poured his uncle half a tankard of cider. Half a tankard too much.

"Thankee," Lem said, giving him a smile that was, despite his fetid teeth, sweetly reminiscent of Tom's mother. "Though it won't help business serving half cups of drink."

"You're welcome that it's free," Tom said. "Set right here while I go and greet the guests."

They were two men and a woman, dusty and gregarious. It was already late morning and they were the first travelers of the day, an unusual thing for spring when the road was clear to ride, but understandable in light of the continuing Maimer attacks. Tom crossed the room with his tavern-keeper's smile. He introduced himself and shook their hands, encouraging them to sit and apologizing that he needed to run upstairs.

"I won't be a minute," he said. "Make yourselves at home."

"Many do," Lem said, tankard to his mouth so he echoed in the pewter.

Tom hastened upstairs, wary of leaving his uncle unchaperoned and suddenly unsure whether he had relocked the bar. Straight to Bess's door, which was shut. He knocked and entered. The room was naturally lit and sparsely furnished, with enough dried flowers on the wall to make it both feminine and morbid. Bess hid in a shadow just beyond the window, waiting in the hope that Lemuel would leave.

She started when Tom entered, lighting her cheek with sun and looking pretty in her cap and blue-striped skirt. She clasped her hands tight for self-reassurance.

"I'm sorry, Tom," she said and stared at him beseechingly, seemingly embarrassed and afraid to disappoint him.

Tom loved his cousin dearly, and he found it as strange to play the role of her protector—she was twenty years old, only seven years younger than himself—as he did to play elder to his middle-aged uncle. But he was far too annoyed to shelter her today.

"You're needed downstairs," he said.

"I don't want to see him."

"Neither do I, but he's your father."

She flushed but it was spirit more than weakness that inflamed her. He could tell because he often had the same flush himself.

"This can't go on," Tom said.

"You wouldn't send me back!"

"What's the difference if he's *here* every day?" But seeing how it panicked her, he added, "You can stay. Send him off and get to work. It's why you're living here, remember."

He left her there to follow him down—he'd give her half a minute—and paused to calm his temper when he reached the bottom of the stairs. He twisted on the handrail and pulled until it creaked, wanting it to hold, expecting it to break. He peeked at Lem and the travelers from the kitchen doorway, found them just as he had left them, and jogged outside to check the boiling copper. Another bee stung his neck; they were furious today. He still had time before the wort needed straining, so he left it once more and went to stabilize the house.

Lem and Bess stood at the bar, bound in intimate whispers, while his cousin poured drinks and placed them on a tray. Tom passed them and continued up front to see the guests.

"I've had your company before," he told the oldest of the group, a man with thinning hair and frizzy gray eyebrows. "Last July, if I remember right. Mr. Hoopworth the banker."

"A trip on urgent business," Mr. Hoopworth replied. "Prodigious memory you have!"

"A tavern keep's memory," the second man said. He was delicately formed but confidently voiced, dandified with ruffles on his collar and his cuffs.

"It helps to warm a welcome," Tom answered with a nod. He turned to Mr. Hoopworth again and said, "You liked a cup of smoak."

"He has talked of little else!" said the lady of the group. She was young and very tall, a spitting image of the dandy to her right—probably his sister. She had sweet, distracting dimples. "He has bound us both to try a cup on penalty of lecture. But what precisely is it?"

"A rich black drink made of strong local nuts," Mr. Hoopworth explained.

Bess had filled the tray but been delayed by her father. Tom continued with the talk and hoped the travelers wouldn't notice.

"Is it true that smoak trees are found only in Root?" the lady asked.

"Aye," Tom said. "Last year a merchant tried growing them in Liberty. Every sapling died. They like it here at home."

"With your extraordinary weather," said the dandy. "We have waited several weeks for the road to finally clear."

"I'm glad of open travel," Tom said, forcing cheer. "We could do with fuller tables. Any trouble on the way?"

"We have all our vital parts," the dandy said wryly.

Mr. Hoopworth coughed and gave his companions a censuring frown.

"You mean the Maimers," said the lady, heating up pink from an over-show of courage. "Mr. Hoopworth worries you will frighten me with horrors."

Her youthfulness and pluck reminded Tom of Molly, as a bright piece of brass reminds one of gold. He looked toward the door, picturing the Knoxes' tidy house off the common, where Molly had been staying for the past three weeks and, according to Benjamin, had recovered in body if not entirely in spirit. She still claimed to remember nothing, but although most of the town suspected she was hiding a scandalous past, local interest had diminished owing to the dearth of new developments. Talk was of the Maimers, here and everywhere in Root, and as the last enduring sense of Molly was one of secret trouble, Tom had kept his distance. He had trouble enough already.

"My sister knows the tales," the dandy said. "She has every right to hear them if she's traveling the road."

"I agree," Tom said. "A person ought to know when someone wants her limbs. There was another attack Wednesday the last. A peddler lost his foot. Before that, they got a lawyer—John Pale—and took his tongue."

John Pale had stayed a fortnight, terrified to leave, until he finally rode away, in sickly gray silence, with a company of seven armed trappers bound for Grayport.

"It's terrible," the lady said. "How is it the victims always come to Root?"

"The Maimers don't attack close to Grayport or Liberty," Tom said. "Authorities are thinner out here. Nearly all of the attacks have been within ten miles of the valley."

"Someone ought to ride out and shoot them," Mr. Hoopworth said.

"Convince the sheriff," Tom answered, "and you'll all drink smoak forever on the house."

"You could ride out yourself," said the dandy with a smirk.

Tom took this as bravado, arrogant but harmless. Still, it irked him: he *had* ridden out, more than once. The dandy plucked a short stray fiber from his jacket, preening as if the Maimers were a coffeehouse diversion.

Tom grinned and looked for Bess.

Lem clutched her arm and held her at the bar. Toughened by her childhood, she fought to struggle loose, but he squeezed so hard her eyes began to shine and the drink tray wavered, threatening to crash.

"Excuse me," Tom said, turning from the table.

He crossed the room with blood pumping swiftly to his muscles.

"Let her go," Tom said, grabbing Lem's free wrist so they formed a kind of chain, familial and tense back beside the bar.

"I need her home," Lem said.

"I need her serving drinks."

"She ain't yours to keep."

"Nor am I yours," Bess said, tugging free. Remarkably, she kept the drinks balanced on the tray, though her movement caused the liquid to precariously slosh.

Tom interposed himself so Bess could walk away and said to his uncle, "You've seen her. Now go home."

Lem's spots began to darken. He chested up close, raised his stubbled chin, and said, "I'll tear this place to kindling if you don't send her off."

"You leave a splinter on the floor and I'll get my rifle."

Lem recoiled as if a flash pan had fired in his face. "You would shoot your own blood?"

"Bess is old enough to make her own way," Tom said.

"I've spoken to Sheriff Pitt."

"There's nothing he can do."

"We'll see about that."

Lem's voice had a melodramatic falsity about it, but the threat wasn't idle. Pitt would stab at any weakness. Tom balled his hand and the bee stings throbbed. He could almost hear his wort boiling over in the yard.

Lem stomped away toward the tavern's front door. Bess saw him coming and retreated to the hearth, where she held the empty tray before her like a shield. He watched her as he passed and seemed about to speak when he bumped Mr. Hoopworth, who spilled his cup of smoak.

"Keep your woman close," Lem told the men, "unless you want her stolen."

The young lady gasped, more at Lem than at his words. The dandy stood defensively beside her with a frown, unsure of how to reply, while Mr. Hoopworth sopped around the table with a napkin, trying to keep the drink from spilling into his lap. Tom approached Lem and was prepared to haul him out, but his uncle bowed dramatically and left without encouragement.

"Lemuel Carver," Tom said to the guests. "He hasn't been himself since the pox took his wife."

Bess suppressed her nerves, rushing to replenish Mr. Hoopworth's smoak.

The lady blushed at Tom and said, "Here I was fearing Maimers, when it's you I must be wary of!"

The door was still ajar and Scratch the cat ran in, a streak of ratty fur and scrabble-sharp claws. He hissed running past and sprinted to the kitchen, where they soon heard Nabby yelling strange, ancient curses.

Tom excused himself and said, "I'll see about your food."

He left them all in Bess's care and hurried back to Nabby, who had cornered Scratch in the pantry with a poker from the hearth. Scratch hid behind a barrel, dodging her attack. A slick pink chicken neck quivered in his mouth.

Tom approached Nabby from behind and took the poker, unaware she'd grabbed the fire-heated iron with a cloth. The metal burned his hand, the poker clanked down, and Scratch darted past into the garden with his prize.

"I had him pinned!" Nabby said. "He took the best neck."

Tom plunged his hand into a bucket of cold water. "I won't have you killing cats in the kitchen."

"The beast is not a cat. He was sent, like a curse, and he will give me no rest until—"

"You aren't ruddy cursed any more than I am," Tom said, examining his palm with the stings and the burn, and thinking of Lem and Sheriff Pitt, Bess and Molly and the Maimers, and the guests in need of food while the cook chased a cat.

He left Nabby muttering imprecations over the chicken beaks and walked out back. His copper had been tipped. The brew had doused the flames and pooled upon the ground, where the steaming mud revealed to Tom not the markings of a cat, but his uncle's deep footprints leading to the trees.

⚓

The house of Dr. Benjamin Knox and his wife, Abigail, had sturdy clapboard walls and a high, peaked roof, and it stood upon a quarter-acre plot—mostly gardened—at the corner of Center and Milk Streets in the heart of the close-packed town.

Leafy vines covered the trellis up the side of the house. Molly had watched them grow from nothing during her weeks of convalescence and seen their tendrils uncoil right before her eyes. Spring in Root astonished her. Trees burst green, flowers leapt to bloom, and early fruits and berries looked ripe enough to pick. Breezy warmth, juicy vines—weeks ago, she'd hidden in a snowbound cabin. Had it only been a month since the winter disappeared?

Molly scanned the garden for renegade stalkers. These were short, sinuous weeds that uprooted themselves and crawled with reaching feelers to fatally suck the fluids of the garden's stationary plants. Benjamin knelt in a shady patch of manure and clipped the newly grown feelers off a mass of writhing stalkers, but many others had spread throughout the garden overnight and had to be collected. They were not to be killed; once crippled and controlled, Benjamin had told her, stalkers clung together and eventually grew leaves of medicinal value. She spotted one now among the skinwort, allowed the feelers to twine around her wrist, and carried it back to Benjamin for pruning and replanting. He cut the feelers with his knife, took the weed, and smiled up at her.

Benjamin was Molly's only friend in Root—her only friend at

all—and for weeks he had kept her close in his care. They breakfasted and supped together, remaining in the garden or the house during the day and then conversing over tea in the parlor every evening. He enjoyed reading music and would often hum the tunes. He had tried for many years to learn the violin but suffered awkward fingers, which also caused him difficulty with writing and, he freely admitted, with stitches and incisions. But just as his medical knowledge compensated for his lack of dexterity, his passion for hearing music on the page compensated, in part, for his inability to play it.

One night the previous week, Benjamin had hummed a piece to himself and Molly had exclaimed, "That's Flumat!"

Benjamin, much surprised, had double-checked the sheet.

"It is. It is indeed!" he said. "But how is it familiar?"

Molly almost blurted she had learned it from her brother, but she pinched herself fiercely on the wrist and said, "I have a memory for music. Like remembering a dream."

He waited patiently for more, reading her expression like an unknown cadenza, and the floor appeared to shrink and draw their chairs nearer together. But on that particular evening, his wish to know her secrets paled before his delight at finding a companion, unheard-of in Root, who was acquainted with the music ever playing in his mind. From that night forth, they had spoken of Brondel, Hark, Riber, Frederini, and Gorelli, often reading the sheets together until Molly—much to Abigail's displeasure—started to hum throughout the day as absentmindedly as Benjamin.

Neither of the Knoxes, Molly knew, believed her memory loss was genuine. Benjamin didn't press, or rather pressed with gracious care. Abigail, however, came at her with knives.

Just that morning over breakfast, Molly was finishing her eggs when Abigail said, "I have another, if you're hungry."

"No, but thank you, Mrs. Knox."

"A wasted egg. If you are finished with your breakfast, you may help me beat the rugs."

"I continue to prescribe no strenuous activity after meals," Benjamin said from behind a month-old newspaper he had borrowed from the tavern.

Abigail pursed her skinny lips—she seemed, in fact, to purse her whole body—and said as she cleared the table, "You encouraged Sarah Crook to go about her work," referring to an elderly widow who had recently been kicked unconscious by a horse.

"A man in Grayport has invented an optical device," Benjamin read, "that detects nascent fevers."

"An honesty device would prove more useful," Abigail replied.

Molly did her best to finish up her eggs. The hard-boiled yolk clung drily at her windpipe.

Benjamin folded the paper and stared at the wall, seeming to consider the materials of fever glasses. "There are numerous diverse manifestations of mental darkness," he began.

"Including voluntary," Abigail said, and promptly left the room.

Molly drank tea and dislodged the egg.

"I am crippling stalkers today," Benjamin told her with a smile. "Would you like to assist me?"

"Yes," she said, standing up and looking to the garden.

"She can cripple stalkers but cannot beat a rug," came Abigail's voice from two rooms away.

Indeed, Molly did feel strong enough to work when she was asked, or at the very least recovered from her most dramatic symptoms—the tenderness, swelling, and after-bleeding of her pregnancy, which she had struggled to conceal from Benjamin and Abigail. The air today soothed her like a childhood bath. Birds familiar and exotic swooped past, flashing colors: goldfinches, cardinals, something pearl, something blue. She pressed her hands into the earth, enjoying the fatness of the worms and the feel of healthy soil, and yet an emptiness remained, a hollowness of body and of life altogether, as if she had possessed a sixth sense and now, having lost it, found her customary senses too predictable and drab.

She captured the last of the runaway stalkers and watched Benjamin cripple and replant them. The weeds were calmer now, defeated—deprived, like herself, of their ability to flee, but at any rate safe within the good doctor's care.

"They will root themselves again and grow more docile," Benjamin said as he tamped the soil with his palms, "so long as they are kept sufficiently moist."

"The rain will help," Molly said.

Benjamin stood and cupped his eyes against the daylight. The sky looked enormous: high blue, bright as life, without a single passing cloud or any trace of wind. He tilted his head and asked, "Why do you say it will rain?"

"The blades of grass look sharper and they're leaning to the west," Molly said. "I noticed it a week ago, just before a storm."

"Yes!" Benjamin said, clapping his hands and almost jigging. He rushed her with ebullience, eyeglasses flashing in the sun. "I have noted it a hundred times. The grass begins to point, the leaves raise their palms, and the white-throated sparrows sing a full octave higher."

Molly had failed to note the sparrows but believed it was true. She had seen her fill of marvels since journeying to Floria, and even in a country so oddly unfamiliar, Root seemed a brighter cornucopia of wonders. Flower floods, walking weeds, multicolored air—of *course* the grass and birds heralded the storms.

"Does no one else notice?" Molly asked.

"The pointing grass?"

"The rarity and queerness."

"Rare and queer! So it is! Most of the townspeople were born here and know of little else. That which travelers and transplants look upon as curious, the locals see as common as the hairs within their nostrils."

"Are you a transplant?" she asked.

"I was born and breeched in Grayport."

"Why is Root . . . different?"

"Why, indeed?" Benjamin replied. "I have notes and observations, legends and accounts, theories geographic, biologic, astronomic. Nowhere else, save perhaps the sea, are the mysteries of nature so abundantly in evidence, to say nothing of our more supernatural phenomena. The presence of ghosts is broadly accepted, and the local Elkinaki tell of a figure in the forest—the Colorless Man—who is strikingly similar to the devil of Scripture. Many in Root claim to have seen him as a thin, crooked shadow in the trees, in their dreams, or at the ends of their own benighted beds. Their stories are amazingly consistent, but how does one substantiate the wholly insubstantial?"

"Why are you whispering?" Molly asked.

"Abigail's hearing is acute," Benjamin said, leaning closer. "She tolerates my inquisitiveness to a degree, but she is devoutly Lumenist and considers my probing into spiritual matters prideful, even insolent to God."

"But do you believe in such things? Ghosts and crooked shadow men?"

"Truth often hides within a skein of superstition. Nabby, the cook at the Orange, is a fount of numinous wisdom and is, herself, almost supernaturally long-lived . . . But that reminds me! The nyx is efflorescing." Benjamin crossed the garden to a blossoming purple shrub. He cut a sprig with his knife and held it up to show her. "Nabby insists the petals, rubbed upon her eyelids, allow her to discover witches in disguise. It flowers only for a day—even now, the bloom is fading. I must take it to her at once or she will grouse at me the whole year through," he said with a smile. "I think you may accompany me today. You have been cooped up enough and must be curious to see beyond the window of the parlor."

"Yes!" Molly said, precisely as a leaden cloud, a forerunner of the approaching storm, dimmed the glaring sun.

She hadn't seen Tom since his one brief visit to the house, but even three weeks later, he seemed to her as present as he had been that morning in the river when she floated in his arms, buoyant with his warmth. He was busy at the tavern, Benjamin had told her. She worried that he remembered her as cold, dead weight. But, oh!—how she would like to speak with him again, and to find in him, perhaps, another kind friend.

Abigail walked out the back door carrying Benjamin's medical bag and said, "You're wanted at the smithy. Luger crushed his foot."

She had tied her hair back strictly so her forehead stretched, heightening her eyebrows. It gave her a look of supercilious attentiveness, recalling Mrs. Wickware, and yet her heron's neck and poise were reminiscent of Frances, instilling in Molly a dual urge to hug her and recoil.

Benjamin took his bag and left for the smithy at once, his rumi-native mood giving way to action, and after he was gone Abigail said to Molly, "There are several more stalkers mangling the pepperstem. I trust that you can cripple them yourself unassisted. When you're fin-ished, you may come inside and help me boil linen."

She went inside without waiting for an answer, and Molly turned to the pepperstem, where three more stalkers had indeed been over-looked. It took her five minutes to extricate and replant them, and then she noticed the sprig of nyx that Benjamin had left behind, its small purple blossoms looking duller than before. She picked the flowers up and ran around the front of the house, but Benjamin had taken his horse and ridden out of sight.

Wind gusted up Center Street, swirling petticoats and dust, and there was thunder in the west and a smell of scoured tin. Gray-green clouds darkened and descended. The tavern stood in the distance on its hillock near the river. She could make it there and back in very little time; why not go alone? She wasn't a prisoner, after all. Yet she doubted Abigail would allow her to leave instead of boiling linen, so she ran down the street without bothering to ask, hoping to deliver the nyx, say hello to Tom, and hurry back to the house before her absence was discovered.

She passed the common where the cows chewed the moist new grass. Next came the meetinghouse, bone white and fronted by a stee-ple, rarely used for several years—so Abigail had told her—since the local minister had been eaten by a catamount. A confidential air deep-ened off the common, partly from the overarching trees along the street but largely from the neatness and compactness of the houses. Most were single story, with a sharp peaked attic—a partial second level where inhabitants would sleep. All were simple in design, with pairs of windows at the front, central chimneys, white clapboards, and var-iously colored trim—crimson, green, indigo, buttercream, black.

However similar in style, they had character from age and many features of disfigurement. A window cloaked in ivy leaves fluttering with birds. A mangled weathervane, its arrow pointing up as if to blame. One small house, immaculately clean, had settled at an angle and tilted to the left, enough so that a ball might roll across its floor.

Another, lacking shade, looked permanently parched. Still another looked warped from a lifetime of rain. Molly tried to imagine the differences inside—how it felt to look out instead of looking in.

Wind blew her east, down the street toward the river. Branches swayed and lightning flickered in the storm-heavy dark. Every citizen in sight was hurrying indoors and no one paid attention as she sprinted past, feeling weightless with the gusts shoving at her back.

She reached the end of Center Street and looked across the river, where the vast eastern forest seemed to spread out forever. Lightning lit the water and the woods stark white. Thunder cracked close, sounding like a pistol shot. She smelled the burnt powder, felt the tremor up her arm—only memories, but strong enough to make her think of Nicholas.

Ice-sharp rain needled at her face, and the wind bent the trees and whitecapped the river. She ran against the gusts, up a slope and sopping wet. She couldn't see a thing through the broad sheets of rain. Hail fell in bursts, coating patches of the ground and pinging off her forehead and cleavage, hard as glass. It annihilated the sprig of nyx—nothing remained except for the stems—and Molly wiped her face and tried to see the tavern. A broad fork of lightning fractured overhead. She saw an old wooden sign swinging off a post: a faded orange, stuck with cloves. Beyond it, glowing windows.

Then a woman ran toward her from behind, drenched and laughing. She was young and unafraid and splashing up mud, a pretty silhouette emerging from the storm.

"Come on!" the woman said.

Molly took her hand. They hiked their skirts, ran beneath a sycamore tree, and raced toward the tavern's storm-flickered door.

Chapter Fourteen

The young woman kept Molly's hand and pulled her up the stairs inside the tavern's front door, looking backward with a fling of wet brown hair and laughing as if the storm was the best kind of fun. Molly glimpsed the taproom's lantern-lit chairs and followed her up, into the darkened staircase, down the second-story hall, and into a tiny room.

The woman closed the door. She passed the rain-lashed window overlooking Root and lit a candle with a tinderbox. The room glowed alive. The walls were pale, creamy green and decorated with a dozen dried bouquets. Atop a tidy chest of drawers lay a hairbrush, a hand mirror, and a picture book of Rougian dresses. Molly sneezed and dripped water on the threadbare rug.

"I'm Bess," the woman said with candlelit eyes. She popped off her shoes and dropped her garters and her stockings. "And you," she said, "are Molly. I saw you when they pulled you from the river. Tom's my cousin. I've wanted to meet you since he saved you but it's work, work, work, clean this and carry that. Tom is always seven places in his head and not a one of them is fun. Not to call it fun—the danger you were in—but oh, I'm glad to meet you! Were you really almost dead?"

Molly backed against the door, overwhelmed and yet delighted by the breathless introduction. They were of equal height and weight, similarly aged. Molly had darker hair and whiter skin—Bess looked permanently sun-kissed—and yet they resembled each other enough, even in their contrasts, to make them like the subjects of the same bold painter.

Bess continued shedding clothes with sisterly immodesty, too diverted by her own flying thoughts to wait for answers. "You truly don't remember where you came from?" she asked, stepping out of her sodden skirts. "What were you doing in the river? Maybe you were poisoned! Isn't it maddening and thrilling? You could be anyone, after all." Bess removed her stays and stood in nothing but her shift. It showed her body, pretty and lean with dimpled knees and tiny breasts. "It's like misplacing a favorite locket and retracing where you've been, except you can't remember where you've been and the locket is really yourself."

She hung her clothes to drip in front of the unlit hearth, then tugged a sheet off her bed and handed a corner to Molly so the two could dry their hair beneath the canopy of linen. Then she handed off the sheet and said, "I need to change my shift."

Here she finally paused and waited for Molly to turn. Molly averted her eyes but there was something—Bess's reticence? her jittery tapping foot?—that made her sneak a look when Bess dropped her shift. Her naked ribs and spine wavered with the candle. She had welts across her back, not quite scars and not quite fresh. Hail beat the roof and skittered down the shingles. Rain lashed the glass. Molly squeezed the locket at her chest and looked away.

Bess finished dressing in a clean, dry shift and said, "It's laundry day—I haven't any shifts for you to borrow. At least wring your skirts out and change your muddy stockings."

Bess pulled a fresh pair of stockings from her drawer, guided Molly into a chair, and knelt down before her. After twisting Molly's hems and taking off her shoes, Bess startled her by reaching up to untie her garters. She peeled the filthy stockings off Molly's cold legs and held her feet against her own bare knees, looking up.

"Thank you," Molly said, shivering in the pause.

The thunder had abated to a deep, constant rumble, and the windswept rain hushed around the room. Molly's soles began to warm. A light from outdoors made the room look greener, giving a hint of renewal to the withered flowers on the walls and infusing Bess's face with weird, ghostly tones.

Bess settled on her heels and said, "You must remember family."

Molly shook her head.

"Your parents?" Bess said. "A sister or a brother?"

"No."

"They say you came from Umber and you really do remember and you're only keeping secrets. If it's true, you can tell me," Bess offered in a whisper.

Molly stood and crossed the room, goosefleshed and bumping into the corner of the bed. She backed against the windowpanes and hugged herself tightly, hearing Abigail's voice condemning her deceits, and she was just about to stammer out another weak lie when Bess seized her arm and tugged her from the window.

"What are you doing?" Molly asked.

"St. Verna's Fire!"

Molly twirled around to look and marveled at the source of the peculiar tinted light. The rain and wind had lessened and the lightning had subsided, but the gloom was faintly lit by strangely glowing objects. Part of a tree, from its uppermost leaves to its middle, smoldered green like embers through a stained-glass pane. The leaves remained intact while the light moved and spread.

"Keep away from the window," Bess said. "It isn't safe."

But Molly drifted forward, curious and awed, and Bess ignored her own advice and followed at her side. The meetinghouse steeple was a pale green spire. Several peaked roofs, puddles in the road, fence posts, and barrel stacks streamed luminescence. A pushcart filled until the color overflowed. The light kept shifting, fading in one place and surging up brighter somewhere else. Molly touched the windowpane and filaments appeared, glowing and electric where her fingers met the glass. She felt a tingle, pulled away, and tried a second time.

"What is it?"

"It's a kind of clinging lightning," Bess said. "Dr. Benjamin obsesses. How I hope he sees it!"

"It's gorgeous," Molly said.

"Look! It's gotten Scratch!"

A cat ran below from the river past the tavern, trailing fuzzy sparks and yowling out of sight.

"The poor thing!" Molly said.

"Scratch has weathered worse."

The darkened figure of a boy appeared beyond the sycamore. He ran toward the tavern, looking every which way, until the glow gathered in and lit itself upon him. It started with his hands and rippled to his face and then he stopped. Light drifted like vapor off his head.

Molly ran toward the door.

"No, you can't!" Bess said.

Molly left the room and hurried up the hall as Bess began clattering through her drawers for more to wear. She ran downstairs, almost falling on an oddly warped step near the bottom. Static shocked her when she reached toward the handle of the door.

Someone grabbed her arm. Molly shrieked. It was Tom.

"There's a boy—" she said.

"I know."

"But someone has to—"

"Don't," he said.

He smelled of horse and pinewood and fiery agitation. Molly felt his pleasurable wringing of her arm, tight as when he'd held her in the middle of the river.

"Let me go!" she said.

"It's dangerous. You can't."

She tried to hit him. Tom caught her slap and then her hair was in her face and Molly steamed, red and heaving in the cramped little stairwell. No matter how she squirmed, Tom's hold could not be broken. She could shout or kick or struggle but she knew it wouldn't work, so she kissed him very hard and blew directly into his mouth. She had done it once to Frances; it had startled her immensely. Tom reacted just the same and let her go. Molly bolted.

Out the door and into the rain—she saw the child all afire. Tom shouted and pursued her but she'd never lost a race, and now she felt the spur of furious defiance. *Cowards!* Molly thought. *To leave a child in the storm!* She cut her heel on a stick and slipped around in the mud but she was close enough to see the boy's terrified expression.

"No!" he cried. He raised his hands and warded her away.

He's only frightened, Molly thought, neither heeding him nor slowing.

Tom pounded up behind her, faster than expected. The boy was straight ahead, spectral green and sizzling. Molly reached to grab him and connected with his hands. She saw a flash and heard a crack—had something hit her head?—and then the ground was falling upward and the green went black.

⚛

"Her heart is beating."

"Dr. Knox!"

"Is she breathing?"

"Doctor, my *son.*"

"Quiet, plea—"

"I'll not be quiet! She can die for all I care!"

Voices came to her in wool—heavy, wet, dense—with a fine, high ring. Molly opened her eyes and Benjamin was close, kneeling over her and smiling. He was rain-soaked and dripping with his hand below her ear, reading Molly's pulse and holding her head above the floor. Bess was muddy in a robe and peered over his shoulder, looking powerfully relieved that Molly had revived. Tom was at her side. His hair was wet and ratty, he was scarecrow stiff, and he appraised her with a look of hard-bitten fury. Molly wondered if he'd clubbed her on the head when she was running.

Wishbones dangled from the rafters overhead. How had she gotten inside, in what appeared to be the taproom? A man with frizzy eyebrows stood before a small group of patrons, all of whom regarded her with kindly curiosity, and somewhere out of sight, a woman called hysterically—and angrily, at length—for Dr. Benjamin's attention.

The boy! Molly thought, sitting with a jolt.

Her body felt heavy and her skull was hard to lift, full of odd motion like a half-set pudding. Molly groaned. Her vision wavered and her limbs throbbed and tingled. A smell of hammered metal, very like a smithy, burned her nose when she exhaled, as if the odor were inside her.

"The boy," Molly said. "What happened to the boy?"

"Nearly dead!" cried the out-of-sight woman with conviction.

"He is well," Benjamin said.

Before he could elaborate, the woman carried on, saying the boy was *not* well but deaf as stone, and cooked from skin to marrow, and if the doctor insisted on caring for the girl instead of her own innocent son—

"Mrs. *Downs*," Tom said, so coldly that the woman stopped, leaving nothing but the ringing in Molly's sore head.

She turned and saw the boy behind her near the bar, grubby from the storm but otherwise intact. His mother, Mrs. Downs, stooped tearfully beside him. She was an ample, frilly woman with a wide straw hat, the brim of which rested on the boy's wild hair. She looked at Molly with ferocity but dithered as she stared, as if surprised to see a girl rather than a devil.

"Are you deaf as stone?" Benjamin asked the boy.

"No, sir."

"Do you suffer any pain?"

"Only prickles," said the boy, "like I slept right strange."

"I assure you, Mrs. Downs, you have nothing grave to fear."

"I don't understand," Molly mumbled at her feet.

"It was St. Verna's Fire," Benjamin said, unabashedly delighted. He appeared to struggle greatly not to question her at once about its character, its force, its bodily effects. "The charge is quite benign, equipollent I would say to commonplace static, till an uncharged object— you, in this particular instance—releases and ignites its marvelous potential. It is rare," he continued, "but familiar here in Root. The charge would have harmlessly diffused in several minutes."

"I'm sorry!" Molly said directly to the boy.

He responded with a scowl and rubbed the prickles from his arm. He blamed her, Molly knew—he had tried to ward her off—and his resentment made her ribs tighten like a corset. Bess caressed Molly's back but the pressure hurt her muscles.

"Please, you must believe me," Molly said. "I didn't know."

Tom stepped up and said, "I told you it was dangerous."

His shadowy face and untied hair gave him a savage aura but his anger lacked conviction and he shifted, self-aware, as if the issue weren't the lightning but the fact that she had kissed him.

"She didn't know the nature of the danger," Benjamin said.

"I told her not to go."

"I thought . . . ," Molly said but quickly shut her mouth.

"What?" Tom said, leaning in close.

She forced herself to straighten up. He tried to stare her down. The tingle in her limbs traveled to her heart until her blood felt charged, hot enough to hiss.

"I only meant to help," she said. "I thought you were a coward."

The room collectively inhaled and everyone looked at Tom. He moved his lips as if to speak and seemed to stammer in his thoughts, by turns offended and surprised and finally dumb as wood.

"Insolence!" said Mrs. Downs. "You were warned and acted anyway with reckless disregard. I have more than half a mind to speak to Sheriff Pitt and see you held accountable."

Tom reacted as if she'd thrown a burning log across the room, striding away to placate her and, as far as could be heard above the reignited chatter, defending Molly's act from criminal complaint. The curious patrons returned to their table in the front of the taproom. Benjamin sat Molly in a chair beside the hearth where she could warm herself, and Bess brought her a hot mulled cider that settled her nerves, if only slightly, after standing up to Tom.

"He has a temper, but you mustn't take it to heart," Bess said, holding Molly's hand while Benjamin reexamined her pupils, pulse, and ears.

"How long was I unconscious?"

"Thirteen minutes!" Bess said, and she explained how they had dragged her and the boy inside, the latter recovering quickly when his mother arrived in a panic, having witnessed the event from a nearby house. Ichabod had ridden off and hurried back with Benjamin, who gladly braved the storm amid the luminous display.

"And here you are, right as science," Benjamin told her with a wink. "You must describe it to me in detail this evening after dinner."

Molly's hearing had improved, the ringing had decreased, and although her tingling pain had given way to aches, she cozied into her chair, thankful for the fire and the sweet warm cider. Even the ire of Tom and Mrs. Downs couldn't mar the tavern's atmosphere of venerable wood, kitchen fragrances, and safety. She would have gladly spent an hour in the taproom with Bess, but Abigail arrived. Molly ducked her head.

Mrs. Downs leapt up and flounced across the room. Abigail, drizzly and besmirched from the weather, showed inimitable control when Mrs. Downs blocked her at the entrance of the taproom and said, "Here at last! She nearly killed my boy and shows remorse by disrespecting me and Tom. If I cannot go to the sheriff, you have all the more to answer for, Abigail Knox. She is yours. You took her in and she is yours to mind and govern!"

"I will not respond to raving," Abigail said.

She passed Mrs. Downs, who turned a dumbfounded scarlet, and walked toward Molly with the same cold poise.

"What has happened?" she asked Benjamin.

Mrs. Downs began to answer very shrilly from the door.

"I will thank you for your silence," Abigail told her, "while I hear it plainly told."

Mrs. Downs was so incensed she took the boy and left, grumbling all the way, while everyone in the tavern—Molly, Tom, Bess, and the patrons—listened patiently to Benjamin's meticulous account. Abigail stood and watched Molly through the telling. Tom lit a pipe but then forgot to smoke it. Finding it dead when Benjamin finished the story, he put it down, poured himself a rum, and drank with a frown. He hadn't looked at Molly since her challenge from the floor and seemed to avoid doing so now.

"The boy is well enough, it seems, to be dragged from the tavern," Abigail said. Then, to Molly, "Are you hurt?"

"No," Molly croaked.

Abigail inquired what had brought her to the tavern, and Molly explained about the nyx she'd tried delivering for Benjamin.

"Without informing me."

"I thought you wouldn't let me."

"Take her home," Tom said.

He spoke it so indifferently, it drained Molly's breath and the words sank darkly to the bottom of her stomach. Abigail turned to look at Tom without reply. Her customary edge at being told what to do was blunted by the fact—as Mrs. Downs had pointed out—that Molly was hers to keep. She *had* to take her home.

Bess retrieved Molly's shoes from the bedroom upstairs. Molly put them on and Benjamin helped her stand. Abigail reminded him he was likely needed elsewhere following the storm, and then she blinked once at Molly, pivoted in place, and walked toward the door, expecting her to follow.

"Bess," Tom said. "Help Nabby in the kitchen."

She squeezed Molly's hand, reluctant to abandon her, but Molly turned away from her new friend's attention, fearing sympathy and tenderness would only make her cry.

"Come see me again," Bess said before retreating to the kitchen.

And what could Molly do but follow Abigail home when there was nowhere else to go and no one else would have her?

<p>

The Knoxes' cleanly painted walls and uncluttered rooms looked spartan, even stark, after the warm and motley palette of the tavern. Benjamin sent word that he had bones to set, an adze-wound to dress, and a baby to deliver before returning home. Molly helped with chores without being asked and Abigail allowed it, neither lecturing nor guiding. The women supped without speaking, and once night had fallen and the major work was done, they sat making candles in the firelit kitchen.

A cauldron of water and candlefruit had simmered in the hearth throughout the afternoon. The air was swampy damp, the window-panes wet. Abigail arranged the molds, explained the process to Molly, and sat in a corner rocking chair to mend a yellow stomacher. Molly tied the wicks and hung them in the molds, and she had begun to pour the tallow with a small tin dipper when Abigail, immobile in the rocker, spoke her mind.

"That was a brave and reckless thing you did today," she said with a tug of her thread. "I cannot fault your good intention. Even your willfulness with Tom should be excused. You followed conscience. Your docility and work today are also to your credit. It is all that I have hoped since we opened up our home."

Molly focused on the candle wax filling up the molds.

"Home is duty," Abigail continued, looking around the kitchen at the cabinets and the cauldron. "A duty to our own and to anyone who enters. Root is home, too. Floria is home. The world is home, and all of us have duties. We have bonds."

Molly tugged on one of the wicks. It moved within the wax, which was softer than it looked and almost liquid down the center. The fragrance of the candlefruit reminded her of snow and Molly shivered in the heat, remembering the cabin she had last called home.

"Threats are ever at the door," Abigail said. "The proverbial wolves of hunger, sickness, grief . . . to say nothing of actual wolves, summer storms, and killing cold. We have had hostile natives and brigands on the road. Some believe the devil himself lurks within our woods."

Abigail seemed to be unbosoming a day's worth of thought. It might have sounded maternal in a more maternal voice. Molly watched her sew, pretending she was Frances, but the needle-bright words recalled Mrs. Wickware.

"A savage place, our little town, hard enough to break the hardiest of spirits. Fewer would endure it if not for the singular blessings God bestows on us in balance. Our crops are abundant, our animals are hale, and the seasonal bounty gives us more than we deserve. But nothing comes for free. Nothing is taken for granted."

Molly turned away to face the cauldron at the fire, where she stirred the floating wax into spirals with the ladle. Bubbles bulged up, thick and hot, and didn't pop.

"With threats from every side," Abigail concluded, "we are very sorely tested when we harbor more within."

Molly slapped bubbles. "Do you see me as a threat?"

"How can I know?" Abigail said. She laid the stomacher aside and held the needle in her fist. "You may be blameless as a lamb. But I have rarely known an innocent who shrouds herself in lies."

Molly filled the ladle with a fresh load of wax. She poured and skimmed it up again, watching how it flowed. "Such an effort," she replied, "to wheedle out my secrets. Have you kept me out of kindness or to stifle me with lectures?"

Abigail stood and set her empty chair rocking. "You have lived with us a month and yet remain a perfect stranger. Were you always such a creature in your own lost home? Have you ever trusted anyone?"

"My brother—"

"Oh, a brother!" Abigail shone. "And what's become of him, now that you remember? Did you burden him as well until he finally cast you out?"

"He's dead!" Molly cried. "He's dead and I'm alone! You talk about trust and safety in a home, and then you hector and belittle me and label me a liar. If you want to drive me out, go ahead and say so!"

She flung the ladled wax far across the room, splattering the table and the wall pearly green. Abigail blenched and landed in her chair, as shocked as if the wax were St. Verna's Fire.

Molly fled the kitchen into the starlit night. She hurried through the garden, swatting at her tears, and then she ran unseen down the road toward the ferry, and the river, and the unknown dark that lay beyond.

Chapter Fifteen

The street was dry but held the morning's rain beneath its crust, giving it the unpredictable slipperiness of clay. Most townspeople had already gone inside, and half the houses Molly passed were quiet, dark, or shuttered. But in the lack of talk and bustle, night awakened like an owl. Something filled the shadows, even here between the homes, just as animals and doubt filled shadows in a forest.

Molly felt alert: feral and nocturnal. She was keyed to smell and sound, aware of every dung heap and after-meal aroma, hearing scraps of conversations, night birds, and frogs. But no one stopped her as she ran—a threat she dreaded and desired—and when she came again to the edge of the Antler River, her heart kept thumping and her legs kept moving. She jogged along the riverside, following the berm. She was tired, so tired from her day but too awake to think of resting. There was nowhere left to rest.

"He's dead!" she'd yelled at Abigail. The night yelled it back. It answered every question, every momentary hope. *Go back to Abigail.* He's dead! *Return to Grayport.* He's dead! *Sail for Bruntland, back to Father. Write to Frances.* No, he's dead. Root would never let her be until she finally told the truth, and then the truth of what had happened would destroy her altogether.

Dampness hung around the riverside. She sweated a musky vapor that reminded her of flesh—the flavor of a kiss, a body on her body. Being filled. Growing round. Pushing out and falling empty. So much life, full and floral, now as inky as the river. Molly stopped and held her stomach, thinking she would vomit, but the feeling stayed within her like nausea under nausea.

She was standing by the ferry. Up the road, very near, stood the tavern in the night, warm and solid with its window lights amber on the ground. There'd be patrons in the taproom talking over beer, smoking pipes, eating chicken or a fresh-baked pie. Any stranger from the road was welcome to a bed but even there she wasn't wanted. Tom would send her off again.

The road through the forest ran in two directions. Behind her to the west, the way led to Grayport, a place she couldn't possibly return to alone. Opposite the river it would lead her to Liberty, an unfamiliar city but her only clear option if she meant to leave Root.

Molly crept toward the ferry, loosed the tether, and grabbed the pole. The ferry was essentially a raft on canoes. It was six feet wide and twelve feet long, big enough for horses, difficult to tip. She drove the pole underwater, jammed it into the riverbed, and walked front to back so the deck moved beneath her. Once she reached the back, she raised the pole and did it again.

Ropes from either end were fastened to a ring. The ring rode the anchor line, the bank-to-bank rope Tom had hooked the day he rescued her, and all that kept the raft from drifting in the current. The farther out she went, the more the line bowed until the ring ropes creaked, seeming taut enough to break. She felt petite, so alone on such an oversized platform, especially once she made it to the middle of the river and the pole was barely long enough to reach the lowering depth. Benjamin had told her of the falls to the south and she imagined going over in the great misty roar, being buried underwater, floating onward to the sea.

Panic swirled inside her but she forced herself to move again, remembering the courage she had summoned back in Umber when she stood before the harbor, reassured by her brother, and climbed aboard the skiff and into the *Cleaver* off to Floria. *But where did courage lead me?* Molly wondered as she floated and the ferry, and the current, and the world moved beneath her.

Soon the water flowed more gently and the anchor line rose. She smelled the great, green pines and the moisture of the forest. Once the ferry bumped the dock and Molly tied it to the post, she stared across the clearing that would lead her to the woods, where the road disappeared into a chasm in the trees.

A universe of trees in a universe of night, a million dark spires, an infinity of leaves—even eagles in the day would fail to see the limit of the forest, with the town, like a dimple, in the center. That the cities lay beyond it seemed an element of faith. All a traveler could do was trust in one direction.

Silver-blue lights hovered in the clearing. They were wisps of flame, smaller than her hands, and Molly felt compelled to see one up close. She stepped toward the nearest wisp and watched it bob away; she tried again, and then again, until it led her into the reeds and both her feet were in the water. Molly blinked her eyes. The wisp glimmered beautifully, as if to lead her on—as if to draw her into the current where the flow would drag her down.

She saw the house lights a quarter mile off beyond the river, much fainter than the phantom lights hovering around her. She regretted leaving Benjamin behind without a word. A passing whiff of candlefruit she'd spilled upon her sleeve made even Abigail a person she was hesitant to leave. She wondered what would happen when they found she'd taken the ferry. Nothing, she decided. Nobody would care.

She left the river and the wisps and crossed the clearing, walking briskly to outpace her fear of entering the woods, which rose above her in a great dark wall as she approached. The way had not been cleared so much as woven through the trees. Creeping vines snared her feet. Thorns caught her skirts. The farther in she went, the more the forest closed around her till the road veered left and she was thoroughly surrounded, feeling as far away from Root as anywhere on earth.

Long, twisted branches seemed to grapple overhead. There were nuts the size of apples, pine needles stiff enough to penetrate cloth. She passed an evergreen with sap oozing audibly out of the trunk. Stones and lumpy roots protruded from the ground, and there were holes and ferns and mounds of grass, moss, and tangling weeds. She listened tensely as she walked, hearing snaps and rustling swishes. Several times she turned, sensing movement at her back, and lost her sense of direction when the road seemed to vanish in the dark.

The smell of skunk grew alarming, strong enough to gag her. She trampled a prodigious heap of scat, maybe a bear's. There was eyeshine, there behind a dense mass of bracken, but from what breed of creature, and from what source of light?

"Man is the dominant animal," she told herself aloud, recalling a thing that Nicholas used to say upon his horse.

She heard an echo overhead and stumbled backward in surprise. A scruffy black bird shifted on a branch, peering down at her intensely with its unblinking eyes.

"Man is the dominant animal," it said to her again, croaking in a crude imitation of her voice.

She hurried on, and walked and walked, and jogged until she panted. It was two days to Liberty by horse. Maybe three. Benjamin had told her there were inns along the way but it was possible she wouldn't reach the first till after dawn. She needed money, needed food. She would need another name. But then in Liberty she might begin again and get it right. Another full city for another new life, unless her secret sprang a leak or someone found her, someone who knew.

She thought her eyes were getting tired or the woods were growing thicker. The way was growing more and more difficult to see. Her vision blurred and clarified every other minute and the darkness had texture, pooling on the ground and rising like mist. There were drifting clouds of blindness, more than ordinary dark. She entered one of these, lost her sight completely, and was forced to raise her arms to keep from crashing into trees.

She moved through several patches of the terrible miasmas till they finally disappeared and normal dark returned. The night chilled her skin and clung to her like dew. The earlier sounds of wildlife had given way to stillness, total and uncanny, sprawling out forever.

Then a shadow moved, thirty paces ahead. She thought it was another of the strange, drifting clouds until it gradually resolved. She almost yelped, almost ran.

It was a man upon a horse, motionless and tall. He wore a tricorne and cloak, and Molly couldn't see his face. The shock of his emergence turned to terror of his silence. It was one thing for Molly not to speak in her surprise, another for a rider who had sat and watched her coming. He moved the horse a quarter turn to view her more directly while a second horse appeared and blocked the way behind her. How could she have missed him, having walked straight by? She was caught between the riders now, with woods on either side. They moved to close her in, still without a word.

They were dressed all in black. The rider at her rear wore a tricorne, too, but it was spoiled out of shape as if he'd ridden in the rain. Both riders wore masks that hid their eyes and noses, and it might have looked absurd—too sincerely evil—if not for the savage desolation of the forest and, conversely, the politeness of the first rider's voice.

"What are you doing here," he asked, "alone without a horse?"

Molly tried to speak but didn't have the air. She paused to take a breath. It filled her up but dazed her head.

"I'm traveling with others, five together out of Root. We're making our way to Liberty. I walked ahead to gather my thoughts. Listen," Molly said. "I hear them coming now."

The rider at her back made a low, chuckling moan. The man in front of her, apparently the leader, cocked an ear.

"I hear nothing but a lot of sunny talk," he said at last. "Do you know who we are?"

Molly felt the answer in her mind. Just a word, and yet it fluttered like a bat wing, shuddering her vision. Benjamin had told her, and she'd thought of it at night, in the dark before sleep, until it seemed to her that speaking it would cause them to appear.

"Maimers," Molly said.

She smelled the horses, heard the swishing of the first rider's cloak. Her fear did not diminish or increase but rather sharpened.

"Do you know our reputation?"

"That you're bloody-minded thieves."

The leader laughed but it was odd, as if the mask pinched his nose. His partner creaked his saddle and dismounted with a hop. She would have watched as he approached her, but the leader spoke again.

"Maybe you think the tales are fanciful."

"You're real enough that everyone in Root wants your skin. I heard that there were more of you."

"We're everywhere," he said. "Patient as the trees, quiet as the shadows."

He spoke to her with cheer as if admiring her pluck, like a cook who talks to chickens soon to lose their heads. His companion stepped behind her, so close she couldn't turn, and pulled back her arms until her shoulder blades squeezed.

"Let me go," she said. "I haven't got a thing for you to steal."

"You have clothes," her captor whispered. "You have parts like any other."

He quickly moved in front of her, releasing one of her arms and twisting on the other. Then he grabbed her by the wrists and held them tight behind her back so they were standing, pressed together, hip to hip and eye to eye. He was shorter than the leader—roughly Molly's height—but as solid in the middle as a well-packed barrel.

The leader stooped toward her, leaning from his mount, appearing to experience a quiver in his conscience. He stared without a word, too far away to see her clearly in the dark and yet attempting to discern something showing in her face. He approached her on the horse, staring harder as he came.

His partner shoved her down and Molly landed on her back. He straddled her and held her to the ground by her neck. The branches overhead looked infinite and crazed.

"What'll it be?" he asked.

He drew a knife and held it by her chin. Molly bit his hand. He snarled and shook her off, and after licking at the blood and spitting in the dirt, he flipped the knife to use the bottom of the handle like a pestle.

"Smile," he said.

She struck at him and clawed and knocked his hat behind his head. His eyes were all iris, showing nothing of the whites.

"Wait," the leader said. He was off his horse and bending down close to see her face, and then he turned toward his horse and grabbed a length of rope.

Molly struggled even harder in the moment of distraction but the brute palmed her face, mashing in her cheeks.

The leader tossed the rope and said, "We're taking her along."

"You ain't swallowing her shite about companions on the road!"

"Tie her up, you block of meat. Lickety split. You'll thank me later."

"Bah!" his partner said, kneeling on her gut and tying up her wrists. "I'll have more than just your teeth before the night is done."

He hauled her to her feet and shoved her hard against his horse. The creature snorted in alarm, as if accustomed to abuse. He pulled a sack from one of his saddlebags and yanked it over her head. The cloth smelled of onion, like the man's own sweat. Molly tottered in her blindness, gasped for air, and stumbled forward, but he guided her foot to the stirrup and lifted her onto the horse. He climbed and sat behind her and the horse grew distressed. It was a gangly, droopy specimen and strained beneath the weight, and when the Maimer reached around her and began to tug the reins, Molly felt the tremor in the poor beast's neck.

In spite of being tied, she could pet the horse's mane. He calmed beneath her touch but she couldn't calm herself. The scratchy heat of the bag was stifling, and her minutes of reprieve would only lead to worse. She thought of the stories she had heard, the fear and mutilation of the victims they'd released . . . What was done to those they kept? Who would know she'd disappeared?

Her day appeared in flickers like the branches of a lightning bolt. She thought of Tom's scowl and the young boy's frown, of Abigail's red flush of anger in the kitchen. She had tried. She had tried and it had all led to this, and now the Maimer held the reins with his knuckles on her breasts.

"My balls are hard as fists," he whispered in her ear.

Molly flung her head back, hard against his nose. She heard it crunch the cartilage. He groaned and pulled his hands away. The horse reared up, and when the Maimer tumbled off and thudded down behind her, Molly took the reins and galloped up the road.

She leaned down close and found the stirrups with her toes, but Molly couldn't have slowed his panicked running if she tried. She held the reins tight and fought to keep her balance, blinded by the sack and barely in control.

Were they rushing back to Root or deeper into the woods? She heard the leader on his own strong horse in hot pursuit. The pounding of the two sets of hooves overlapped and the air pressed the sack more tightly to her face. Any moment she'd be battered by a low-slung branch. She waited for a pistol shot to hit her in the back.

She tried to shake the sack away and dizzied herself severely, and it felt as if the horse were spiraling or falling. When the sack was finally off, she saw the trees blurring past, the shrubs and obstacles and holes they miraculously cleared. The leader rode beside her, narrowing the way. Molly spurred harder but the Maimer snatched her reins and the horses slowed with a battery of hooves. Molly jumped off and landed in a bush, but after scratching up her arms in the fight against the branches, she was clear of the entanglement and running for the trees.

The Maimer caught her hair and jerked her off her feet. He stamped his boot upon her chest and held her down against the roots, forcing out her breath while he tied a longer rope around her wrists like a tether. Then he hauled her up and pulled her to the horses in the road.

She was panting and her heartbeat thumped like a rabbit, but he still hadn't spoken, hadn't struck her in his anger. He was stealing her, of course, and yet he treated her with care, like property he couldn't afford to break. She had the ludicrous suspicion he was working for her father, who'd perhaps sought her out with advertised reward. But no, she thought. Impossible. Her father would have shot such mercenary men. This was something else more immediate and grim.

He forced her onto the horse without threat or explanation. It maddened her to know that he was thinking in the dark, full of judgments and ideas about her actions and appearance. Suddenly his mask looked ridiculous and cheap. He was short beside the horse, a coward in disguise. She yanked the tether from his hand, just to prove she could.

He picked the rope up and spat, yet the spitting seemed an act—a cool bit of flair to show he wasn't irked. He wound the rope around his arm, slipped the end between the loops, formed a barrel knot and said, "Try pulling that."

Molly looped her portion of the rope around her pommel.

"Hyah!" she said, and drove her heels.

The horse launched off. The Maimer dropped her reins but couldn't drop the tether, and it tugged him off his feet so he was hanging by his arm. His hat blew away and he was twisting at her side. The line was short enough to keep him at the horse's rear flank with his head at Molly's thigh, boots dragging on the ground. He was jostled by the horse's leg without being trampled, but the hooves were likely clipping him; his wrist was surely broken.

Out of courage or belligerence, he didn't cry or plead. Molly almost pitied him—she didn't want to kill him—when she scraped him past a thornbush, tearing up his coat, and whipped him with a passing branch and bounced him over rocks.

Once again she wasn't certain which direction she was riding. Any second they could come upon the Maimer she'd unhorsed. The road was unfamiliar, all a blur of passing forest with the mists of sudden blindness and the Maimer at her side. He managed to grab her ankle and she couldn't shake him off. The horse was tiring. The ride began to tire Molly, too, after such an endless day and such a tempest of emotion.

She squinted in the wind and fought to keep her balance. If they stopped or if the Maimer finally pulled her off the saddle, they would still be tied together with a knot she couldn't slip. Her only option was to ride and improvise the rest.

Chapter Sixteen

Tom settled by the hearth, cozy with his pipe and savoring the best but often saddest part of the night, when all he had to do was sit and smoke alone. The last remaining patrons, seven rowdy craftsmen traveling to Grayport, had finished a late-night meal and finally settled down. Someone knocked. Tom tensed, rising quickly from his chair. Very few riders braved the road after dark, and the early-rising citizens were mostly early sleepers. Tom and Bess exchanged a look: the knock was likely trouble.

He walked to the door, expecting Sheriff Pitt or another poor soul missing a limb—which of the two he dreaded more, he almost couldn't say—and asked who it was before unfastening the lock.

"It's Benjamin," he heard, muffled through the door.

Tom opened to his friend's worry-worn face. Benjamin had run—he was strongly out of breath—and hadn't changed his clothes since the midmorning storm. He was caked with dried mud and even his hands looked dirty: extraordinary, given the doctor's mania for cleanliness.

"Is Molly here?" he asked.

"Why would she be here?"

"I couldn't think of any other place she would have gone."

"She ran off again?" Tom said. "Someone needs to hang a bell on that girl."

Bess joined them at the door. "Molly would have come to me before she went to Tom."

She had sniped all day, every chance she got. Earlier in the evening, Tom had almost dropped a firkin of beer and Ichabod had rushed to grab the other end. "Don't try to *help*," Bess had said. "You'll be ostracized." Tom had not responded to his cousin's many barbs, but there were jabs and pricks aplenty in his inner conversations. His parents had rarely tossed anyone out of the tavern, and now he had thrown out the sheriff, his uncle, and Molly in the last month alone. His father would have tossed all three. Not his mother. Tom hardened at the thought of which of them he'd mirrored.

"I shouldn't have scolded her," he said to Bess. "I didn't think she'd vanish."

"It was Abby," Benjamin said, his face a blend of pique and conjugal embarrassment. "She was holding Molly's feet to the fire—metaphorically, of course—although our treatment of her here assuredly contributed."

Benjamin's use of "our" was obviously tact.

Ichabod bumbled downstairs from his room, wearing a nightcap and shift but also his boots and breeches, having gotten into bed, it seemed, and gotten back up. He must have heard the knock and looked out the window; something outside had roused him into action.

"What?" Tom said.

Someone took the ferry, Ichabod signed.

"Who? When was this?"

Ichabod shrugged.

"Ruddy hell," Tom said.

Bess clasped her hands. "Oh, she can't be on the road!"

Benjamin's complexion was a blank side of paper with his thoughts, all ascramble, being scratched inside his head. Tom closed his eyes, partly from annoyance, partly to imagine Molly entering the woods. He crossed the room and went to the closet for his rifle and his cartridge bag. The patrons quit talking and regarded him intently.

"Nothing to worry yourself about," he said. "A woman ran away."

One of the guests, a grimy tinker, said, "Zounds! She must be dangerous."

They laughed and drank and talked about their girlfriends and wives, making several awful puns on pistols, cocks, and ramrods.

Ichabod ran down to the river to fetch the ferry. Tom loaded a second gun for Benjamin, who hurried out back to saddle a pair of horses, and turned toward the guests. "Bess'll show you to your beds whenever you're ready. You're welcome to stay down here until I'm back."

The table wished him luck with his runaway skirt, turning boisterous again and speaking of Bess and beds.

Tom said to Bess, "If they're trouble, call for Nabby."

"I can handle them," she said, tough and supple as a switch. "Bring her back."

"That I will."

"I might forgive you if she's safe."

Bess kissed him on the cheek very hard. It hurt his gums.

He crossed the taproom into the kitchen and said to Nabby, "Keep an eye on things."

Nabby, unfazed at his leaving with a rifle, sat spinning wool with the Book of Light beside her. She had never been known to read it but considered it a talisman, and she could quote John Lumen and the prophets word for word. Now she said above the treadle creak, "We're running out of firewood."

"I'm off to find Molly," Tom said. "She left the Knoxes. Took the ferry on her own and crossed the river into the woods."

"Then careful of the devil's shroud and anybody crooked."

He walked out back to meet Benjamin at the barn. The starlight was clear despite the humid warmth. His back felt firmer with the rifle at his shoulder, and the stables smelled alive, full of strong, shuffling horses. Benjamin chose a reliable gray, young but hard to spook, and Tom mounted Bones, who sensed his master's mood and copied it at once, growing dignified but lusty, steady but electric. They cantered around the Orange, down the road toward the river.

Ichabod had rowed a small boat to the opposite shore and was already back with the stolen ferry. None of them spoke as they led the horses onto the raft and started off. Benjamin checked his pistol. Ichabod poled, walking firmly fore and aft, and Tom loaded his rifle without taking his eyes off the dark forest road.

"She said she had a brother," Benjamin told him as they crossed. "She said that he was dead."

"Does Abigail know?"

"Abby drew the splinter. She had picked for quite a while, opening the wound. Molly shouted it and fled in violent agitation. Abigail is utterly beside herself with guilt."

Tom withheld his doubt of Abigail's remorse. Benjamin apparently perceived this and sniffed.

"Pitt'll find out," Tom said. "Sure as sin."

"First things first," Benjamin replied.

His patience and diminutive stature were deceptive. Tom had known Benjamin to ride many leagues without rest, hike valleys and hills during blizzards, and brave the perils of night, storm, fire, and contagion when he needed to. The doctor wouldn't quit until he found his missing patient. Tom considered him a brother, like his brother out at sea. How had Molly lost her own? He wondered what secrets could be dangerous enough to drive her into the godforsaken forest after dark.

They reached the bank and disembarked, and once they had led their horses to the road and mounted up, Tom said to Ichabod, "Stay until we're back. Keep your eyes and ears sharp, and don't go chasing after will-o'-wisps."

Ichabod stood like a sentry on the dock. For reasons unknown, he never used a gun, but Tom had seen him knock down apples with the ferry pole. Surely he could knock an unfriendly head.

Tom and Benjamin started slowly, entering the woods as if entering a tomb. They listened hard for hoofbeats or voices in the depths. Bones was sensitive to every faint crackle, snap, and smell. He swiveled his ears and flared his nostrils but was otherwise calm, and he avoided tree limbs and pitfalls without Tom's guidance as they quickened to a trot with Benjamin behind. The quicker they went, the sooner they would catch her on the road, but Tom was worried they would pass her; she was liable to hide from riders. Worse, she might be trampled if they came upon her suddenly.

Devil's shroud was everywhere tonight as Nabby had warned,

blinding them at intervals and frightening the horses. Benjamin had a long-abiding passion for the mists—some theories he had tested, others he had not—but he made no mention of them now. On they rode.

Bones raised his head and slowed the pace unbidden. The horses stopped together, side by side, and blocked the road. They heard a rider coming fast, dead ahead and not yet visible in the dark. Fifty yards away, Tom guessed, maybe closer. He aimed his rifle up the road and Benjamin cocked his pistol. Bones splayed his forelegs and braced for what was coming.

"Stop!" Tom yelled.

His rifle barrel shook. He hadn't shot a man in years—three to be exact—and took a long, deep breath before he tightened on the trigger. When the rider didn't slow, he aimed for the shoulder.

"Wait!" Benjamin said, lowering his gun.

The horse stopped fast, the rider's hair fluffed forward.

"Help!" Molly said.

Tom was off Bones the second he saw the figure clinging to the horse, or rather dangling by his arm. The man staggered up, badly tangled in his cloak and wearing a mask that had slipped halfway down his face. It covered his mouth instead of his eyes, and he was too dazed and furious to notice Tom and Benjamin. He lunged at Molly's leg and Molly kicked him off. Tom bopped him on the head with the rifle and he turned, groaning when the muzzle touched him on the chest.

When Molly climbed down, the Maimer's arm jerked toward her. Tom backed up and almost pulled the trigger.

"We're tied together," Molly said.

Benjamin went to her side, used a knife to free her wrists, and pulled her into a hug. Tom gathered up the rope still fastened to the Maimer, ordered him to turn, and bound his arms behind his back. One of the arms was limp: a shoulder out of joint. Tom tied it extra tight.

Molly managed to appear both vulnerable and strong, wary of the Maimer—and possibly of Tom—but upright and facing them and seemingly unharmed. She crossed her arms with confidence, or hugged herself with fear.

"What are you doing here?" she asked.

"We came for you," Tom said. He frowned in agitation, not only because of the Maimer and the mystery of his capture, but also because of the flustering relief he wanted to hide—relief that Molly was safe, after his fear of having lost her.

Tom pulled the Maimer to Bones and tethered him to the saddle. He pulled the mask fully off and scrutinized the face, unfamiliar with its narrow eyes and long crooked nose.

"Try to run," Tom said, "I'll shoot your leg and drag you."

"There were two," Molly said, surprising Tom anew. "The other one's a long way back without a horse."

He considered going after the man, and yet as impressive as it was that Molly alone had bested two, there were usually four or five. They couldn't risk being ambushed.

"We're leaving," he decided, climbing onto Bones.

Molly sat on the Maimer's horse and Benjamin rode beside her. The Maimer limped along under Tom's pointed rifle. Their pace was nerve-rackingly slow, especially in the devil's shroud where anyone could jump them. Tom frequently interrupted Molly's tale of the attack—amazing as it was—to listen for pursuers.

When they finally emerged from the woods, Ichabod charged them with the pole as if to lance them. He recognized his friends and lowered the weapon with a smile. Then he saw the Maimer, raised the pole again, and froze; Nabby had filled his head with tales and superstitions, and she had convinced Ichabod, along with others in the town, that the Maimers weren't men but demons from beyond. Even Tom kept reminding himself the man was only a thief, not the vaporizing terror he had known by reputation.

Ichabod retreated and busied himself at the dock. He tied Benjamin's and Molly's horses to the anchor-line support and led Bones onto the ferry, feeding him an apple. Tom secured the Maimer to the side rail of the raft, waited for Benjamin to take over guarding him, and guided Molly off the dock. The chivalry was needless—she had, after all, taken the raft alone—but served as an apology for driving her away.

She clung to Tom's arm when they started across to Root, seeming smaller than before despite her unexpected coup. She relaxed him, which was risky when he needed to be watchful, and concerned him, which was foolish since he had her safe and sound. She smelled of candlefruit but also like a child who'd been crying. A group of townspeople stood on the opposite bank of the river, talking amongst themselves and holding lanterns in the dark. He would never hear the end of it—the two of them *again*.

The Maimer looked at Molly with a curious expression. Hostile, yes, but loaded with an undercover meaning, not quite intimate but close enough to question it. Tom turned his face down, pretending not to watch her. She was staring at the Maimer with the same mysterious glow. Molly noticed Tom's attention, blinked, and turned away, but not before he sensed the link between them: recognition.

They reached the crowded dock. Twenty-odd citizens, presumably roused by Abigail, had come to the river with guns and lights, ready to assist. They'd probably gone to the tavern, learned that Tom and Benjamin had already left, and stood at the bank debating how to proceed without the ferry.

Sheriff Pitt stepped forward. "What in hell's going on?"

Tom addressed the crowd. "Molly caught a Maimer. Broke a second Maimer's nose."

Greater shock would not have been felt if Tom had popped his head off, held it up alive, and sung a verse of "Green Leaves." Everybody hushed. They looked from Molly to the Maimer with open mouths, squinty eyes, or stupefied mixtures of the two, and only Pitt recovered his wits quickly enough to board the ferry, pistol in hand, and point it at the prisoner's chest as Tom led him off. Once the lanterns showed the villain was an ordinary man, the crowd found its courage and began to swarm around, following them to the Orange with Pitt at the head, Molly and Benjamin arm in arm, and the Maimer being scrutinized and pushed along the way.

Ichabod returned with one of the men to get the horses they had left on the opposite bank, while another of the group guided Bones to the stables. Tom looked at Molly and considered her escape again. Why had she been bound instead of maimed like the others? Why had the Maimer failed to shoot her when she stole the horse and fled? He watched her so long, dwelling on her shifting eyes and marvelous tousled hair, that he allowed Sheriff Pitt to enter the tavern as if he owned it.

"Bring him into the taproom," he called back to Tom.

Bess had opened the door and promptly stepped aside, and she seemed more surprised by Tom following orders than she was about the horde surging inward with a prisoner. When Molly passed by, Bess pulled her to her side. The Orange's guests had stayed awake and looked rewarded by the spectacle. They stood and sloshed their drinks, tipsy but engaged, while some of the townspeople strong-armed the Maimer into a chair.

The taproom could easily accommodate the crowd but they clustered up tight and made it claustrophobic. Tom and Pitt shouldered through and backed them all away. Benjamin and Bess seated Molly near the bar. They gave her a cup of cider, which she drank two-handed, emptying the tankard with a long, hearty draft. Tom tied the Maimer to the chair. He turned to the group and raised his hand, silencing the chatter. Then he told them what had happened, just as Molly had recounted. By the time he finished talking, every eye was on her.

"She's a pistol!"

"Give her a medal."

"Well done, you plucky girl."

"Call her Miss, you fucking boor."

"We ought to make her sheriff," someone shouted from the back.

The last, cutting through, slashed Pitt's façade. Tom focused on the Maimer, so as not to crack a smile. Baiting Pitt wouldn't help tonight—he knew the greater danger.

Pitt was baited all the same. He told Molly, "It was a ripe piece of luck. They might have cut you into ribbons. You were foolish to run off, risking other people's lives."

Molly didn't answer, didn't duck or look abashed. The crowd was on her side and, after everything she'd suffered, being lectured by the sheriff was a small thing to bear.

"Leave her be," Bess said, and everyone agreed.

Pitt flushed and turned his furious attention to the Maimer, asking questions that the whole bristling crowd wanted answers to. What was his name? Who were his companions? Where were the others hiding? The Maimer stared ahead without a ripple of acknowledgment. The crowd grew impatient and began pressing in, and Tom and Pitt were shoved together, touching boots with the prisoner.

"You took a man's tongue and even *he* said more" came a voice from the back.

"We should start trimming pieces till he talks," said another.

That caused a ripple. The Maimer had been lulled by the bland interrogation; now he looked at Tom and Pitt with wide, veiny eyes, seeking reassurance from the safety of the law. There was a tumult in the crowd as someone raised a knife, which was passed hand to hand until it came to Tom's side, jabbing forward so dramatically the Maimer flinched away.

"Chop a finger!"

"Take an ear!"

"He wouldn't hear the questions."

"'Course he would, you dolt. He'd still have the hole."

Tom and Pitt reached together for the outthrust knife. Pitt got it first and Tom grabbed his wrist. They traded urgent looks and Tom let him have it.

"Back up," they said together, surprising the crowd with unity. The people did as they were told and cleared a wider space, softening the crush and leaving Tom, Pitt, and the Maimer in a spotlit gap.

"He's a butcher and a rogue!" someone said.

"He's got it coming!"

Reasons came forth—frightened children, ruined travel, body parts and property the bastard had to pay for—and when the circle tightened up again and words would not suffice, Tom unslung his rifle and said, "No one's cutting him up."

A farmer at the front, named Hooker, grabbed the gun. They stood together, face-to-face, hands upon the rifle. Tom saw the fury and the fear in Hooker's eyes and so he head-butted him, knocking a bit of sense—or stupefaction—into the farmer's big skull. He took the gun back and stiffened, daring anyone else to try. Hooker rubbed his head, angry but embarrassed.

"Tavern's closed," Tom said. "Everybody out. We'll lock him upstairs and do it lawful come morning."

Tom's fearless reputation from the war, coupled with his temper, gave the order more power than the crowd's indignation. They respected him and dreaded being banished from the tavern, and when Pitt backed him up and said, "You heard him, off you go," the disappointed crowd grumbled to the door.

Even the travelers stood to go, carrying their drinks.

"Not you," Tom said.

They sat and looked chastened.

Once the townspeople left, Tom locked the door and returned to the taproom, where he walked around Pitt without acknowledging their teamwork. He felt profoundly self-conscious after countering the mob, as if by opening his mouth he'd opened himself to judgment.

Molly and Bess sat in the corner holding hands, warm and sisterly. The Maimer slumped forward in the chair, not blinking. His face was moist and grimy, he was trembling at the knees, and his dislocated shoulder sagged pitiably low.

Tom said to Benjamin, "You need to check his wounds?"

"Breaks and bruises," Benjamin said. "He'll survive until the morning."

It was a cross-grained answer from a doctor sworn to heal, betraying his resentment of a man who lived to injure.

"Get up," Tom said to the Maimer.

He made the prisoner stand without untying him from the chair, forcing him to stoop with the angle of the seat back. They crossed the taproom and started up the stairs with Pitt behind them. Criminals were commonly held in the tavern, and the Orange had a room well suited to the purpose: small and unfurnished, holding nothing but a corncob mattress, with window bars and a heavy, lockable door. They led the Maimer into the room and kept him fastened to the chair.

After Tom had shut the door and left him in the dark, Pitt said, "You're sure that lock is strong enough?"

"My knots are," Tom said.

He had misgivings about the prisoner altogether, truth be told, and when Ichabod returned from ferrying the horses, Tom sent him upstairs to guard the room. Back downstairs, he told the travelers, "Go to bed," and they immediately complied. Nabby emerged from the kitchen,

having spent the whole time spinning out flax, and started dousing
lights until the shadows spread to dimness. The hearth light pulsed,
a minor flame with ticking embers. Benjamin, Pitt, and Bess stood at
the bar and grew obscure. Molly alone faced the fire and was soft gold-
orange.

Tom stepped beside her and she seemed to hold her breath. "I'm
sorry I treated you hard this morning. You're welcome to stay the night
if Benjamin agrees," he said, ostensibly to free her from the wiry hooks
of Abigail, primarily to keep her under his own watchful eye.

"It might be for the best," Benjamin decided.

"Thank you," Molly said and subtly clasped her hands, showing
fear as much as gratitude. She seemed to feel Tom's doubts.

Bess crossed the room and hugged Tom around the arms. "I love
you, coz," she said, and kissed him on the cheek, and there were suddenly too many skirts and too much snug affection, given the hardness of the problems he had welcomed into his home.

"Be back at dawn," he said to Pitt, "before the town comes to get
him. Bring as many trusty men as you can find to keep the peace."

The hearth log collapsed and the fire died down. The room's red
glow was like a second, deeper sunset, heralding a night more dangerous and dark. Pitt's scarlet coat turned the shade of old blood.
Instead of growing surly at the summary dismissal, the sheriff nodded his head, puffed his chest military-style, and strode toward the
door with dignified exhaustion. Tom saw him out and resecured the
door while Bess took the last empty dishes to the kitchen.

Molly and Nabby examined each other in wary, intimate silence,
as if the oldest woman in Root were actually a witch, viewing the new-
est woman in Root as either a rival or a pupil.

"The child ghost distrusts you," Nabby finally said, "but shouldn't
harm you in your sleep, so long as you behave."

With that, she went to her own small room off the kitchen.

Benjamin spoke to Molly, too privately for Tom to overhear, presumably to offer an apology for Abigail. He hugged her once more,
crossed the room, and said to Tom, "Keep an eye on her tonight."

"I mean to," he said. "I could use you here tomorrow."

"I'll be here at first light," Benjamin assured him, straightening his glasses and appearing, as he did so, to straighten out his thoughts. "Tom," he said discreetly. "The Maimer will be judged by a town pre-decided. Either silence or confession will secure his noose. When he hangs, all he knows and hasn't spoken hangs with him. If we hope to learn enough to thwart more attacks, you must convince him to divulge whatever secrets he is keeping."

"How?" Tom said.

"Abigail would counsel him to think upon his soul. He may con-sider it at night, when fear of hell is more enfleshed."

Tom thought it futile but refrained from contradicting him. He shook his friend's hand, walked him out, and locked the front door one last time. Bess took Molly to the privy out back, and once the women had said good night and gone to Bess's room upstairs, Tom relieved himself in the garden and thought of the Maimer tied to the chair.

"Let him piss himself," he thought, lacing up and going in.

After confirming that every door and window was secure, he stirred down the hearth and carried a candle and a pistol upstairs, where Ichabod was still keeping guard at the prisoner's door.

"Go on to bed," Tom said. "I need you vital in the morning."

Ichabod retired and Tom remained a minute on his own, hearing nothing from the Maimer but occasional creaks and moans. He went to his own room down the hall and listened to the tavern, waiting for an unfamiliar shifting in the timbers, and it was now the hectic day hit him full bore. He wobbled at the knees, and yawned until his vision blurred, and longed to get in bed but didn't dare—not tonight.

He occupied himself by reconsidering what had happened, word by word and detail by detail, and he had been musing for a while, half sleeping on his feet, when he sensed a subtle change in the character of the silence. Judging by the candle, half an hour had elapsed. He thought he heard a sound. What it was he couldn't say.

He opened the door and checked the empty hall, then crept toward the prisoner's room, pistol in hand and traversing the dark by mem-ory, avoiding the one warped floorboard that squeaked against the joists. The crack at the base of the prisoner's door flickered from within. He paused and heard the S's of a rush of whispered words.

He didn't bother with the key. The lock was disengaged—he could feel it—so he raised the gun and held his breath and opened the door abruptly.

A candle on the floor showed the Maimer in his chair. Molly held the knife that Pitt had left behind. She removed it from the Maimer's throat and dropped it in surprise. It wasn't the gun she seemed to fear, or even Tom's reaction, but the loss of what had brought her there— the loss of some advantage.

She had been crying but contained herself and backed toward the corner. The Maimer wasn't cut. He smiled in relief, but his eyes looked frightened and his cheek flesh twitched. The door had moved the candle flame; shadows grew and shifted. Molly's face seemed to pulse, her tears lightly glistened, and her wide-open eyes had their own clear fire.

Tom stepped toward her, kicking the candle in distraction and grabbing her arm in the dark. Molly pulled away. He didn't want a struggle with the Maimer right beside them so he backed toward the door and said, "Downstairs. Now."

Once he had her out of the room, he locked the door a second time—lot of ruddy good the first time had done—and led her down the stairs as quietly as he could. Molly stepped on every loose board along the way, including the third-to-last step with its low, mournful groan.

He sat her at a table in the middle of the taproom. Nabby's door opened in the shadows off the kitchen.

"Only me," Tom said.

Nabby mumbled and retreated.

He stirred the embers in the hearth, lit a taper, and ignited a whale-oil lantern hanging from a rafter. The light was pure and gentle, like a touch of summer dawn. Molly watched the flame, distant but alert, her illuminated face seeming younger in the glow but older in expression. She was difficult to read.

He put a kettle in the hearth and ground smoak behind the bar. The nuts were tough to pulverize and Tom muscled in, using so much force he almost bent the grinder's handle. It was a violent sound but yielded fluffy powder in the box, which he spooned into cups and stirred with boiling water. Molly didn't move when he set a cup before her, and he stood a minute longer, looking down at her and breathing in the aromatic steam.

Then he sat and held her hand, both gentle and direct. She was hot beneath his palm.

"Drink," he said.

He squeezed her hand. She sighed and took a sip.

It might have been Elkinaki firewater, to judge by her wince. That was everyone's reaction to a first taste of smoak—its bitter-rich, cinnamony, burnt-black flavor—but he'd bet a silver plate she would crave it ever after. Molly put it down and looked considerably sharper. Her breath intermingled with the fragrance of the smoak and made a spice so potent that his skin began to tingle.

"You're good at picking locks," he said.

"I learned it growing up."

"With other people's locks?"

"No, at home," Molly said.

Tom released her hand and drank his smoak, leaning back.

"Tell me about that."

"Not now."

"You want to reconsider," Tom said. "Because I know it ain't your memory that's keeping you from talking. I already think the worst, and I don't want to. I truly don't."

The lantern just behind him threw his shadow on her bosom, darkening the leaf-print pattern of her gown.

"You know him," Tom said.

"I've seen him before."

"He's seen you, too."

"Yes."

"Where?"

Molly tremored when she spoke but looked defensively resolved, like a person loath to fight finally putting up her fists. "In Grayport," she said.

"You lived there?"

She nodded.

"With your brother," Tom said.

Molly gripped her cup. Her eyes shone brightly, not as if to cry but rather as if her feelings had been heated, like an oil. Tom leaned against the table. They were close, knee to knee.

"You're trying to decide if you should trust me," Tom said. "Here's how it is. You haven't got a choice. Keeping secrets anymore ain't a God-given right."

Molly clamped her lips and didn't speak for half a minute. Then her shoulders drooped, her face collapsed, and out the story came.

Chapter Seventeen

Molly and Nicholas disembarked the *Cleaver* on a cold November afternoon, having traveled from the warm Bruntish summer to the first light snow of Florian autumn.

Grayport, the oldest city on the continent, stood against the harbor like a miniature Umber, with the Arrowhead River flowing along the west and the wooded frontier encircling its borders. The city drew its name from a rare form of salt—a mineral in the bay that evaporated with the water and effloresced, like fuzzy crystal mold, anywhere the rain or mist carried it from the harbor. Drifts and pillars of the salt could be seen around the docks, trees stood gray and yet surprisingly survived, and the buildings looked far more aged than they were. Grime and patchwork were everywhere and gave the houses and the port a workmanlike appeal, as of structures roughly used and practically repaired. It was a lived-in city, now to be their home.

Despite Molly's affection for Captain Veer and the crew, she said her goodbyes quickly—though tearfully with kind Mr. Knacker—and the siblings hurried off, eager to leave the ship's stinking confines, the sailors' questions about their prospects, and the pall of Mr. Fen's unexplained death.

Nicholas's health had largely rebounded but his strength, such as it was, had not entirely returned. Molly dragged their trunk, all they owned in the world, and scraped a trail in the clean inch of snow upon the wharf. She marveled at the firm, still planks beneath her feet, the unfamiliar gravity of ground that didn't tip. The weather made the city beyond the docks as blurry as the ships in the white-gray harbor. The air was clean and cold, the smell of people, cod, rotten wood, and even her own unwashed body given freshness by the sea. There were tables of vegetables and fish; barrels, crates, and carts; cats and dogs and fearless gulls; drunks and raggedy children. Hawkers sized them up, some with offers of goods or greetings of dubious intent, but by and large they were no more regarded than anyone else around the dockyard.

Nicholas strode ahead and almost lost her in the crowd. Twice she said, "Nicholas," and twice he didn't turn. Molly dragged on, frazzled and alert, and saw her brother more than thirty paces off and never slowing. Wind razored through her cloak. The snow chilled her toes. She stamped her feet to warm them up and dropped the trunk, becoming an obstacle in the walkway and refusing to move another step, ignoring the grumbling passersby and balling up her fists.

"Jacob Smith!" she yelled.

Her brother stopped and turned. He made his way back with quick deliberate steps, a thin dark figure in the crosswind of flurries, as cool as she was hot, and maddeningly blank. Each was all the other had, and he had very nearly left her, merely to reinforce the lesson of their names.

"No one's listening!" she said. "No one cares who we are!"

"We talked about this," Nicholas replied.

"We're here without a friend or anyplace to go, and you're prepared to walk away because I called you by your name!" Her shout drew the hesitant attention of a constable, a portly man with fat silver buttons on his greatcoat. "Nicholas, Nicholas, Nicholas!" Molly yelled to prove her point. No one listened. No one cared. In fact, her overcooked dramatics turned the constable away, as she appeared to be a wife giving fire to her husband, something far too common to arouse the law's suspicions.

Nicholas slumped and bowed his head.

"I'm sorry," he said to her shoes.

The frailty of his will—an inner slump to match the outer, which she couldn't remember seeing in her brother all his life—frostbit her hopes. They were equals now, tiny and encumbered by their freedom, as reliant on her wits as on Nicholas's.

He tried to hide a cough. Molly's stomach swooped and growled. She had caught a whiff of bread that made her ravenously hungry, and rather than console her brother in his doubt, she picked up the trunk and followed the aroma, keeping Nicholas behind her as she wove through the crowd.

The smell disappeared. She had possibly imagined it, but now that she was leading she was warmer, more determined, and she came upon a cart of plump frozen apples. The vendor was a man with pink protruding eyes, very like the snow-packed fruits he was selling. He stared with terrible acuity at everyone who passed, assessing whether they were customers or thieves, giving the same sharp look to well-dressed matrons as he did to wily children and a lean mongrel dog.

Molly hadn't tasted apples since they'd sailed from Umber—only hardtack and salted meat and vegetables the likes of which she wouldn't have fed to hogs. Nicholas stood beside her, out of breath and shivering hard. The apple seller glared.

Molly smiled and said, "Good day."

"Good day," the seller answered. "Rosy apple for you, miss?"

"I haven't any money," Molly said.

The seller blinked, or rather puckered at the eyes without closing up the lids. Molly opened the trunk and found a beaver cap mashed among the clothes.

"What are you doing?" Nicholas asked.

"I'm going to sing for coins."

Her brother cocked a brow and said, "Molly. You cannot."

It was true. She couldn't sing. Even Frances had discouraged her—Frances, who encouraged her to dance, which Molly excelled at, and to practice speaking Rouge, which Molly learned with much complaint, and to swim and ride her horse and play the harpsichord with Nicholas: anything to keep her out of trouble with her father. Anything but sing. She could read a sheet, name a pitch, and memorize a tune, but though her speaking voice was sweet and bright, her singing voice was not.

"Torturous," her father had called it. "Discordant," said her brother. "It is a gift God withheld," Frances gingerly suggested.

Molly would sooner win a coin juggling cats or eating fire. She
set the cap upside down in the snow, ushered Nicholas behind her, and
stood on the trunk. Then she swelled her chest and sang:

> 'Twas on the deep Eccentric
> Midst extraordinary gales
> A sailor tumbled overboard
> Among the sharks and whales!
> He vanished in a blink
> So headlong down went he
> And went out of sight
> Like a wrinkle of light
> In the darkness of the sea!

"God's blood!" a passing trader said, covering his ears. The fishmongers stared, openmouthed as mackerel. A rope beater paused in
the beating of his rope.

> We lowered a boat to find his corpse
> And mourn whate'er we could
> When up he bobbed and split the waves
> Like a buoyant piece of wood!

The apple seller tried to speak but choked and started hacking. Two
women carrying baskets, who'd been coming toward the cart, frowned
at Molly haughtily and walked the opposite way. Others shuffled off
and kept their distance on the dock until the apple man and half the
neighboring merchants were abandoned.

"Cut that out!"

"You're killing business!"

"And me ears!"

"Scat, be off!"

> My fellows, said the sailor,
> Do not grieve for me

I'm married to a mermaid
In the sweet Eccentric Sea!

The apple seller grasped at her with cold, bony hands. His eyes were wider now, and raw, and threatening to pop. A burly man, slimy-aproned with a foul stink of fish, took her other arm and forced her off the trunk, saying, "Tha's enough now. You's injuring me finer sensibilities."

Molly kept singing over all their protestations. A bearded sailor with a sad, flat face produced a copper, dropped it into the cap, and said, "Buy yourself a muzzle."

Molly stopped and took the cap and looked for Nicholas, who'd vanished. In the sudden lack of song, she heard the hiss of falling snow. She curtsied to the vendors and left the dock, dragging the trunk.

Nicholas met her beside a dray at the start of the city proper, holding four grand apples he had stolen undetected. Molly laughed and flashed the coin. Nicholas grinned and bowed.

They put the apples in the trunk, all but one that Molly ate as they walked the narrow, mazy streets of center Grayport. The closeness of the buildings lent both snugness and constraint to the city, a sense that everyone was safe but too close packed, like people on a ship with overstuffed cabins. Opportunity was everywhere but so was competition, and although it seemed a perfect place for runaways to hide, it also seemed a place where someone vulnerable could vanish.

Molly and Nicholas were jostled by people who seemed fresher and more cavalier than the citizens of Umber. It was freedom, Molly thought, from the governance of Bruntland, a mother country too far away to fully parent. Everyone they saw showed vitality and purpose. Even the drunks and beggars seemed to know where they were going.

The siblings spent their copper on a hearty loaf of bread. They tore it into chunks and chewed it as they walked, but their hours of discovery were terribly fatiguing, and they could linger only so long in shops or public houses without a show of money. The snow eventually stopped but the temperature plummeted in the late-day sun. Dragging the trunk had worn Molly out and Nicholas was wan. They came to a tavern at the outskirts of the city, where the streets petered out to show the wilderness beyond. The sky was bloody wool. A lamplighter passed, igniting salt-encrusted lanterns, and the streets looked cozy in the hard-biting cold. They heard a fiddle and a hornpipe playing in the tavern, smelled the meat and pies and biscuits, watched the patrons come and go.

Nicholas took Molly's hand and led her to a church. It was tiny, gray and black with a tall sharp steeple. They went inside and huddled in a corner in the dark. Molly wiped her eyes, looking up beyond the rafters. Nicholas thought and thought, staring at the floor.

⚜

They lived by hook or crook for the first few days, stealing what they could and begging for the rest, until they each found employment and rented a small, drafty flat in the rougher section of Grayport's central district. By midwinter, Molly had worked as a scullery maid, a seamstress, and a serving girl in three separate taverns. She had been fired from every position for cheek and ungovernability, and had been forced to start again each time without references.

One evening after a long, futile search for new employment, Molly walked to the Customs House, a noble brick building, four stories high, with a newly added portico and a clock tower overlooking the waterfront. Nicholas had found clerical work there, thanks to his aptitude with figures and his fluency in several languages: qualities of worth in a city with so many foreign sailors, so many ledgers and restrictions. It was a position Nicholas loathed but one he had to keep; even when Molly held a job, they could barely pay the rent.

The sun had set on all but the face of the Customs House clock, and Molly paced the shadowy docks and gazed across the sea. She had a vision of her father, well-attired, in his study.

News of the Bread Riot Massacre had arrived from Umber in early winter. Seventeen dead, dozens more wounded. Inquests were held and protests were staged, but ultimately the rioters were demonized, having instigated the bloodshed with countless acts of violence, theft, and vandalism. To stabilize the peace, fixed prices were enforced once more throughout the markets and Umber carried on, bruised but not destroyed. General Bell, so recently the nation's savior in war, was generally portrayed as a hero and a victim. Molly didn't know whether he had remained in Worthington Square. For all she knew, the home she'd come to miss was nonexistent.

She left the wharf at nightfall and met Nicholas at the Customs House door. Her appearance there surprised him for only a moment. Then he said with leaden certainty, "Another fruitless day. Perhaps it's you, and not employers, who are being too selective."

"I can always be a laundress. How I'd love to be a governess," she said, feigning hope.

Nicholas wounded her with laughter. "Who would trust you with their linens, let alone their children? The streets would soon be full of underboiled urchins."

They began walking home through the tight-knit crowd in a city still foreign, still coldly unfamiliar. Little coin and many worries were the whole of their existence. Molly glowered at a coffeehouse stuffed with rosy people. Salty gray slush leaked through her shoes.

A fellow with a long crooked nose bumped her shoulder.

"Excuse me, miss!" he said. "I wasn't looking, thousand pardons."

When she turned around to answer, he had blended with the crowd.

"Open your cloak," Nicholas said, reaching for her collar.

"What are you doing? Nicholas, stop."

He pried apart her hands, saw her throat, and narrowed his eyes. "Wait for me at home," he said.

Before she understood or could summon a reply, Nicholas had walked away and she was suddenly alone.

She called his name and followed him, but no—he'd turned a corner. Then a horse was in her way and she was forced to move aside, and it was only upon refastening her cloak that she discovered her locket was gone. The only valuable thing she owned, with Nicholas's tooth! She hurried through the streets, unsure of where to go, less concerned about the locket than she was about her brother as he chased a practiced thief to God knew where. What if there were others? Didn't thieves have dens? What if Nicholas were cornered in an unlit yard, bludgeoned in a house, and never seen again?

For almost two hours she checked the side roads, marketplace, and docks, all the time with billowing dread that she had lost him altogether. How would she survive without a job or ready money, having no place to live and no means of sailing back?

"Rotten spoiled girl!" she said, upbraiding herself for selfishness and drawing wary looks.

When the cold shrank her down and the search was clearly useless, she returned to their icy flat, shivering and despondent. Watchmen rarely patrolled their part of the city and the streets were barely lit. She braved a shortcut between a pair of derelict houses, where the weeds were frozen dead and snagged her skirt, and climbed the creaking outdoor stairs to their door, relieved she had a key but jealous of the landlady's late mutton supper. Molly paused a moment, savoring the wonderful aroma. She considered going down and begging for a plate, but how could she indulge herself with Nicholas in danger? So she turned the frozen key to face the dark, spartan flat.

She opened the door to heat and light. A lantern burned, the iron stove was full of burning coals, and Nicholas sat at the table with a roasted chicken, a golden loaf of bread, and a bottle of wine he had opened but not yet poured.

She rushed to hug him in his chair and he was warm, very warm. He backed her off and rubbed her hands to foster circulation. Molly cried in her relief, and laughed, and said in anger, "I've been searching half the city, thinking you were dead, and here you are with dinner! O, you hardhearted fiend!"

"I said to wait at home," he answered, unperturbed.

She called him many things and cursed him many ways. Nicholas took her cloak and stood her at the stove. He poured her a cup of wine—they had tin instead of glass—and Molly gulped it down with no awareness of its flavor.

Nicholas held her locket up. It dangled by its ribbon, delicate and twisting, glinting in the light.

"Oh!" Molly said. "But how—"

"I used persuasion."

Molly stood with jellied legs, recalling Mr. Fen.

"Is he jailed? Is he—"

"Free. Not to trouble us again."

He handed her the locket, poured his own cup of wine, and sipped it with attention, savoring the vintage.

☧

Two days later, Molly sat alone in the flat mending a tear in Nicholas's only spare shirt. She daydreamed of Frances, who had taught her how to sew and had been doing so herself, in the little green room of the country manor, on the evening Lord Bell had announced her dismissal. Molly longed to write her letters but Nicholas wouldn't allow it. What if Frances's employers intercepted such a letter? What if Lord Bell had asked for their assistance, hoping to discover the location of his children? Molly understood but would have risked it anyway, and she had spent a quarter hour recalling the sound of Frances's voice, and how she used to dab her nose with a monogrammed handkerchief, when someone ascended the outdoor stairs and knocked upon the door of the flat.

No one ever knocked. No one visited at all. Nicholas wasn't due for at least another hour, having planned to finish his day at the Customs House and inquire after a printmaking job across the city. In Molly's reverie, the daylight had fallen to the dark, and now the person at the door was playing with the lock. She stood and grabbed the shovel used for cleaning out the stove. It was iron, square-headed with a reassuring heft. She raised it when the lock and then the door gently opened.

In walked a stranger, magisterial and tall, and she might have cracked his skull if not for his ebony skin.

Rich, Molly thought. *From the bright Aquatic Islands.*

Aquarians were a prominent minority in Grayport, hailing from a small, wealthy country in the Solar Ocean. Molly had seen them often in the city that winter, riding carriages or walking from the harbor to the Customs House. Not every Aquarian was affluent, but they were foreign and imposing and possessed of native pride. One assumed a higher pedigree and generally the assumption was correct; Molly—poor and plain—was outside their sphere.

"Good evening, Mrs. Smith," the stranger said, doffing his hat with a bow and exposing his head to the shovel. "My apologies for entering so. I knocked and no one answered."

He addressed her with the slow, melodic accent of his country. It was a voice that took its time without being dull, rather like a cello at a comfortable andante. He was sensibly dressed for winter in a bearskin hat, knee-high boots, and a fur-shouldered coat that added to his broadness. Molly backed away, speechlessly confused, until the stove felt near enough to scald her derrière.

"My name is Kofi Baa," he said. "I am a shipowner residing here in Grayport. Your husband suffered injuries in aid of me tonight. A hired man is carrying him up even now."

Molly dropped the shovel. Kofi Baa stepped aside, untroubled by the clang, and she had nearly reached the stairs when a short, swarthy man carried Nicholas inside.

"Jacob!" Molly cried.

Nicholas smiled coyly. His carrier had the misshapen nose and knuckles of a boxer, but he placed her brother upright in a chair as gently as he might have placed a child. Nicholas's forearm was crudely wrapped and bloody.

"What happened?" Molly asked, kneeling at his feet.

Nicholas gave her a look as if to say: *Best behavior.*

Kofi handed the swarthy man a large silver coin and said, "We thank you for your efforts."

The man bowed and left.

Kofi closed the door and said to Molly, "Please allow me to explain so your husband may collect himself. This evening I followed a familiar shortcut after business at the Customs House, unwise of me in retrospect, and found myself at knifepoint, alone beyond the docks, at the mercy of a brigand who demanded all I had. He seemed inclined to use the knife when your husband, silent as a grave cat, tackled him and grappled with the man upon the ground. I admit to being startled by the unexpected rescue. By the time I gained my wits, the villain had escaped. Your husband broke his ankle and was slashed along the arm."

Tackled, Molly thought, *and grappled on the ground?* If not for the sincerity of Kofi Baa's telling, she'd have laughed at the absurdity. Her brother in a brawl!

"I used my handkerchief to bind the wound," Kofi said, "and summoned a passing jack, just departed, to assist us."

"But you must see a doctor!" Molly told her brother.

Nicholas touched her cheek, very like a spouse.

"I have already sent for one," Kofi said. "He will be ably stitched and splinted."

"Thank you," Nicholas told him. "Molly, don't be frightened. We could all use a drink, if I may trouble you to pour."

"Yes, of course," Molly mumbled, suddenly aware of the flat's crooked squalor. It was tiny and dim with cracked plaster walls, a very low ceiling with a fur of old salt, and no furniture aside from the table, chairs, and two lumpy mattresses positioned near the stove.

Molly uncorked their one bottle of wine and poured it into a pair of cups—the only two they owned—for Nicholas and their guest. Kofi recognized the shortage and said, "Formality should never do disservice to a lady."

He handed her his cup, gave the second cup to Nicholas, bowed to each in turn, and drank directly from the bottle. Then he encouraged Molly to sit while he stood beside the stove, making easy conversation while they waited for the doctor.

Nicholas spoke of the Customs House—small talk, at first, to pass the empty minutes but increasingly precise as Kofi asked questions. They spoke of trade with New Solido, of markets still reeling from the war against the Rouge. Nicholas clarified a thorny regulation concerning the export of lumber and shared a loophole, little known but perfectly legal, that would save Kofi a great deal of trouble.

"Once again I am indebted for your help," Kofi said. "You must allow me to perform some service in return."

Here, Molly thought, was the chance she had prayed for. But Nicholas looked abashed, showing a strange combination of humility and pride, and seemed about to decline when they were interrupted by the arrival of the doctor.

He was a tightly wound, squinty little man of roughly sixty, brisk in social niceties but masterful in skill. Molly and Kofi watched as he examined Nicholas's injuries—the ankle was not so badly broken, but the cut was rather deep—and her brother closed his eyes and went to a place of abstract thought, wincing only slightly, as the doctor sewed his arm with a long, arced needle.

Molly warmed to Kofi. He was gentle and expansive and accorded her the mannerly attention of a suitor. To lie to his face seemed grossly disrespectful. Nevertheless she did, telling the well-practiced story she had used since the *Cleaver,* because although they had meant to live as brother and sister in the city, their artificial marriage had gained a life of its own. They had foolishly presented themselves to their landlady as husband and wife, and it was she who had introduced Nicholas to a clerk she knew in the Customs House—a clerk who found the married "Jacob Smith" a good position. Now a mounting house of cards was built upon the lie, and so she told Kofi Baa that her parents were deceased; that Jacob, born to affluence, had married her against his family's wishes; and that they had sailed for Grayport to start a life upon their own terms, however great the struggle.

Kofi, too, had sailed away from home when he was young.

"My great mistake was pride," he said, widening his stance. "Refusing any aid, I almost starved when I arrived. But certain forms of charity are not the same as pity. Had I not been offered help and seen the opportunity, I might have sailed home, sorely beaten by the world."

The doctor finished sewing Nicholas's arm. He secured the fractured ankle, first with a bandage and then with a wooden splint, clad in leather, that fit together as a two-piece shell around the leg. Nicholas thanked him, as did Molly, but the doctor packed his instruments and seemed not to hear, the way a joiner might ignore a newly finished chair. He laid a cheap wooden crutch in Nicholas's lap.

Kofi escorted him out and paid him on the stairs, and then he walked back in and clasped Nicholas's hand.

"I must be off," Kofi said, "but this will not be forgotten." The timbre of his voice warmed Molly's bones. "I will see you at the Customs House tomorrow afternoon, when again"—here he bowed—"I will ask for your assistance."

"I look forward to it," Nicholas said. "Will you be safe walking home?"

"My father used to say, 'Fools are luckier than cowards.'" He kissed Molly's hand between her first and second knuckles. "A pleasure to meet you, Mrs. Smith."

"You as well, Mr. Baa."

She saw him out, closed the door, and waited until his footsteps were safely off the stairs. When a very long sigh failed to dissipate the tension, Molly mussed her hair like an uncouth child. She kicked her shoes across the floor and strode toward her brother, who was sliding off the chair, peaked and depleted.

Molly gawked at him and said, "What on earth just happened?"

"Fortune paid a visit," Nicholas replied.

<p>

Nicholas studied his cast and seemed amazed by what had occurred. He explained to Molly that he had been delayed an extra hour at the Customs House and left after dark. Eager to reach the printer who had advertised a job, he took a shortcut between the storehouses at the far end of the dockyard and noticed, near a shadowy stack of crates, a well-dressed man being cornered by a thief. Discovering the crime triggered something primal. He ran swiftly and tackled the assailant without thought, emboldened, he supposed, by his capture of the locket thief several days before.

"It galls me," Nicholas said, "that rogues play with gold while you and I, of better character, sup with wooden spoons. I vowed in Umber that I wouldn't let us fall to disadvantage. Tonight, as with the locket thief, I exercised my strength."

His ankle had been broken in the fight but he hadn't felt the cut, not until the assailant—much surprised—fled for safety and left Nicholas and Kofi on their own. Molly visualized the scene but struggled to digest it. The knife could just as easily have plunged through Nicholas's heart. She made him promise to desist from fighting *all* the city's villains, and late in the night, once he was asleep, she wondered what she would have done in his place. It seemed inevitable that dangers would continue to beset them, that eventually she'd have to face a threat on her own.

Nicholas hobbled to work the following day and returned that night with extraordinary news. True to his word, Kofi Baa had met him at the Customs House, not only with additional questions about lumber and fur exportation, but with a great many questions about Nicholas himself.

Mr. Baa controlled numerous ventures in Grayport, among them a translation office whose sole employee had recently died of gangrene. Reliable translation of foreign correspondence was increasingly vital with so many thriving markets and overseas contracts, and upon determining that Nicholas did not desire a future in the Customs House, Kofi offered him not only the dead man's position but also the newly vacant quarters over the office. The salary was modest but the rent would be waived; the office was located in the better part of the city, only minutes from the best markets; and Nicholas, so often ill, could go to work on bitter days simply by walking downstairs. To quell the fear of charity, Kofi explained that Nicholas's erudition, polyglotism, and attention to detail suited him ideally to the venture's clientele. That Molly spoke Rouge, and was at least passably fluent in Violinish and Solidon, was an added piece of luck. She could translate, too, and copy critical documents.

Nicholas accepted. In two days' time, he and Molly were living in well-furnished rooms, purchasing their first new clothes since arriving in Grayport, and dining on wholesome food before a clean, cheerful hearth. Molly took a bath and overslept in downy blankets. Nicholas got to work, examining Kofi's backlog of foreign correspondence and leaving Molly alone to explore the wintry city, now with money in her pocket, and discover that it wasn't so hostile after all.

Merchants spoke to her and smiled, sensing she could pay. The falling snow was lovelier, reminding her of warmth in their sweetly settled home, and even the taverns felt safer when she ducked inside, escaping the cold because she could, and sat before a fiddler with a cup of hot chocolate.

But her freedom was withheld as soon as she embraced it. Nicholas began to focus on Kofi Baa's most pressing contracts and letters, leaving Molly to translate the rest and mind the public office, a quiet brown room that faced the vibrant street. There she sat for hours, day after day. She greeted customers and accepted their paperwork and payments. Messages of particular sensitivity were handled by her brother, who made her translate and copy the most flavorless, abstruse documents to and from Rouge. How she would have liked to wander in the snow—to make a friend, climb a tower, ride a horse beyond the city!

The doldrums only deepened once the office was established and her brother devoted himself to more delicate work in the rear parlor. Kofi Baa had benefited greatly from Nicholas's varied expertise, and he began referring colleagues with questions about shipping regulations, tariffs, and taxes. Her brother read day and night, bolstering his knowledge, and by winter's end, not a day was passing without several respectable businesspersons coming to Nicholas for advice or arbitration—some professional, some private, none of which he spoke about specifically with Molly.

"A property dispute beyond the purview of the courts," he might say, or "Familial concerns," or "Sensitive relations." He was something like a lawyer, or a scholar, or a minister, and those who visited the office and met him in the parlor entered nervously, or grimly, and departed much at ease.

One night, Molly woke in the dark and sat up in bed. It was summer by then and depressingly hot. The overripe city rarely freshened with the breeze, which wafted from the west instead of from the sea so that its greatest effect was to move the smell of humid dung, sweat, and fishy remains from one stifling district to another. Molly's window was open, and although it was late and quiet on the street, she felt that she'd been woken by an unfamiliar sound. Her senses twitched and flickered, and her heartbeat thumped, as if she'd woken from a nightmare and parts had followed her out.

"Nicholas," she whispered to his door across the room.

She heard a sound downstairs: someone moving in the office.

"Nicholas!" she said.

The sound below her ceased. Had her voice carried down? She couldn't leave the bed and risk creaking on the floor. Before deciding what to do, she heard the telltale hinges of the office door, so she knelt upon the bed and leaned toward the window, peeking down with only her forehead and eyes above the sill.

She saw a man leave the office, just below her in the dark. He shut the door behind him and stood for a moment, facing south and show-ing the back of his head. He had black sweaty hair and too-tight breeches, and when he turned and started north, Molly knew him at once by his long, crooked nose.

She sprang from bed and opened the door to Nicholas's room. He wasn't there. Molly wavered in her panic, considering first a cry of "Help!" to summon a constable or watchman but afraid, at such an hour, it would only bring the locket thief back toward the house.

She hurried down the darkened stairs, unable to see the steps, and opened the door to the lower parlor. There were shadows on the floor from a single lit candle. For an instant every one of them was Nicho-las's body—there a foot, there his head, there a small pool of blood—and finding they were nothing only heightened Molly's dread. He had to be in the office, where the locket thief had been. She crossed the parlor to the door, and then she braced herself and paused, hand heavy on the knob, with a great dull wedge in the middle of her chest.

She opened the door and shrieked. Nicholas stood before her.

He wasn't a bit surprised and must have heard her coming, and she wondered why he hadn't called out to reassure her.

"What are you doing?" Molly asked, breathy and aggressive. "He was here, I saw him leave! The locket thief!"

"Molly—"

"Tell the truth!"

Was it worry or a thin blade of fear in his eyes? She grabbed his arms and felt them stiffen in his loose silk sleeves. His expression did the opposite, softening within but staying hard upon the surface.

"Don't concern yourself," he said.

"Are we in danger? Did he threaten you?" she asked. "Was it *him*?"

He stepped toward her as she held his arms and backed her into the parlor. He had strengthened over the summer and was harder to resist. Humidity engulfed them and the candlelight throbbed.

"Trust me," Nicholas said. "I have everything in hand."

Chapter Eighteen

That was how she recognized the Maimer in the Orange. He was the locket thief, familiar with his long, crooked nose.

Molly told Tom a version of the story, carefully trimmed but with enough good meat to give it substance—enough, she hoped, to sate his curiosity for now. She told him nothing of their lives back in Umber, nothing about their false identities or masquerade marriage. She called Nicholas her brother and used his real name, and she referred to Kofi Baa as "a trader from Aquaria." It had been strange to let the story blossom in her mind again, knowing both the seed and the eventual corruption. Her surface had been cool, her insides boiling. There were questions she herself had not yet answered—pieces of her past she couldn't fit together—and she scarcely knew which part of the truth would compromise her worst.

In essence, Tom learned that the siblings Molly and Nicholas had arrived by ship and struggled in Grayport, had been employed by a benevolent Aquarian, and had apparently fallen foul of a street thief who would, in time, become the Maimer currently imprisoned upstairs.

Tom leaned backward, one hand on his cup, the other on the pipe clamped in his teeth. Smoke obscured his face. The lantern hung behind him; she was lit and he was not. Molly's mouth had gummed up, and she had already finished her drink. She didn't remember doing so and tried to take a sip, but all she got was smoak grounds, gritty on her tongue. She craved another cup. How the flavor had relaxed her—it felt as if she'd drunk a little portion of the tavern. Oh, to be a stranger! Just an ordinary woman in the taproom with Tom, sharing smoak and conversation, free from scrutiny and doubt.

She flipped the cup and let the grounds ooze slowly in her hand, and then she moved them with her finger, drawing symbols in her palm. Tom kept smoking. His tobacco glowed and crackled.

Did he believe a word she'd said? Did he expect her to continue? His silence seemed to indicate that she hadn't confessed enough, and he would sit, and wait for more, until the pipe went cold.

⌘

Tom smoked a while longer, trying to fill in the blanks and sift the truth of Molly's story. She had answered what he'd asked, telling him how she knew the Maimer, and given him more of her recent past than she had confided to anyone in Root, including Benjamin and Bess. But damned if she had told him anything of worth.

She sat the way a water drop dangles off a spout, perfect and precarious as long as it can hold. He laid the pipe beside his cup and said, "You never learned more about the visit that night?"

"My brother was secretive," she said. "Even as a child."

"You're sure the people he met in the parlor were respectable?"

"No," Molly said, glimmeringly honest.

"Private business," he mumbled, low enough that Molly leaned forward into his words. Tom leaned, too, and they continued up close, the way a couple might converse when they're surrounded by a crowd. "Now and then," he said, "backroom talk makes an enemy or two. Or maybe the thief upstairs harbored some resentment. However Nicholas got your locket back, it wasn't by asking nicely. Once your brother had money and some upper-crust connections, he'd have made a fat target for a criminal with a grudge."

Molly touched the smoak grounds smeared around her palm. "I'm sure you're right."

"You don't believe it, though."

She stared at him and sighed. "No, I don't."

"Why not?"

"People didn't take advantage of Nicholas."

"Everyone's vulnerable."

"You didn't know my brother."

"But he's dead," Tom said, very bluntly, to disarm her.

Molly looked down, wiping her hand on the table with no apparent notice of the mess she was making. He took her hand in both of his own and didn't let go when she instinctively recoiled. He smelled the warm smoak. She would taste like it, too—cinnamony and rich—and he had urges that were smudging up his line of proper thinking.

"How did your brother die?" he asked. Her hand spiked a fever. Tom felt it up his arm, through his shoulder, to his chest. "Did the Maimer upstairs kill him?"

"No," she said.

"Was he after you on purpose in the woods?"

"Not at first."

"That's hard to swallow," Tom said, believing her regardless. "Was he the one who threw you into the river?"

"No," Molly said.

Then who? he almost shouted, having come to it again—the ending of the riddle she had started to reveal. He'd known enough bile and desperation to understand violence. He had shot men dead in and out of war, and yearned for vile things in and out of dreams, but what kind of man, crooked providence, or fate could have cast Molly off like rubbish in the flood?

He dropped her hand and filled the emptiness by picking up his cup, and after finishing the drink he clapped the grounds on the tabletop. Elkinaki read the present, not the future, in the dregs. "Everything is present," he'd been told when he was young, talking with a squaw named Running at the Mouth. He used to disagree, when all his life lay ahead, but found it comforting tonight to read the symbols and the signs. He saw a woman's open gown, or a house made of mud, and felt his nerves prickle up toward the Maimer in the holding room.

"Come on," he said, standing up to unhook the lantern. "Let's see if he'll talk to us together."

Tom walked around the table and held her under the armpits. She sagged when he raised her, like a loose sack of corn, shifting in his grip and difficult to lift.

"You have a taste for torture?" he asked.

She stared at him and tensed. It helped him pick her up.

"The town is coming tomorrow, and they won't come to talk," he said. "They'll carve him up and hang him, good people as they are, and others not so good, and some of them—like me and Sheriff Pitt—plain and simple outnumbered. But they might skip torture if he tells us where the rest of them are hiding. And he might just tell us"—Tom pulled her up close—"if we use the facts you told me, any kind of leverage, to convince him that we know a lot more walking in."

He doubted it would work, but it was doubly worth a shot. Something more of Molly might be learned if they confronted him, and Tom was frankly surprised when she took the lantern from his hand and led the way upstairs, determined, risk be damned, to save the Maimer from unnecessary violence in the morning.

They reached the top of the stairs and stood at the prisoner's door. Molly pressed beside him, radiating oil-light and swelling as she breathed, and he imagined leading her on toward his own small room. Instead he fitted the key and turned it in the lock.

Something knocked his head as soon as he opened the door.

He fell and grabbed the air and banged against the wall. The key tinked down, Molly shrieked beside him, and the lantern light swooped and made the hall warp and fluctuate.

"*Braaah,*" Tom said, fighting to his feet.

He heard a thundering beyond him on the stairs, going down.

They'd left the knife behind—the goddamned knife Molly had dropped. The Maimer must have freed himself and hit him with the chair.

"He's gone!" Molly said, fallen near the stairs.

He shook his battered head and got tangled in her skirts, almost falling over till she stood and helped him up, and after bracing on her arm he stomped downstairs, fighting dizziness and planting every step to keep his balance. The tavern's front door was open to the night. Bess and Ichabod were coming; he could hear their frantic footsteps pounding overhead. He ran to the closet for his gun and there was

Nabby with a candle, standing in a moth-eaten shawl beside the bar. She frowned with disapproval as if she'd caught him getting drunk, and somewhere in his addlepated brain he felt ashamed.

He grabbed his loaded rifle and hurried out the door. His thoughts were coming clearer and his wooziness was gone, but he couldn't understand the blood upon his hands.

The moon was as bright as the candlelit tavern, and he focused on the houses and the trees. His ears were sharp—he heard the sound of running to the right, and when he turned he saw the small, distant figure in the dark.

The Maimer had a thirty-second lead, maybe more, but had a limp from being dragged by Molly and the horse. He kept along the river's edge, heading for the woods. Tom ran along the hill and looked toward a clearing where the water swamped in, just before the trees. It would bog the Maimer down or turn him from the bank, leaving him exposed long enough to shoot.

Molly followed out and called Tom's name.

The Maimer, just a shadow in a blur of silhouettes, hit the marshy ground and floundered with a splash. Tom stopped. He held his breath to steady the rifle on his shoulder. When the Maimer lunged right, Tom would shoot him in the leg, assuming he could still make the shot at such a range. It was at least fifty yards, no wind, high to low.

Instead of going right, the Maimer went left, apparently deciding he would swim across the river. It happened so quickly, Tom shot him in the back.

He didn't see the impact, owing to the smoke, but he knew it like a well-struck nail beneath a hammer. There was a lightning flash of joy, the shot's echo in the valley, then a deep, black quiet and the body face-down. The bullet had thrown the Maimer forward off the bank. Now the river took him gently, even sweetly in the flow. The body briefly snagged in a thin patch of reeds, made a slow quarter turn, and floated out of sight.

Perfect shot, Tom thought, too alive to feel its meaning.

Molly ran up, panting and astonished. Tom leaned against his rifle while she tried to see the body, unsure if she was sorry or relieved that it was gone. Seven miles to the Dunderakwa Falls and then oblivion. He fought the urge to hold her when the night swirled around him.

"You're cut," he said, discovering a wound along her forearm and finally understanding how his hands had gotten bloody.

"He slashed me on the stairs," she said. "I almost dropped the lantern."

Tom slung the rifle onto his shoulder. Molly slumped. They walked together, with her uninjured arm around his neck. He hugged her waist and kept his other hand pressed on her cut, and there it was again, the heat of her like radiance or fever, more alarmingly direct from the flow of Molly's blood.

Past the hilly undulations leading to the Orange, houses up the road flickered from within. People had been roused by the midnight shot, and Tom was thankful for the last few minutes of obscurity. Ichabod and Bess, waiting at the tavern, were startled by the blood, wondering who'd been shot. As the situation's import hammered into Tom, he knew what had to be done and handed Molly off to Bess, and then he left them on the grass and hurried inside.

He went to the kitchen and rinsed his hands in a basin. Nabby materialized beside him, spectral and decrepit with her bristly gray hair, and used a rag to wipe the mess he was leaving on the table.

He found a length of rope in the storeroom and ran upstairs. The holding room door was open as he'd left it. He tied the new rope exactly like the other. Then he dropped it near the chair, hid the rope the Maimer had cut, picked the key off the floor, and locked himself inside.

He stood in the dark and breathed. Muffled voices spoke below. He raised his heel and kicked the door, right beside the knob. He kicked again, and then again, until the wood began to fracture and the bangs shook the room. The fifth and hardest blow cracked the frame and broke the lock. He opened the door and left it hanging crooked off the hinges, walked downstairs, and found them huddled at the bottom—Molly, Bess, Ichabod, and Nabby looking up, seeming to believe that he was dangerous or mad.

His forehead ached and now his foot throbbed, too. It pained him to have broken part of the tavern on purpose and to see Molly's blood dribbled on the steps. When he reached the group below, Ichabod retreated halfway out the door, Nabby waited with a bucket, and Bess held her ground with tremulous concern.

"Here's what happened," Tom said. "Molly and I were talking in the taproom. The prisoner slipped his bonds, broke the door, and ran downstairs. He hit me in the head, grabbed a knife, and cut Molly on the way out. I shot him near the river and his body floated off."

Before anyone could answer, he led Molly by the hand into the far corner of the taproom, gently as he could but brooking no resistance.

"I haven't dressed the wound!" Bess said. "She needs stitching."

"That can wait," Tom said, hard enough to quell her.

He and Molly stood in private, out of the light and out of earshot. He lowered his face and raised her chin and whispered to her mouth.

"You told me the truth tonight," he said. "Part of it, at least. My father used to give me a coin for a good piece of honesty."

She smiled, false and sad. "Are you going to give me a coin?"

"I'll give you a place to live," he said. "You can stay upstairs with Bess and help around the tavern. Long as you keep being honest and do whatever you're told. No more causing trouble or disobeying orders. I can't have it, not with Pitt breathing down my neck. Especially after this."

Molly held her cut. She moved her thumb in little circles in the blood that slicked her arm, as if the movement were a comfort, or a symbol of her thoughts. She was a girl who played with injury, and now he meant to keep her.

"I have no reason to do this," he said.

Molly nodded.

"There's a world of reasons not to. And as for you recognizing the Maimer, that's between us. Don't even tell Benjamin."

"I trust him," Molly said.

"It's Abigail I worry about. Benjamin wouldn't tell her if we said to keep it secret, but I hate to put a thing between a man and his wife."

But there was more to it than Abigail. A fear of looking foolish? He would learn whatever he could by way of inquiries to Grayport but hoped that Molly would trust him—him alone—with all the rest, at least until he had a better handle on the facts.

"How's your arm?" he asked.

"It hurts. How's your head?"

"Like a ruddy fucking anvil."

Molly touched the knot, very cautiously and sweetly.

"I'm sorry," she said. "It was me who left the knife behind."

"I should have picked it up. But it was him who went and used it."

Then, with nothing left to do but face the repercussions, Tom was bleary and dejected. It was too late to sleep. Dawn was coming soon, along with Pitt and all the town, and so he clung to this—to Molly and their own private space—aware that Nabby, Bess, and Ichabod were watching them intently as they stood, face-to-face, bound in secrecy and trouble.

Chapter Nineteen

Molly lived and worked in the tavern through spring and into summer, when the farms and woodland flourished around the homes with bright, luxuriant growth. There was so much vegetation even the air felt green. Pumpkins swelled. Apples sagged branches in the orchard. Some of the deadwood boards inside the Orange sprouted twigs, and the taproom's walls were graced with tiny leaves. Summer in Grayport and Umber had not been so intense, and Molly was daily astonished by the swelter, the heat-fueled storms, the profusion of fruits and berries, and the fact that such abundance would perish overnight, she'd been told, when the valley's season of deadfall arrived instead of autumn.

One night after the umpteenth squall of the day, Molly opened the windows she had closed against the rain, wishing she could run to Echo Pond and swim the stickiness away. Navigating deftly through the tavern's packed crowd, she was enveloped in a haze of beer and perspiration. She reached the bar at the rear of the taproom and stood beside Bess. They had become like sisters since Molly moved into the Orange, working together, sharing a room, and gabbing nonstop, much to Tom's annoyance.

Bess leaned close to speak in Molly's ear. She smelled of fresh-chewed mint and warm summer honey, and she kept her eyes focused on the fiddler near the hearth. "I can't stop looking at his fingers when he plays."

His name was Lucas and his hands looked spidery and strong. He played his jigs with sadness and his ballads with élan, and Bess had all but borne his children in a fortnight of pining.

"You've missed your chance," Molly said. "I'm taking him myself."

"You wouldn't!" Bess whispered.

"I'll tell him that I'm musical and ask for private lessons."

Bess twisted Molly's arm, pleasurably hard, where the Maimer's cut had healed but hadn't stopped itching. Molly laughed and drew the looks of merry-minded patrons. Lucas kept fiddling "Tom Scarlett," Bess's favorite.

"Oh, you're right," Bess said. "I've waited too long. Except he's only ever here with everybody watching."

"Forget what people think."

"*You're* one to talk."

Increasingly of late, Bess was peppering conversations with hints of irritation—or injury—so that Molly didn't trust her with her own many secrets. No one believed in her amnesia anymore, but her capture of a Maimer had improved her reputation, and although it was widely assumed that her past was in some way disreputable, she was generally seen as a victim of circumstance rather than a menace.

Lucas finished his song and paused to wipe his face. Benjamin approached him with a thick roll of papers.

Molly filled a tankard from the cider tap, handed it to Bess, and pulled her startled friend before objections could be made. They squished through the crowd to Benjamin and Lucas. Bess tried to escape but Molly wouldn't let her.

Benjamin attempted—not for the first time—to convince Lucas to play a piece from his own dear collection of music. The fiddler listened as politely as Benjamin persuaded, but he finally insisted that he lacked sufficient skill.

"I could tutor you," Benjamin said. "I am certain you could learn to scrape a passable sonata. Perhaps not one of Hark's, but there are many by Gorelli. You could practice the *Folia*."

"You think too well of me, Dr. Knox," Lucas said and smiled, noticing Bess despite her effort to retreat behind Molly.

Benjamin raised his sheets to try again when Molly said, "We won't have music at all if he collapses from the heat."

She twirled behind Bess and pushed her forward with the cider.

"Thankee, Bess," Lucas said, and took it with a wink.

Bess hiccupped through a laugh and nearly died: he knew her name.

"May I speak with you, Doctor?" Molly said. "I'm sorry to interrupt, but it's a matter of terrible urgency."

Benjamin turned professional at once, allowing himself to be dragged to the kitchen, where Nabby faced the hearth fire, sharpening a knife. Her withered face flickered like a warning of perdition. Molly explained why she had led Benjamin away, and he looked from the kitchen to the taproom, where Lucas held his fiddle up so Bess could pluck the strings.

"Infatuation," Benjamin said. "One of the few common pains for which the cure, if one existed, would be ardently rejected."

Nabby whisked her blade across a whetstone and said, "There's wickedness in love."

"Bite your tongue," Molly said.

Nabby went to a table strewn with vegetables and organs. "Ask the child," she continued, speaking of the tavern ghost. "She knew a touch of love and took it to her doom."

"Is she here?" Molly asked.

Nabby pointed with her blade toward the middle of the hearth, where the drippings from a chicken crackled in the flames.

"Will she tell me her name tonight?" Molly asked.

"She'll tell you when she trusts you."

Molly scrutinized the hearthstones, uncertain of where to look; Benjamin, more intrigued by living beings who would speak to empty air, adjusted his glasses and focused on the women.

He said to Molly, "You perceive her with your senses?"

"Like a fragrance," Molly said, and yet it wasn't quite a scent but rather a fleeting saturation. It reminded her of things she had honestly forgotten in the hours of delirium that followed giving birth: her hand upon a heartbeat, a tugging at her breast. She couldn't ascertain if the memories were real. Had she kissed her own baby on the head before she lost her?

Molly believed the ghost would know, and she longed for other answers, but Nabby said the child still considered her a stranger. If only there were a way to win the spirit's trust. But now was not the time—she needed to hold herself together—so she went to the kitchen door again and looked across the taproom. The noisy hurly-burly of the drinkers perked her up.

"Can you describe the ghostly fragrance?" Benjamin asked her from behind.

"Lem," Molly said.

"Lemuel Carver, did you say? Like the odor of corruption, or a stench of perspiration?"

"No, he's here," Molly answered, pulling Benjamin toward her. "He's staggering drunk. There, he's coming in the door."

Benjamin craned his neck to see beyond the crowd. Lem shoved in, heavy-limbed, to find his daughter. Some of the drinkers swore and grumbled when he bumped them out of his way but nobody confronted him—a leatherbound giant with a three-week beard and a slaughterhouse mien.

"Go get Tom from the stables. I'll get Bess," Molly said. Benjamin hurried out the back, leaning forward like a turkey. Molly wove a path to Lucas and Bess and said, "Your father's here, come on."

There wasn't any time. Lem cleaved the crowd, swept Molly out of the way, and closed a brawny hand around the meat of Bess's arm. He smelled like pickled tongue and had a ghastly, peeling sunburn.

"You're coming home now or I will tan your fucking hide," he slurred.

Bess shrank back with teary, frantic eyes.

"Let her go!" Molly said.

The nearest patrons were either too surprised or too familiar with Lem to intervene. Lucas stepped forward, more from startlement than nerve, and laid his long fingers on the bulk of Lem's shoulder.

"Mr. Carver," he began.

Lem grabbed his throat. Bess shrieked and twisted free. The crowd erupted into shouts and two of the nearest men, able-bodied masons, futilely attempted to relax Lem's grip.

Lucas reddened in the face and dropped his fiddle. Molly picked it up, held it by the neck, and swung it at the back of Lem's enormous head. It fractured with a twang, musical and strange. Lem let go of the fiddler's throat and backhanded Molly. She staggered, smelling blood. He raised his arm to hit her again but Tom arrived, threw a punch, and caught him in the liver, up beneath the ribs, with a hard-packed thump. Lem doubled over.

Tom seized him by the collar and the back of his breeches, the masons held his arms, and then they all dragged him out through the kitchen into the yard. Molly held a napkin to her nose and followed Bess, who looked as if she and not her father had been bludgeoned by the fiddle.

"Get him in the stocks," Tom said behind the tavern.

The stocks were near the garden, just beyond the door light, tall enough to make a prisoner stand but low enough to force him into a stoop. The masons got Lem positioned in the notches. Tom clapped the stocks shut and locked the boards in place. Lem's agony and drunkenness were wearing off together and he growled, shook the padlock, and drooled into his beard.

Bess held her fist very tightly to her lips. Molly stood beside her, trying to stop her nosebleed. Half the tavern followed them out and Lem's fury hit a crescendo. He would either break the stocks or snap his neck with so much thrashing.

Tom dropped a bucket into the well and drew it up. He was hulking when he carried it—mightier than Lem in Molly's estimation—and formidably calm as he walked toward the stocks. Tom splashed him in the face. "Sober up and settle down," he said.

Incredibly, it worked; Lem began to moan, sagging as his beard dribbled water in the mud. Molly's nose had bloodied the napkin and her whole head pulsed. Mosquitoes buzzed her ears but formed a cloud around Lem, whose tannery stink and helplessness attracted them in force.

"It's over," Tom said, backing everybody in.

Nabby was beside herself at having so much traffic in her kitchen. She tried to shoo them out when they turned to come inside again, but instead they heeded Tom, suffered Nabby's hexes as they tromped back through, and returned to the stifling taproom, where nobody was left to serve drinks or keep the peace.

"You all right?" Tom said to Molly.

"It's only a nosebleed."

He turned and asked Bess, "What about you?"

She bubbled into sobs, as full of fury as of sadness. Tom hugged her close and let her blubber on his chest.

"Take her in," he told Molly, speaking to her gently through a fissure in his anger. "And have Benjamin look at your nose. Will you do that for me?"

Molly nodded, pried Bess away from Tom, and led her into the kitchen, where they both rinsed their faces.

"Not a week goes by you don't bloody up my kitchen," Nabby said, but she was quick to hand Bess a restorative cup of wine.

Tom remained outside and Lem resumed shouting. Molly guided Bess out of earshot and into the taproom, where Benjamin stood examining Lucas, who held a glass of rum with badly trembling hands. His collar was torn. Angry red marks had risen on his neck. He pursed his lips and puffed, as if to breathe were still a challenge, and his fiddle lay demolished in a pool of spilled cider.

Bess's eyes were round and raw.

"Nothing cracked or crushed," Benjamin told the women, studying his patient with a palliative smile.

"I'm sorry about your fiddle," Molly said with all her heart.

Lucas stooped and gathered it up, a mess of strings and fractured maple with the scroll still intact atop the separated neck. He looked at Molly sharply, as if she had broken it for sport, and glared at Bess as if she'd grown a beard and stank of rotten hides. When he stood and carried his poor, crumpled fiddle to the door, Bess collapsed into his empty chair and cried without reserve.

Cracked and crushed, Molly thought, recalling Benjamin's words, and cursed the spineless fiddler for abandoning her friend.

Sheriff Pitt strode in—scarlet-vested, flush with pomp—just as Lucas slouched out.

"What the deuce happened now?"

☙

Tom breathed a gnat and bottled up a cough. The heavy dark air was full of barn musk and plant steam, and between the background chatter of the tavern and Lem's protestations, a pressurized quiet filled Tom's mind, thoughtless and profound, until he felt he'd either explode or stay that way forever. Then Pitt showed up.

"I see you treat your kin contemptuously, too," the sheriff said.

Pitt crossed the yard halfway to Lem, who gentled down quickly in the presence of the law.

"He walked in fighting," Tom said.

"He's peaceable now."

"That's because he's in the goddamned stocks."

Pitt grinned. It broadened his cheeks and made his head look thicker. "I'm surprised you managed to hold him," he said, "instead of shooting him in the back and letting him float to kingdom come."

He plucked the key from Tom's hand and unlocked the stocks.

Lem stepped away, slipping in his crapulence and landing in the mud. He wiped mosquitoes off his face, smearing himself with filth, and looked a perfect drunken wreck when he tottered to his feet. For a second his contrition seemed entirely sincere, and in his sweetness and distress he briefly resembled his sister. Tom felt the pang, remembering his mother, but he wouldn't bow to gold-leaf memories tonight.

"Tell me what happened," Pitt said.

"I was being a concerned *father,* is all," Lem said, beady-eyed, sounding as if he'd memorized the words. "I come to the tavern and that fiddler boy is groping up my Bessie. 'Fore I know it, he attacks me."

"Was that the way of it, Tom?"

"Not ruddy likely. I didn't see the start of it," he had to admit. "Benjamin called me in and Lem was hitting Molly."

Pitt turned to fetch the doctor but he had already appeared, having patiently observed the situation from the kitchen. He lent an air of reason with his scholar-prim demeanor. Pitt looked relieved to see him at the door.

"I was summoning Tom from the stables," Benjamin said, "and

missed the first spark. I will attest that Lem arrived in high intoxication. Young Lucas had been seized about the neck and might have suffered worse—asphyxia, for instance, or compression of the larynx—if not for Molly and Tom's intervention. Fourscore witnesses will verify the facts."

"I only come to see my daughter," Lem muttered with deflation. If Tom had closed his eyes to visualize the speaker, he might have imagined a well-mannered giant, ignorant but dignified, standing hat in hand with guileless intent. "I don't see her no more, now that Tom has stole her off."

"She ain't a branded heifer," Tom said. "She's here of her own accord."

He stood with Lem and Pitt, close enough to punch. Another squall was bearing down, invisible in the dark but sounding like wind with the rainfall rushing through the trees across the river. Pitt inhaled dramatically, averting his nose so as not to smell Lemuel directly.

"Go inside," he said to Benjamin, who left without a word, and then it was just the three of them and Tom was on his own. "Bess is old enough to choose," Pitt said to Lem. "And let's not pretend you haven't caused trouble before."

Every now and then, the son of a bitch showed common sense.

But then he said to Tom, "That doesn't make her being here seemly. This isn't the first complaint I've had about your boarders."

"Is that right."

"Two young women living under your roof," Pitt continued. "Folks would like to know the genuine thrust of the arrangement."

"Folks," Tom said. "Is this a formal complaint or just talk?"

"Call it a friendly warning." The lanterns in the kitchen lit the side of Pitt's head, showing half his face and leaving the other half eclipsed. "Get your house in order before it becomes a question of considering your license. I'm meeting with the governor next month and it's my duty to mention any municipal concerns that need addressing."

"Since when is hiring women a municipal concern?" Tom asked, backing Pitt up toward a shadowy pile of manure.

"I'll make a list of incidents and nail it to your door," Pitt said, presumably in jest. "You know I'll have to speak about the prisoner who escaped."

There had been three more attacks in the intervening weeks, and comments had been made, rarely to Tom's face, that his failure to keep the Maimer secure had cost the town a vital advantage. Throughout the exchange, Lem had done his best to keep himself steady, but he suddenly lost his balance and stumbled into Pitt, who managed to prop him up but trampled the manure.

"You're made for each other," Tom said without amusement.

Pitt scowled at Lem and said, "Go home and sober up."

"I don't suppose you'll reimburse me for the mess you caused tonight," Tom said to his uncle.

"Not until you reimburse me for my Bessie," Lem said.

"I'll let her know you're willing to barter. You can leave from out here. I don't want you tracking filth through the tavern. You, too," he said to Pitt, who only now looked down and saw what he was standing in.

Pitt nodded at his shoes as if this, exactly this, was what he expected from the Orange, and Tom himself couldn't help regarding his property as a place where, yes, shit like this and people like his uncle were bound to appear.

Lem clomped away; drunk or not, it was the only way the man ever walked. Pitt wiped his feet in the grass, rather too close to the door, and left Tom alone as rain began to fall, drenching and warm and somehow stagnant in the dark.

Folks, Tom thought, recalling Pitt's word.

It was Abigail still, slipping thoughts in people's heads. She had publicly supported Bess's moving in, but for Tom to harbor Molly was something else entirely, despite the fact that she herself and Benjamin had done so. She had questioned every traveler she met throughout the summer, pointing Molly out whenever she could and mentioning "the dead brother," never suspecting that Tom knew more than he admitted and was already making his own quiet inquiries to travelers.

The rain stopped as briskly as it had come. Instead of freshening him up, it had spattered mud on his stockings and left him with the steaming, clingy weight of sodden clothes. The tavern stood before him, its stone foundation muddied like his legs, its clapboards deeply weathered by a thousand other rainfalls. To the right of where he stood, the storeroom and secondary bedrooms—an addition to the original building, one that predated even his parents' ownership of the tavern— made an L-shaped enclosure in a portion of the yard. It was cozy and secluded, and it recalled him to his childhood and other rainy nights when he used to help his father with the horses in the stables.

So many memories of his father had an element of dark: a reas- suring figure in the brightness of a door, a shadow in the barn, a body on the floor. After carrying the straw and mucking out the stalls, Tom would run toward the lantern in the kitchen—this very kitchen, with the very same lantern—and forget to take his shoes off. He remem- bered how his mother's laugh lines sagged in disappointment when she turned to find him sullying her newly swept floor, and how she met him in the light, and lectured him again, but handed him a fresh- baked cracknell all the same.

He tasted caraway seeds and smelled the flour on her apron. This was home and there was more to it than licenses and sentiment. His father had died for it and his brother had abandoned it, but his mother had lived for the Orange and given it to Tom, and neither governor nor grief would take it from his hands.

Chapter Twenty

Later that night, after everyone had gone, Molly found Tom alone in the taproom. He sat at a table near the window and watched a shower of rain. A lone, stumpy candle in the middle of the room was scarcely bright enough to qualify as illumination, and the saturated heat was like the air beneath a blanket.

"How's Bess?" he asked.

"Sleeping," Molly said.

So were Ichabod and Nabby and the handful of travelers. She flapped the front of her gown to ventilate her breasts and grazed her left nipple. That was all it took to overwhelm her senses and she wobbled off center, like a pudding set aquiver. It astonished her to be so affected. After last winter, she'd believed the urge had died but here it was, resurrected like an everlasting body.

Molly stood beside Tom with her belly near his ear. She reached toward his tied-back hair without his noticing.

"Why was she talking to Lucas?" he asked.

"She's been saving her money for fiddle lessons."

"I didn't know that."

"I'm teasing you," she said, and then she did grab his ponytail, squeezing it and giving it the gentlest of tugs. "She fancies him."

"I didn't know that, either," Tom said without turning.

Molly released his hair, disappointed that her boldness hadn't prompted a reaction.

"I reckon Lem scared him off," Tom said.

"Then he wasn't much of a man."

"Most men have the sense to keep clear of a woman with that much trouble clinging to her skirts."

"Not you."

"It's one of my reckless virtues," Tom said, looking up at her with nothing like virtue in his eyes, as if her skirts, then and there, were smoldering off her body. Molly drew a chair and sat beside him, knee to thigh.

"What will you do about Bess and Lem?"

Tom sighed. "There isn't much I can do. I won't send her off, but neither will I fight him outright unless I have to. They're all the family I got, at least around here."

"Your brother at sea—"

"Winward," Tom said, smiling just to say it. "People call him Win. He was smart enough to leave and not look back."

"Don't you love Root?"

"I do. I love the Orange. There's a history to home, but every history has hurts. Ever seen the gash on the outside door?"

Molly nodded. She had probed it with her finger only last week.

"That's a hatchet cut," he said. "I could show you seven bullet holes peppering the walls. Bloodstains from accidents and childbirth and fights. A quarter of the tavern caught fire one year. You can still see the burns on the underlying frame."

She knew the scorched wood, a few of the bullet holes, and many of the stains, some of which she'd made with her own spilled blood. She knew the black glove nailed to the parlor wall and the sinister face lurking in the hearth stones. She also knew the exact number of wishbones hanging in the taproom, the hidden panel in the upstairs hall, and the cobwebbed passage that led to the secret part of the cellar. She didn't know most of the stories behind the details, and considering how often she discovered something new—a roughly carved symbol, or the window outside that didn't correspond to any known room—it seemed the Orange had the history of many homes combined.

Tom fell as silent as the furniture around them.

"How did your parents die?" she asked.

"You don't know this yet?"

There were countless questions Molly had withheld throughout the summer, especially those related to her regular companions. She knew nothing about Ichabod's muteness, little of Benjamin and Abigail's past, and almost none of Tom's life aside from what she saw directly. Having secrets of her own made her hesitant to ask.

"You know about the war," Tom said.

Molly nodded. She knew it verse and chorus from the papers back in Umber, when she used to study the articles for news about her father.

Tom looked out the window instead of at her, giving an oddly distant feel to everything he told her.

"I served for three years in the army and wound up at Fort Pine," he said. "That's fifty leagues north of here, mostly wilderness except for the odd settlement or two. The Rouge had found a passage from the sea to the northern Antler. They meant to run ships from the mountains to the Arrowhead River, straight down to Grayport—it would have won the war. We were a skeleton division holding Fort Pine, barely enough to man the cannons. Our captain had died of knotgut, our food and ammunition were low, and the Kraw had hemmed us in so we couldn't send for reinforcements. We knew the Rouge were coming, and we knew General Bell and his men were only a two-day march to the west, completely unaware—"

Molly bumped his leg, rising from her chair. She had mostly held her breath since he mentioned Fort Pine, but on hearing her father's name, she walked toward the bar to gather her composure.

"What?" Tom asked.

"I thought you'd like a drink," she said, thankful of the dark.

Of course the bar was locked. She walked back to get his key and he was sitting there, perplexed, seeming worried he had rambled and annoyed that she was up.

"I want to hear it all and mean to settle in," she said.

Molly took the key and unlocked the bar. Tom waited, silhouetted by a quick flash of lightning while she poured them each a rum, drank her own, and poured again. The heat felt thicker at the level of her head. She took the glasses back and sat. Her legs were made of wax.

"You needed reinforcements but the Kraw had hemmed you in," she said. "What are they like?"

"The Kraw?" he asked, holding his rum and leaning away from her exaggerated interest. "Hard," he said. "Sharp. Like a thicket made of knives. The warriors are women."

"People say they aren't human."

"They're human," Tom said. "I admit to having wondered. The Elkinaki say the Kraw are so connected to the forest, they sicken when they leave it, like uprooted trees."

Tom took a drink and swished before he swallowed.

"They were all around the fort, and fearsome good at hiding. A man could try to run and get a message through to Bell, but even with sharpshooters clearing the way, it was more than likely suicide. A week before the siege, I'd gotten word my mother had died of fever. My father was already dead, and there had been rumors that my brother's ship had sunk at Point Dureef. I suppose I fell victim to despair," Tom said. "But it felt like rage. I hated the Rouge for starting the war. I hated the Kraw for pinning us in. I hated General Bell for camping so close and not knowing how desperate we had gotten at the fort. I put it all on him. I wanted him to know.

"I left at first light, before the sun was rightly up. There was a secret way out, a hidden door that got me into shrubs around the fort. The forest smelled rank and overgrown, like a poison. All I meant to do was run until I died. I took off straight toward the tree line, sprinting through the clearing with a knife and two pistols. The Kraw appeared out of nowhere, shadows in the shadows. I shot the first, missed the second, dropped the guns, and ran as fast as I could. An arrow hit my leg. I broke it off with the point still buried in my thigh. A few of them chased me. They were silent—it was eerie how they moved. Sharpshooters hit them from the fort and cleared the way, but one of the shooters wasn't so sharp and hit *me* in the shoulder, right before I made it to the trees. The bullet spun me and I landed in a patch of high ferns, with the Kraw it should have killed coming right behind me.

"The fall dazed me and she caught me—I must have looked dead. I didn't see her but I smelled her, and the strange thing about it was she smelled like home. Exactly like this," Tom said, putting his palms upon the table, close to Molly's own. "Smoky and familiar. I imagined I was here. I felt her leaning over me and thought about my mother. Then she tried to scalp me—sliced a quarter way back before I stabbed her in the gut. I didn't feel her knife until her body fell away."

He tipped his forehead down for Molly to examine. She ran her fingers over the scar, slightly crooked, slightly raised, and moved the skin upon the bone with a fascinated shiver. She wondered if he'd ever let another person touch it.

"Did you feel your own skull?"

"I don't remember," Tom said.

He traced the scar with his thumb, with his elbows on the table and a thin line of sweat running from his temple.

"I left the fort ready to die," he said. "The pain changed my mind. So off I went with a bullet in my shoulder, an arrowhead buried in my leg, and so much blood in my face I couldn't wipe it off. I heard another round of shots—a few more Kraw the sharpshooters hit—and then I was clear of the worst and running in the forest. Eventually I stopped and tore my sleeves to make a bandage so my scalp wouldn't keep flapping open as I ran. When I made it to Bell's encampment, I wouldn't drink or sit until I delivered the message in person. I met the general in a tent, gave him the letter, and collapsed. I gathered he was powerfully impressed by my arrival."

Tom gulped his rum so unslakably and firmly, he seemed prepared to swallow the glass or crush it in his hand. He stood and opened a window. Fresher, cooler air wafted in and gave them breath. Molly watched him sit again. His weight creaked the chair. She could still feel his scar like blisters on her fingers.

"I slept for three days and woke to news that General Bell had marched to Fort Pine," he said. "The Rouge sailed down, expecting no resistance, and were blown to smithereens. It turned the war in Bruntland's favor. Bell visited me later and gave me a commendation."

"What did you think of him?" she asked.

"An angry man. Rigid. Like he wasn't used to anything but standing up straight. He admired my wounds. He even touched my scalp the way you touched my scar. We shared a bottle of port and talked about the war, but something in his being there, something in his crispness or his confidence enraged me. I tried to disillusion him. I talked about my mother, how I'd left the fort assuming, even wishing, I'd be killed. I thought he'd be disgusted and consider it unsoldierly. But then he talked about his wife, who had died giving birth, and his son and daughter, who were waiting back in Umber."

"What did he say?" Molly whispered.

"He said he hoped his own death would inspire them to greatness—only nothing quite as bloody. We toasted to their health."

Tom fell into a reverie, accompanied it seemed by the spirit of his mother, and the voice of General Bell, and the old glass of port. In the hour when her father had been toasting to her health, she'd been reveling with Nicholas and toasting their ascension. Was it possible the same was happening again—that her father, worlds away, was thinking of her now, never dreaming what fates he had driven her and Nicholas to follow?

"After the war," Tom said, "people saw me different. They asked for my advice, came to me for help. They put me at the head of Root's militia. More than a few suggested I run for office. And it burned James Pitt, who'd joined another regiment and served without injury or recognition. No fault of his own. He'd been willing to fight. The war played out a different way, that was all, and he marched back home the same as when he left."

"It's small of him to hate you for it," Molly said.

"He hated me before. The war deepened the trench."

He stood again, fetched the tobacco rope hanging near the hearth, and laid it on the table. She watched him cut coin-sized disks off the rope and dice them very finely with his knife while he spoke.

"Pitt's father used to own this place when we were boys," Tom said. "Our mothers were friends. They knew each other in Grayport before the Pitts moved here and built the tavern for their home and livelihood. There was need of a tavern here, but Mr. Pitt had made his money in shipping and didn't know a lick about brewing. He had contempt for most of the locals, too, which didn't help business, and a run of bad luck. Part of the roof collapsed one winter. The storeroom burned. He fell into debt, was facing jail and worse from some of his creditors, so he took their savings back to Grayport and gambled on a high-risk shipment overseas, right as the Rouge and pirates started playing havoc with the trade routes. Even if the shipment got through, he needed half a year to see a big enough return."

Tom returned the tobacco rope to its hook. He carried the candle from the middle of the room and set the pewter holder on the table. Then he gently stuffed his pipe, inverted the bulb over the flame, and drew until it crackled. Molly squinted at the candle after sitting in the dark, enjoying how the light seemed to hold them in its aura.

"Mr. Pitt's wife confided in my mother, who sympathized and wanted to help. My parents had talked about moving to Root. There were opportunities here—less competition than the city, cheap land. My father had made some money as a brewer in the city. He offered to buy the tavern—temporarily, to keep it from the creditors—and get it into shape while the Pitts stayed in Grayport to settle their affairs. Mr. Pitt agreed. He took the proceeds and paid down a number of his debts. The plan was when the shipment made Mr. Pitt's fortune, my father would sell the tavern back and be paid an extra sum for his assistance, more than enough to settle our family permanently in Root . . . But you have to understand," Tom said gravely, "no one, including Mr. Pitt himself, honestly expected that shipment to succeed."

Molly's heart thumped warmer from the rum she had drunk. She breathed the pipe smoke, a fragrance she had come to adore, and listened with the dread and fascination of a child.

"My father called this place home as soon as we arrived," Tom said. "He rebuilt the storeroom, hired Nabby as a cook, and brewed better beer than Root had ever tasted. He was one of the first to roast smoaknuts. He learned it from the Elkinaki. People liked him. By the end of the winter, the tavern was a popular place, and when the road cleared in spring, he started making money."

Tom smoked to calm down, gazing at the ember, but he coughed as if he'd never smoked a pipe and couldn't take it. Another pulse of lightning came without sound and the rain dripped softly from the eaves above the window.

"The shipment got through," Tom said slowly. "Mr. Pitt was in the black. But people in Root liked the tavern just the way it was. So did my father. When the Pitts returned from Grayport prepared to buy it back, my father wouldn't sell. Mr. Pitt was furious. He built this place, he said. 'And wrecked it,' said my father. 'It was me who built it up again and saved you from the creditors.' Mr. Pitt returned to Grayport and fought it with a lawyer, but the law stood against him. There was nothing he could do. So he rode back to Root, brought a pistol, and shot my father dead in front of thirty-seven witnesses."

He said the word "dead" with a visible deflation. Molly dug her fingernails fiercely into her knees.

"How old were you?" she asked.

"Ten," Tom said, cradling his pipe so his hand seemed to smoke. "I was back behind the bar, tapping a keg of ale. My brother was in the stables. Our father made us work like any other hands. We groused a lot but loved the way he treated us like men. I was struggling with the tap and looked to him for help. He was five paces off, standing near my mother with his back toward the door. I suppose he looked like me—the way I look now. My mother was pretty but frail. She had a crooked leg from birth. It made her stand with her right side lower than her left, but she learned to tilt her head a certain way in compensation. It made her look thoughtful, like the tilt was curiosity."

Tom stared back in the direction of the bar as if his mother, even now, were curiously watching.

"Mr. Pitt walked in. I saw him in the crowd but couldn't place him right away. He didn't have his wig and I had never seen him bald. He'd ridden nonstop from Grayport, changing horses on the way, and he was so exhausted that his eyes looked punched. 'Orange,' he said, and raised the gun. My father turned his chest directly into the shot. I thought my ears had burst. I'd never heard a pistol fired indoors. My father fell back, like the sound had knocked him over, with a pained look of outrage twisting up his face. I don't recall seeing any blood. Only smoke."

Molly squeezed her trigger finger inward with her thumb. Her knuckle cracked. The smell of burnt sulfur stung her nose.

"A group of men tackled Mr. Pitt," Tom said. "Someone dragged me out—I don't remember who—and I couldn't see my mother. When I didn't hear her crying, I thought my father might be all right. The place was in an uproar, my ears were numb, and I kept expecting my mother to call for me or Win, tell us not to worry. It was only when they got me outside I heard her screaming."

Tom's voice sounded peaceful, almost casual to Molly, as if the story wasn't his but something he'd been told. Seventeen years had passed since it happened—seventeen years of living with the shot. He hadn't moved beyond it, Molly thought. He'd grown around it, like the flesh around the sharpshooter's bullet in his shoulder.

"Mr. Pitt was tried and hanged," Tom said. "My mother stayed home—she wouldn't get out of bed—but me and Win sneaked out. I sat in the crook of a tree, a long way off from the crowd, and started crying when I saw him. They had him on a horse with the rope around a branch, and someone smacked the horse to make it bolt. At first I thought the smack was his neck getting cracked. It made me stop crying but the plainness of it scared me, how he dangled from the rope and twitched until he died. Then I noticed James Pitt standing with his mother. He was ten like me and looking at his father. I watched him so long, he finally stared back. He'd been crying, too, but then he wasn't anymore. We've been looking at each other that way ever since."

Tom scraped his chair a leg's length back and sized Molly up, as if her body, not her face, would show the depth of her reaction. Silence was her answer, and a heartsore chill, for both ten-year-old Tom and ten-year-old Pitt, as well as for the losses in her own private memories.

"Our family ran the tavern after that," Tom said. "We hired hands to do the work we couldn't fully manage, but me and Win grew up fast and my mother was determined. She was never very strong but she was tough, and even the locals who had sided with the Pitts didn't hold the outcome against her. When the war broke out, my brother went to sea and I joined the army. We wanted to see the world. My mother encouraged it. But when she died here alone, I blamed myself for leaving."

"I left my father," Molly said, as if a tourniquet had slipped and opened up the flow. "I thought he might have died the day I ran away."

Tom sat straight and gripped her with his eyes. His stare was so direct, Molly's face began to ache. She concentrated desperately to steady her expression.

"Did he?" Tom asked.

"No. He's still alive."

"Why did you leave?"

"Imagine Lem," Molly said, "with influence and wealth."

"That's hard to do."

"Then think of a nobleman who cracks a child's tooth." She thought of hugging him the day he said goodbye and left for Floria, of reaching for his saber when he dragged her on the floor. Love made her miss him, love and all its afterbirth. "I left to see the world and start new. Same as you."

"I didn't find what I expected," Tom said.

"Neither did I."

The tourniquet inside her reasserted force, causing her to hunch and put a hand upon her breastbone. Tom was too depleted to pursue it any further. He regarded her with something more than bottled curiosity—compassion, or a sense that she resembled General Bell?

"What happened to Pitt and his mother?" Molly asked.

"Back to Grayport first," Tom said. "His mother eventually moved south to live with family. She died two years ago. When Pitt came of age, he tried to buy the tavern from my mother. She was kind to him. She pitied him but wouldn't agree to sell. He stayed here in Root, bought a house, and went to war. He was sheriff after that, proud of having clout. But he wants this place. He's never let it go. He says he has the money. Says he has a right."

"Was your father right to keep it?"

"No," Tom said. "He broke his word and all of us suffered. I hated him for that. But as far as I'm concerned, James Pitt lost his rights when his father shot mine."

Molly couldn't decide where the truer claim lay. Had she any better right to claim the tavern as her own? She stood and hugged Tom. He didn't hug back. Then she knelt and laid her head very softly in his lap, as she used to do with Frances when her governess was sewing, and she looked out sideways, admiring the Orange and imagining, believing, she were really safe at home.

Chapter Twenty-One

Root ripened in September. Threadbare clouds made the sky seem bluer, and the forest's ravishing colors spread forever to the east. The temper trees shed their clothes impulsively, in tantrums, dropping every last leaf in ten or twenty minutes. Molly could see one now, all a blur in fiery red, and wished she were standing underneath it in the rush.

It was Muster Day and most of Root had gathered near the Orange, filling the grounds between the road and the tavern with vegetable carts, livestock, handicrafts, and other wares. There were watermelons big as hogs and pumpkins big as wagon wheels. Tinkers, farriers, and cobblers plied their trades; children played at hoops; citizens raced and boxed; and although Molly was working with Bess to keep the tavern drinks flowing, she had reveled in the sights and smells, the bustle and variety.

Now she stood above the road and watched Root's militia, who assembled twice a year to practice basic drills. Tom had spent the day as captain of the troops. He had never looked more handsome than he did in his greenspun uniform, his boots cleanly oiled and his hat freshly curled. Neither had he looked more livid and explosive. Things had gone badly from the opening roll call, when a quarter of the volunteers failed to arrive on time. Many were unprepared. Others forgot their guns. Marches were disorganized, volleys were delayed and out of sync, and there was too much conversation, laughter, and mutinous grumbling. As soon as Tom corrected one shortcoming, another would emerge, and although some of the onlookers and volunteers had begun to question his ability to captain, the troops' ineptitude struck Molly as unnaturally consistent, almost as if the problems had an organizing hand.

She was thinking of it now, suspecting Sheriff Pitt, when she recognized a man she'd met with Nicholas in Grayport.

The man was fifty paces off, short and round with widely splayed feet and a pronounced flatness to his head. It gave him the appearance of a cross-sawn trunk, and his name was Mr. Bole, which heightened the effect. He had been one of her brother's clients—Molly had translated pages of his dreary correspondence—and had hung about the office making friendly conversation. Now he noticed her, too, and smiled in recognition. She ducked and hastened off and hoped he wouldn't follow.

Cravens spiraled by, making Molly flinch. These were tiny black birds that traveled by the hundred, terrified of everything and huddled into swarms. They flew toward a tree but the tree scared them off, and so they whirled, dark and fluid, in a smooth gorgeous panic.

Mr. Bole was on the move, waddling toward her. Molly zigzagged quickly through the Muster Day crowd. She walked behind a row of smoking metal drums, where a dozen men and women raked coals, added fuel, and roasted mounds of gathered smoaknuts to package for the winter. She continued around the side of the tavern, hidden by the smoak-roasters' haze and coming to a cannon that was butted against the storeroom wall. The barrel pointed out across the river to the woods. She crouched behind its wheel and hoped she hadn't been followed.

From her vantage point overlooking the bank, she could see a mile of the sun-gilt water in either direction. In the distance to the south, on the town's side of the Antler, black-leaved smoak trees darkened like a burn. She had visited the smoakwood to help gather nuts. There the trees stood towering and twisted and majestic, and the shade held an ancient smell of cinnamon and soot. The quiet had a past there. Birds seemed to listen. *Good death*, she had thought, pressing on the soil, sensing in the gloom a hint of resurrection.

But even here in town with all the colors in profusion, there was something overripe and dreadful in the glory. Deadfall was coming. People talked about it constantly: a brutal freeze that would put an end to summer overnight. Benjamin insisted it could happen any day now, earlier than usual, according to the signs. The moon's double halo. Caterpillar hues. The suicide weeds were already strangling themselves, and many people in the town had claimed to see the Colorless Man—one of the truest indications, Nabby and Benjamin agreed, that the season of adversity would soon be upon them.

Molly heard footsteps coming up behind her. It was Ichabod, flailing like a windmill and warding her away with broad, emphatic gestures. He shoved himself between her and the cannon, putting his hand upon her shoulder as he tried to catch his breath. Molly stepped back to give him room for explanation; she had learned to read his signs as well as anyone in Root.

"This is dangerous," he signed. "Primed and loaded, ready to fire, and look—the barrel is loose."

Molly saw where the trunnions had nearly broken free of the carriage.

"But why were you afraid?" she asked, studying the cannon. It was old, without a flintlock hammer to ignite it. "I couldn't have set it off unless I had a light."

She had, in recent days alone, disturbed a waterwasp hive, accidentally burned a patron's ear, fallen from the hayloft, and ruptured a keg of beer.

Ichabod led her away from the gun.

"I'm not a *fuse*," she said.

They stood together where the crowd was visible again. The militia's drills had ended and the volunteers trooped with added vim toward the tavern, seeking drink and conversation and reprieve, earned or not, from Captain Tom Orange's cantankerous command. Molly spotted Bess, pink and pretty in her calico dress beneath the sycamore, filling up tankards from a kilderkin of cider. Mr. Bole was there, too, asking Bess questions.

"I have to go," Molly told Ichabod.

She cut across the lawn and yanked her friend's arm.

"*There* you are," Bess said, refusing to be budged. "You should've joined the ranks if you wanted to stare at the captain all day."

Before Molly could lead her away, Mr. Bole asserted himself and said, "Mrs. Smith!"

He was middle-aged. His wig was triply curled on either side. He was nervously delighted, like a child with a present, and he shook her hand emphatically and spoke for all to hear.

"How wonderful to see you! I haven't returned to Grayport in more than a year. I've only come to Root to buy a bag of smoak—a yearly sojourn, a pleasurable trip before the cold. I moved to Liberty, remember. But of course you do!" he said, his face a summer day of bonhomie and wealth. "My *venture* has been utterly successful," he continued, loading "venture" up with meaning she could scarcely comprehend. "Utterly, euphorically successful, through and through. I owe your husband a marvelous debt, one I am delighted to—"

"I have no husband," Molly said, aware of some attention from the crowd, including Bess. "I'm sorry, you're mistaken. I'm afraid we haven't met."

"Oh, I see. Perfect strangers, then," Mr. Bole replied, giving her a wink that made his crow's feet smile. "But what are you doing here in Root?"

The militia thronged up around the table full of tankards, and the demand was so great that Bess continued pouring, even as she listened in with breathy fascination.

"I told you, you're mistaken," Molly said to Mr. Bole.

He turned sly and put a finger to his nose. "Please forgive me. I mistook you for a woman I knew in Grayport."

She frowned at him and whispered in his ear, "Go away."

Mr. Bole appeared wounded and surprised but then retreated, shuffling off to buy his sack of fresh-roasted smoak.

"Who was *that*?" Bess asked.

"No one. Just a traveler," Molly said. "Someone drunk."

"He didn't seem—"

"Ruddy fucking hell," Tom said behind them, raspy from a day's worth of hollering commands. His rifle's bayonet jabbed above his shoulder, and the muscles in his neck looked firm enough to strum. "I ain't paying you to talk," he said, walking to the table.

"What *are* you paying 'em for?" asked a farmer with a grin.

"I'm pouring quick as I can," Bess told Tom. "I won't pour quicker just because you're scowling."

"I ain't scowling."

"You are," Bess said. "It makes you special handsome. Ain't my cousin handsome?"

A militiawoman clapped Tom's back. "He's a keeper."

"Lousy captain, though," someone else mumbled in the crowd. "No wonder we were told to show up late."

Whoever said it didn't show himself but hurried out of sight. Several troops drinking cider traded shifty looks, as if they knew a bit more and didn't want to say.

Molly watched Tom. He seemed, as he considered what he'd heard and what it meant, to reenact the whole disastrous muster in his mind. He upended his rifle and stabbed the bayonet into the ground. Then he removed his hat and coat and hung them on the stock, and laid his ammo bag, powder horn, and knife at Molly's feet. Divested of his uniform and weapon, he seemed less a captain, more an ordinary man. Her nerves began to settle until he smiled at her and said, "I'm going to beat the sheriff to a red bubbling mash."

He laughed as if he'd bottled one laugh for many years and all the waiting had fermented it into something black and poisonous.

"Stop," she said. "Don't. Come inside and have a drink."

Tom began to walk, heedless of her plea.

"I won't let you do this," she said, and blocked his way.

"I've told you more than once," Tom said. "Learn your place."

"Or what? You'll send me off?"

He put his hands around her ribs and said, "I'll chuck you back in the river." Then he picked her up, turned, and set her to the side.

"Oh!" Molly said, mad enough to spit.

She let him go and briefly hoped he'd get himself arrested. An evening in the stocks was just what he deserved—she'd be first in line to bounce a rotten apple off his head. Then she thought about the tavern license Pitt could try to revoke. Molly tiptoed high to look around the crowd for Benjamin—only he could possibly defuse Tom's temper—but she didn't see either of the Knoxes on the grounds.

She was forced toward the tavern by the last swell of troops, a dusty brown gang of younger, rowdier men who laughed and pushed and looked prepared to tap their own keg. Benjamin wasn't in the taproom. Molly hurried through to the kitchen, where Nabby denied seeing him and upbraided her for gallivanting around instead of working.

"It's urgent," Molly said.

"Is someone dying?"

"No, but Tom—"

"The rabble wants drinks, and who is helping Ichabod? You've left him on his own," Nabby said, "to your shame."

She tried corralling Molly with a whisk of seasoned hazelrod, but Molly escaped to the yard and ran to the side of the tavern, racing around the storeroom and past the broken cannon, where she squinted through the smoak-roast haze and scanned the crowd again.

Pitt's scarlet coat finally caught her eye. He was thirty paces off near the tavern's front door and looking down toward the road with a concentrated smirk. Molly followed his gaze. There was Tom, marching up. He was headed straight for Pitt and undeterred by the bustle. Nothing but a miracle would halt him in his course.

Molly found tongs among the smoak-roast tools. She stooped and took a small burning coal from the pit, holding back her skirts so they wouldn't catch fire. The smoke stung her eyes but kept her well concealed, and she returned to the cannon at a sprint, double-checked that nobody had seen her, and verified the slightly upward angle of the barrel. The shot would clear the river and continue to the forest. No one would be hurt—although she worried about the deer—and so she stood beside the cannon, as far away as she could get, and held the tongs above the touch hole. The coal lit the fuse.

A thundercloud of smoke, stabbing fire, and an earthquake. She fell and clutched her heart, deaf and badly dazed, and thought the barrel had exploded. It was gone, completely gone. All that stood before her was the empty, fractured carriage. How was she alive?

She saw the wall and understood.

✥

Tom heaved another pail of water onto the cannon barrel and touched the iron with his palm, relieved to find it cool but still not trusting it completely. The blast had thrown it backward off its carriage into the storeroom; there had been no fire, but even so the damage was shocking. The hole was a maw of jagged clapboards, and one of the studs had fractured and been thrown in lethal pieces twenty feet back against the room's inner wall. The barrel had shattered several crates and lay at an angle amid the pulverized jars of pickled pigs' feet and snouts. Ichabod entered with another full pail and poured it into the barrel. Something sizzled deep inside. Tom stepped back and looked toward the hole. It afforded a view of the river, radiant and pure, which made the gloomy, acrid wreckage look all the more severe.

Now that they had driven away the gawkers and the Muster Day crowd was starting to disperse, Tom had left Bess in the taproom with a handful of trustworthy militiamen—hard to come by today—to mind the tavern while he, Nabby, and Ichabod surveyed the damage. Molly, God damn her, was conspicuously missing.

Tom heard a scraping from the corner. He dragged a crate aside and Scratch leapt out, growling, with a pig snout clamped in his jaws. A splinter from the blast protruded from his flank. He was damp with blood and vinegar and rippling with emotion. Tom reached toward him, hoping to pull the splinter. Scratch jumped away, giving Ichabod a fright when he darted outside with his hard-won snout.

Tom shook his head. "Ruddy fucking devil."

Pitt crunched in, seemingly on cue. Benjamin and Abigail followed close behind. They stood inside the door just off the kitchen, looking at the cannon barrel lying in the rubble.

"These were in the grass beside the carriage," Pitt said.

He held up a pair of wrought-iron tongs.

"Who would do such a thing and promptly disappear?" Abigail asked, sounding as if the answer were a foregone conclusion. She stepped beside Pitt, leaving little room for Benjamin, who tilted his head to see above her shoulder and offered Tom an apologetic look.

"It could have been anyone," Tom said.

Pitt clipped the air with the tongs and asked, "What was a loaded cannon doing there at all?"

"We moved it out of harm's way."

"Evidently not."

"I'd like to know who sabotaged the carriage in the first place."

"Sabotage," Pitt said. "Like the rifles, and the powder, and the general disarray from opening muster. Those are captain's cares, Tom, not the business of a sheriff."

Tom picked an unbroken bottle off the floor. He drew the cork and drank until the rum warmed his gut. "Unless the sheriff played a part."

Pitt smiled as if his teeth were ready to explode. "I hope you aren't accusing me of purposeful disruption."

"No," Tom lied. "You're naturally inept."

Benjamin edged around Abigail, crunching the debris as he moved. He adjusted his glasses more securely on his head and stood between Tom and Pitt, not quite tall enough to interrupt their stares. "There is the possibility, however unlikely," he said, "that the cannon spontaneously fired. Certain varieties of powder, especially those that utilize the sawdust of smoak—"

"And did the tongs spontaneously tumble from the heavens?" Abigail asked. "We could theorize for hours or confine ourselves to facts. I know you think me wrong to harp upon it so," she said to Tom, "but much of the tavern's recent trouble has an element in common. Can anyone account for Molly at the time of the explosion?"

Ichabod clattered from the wreckage in the corner, stooping as he came so as not to bump the cheeses hanging from the rafters. Nabby raised a lantern to illuminate his gestures; his hands cast elongated shadows on the walls.

"Molly was down at the road," Tom interpreted.

"That isn't what he said," Nabby corrected out of sheer orneriness. "She was with him at the cannon."

Abigail hmph-ed with tight-clamped lips, but Ichabod persisted with another round of signs.

Nabby watched his hands and said, "She left before the shot and talked to Bess beneath the tree. After that, he doesn't know."

Having nothing else to add, Ichabod navigated the dangling cheeses and began shoveling rubble into a large dirty box, looking happy to have tried exonerating Molly.

"Get Bess," Abigail told Nabby.

Nabby fixed her with a grim, sharpened eye and didn't budge.

"I'm here," Bess said, coming from the kitchen with her hair a sweaty ravel. She was breathless from her work and still agog at all the damage, and she wiped her palms firmly on her stained, shabby apron.

Tom put the bottle on a crate. His hand was trembling. He had drunk too fast with nothing in his stomach, and the smoke and pickled pork were giving him a headache. He needed room to think, needed room to breathe.

"You talked to Molly before the shot?"

"So did you," Bess told him, "when you scolded us for gabbing."

"There you have it," Tom said, as if the cannon hadn't fired ten minutes later. Dust motes swirled, causing him to squint.

"It concerns me," Abigail said, "how readily and blindly you protect her."

"You make a lot of folks' business your concern," Tom said. "I would hate to see you branded as a gossip and a meddler."

Benjamin sniffed so hard his nostrils almost shut. Friend or not, Tom was very close to slandering his wife. He swelled his fragile chest, filling out his coat until it looked as if his ribs might fracture from the strain.

Abigail ignored them both and kept on with Bess. "You were with her all the time?"

"No," Bess said. "Tom walked away, and then a funny little man . . . Never mind, it doesn't matter." She fought to hold a giggle at whatever she remembered.

"What?" Tom said.

"There was a man, swore he knew her. He was short, and squatly built, and kept making secret little gestures to his nose. Like this," she said and showed them, smiling as she did so. "At first I thought I'd finally learn a smidgen of her past, but then he acted awful strange and said he knew her husband!"

It was as if another cannon had exploded in the distance.

"Find him," Abigail said.

"You don't think it's true! But he's gone," Bess said. "He and a group of merchants rode away to beat the dark."

"Which direction?" Pitt asked.

"'Cross the ferry, off to Liberty."

Pitt looked from Bess to Abigail and Tom. A gleam lit his eyes, like a tiny pair of demons, and he marched toward the door, better than he'd marched all day during muster.

Tom laughed, and yet it pained him like a rupture in his chest. "You're riding out for this?"

Pitt smiled from the door.

"It's almost dusk," Tom said. "The Maimers'll be out. On second thought, go. Although aside from your coat, I can't think of anything they'd bother cutting off."

Pitt ignored the insult but heeded the warning: night fell swiftly in the woods. "I'll go at dawn," he said.

"She hasn't caused trouble all month," Tom said, stumbling backward with his heels against the barrel of the cannon. "If it's me you want to hit, aim at me direct."

"Housing a woman in need is one thing," Abigail said. "Housing another man's wife . . . "

It was quiet outside and turning violet in the twilight, pregnant with the dark and overripe, overdue. Ichabod was still, Bess was scared to say more, and Nabby held the lantern up and kept her own counsel. Tom looked to Benjamin for sensible support. The doctor sighed as when a wound was past the power of his art.

"Tom," Benjamin said. "It may be time we learned the truth."

Even you, Tom thought, hardened to the marrow. He'd been fighting against the current since he caught her in the river. "People have a right to earn a fresh start."

"Look at the ruin at your feet," Abigail said, surprising Tom briefly with a ring of genuine pity. "She's a firebrand. You shouldn't have to bear—"

"Speak another ill word against a person under my roof," he said, "I'll pick you up and throw you out the goddamned hole."

Abigail recoiled, mostly from the blasphemy.

"You go too far," Benjamin declared. He sounded like a skinny man, delicately boned, whose principles and pride made him physically imposing.

"Get out," Tom said to Pitt and both of the Knoxes. "Come back tomorrow with your hayforks and torches."

Rather than wait for them to move, he shoved them all aside— "Easy!" Pitt said—and exited alone. He walked through the taproom, where a few straggling drinkers smartly kept their mouths shut, and stomped upstairs to look for Molly in her room.

He strode down the hall and opened her door without a knock, ready to hammer out the big and little secrets of her heart. Nobody was there. He'd sworn he wouldn't chase her if she ever ran away again. His cousin's dried flowers gave the room a blush of summer, sweetening the cannon-fire odor he'd been breathing. Molly's stockings hung naked on a chair beside the bed. The ghost of her asleep and laughing and undressing made the room so empty, so Molly-less and still, he caught a glimpse of deadfall congealing in the shadows.

He gritted his eyeteeth hard enough to squeak and went to the stairs again, prepared to gallop off and find the man who said he knew her. Something made him stop: a feeling in his skin. He turned toward his own room and opened up the door.

She sat on the edge of his bed. Her hands were in her lap, furrowing her skirt. She looked at him with lowered chin and upturned eyes, and her complexion seemed softer in the dim, private light. He almost rushed her. Was it to haul her up or squeeze her in relief? Just to feel her. How or why, he couldn't positively say.

He closed them in and said, "You'll never guess what's lying on the storeroom floor."

"I did it," Molly said.

"My God. A chip of honesty. You care to tell me why?"

"Promise you won't be angry."

"I'm a fair ways around that corner already."

"You were going after Pitt," Molly said, standing up. He raised a hand to settle her down, as if she'd stood and shown a gun. "I thought you meant to hurt him."

"You were worrying for *Pitt*?"

"I was worrying for you, you bully-tempered clod! What if you'd attacked him?"

Tom approached her with a huff, lungs full of steam.

"You shot a cannon to distract me? Did you truly think I'd risk—I ain't a clod of any fashion. You might have tried dissuading me."

"I did." Molly frowned. "You said you'd throw me in the river."

Tom made fists until the boil in him cooled, and then he sat on the bed and slouched with Molly standing over him. The twilit blue coming from the window showed him half of her: a hip, the subtle veins along her wrist. He focused on her waist, imagining it full. He knew she'd given birth since Benjamin had told him, yet the news that she was married curdled in his stomach.

"Pitt's riding out to find the man who knew your husband."

The statement cut her legs. She sat beside him, slumping forward. For a moment he believed she would vomit on the floor.

"I don't want to leave."

"Then tell me everything," he said.

Chapter Twenty-Two

"My name is Molly Bell," she said. "I'm General Bell's daughter."

Tom was on her right, their legs a ways apart but inching closer as the mattress sagged. She'd chosen to sit on the side of the bed nearer to the window and could just discern his features as she watched him at an angle, keeping her own expression shadowed and her panic in the dark.

She tried to read his mind: *The man I shared a drink with. Impossible. A lie.* She might have told him she was royalty or born of noble wolves. He widened his eyes and leaned away, squinted, and examined her. His disbelief shifted to a dumbfounded awe and she was trapped again, compelled by his acceptance to continue.

Unable to start at the end, the part she feared to tell, she started with her birth and how the bleeding killed her mother, speaking to the floor and painfully constricted. Tom didn't talk. He didn't once interrupt. She sensed his thoughts reconfiguring with every new fact, his inner ears spiraling with every new turn.

She told of her childhood in Umber, and of Nicholas and Frances, till the loneliness the memories enkindled made her falter. How her father went to war and left them in the care of Mrs. Wickware and Jeremy; how they suffered and rebelled; how their father came home and threatened to divide them; how they fled amid the riot and escaped aboard the *Cleaver*. Tom gestured more than once because her voice kept rising. She tried to quiet down but her spirit wouldn't let her, and her words bubbled out, strong and effervescent. She told him the false names they adopted for the journey. She described Mr. Fen's molestations in the cot and how he vanished in the storm with the purse full of money.

Tom was already conversant with their early days in Grayport. She paused to let him play it through his memory again, now with Nicholas and Molly in their artificial marriage. They had met Kofi Baa and settled in the city, Molly translating, Nicholas doing business in the parlor, and the locket thief had visited her brother in the night.

It was here the truth began and where the crux of it was hidden. Molly took a breath that seemed to go forever, as if her body were a chasm with the world falling in.

⚭

Day upon day, for much of the spring and far too much of early summer, Molly sat with quill and paper in the quiet brown room while interesting strangers—men and women, young and old, most of obvious affluence—passed by her desk to meet her brother in the back.

"They require anonymity," Nicholas told her more than once.

She spoke with them as long as they would allow. Some ignored her. Others humored her—Mr. Bole was always voluble and happy to converse—but she was never able to glean the nature of their visits.

Nicholas's health was enviably strong, as if his work were not depleting him but curing him of weakness. It was Molly who was pale and tired in the mornings. She was cramped and inky-fingered, scratching out letters, and although she counted her blessings after such a frightful winter, there came a point when gratitude was not enough to sate her. Nothing seemed as gorgeous as the street beyond the window or as vivid as a sun-kissed stranger passing by.

Molly longed to socialize but Nicholas forbade it.

"Father may have sent men from Umber to discover us," he said. "We must confine ourselves to necessary interactions."

"Why did we escape, if not to live however we choose?"

"It's only for a time," Nicholas assured her.

Weeks passed. Months. Nicholas grew cagier than ever about his dealings, instructing Molly to avoid not only conversation with his visitors but eye contact, too; and indeed, many who came to the office looked embarrassed to have come. A lady might pass several times before opening the door. A gentleman would fumble with his hat or stammer words. Regulars ignored her altogether when they entered; Molly might have been a candlestick for all that they acknowledged her. Sometimes, irked, she greeted them effusively, asking the leeriest visitors direct questions about their business and commenting on the wigs, hats, cloaks, and eyeglasses she believed were intended as disguises.

Nicholas knew better than to punish or berate her—Molly had balked at his suggestion that she work in a more isolated room—but the clash of wills approached a dangerous strain, until the tension was relieved, at least in part, by a stranger.

"A man named John Summer is coming today," Nicholas told Molly one morning in July. "He is a protégé of Kofi Baa, newly arrived from Aquaria and unfamiliar with Grayport. Mr. Baa is traveling abroad for several months and has asked me to escort Mr. Summer around the city as he establishes his contacts. As I have matters of urgency that cannot be disrupted—"

"Yes," Molly said before he finished the request.

It wasn't quite the unchecked liberty she craved, but she would rather walk the breadth of Grayport with a wearisome companion than spend another day cloistered in the office.

Cheerless. Middle-aged. Dull as old snuff. Molly had limned Mr. Summer long before he came, and so when a different sort of man arrived midmorning, she experienced a tingling rush of blood, strong as rum, in regions of her body not commonly awakened. He was Nicholas's age, slightly older than herself, elegantly thin but vital in his movements. His shirt and waistcoat were new and fashionably rumpled. He wore his hair cropped short, like many from his country, and his skin appeared especially dark in contrast with the day-lit doorway at his back. He opened both hands and showed his upturned palms, the Aquarian way of saying "Please accept me; I accept you."

Molly said hello and returned the Aquarian gesture. Nicholas shook his hand and introduced himself as Jacob, and then they stood and spoke of travel and shipping contacts while Molly kept aside, watching John Summer and studying his face. His mouth seemed naturally inclined toward a smile but he listened to her brother with intense concentration—a gravity at odds with his carefree pose. He smelled of juniper and leather, with a dash of open sea.

Her brother was brief. His loyalty to Kofi Baa extended to this protégé, but Molly sensed impatience, perhaps even competitiveness, in Nicholas's demeanor, and after the necessary pleasantries he wished John Summer success with his visit and retired to the parlor, leaving Molly and their guest to navigate the city.

It was a hot, brilliant day. The streets were dry as baked fish, and people's faces looked salted more than sweaty in the sun. They walked a few blocks with little conversation, acclimating slowly to the energy around them—businesspeople, shopkeepers, artisans, and traders constantly in motion, stirring dust around the cobblestones.

"'John Summer' doesn't sound Aquarian," she said.

He laughed with wary eyes, then sighed without a smile. "I am an orphan. I chose my own name."

Molly thought of when her brother chose "Smith" before the *Cleaver*. She had fought to keep her name; she was Molly through and through.

"What happened to your family?"

"Gone," John said.

She couldn't bring herself to ask whether they were dead or only missing. As they walked from the fruit market to the harbor, he asked about her life and Molly told him, with unconcealed boredom, the well-rehearsed story she and Nicholas had devised. John Summer listened casually but studied her face with ardor; she supposed that, sensing the lie, he trained his interest on the liar.

He was far more engaged when she described how she and her "husband" had met Kofi Baa. He told her his own story of benefaction: a parentless child in Aquaria, he had stowed away on a merchant ship bound for Bruntland and been captured. Instead of being punished when he was brought before Kofi, he was promptly made cabin boy and nurtured on the sea.

"I have been everywhere from Swiftland to Crescencia."

"But you need a guide in Grayport?"

"The city changes every year." John paused to view the harbor they had only just reached, and which appeared more colorful and packed with splendid sails than Molly herself remembered. The season of travel and trade was fully under way, and it seemed that for every person who left for other ports, two more arrived to seek their fortune on the continent—a perpetually new world attracting young, intrepid hopefuls from Solido, Brach, Bruntland, Violinia, and Rouge. They were streaming in now from the harbor to the city with their unfamiliar faces and their unbridled dreams.

John Summer looked as lost—though not as daunted and forlorn—as she and Nicholas had been on the day they disembarked. Molly felt the sunlight washing through her limbs. She looked at John and tried imagining the flavor of his skin, as she would do upon discovering a rare, foreign fruit.

He smiled at the sky, as if he'd noticed her attention. "The world is like a heart full of unknown loves. It is vigorous and strange. A wonder to explore."

"But dangerous."

"Of course," he said, squinting at the sun. "A great adventure. Before I left Aquaria, the world was flat and empty. Then I went to sea and felt the roundness all about me. What if you had lived and died without seeing Floria?"

Or withered in an office, translating Rouge. "Will you stay here long, or sail around the world again?"

He looked at her with sparkles of enticement in his eyes.

"I am traveling north to Kinship in two weeks' time," he said, "facilitating river shipments of merryweather tea for Mr. Baa. Have you tasted merryweather tea?"

"No," Molly said.

"Then you must." He took her hand and led her off toward a coffeehouse, moistening her palm. "It is a cup of many seasons."

So it was, and so was he: a taste of many seasons. So she told herself at night and over a week of daily walks, discovering the city with the spark of an explorer. John Summer was a gentleman—a toying, cavalier, insinuating gentleman—and although he met with numerous importers and river captains to arrange the northern delivery of merryweather tea, he was inclined to roam the streets entirely for pleasure. He and Molly walked to popular landmarks, lunched at various public houses, and followed the whims of curiosity and mood.

They dined on berry-smothered fowl and spoke of the Glacial Islands, which he told her were inhabited by turtles shelled with ice. They shared wine and soup of lamb's head at the Purple Lion, where Molly enjoyed the deference her Aquarian friend commanded. People glanced at them and nodded, seeing luxury not only from his spending, which was loose, but from their free-floating laughter and the halo of their ease. They visited the marketplace for popping-wet kumquats, sugary bananas, and phosphorescent pears. She talked about the waterbreath and bird crabs at sea. John knew both and relished her descriptions, seeming to doubt—with great amusement—her account of scaling the masts.

"Are you such a dauntless climber?"

"All my life," Molly said.

"I quail at any height. Sailors often taunt me."

She led him through the city to the church on Beacon Mount. The building stood alone on the outskirts of Grayport, white and salty gray upon a soft green hill. It was slender, long and plain with green-tinted windows and a fifty-foot steeple with a brass Star of Lumen. They went inside and Molly pulled him up the stairs toward the belfry, John cowering in a hunch but smiling, always smiling, with his slightly gapped teeth and round-hearted verve. The steeple seemed a good deal higher than it was, rising as it did upon the isolated hill with hay carts below, and a tiny fenced graveyard, and horses that appeared as small as dogs from such a height. Behind them spread the vast frontier's rolling trees, in front of them the city and the harbor and the sea. Molly leaned backward with her spine against the rail. The peak above the belfry rose another ten feet.

"I could climb and reach the star," she said, gazing up and swaying as the clouds moved beyond it.

John knelt, afraid to stand, and pulled her in toward the bell.

"I will have my revenge," he said. "What are you afraid of?"

"Restriction," Molly said.

He held her wrists and wouldn't release them. "You must say the secret word."

"What is it?" Molly asked.

"I cannot say."

"I cannot speak it, then."

She watched him as he knelt. His hands were tight as manacles. He couldn't bear the view and stared at her instead, looking up past her bosom to her face with concentration—playful brutishness, it seemed, or guarded desperation.

"Come now. Guess."

"No," Molly said.

"I won't let you go."

"Then we'll stay until the moonrise."

Wind snapped his sleeves and emphasized the height.

"I must devise another way to hold you," John said, releasing her and creeping down the stairs as Molly laughed at him. She rubbed her wrists and briefly grew dizzy from the height.

☙

"Are you showing him the city or the boundaries of the continent?" Nicholas asked irritably one evening, having spent the afternoon on her neglected translations.

"He is hopeless," Molly said. "It's miraculous he finds his way *here* every morning."

"A wonder Kofi Baa thinks so highly of him."

"You needn't be jealous."

"I am nothing of the sort," Nicholas told her. "But I cannot spare you much longer from your work. Shall I remind you how desperate we had become before our current situation?"

"We couldn't afford a spoon without Kofi's help. I should think whatever he asks of us, however inconvenient—"

"Yes, of course," Nicholas said with dubious conviction.

"He needs me one more day"—*Needs,* Molly thought—"and then he travels north to Kinship, eighty leagues away."

"I know where Kinship is."

On a map, out of reach. She saw the papers on her desk, a fort-night's worth of unfinished work: contracts, lists of regulations, correspondence. Translating, copying, interpreting, repeating. Nicholas's quill scratched itself dry. She felt the splitting of the nib, the speckling ink, the crinkling sheets—how flat and parched the future map of summer would become.

John had no additional business prior to his trip, and he and Molly spent the following day on a long, desultory amble through the city. The midmorning sun was painfully direct. Molly's neck began to burn. John was heavy and subdued. They came to a tavern called Pike's Salty Herring, crammed between houses and, with its dingy dark nooks and solitary drinkers, seeming cooler than the summer-bright street. Molly took a booth while John walked through to use the privy out back. She ordered a cider from the keep, a porcine man who rubbed his meaty knuckles.

"What'll your husband want?" he asked.

Molly flushed and said, "The same."

She sat in the booth, snugly shadowed, and watched as John returned and stopped to order at the bar.

"Your wife has beat you to it," said the keep. "Be just a moment."

"Thank you, Mrs. Summer," John said when he rejoined her.

The dark was not enough to hide her from his stare, nor cool enough to moderate the swelter in her clothes. Her toes were wriggly moist deep inside her shoes and Molly smelled herself, slippery and sweet as buttered onions.

They talked for nearly an hour till the cider fizzed her head, and then they left and walked the sultry half mile to his inn. Molly clasped his arm and told him she was faint. It wasn't a ruse. Colors shifted and her vision turned sparkly. John held her close but his voice seemed distant. The distortions didn't pass until he took her inside, sat her in a chair, and fanned her with a newspaper. The owner of the inn brought her rum and water. He offered to summon a doctor.

"No," Molly said. "It's nothing. Too much sun."

The drink revived her enough to stand. They thanked the owner for his care and John led her upstairs so she could rest, close her eyes, and thoroughly recover. It was a tiny room, softly green with ivy-patterned walls. There was a bed, a desk, and two packed trunks beneath a window.

John closed the door. She clapped her hands around his cheeks and kissed him on the mouth, clinging to his body like a warm wet leaf. He pushed her off but held her arms, rebuffing her but keeping her, his grimace so intense she might have called it murderous if not for how his eyelids flickered in alarm.

"He isn't my husband. He's my brother," Molly said. "His name is Nicholas."

It felt as if a sea breeze billowed through her ribs. She'd rarely talked of Nicholas, and John had rarely asked. He must have been suspicious but to say it out loud, in the light and with his cider-sweet flavor on her lips, felt as brash and oddly natural as taking off her clothes. His jaw hung agape. Then it closed. Then it flexed. He inhaled through his nose as if her voice were a fragrance and he wasn't yet sure if it was poisonous or clean.

He pulled her in slowly, dropped her arms, and caught her waist. Molly held his head again, thumbs behind his ears, and kissed him so deeply that he hummed through her tongue. She leaned away and gasped, surprised and out of air. It wasn't as she'd imagined it would be but rather slipperier, and messier, and firmer, and a great deal softer.

"I've wanted to kiss you since we met."

"I know," John said. "I thought of stealing you away."

"You can't."

"I could."

"I'm here," she said—a yes, a no, a compromise.

He backed her through the room, toward the bed against the wall: a little four-poster, uncurtained for the summer, making it appear both cozy and exposed. She leaned against the footboard, trying not to fall, but the board rose only to the bottoms of her thighs and Molly tilted till she reached out and caught him round the hips. He said, "I've found what you're afraid of."

"I'm not afraid of Nicholas."

"That isn't what I meant."

He held her breasts through her stays. She liked the way they flattened and expanded in his palms.

"I don't know what to do."

"Play along," John said.

He took his waistcoat and shirt off. Molly touched his chest. She couldn't feel his heart but she imagined it, enormous. He had mossy black hair around his wide, dark nipples and she wished it weren't there; she couldn't say why. He was skinnier and smoother than he'd seemed fully dressed, which made her think of sticks with the bark peeled away.

"I'll take my clothes off," she said, proud to get it right, embarrassed to be talking but incapable of stopping. She hopped to get her shoes off, blinded by her hair, and struggled with her stomacher, pricking her fingertip and saying, "Oh, these stupid pins."

He turned her at the bed and unlaced her stays. They had such a clumsy time of diligently undressing her, she didn't feel naked till she turned back around, wearing nothing but her stockings, and hugged him both to cover up and give herself away. She rubbed her face around his collarbone, mashing up her nose. She nudged him back and tugged his breeches down, and with it his erection, causing it to pop back up when it was free. Molly laughed. He sucked her breasts, first one and then the other.

"Hmm," she said, gazing at the heat-blurred room.

A cloud of sunny motes swirled around her head. She arched back and tried to keep stable on the mattress but her hands kept sinking and her feet began to slip. The awkwardness distracted her. She worried he would notice but was irritated, too, because he wouldn't help support her.

"Wait," Molly said.

She righted herself and sat. Her bareness on the counterpane delighted her anew, reminding her of dressing in her room when she was little, when her nakedness was simple—something glorious and fun. She rolled her stockings off, dropped them on the floor, and raised her eyes. John's erection stood before her, inches from her nose. She'd never examined one before—its veins, its lurid strangeness—and she leaned in close until her breath moved the hairs. His balls were light and solid when she held them in her hand.

"One's bigger than the other," Molly said, full of wonder.

She made a fist around his penis and began to move the skin. A tiny drop of fluid glistened at the tip. She thought of Mr. Fen's clammy member in the hammock, but she didn't let go when John kissed her mouth again, laid her on the bed, and knelt between her thighs.

He drove his forearms down on either side of Molly's ribcage, knuckles at her armpits, hovering above. She raised her knees and let her legs fall wider when he settled. He was heavy, also taller, with his stubble on her brow. His spine was slightly crooked when she hugged him round the back. He lowered his face and kissed her as he poked around below, aiming with his hips until he pushed himself in.

It didn't want to fit. Suddenly it did. She bit his lip and made him bleed, less from pain than from surprise. He tried to look impassive but the bite had clearly hurt. Her own pain was closer to a throb than a sting, feeling like a bruise that would tenderize later. The bed was too petite; she bumped the wall stretching back. When she moved her face forward so her chin was at his neck, their temples clunked together.

"Sorry!" Molly said.

He thrust and hit a spot, very deep, that made her pelvis ring. She saw her own foot flopping in the air and watched his backside contracting and expanding, hard at work. She tried to pay attention—was he enjoying this? was she?—but there was too much to follow, too many jolts and flashes. It was close but oddly distant. She surrendered, then revived.

John finished quickly, spasming inside her with a bodywide clench. She was pleasantly relieved the experience was over and her inundated thoughts could finally get some air. He was leaden but alert. When his lungs swelled and emptied, Molly listened with a sigh. She rubbed his hair and saw his breeches still bunched around his ankles and he looked much younger than before, like a boy.

Molly sneezed. It startled both of them and shook them into laughter, and he peeled himself off and lay beside her, hip to hip. She felt the spill between her legs and touched it with her fingers.

"Don't be frightened of the blood," he said. "It's natural at first."

"I know. My brother explained . . . " She heard herself and paused. "I didn't have a mother or a governess to ask. Nicholas taught me things to warn me and prepare me."

"And your marriage?"

"It's a ruse. We're hiding from our father."

She listened to his heart, reassuringly alive, and curled against him with the sunlight falling on her knees. The sun was overhead, straight above the roof, and must have been reflecting off something outside. Another window, Molly thought. What if somebody had seen?

John didn't speak. He expected her to talk. The ivy-patterned walls seemed denser as she stared, and his muscles felt tighter than an octopus knot. She could tell him just enough, embroidering the lie. Instead she told him everything, as true as she remembered, till at last his body softened and he stroked her sweaty hair.

⚘

He escorted her home an hour after dark but stopped to let her walk the last stretch alone. To face Nicholas together would exacerbate the risk. Molly pulled him into a shadow for a kiss before she lost him—his plans could not be changed, he left for Kinship tomorrow—and he promised he would think of some solution and return. Molly wasn't sure. Having dallied with adultery, or something very like it in the weeks of his suspicions, he'd failed to act and finally let Molly take the lead. Had the reason been restraint, or had the jeopardy dissuaded him? And how did he view her now—as the artificial wife of a cunning young man whose fortunes, like his own, were bound to Kofi Baa? If their lies and misbehavior reached Kofi's ears . . . Molly's heart sank, imagining their patron's disappointment. All his trust, all their prospects would shrivel in the flame.

"Write," Molly said.

"I will," John assured her.

She drew him from the shadows but his face remained opaque. The nearest burning streetlamp was several doors away and even now, after making love twice and studying him for hours, she couldn't read his body language, couldn't guess his thoughts.

A final kiss and then he left, preoccupied and grave.

Molly found Nicholas waiting in the glum brown office. He sat behind the desk, trimming quills with a penknife, its silver looking fiery and keen beside a candle. His eyes had the same lively flicker as the blade.

She closed the door and felt exposed, as she had been with John Summer, and discovered the exposure made her liberated, strong. Dressed or undressed, fettered or released, she was whole within herself again, completely Molly Bell.

"You'll tell me you're in love and need your freedom," Nicholas said. "Can you tell what I will answer?"

His expression and his tone were pompously serene. There he sat, so certain he was privy to her secrets, and she hesitated, wondering how informed he truly was. His contacts and clients were dispersed throughout the city. Someone might have seen her, Mrs. Jacob Smith, entering the inn on the arm of John Summer and remaining there, cloistered in his room, until the dark.

"I don't care what you answer," Molly said.

"You do."

Nicholas pressed the penknife's blade against his lips, the way a man in contemplation might gesture with a finger. Molly held his gaze but swayed in her resolve. She used a table heaped with books as a low defensive wall, needing something more physical than insolence between them. Molly still viewed him as the brother of her memory, desperate in his privacy and quiet self-reliance. Yet he had aged beyond his years since arriving in the city. He was graying over the ears, hard to rile, hard to gauge, his authority as natural and tailored as a uniform.

"You're becoming like Father," Molly said.

His temple vein bulged. He lowered the knife as if his arm hadn't strength enough to hold it. Then his eyes met the challenge and replied:

I am better.

Molly clutched her hair until it made her think of John, how his hands had combed the strands, catching in the knots.

"I have far too many ties," he said, "to sever all connections, but in time—another year, perhaps—a simpler situation may be carefully arranged."

"A year!" Molly said. "I cannot bear another day!"

He paused and said, "I know," speaking with a mournful twinge that seemed—she may have imagined it—to show a little more than disappointment. Was it fear? "You would risk all we have—"

"Yes," she interrupted.

"—for your own selfish needs."

Her brother said it crisply and she bristled at the words. She stood behind the books and leaned against a stack of them. They formed a kind of stairway, threatening to fall.

"I do as I am told and sit and die of boredom while you jaunt wherever you please, doing God knows what, and what is my reward? A window to the street! My brother as a husband! Is it selfish to be happy, selfish to be free? I'd have loved John Summer if he leeched me and abused me, long as I was anywhere but suffocating here. Don't you see?" Molly asked. "I would sooner leave Grayport than scratch another letter. I would rather board a ship and sail back to Umber."

Nicholas twirled the penknife slowly in his fingers till he grasped it by the middle of the blade, as if to throw it.

"Don't be childish," she said. "Am I supposed to be afraid?"

She was poised when she said it but a feeling came upon her, one of distances expanding, like a long fall of night. Frances and her father, infinitely far. John Summer, less than one mile off, soon to leave. Even the little office opened like a gulf until it seemed they ought to shout to make themselves heard.

Nicholas threw the knife with a deftly snapped wrist. Molly moved aside. It hit the beam between the window frames and wedged in the grain. Molly felt the air disappearing from her lungs. He had honed it—she could see the extra brightness of the edge.

"You might have killed me," Molly gasped.

"I was certain you would move."

"Were you certain of your aim?"

"More than anything," he said.

He walked around the desk and met her near the table, righting the stack of books she had tilted out of place. She picked up a volume— *The Rudiments of Bruntish Grammar*—and considered thumping his head, but when he reached toward the knife, Molly reached for it, too. Her hand covered his own. The blade remained stuck and they were posed, close together, like a married couple standing at the window of their home.

Nicholas turned to face her. "What does John know?"

"He knows I'm miserable and wish to get away," Molly said, hoping that her words would distract him from the dodge.

He had a way of going dead-eyed, lost in concentration, and of instantly reviving when it came time to speak. "I erred," he said, "when we met Kofi Baa. I should have told him we were siblings."

"Wouldn't he understand if we explained ourselves now?"

"He might. He has a kindness in him, near to gullibility. If not for his success, I would think him too naïve. But Kofi himself is not the main concern. In the work from which I've shielded you—oftentimes to guard you—I have made certain enemies."

"Who?" Molly asked, letting go of the knife.

Nicholas tugged it out. "People worse than Kofi. They would thrill to see me scandal-bound or suddenly exposed. I have also made allies who take me at my word. Think if such persons learned our parentage and past."

"We could still keep the secret of our father either way. Must we play at being married?"

"One lie supports another."

"John is coming back," she said.

"When?"

"I don't know."

"Let him go," Nicholas told her. "I will give you greater leave. Don't defy me just now—consider it, at least. You said it isn't John but freedom you desire. This is a dangerous point for both of us, more than you can know. Hold fast awhile longer. It would shatter me to lose you."

Nicholas handed her the knife. She looked to where it had stuck and couldn't find the mark. The cut was either shaded or miraculously healed. Molly shaved a fine wooden coil off the window frame.

"What if it's John himself instead of freedom I desire?"

"We will see when he returns," Nicholas replied.

☙

She hadn't bled in three months. More intuitively, she sensed it, and she didn't need a doctor or a kick to make it real.

Molly had written to John Summer once a week since he left. At first he'd written back. He missed her and was hoping to return with some solution, but he had met with complications, opportunities, delays. His letters came sporadically. She couldn't use Nicholas's couriers, so they kept their correspondence through the ordinary channels, which were slow and indirect and largely unreliable. The distant town of Kinship lacked a formal post office; Molly sent her letters to a tavern called the Hook where they sat, perhaps for days, until he went to pick them up.

She had finally sent the news—she was pregnant, no mistake—and since he hadn't written back in thirteen days, she had no way of knowing if her letter had arrived. Silence was the worst of all replies: a strangulation. She imagined telling Nicholas, or dying like her mother, or surviving with an infant. Would they move? Would they stay? She thought of how it had felt losing her virginity, squeezing him inside until the break made her bleed, and now a whole head and body were expected to emerge. She found herself attuned to every passing infant, admiring their delicacy and sizing up their skulls.

Late at night, she'd lie in bed and smell the chill of early autumn as the crisp brown leaves blew against her window. She'd pray for John's reply and gently rub her belly. Oh, to think of it! The eyes and ears growing in the dark, the miniature heart like a rare, perfect berry. She longed to hum a lullaby but Nicholas would hear, and so she tried to think of sunlight and laughter and relief, of the view atop the *Cleaver* and the bell of Beacon Mount, hoping her emotions were umbilically connected and the comfort she was summoning would nourish them together.

One morning in mid-October, Molly woke to find ice-flowered windows in her room. The sun was cold and white. She had overslept the dawn and Nicholas hadn't woken her, a thing so doubly strange she took it as an omen and hesitated to leave the safety of her blankets. The city's early noise made the house too quiet. She wondered if her baby felt the same inside her womb, sensing all the world's movement and desiring to join it, striving to be out regardless of the risk.

She rose, tight with cold, and dressed in slippers and a robe. The fire wasn't lit and she could almost see her breath. Halfway down the stairs, heat began to rise. She could tell there was someone in the parlor with her brother, and she paused in the darkness at the bottom near the door. They had heard her coming down and stopped their conversation. She considered going back and getting properly dressed but then it seemed as if her baby, with its own strong will, put her hand upon the knob and moved her into the parlor.

Sun dispelled the gloom and there was Nicholas, strictly seated, with the wintry hard expression he had shown to Mr. Fen.

John Summer stood to meet her in a fine green coat. He smiled and his buttons, warm gold, winked and shone. There was fire, there was warmth—there was John come to save her. Molly's baby seemed to gain a new buoyancy within her, and her feet left the floor when he crossed the room and hugged her.

He put her down and held her waist, thumbs around her navel.

Molly wiped her eyes and said, "I thought you'd gone forever."

"So did I," Nicholas said.

John's hands felt wooden through the wrinkles of her shift. They faced Nicholas like a pair of young lovers with a parent.

"Now that all four of us are present," Nicholas said, "we should formulate a practical solution to our crisis. First and foremost, however, I will say congratulations."

The word's warmth, so at odds with the coldness of his voice, left her brittle when he stood and offered her a hand. She took it automatically. He led her to a chair. John held her other hand and followed close behind her and the men seemed prepared to pull her limb from limb.

The three of them sat together, equidistant in their chairs but angled so it seemed that Nicholas was separate. Between them stood a round mahogany table on a rug. Upon it were an oil lamp, paper, and an inkwell. The parlor was a compact, low-ceilinged square with the walls dark red above the ivory-painted wainscot. Countless conversations had occurred here in private. Molly sensed it in the hissing of the logs, like a whisper. It was Nicholas's room, Nicholas's air.

She looked at John Summer, disbelieving he was real. He returned a look of kindness, and apology, and strength.

He said, "I've told your brother everything."

He didn't mean it literally but Molly felt disrobed. She hugged herself and lowered her head, trying not to flush. She felt as if Nicholas had witnessed her and John making love and could observe, as through a windowpane, the baby in her womb.

"I mean to marry you and take you to Kinship," John said. He quickly added, "If you'll have me, poor and faulty as I am."

Molly didn't see her brother roll his eyes, but sensing he had done so dampened the proposal.

"It's far enough to keep us free of scandal," John continued.

"What will happen," Nicholas asked, "when someone who knows us travels north and finds you living with the lovely Mrs. Smith?"

"I will keep her out of sight."

"Like a mistress or a whore?"

John stood and scraped the chair, violently erect. "It was you, was it not, who conceived the false marriage?"

"A necessary ruse."

"Did you really think your sister would be bound to you forever?"

"Evidently not," Nicholas replied.

Was it injury or shame that marred her brother's countenance? His features fell, softening his eyes to leave them fuller, and his cheekbones lengthened, and his brows seemed to frown. He was plain as any page she'd ever had to translate but written in a dialect she didn't understand.

"The three of us could move wherever we like," Molly said.

"My work is here," Nicholas said.

"And mine is north," John agreed.

Nicholas crossed his legs and locked his fingers over his knee. He turned to Molly and said, "You needn't wrestle with the choice between your brother and your lover. You chose many weeks ago. Nature saw it through. You and John must go. I will stay here in Grayport."

For weeks, Molly had tried to think of practical solutions. Uncle Nicholas. Her brother and her lover at her side, with the baby, starting over in an unfamiliar home. Impossible, impossible. She had to go with John. But he was virtually a stranger, much as she adored him, and to live without Nicholas, her brother and her mirror—it was almost too foreign and unthinkable to stomach.

"Your absence will be noted," Nicholas reminded her. "I'll say that you are caring for a relative in need. A sister with paralysis, perhaps, or sudden blindness. But Kinship is far too near," he said to John. "You will have to take her farther to the north or overseas."

John bridled at the order, sitting down but leaning forward. He mastered his distress and said, "I've spent the last three months establishing my livelihood."

"A season," Nicholas said. "Scarcely time to grow a fetus. You will sever ties with Kofi—"

"Kofi Baa will know the truth."

"And he would probably embrace you. But everything I have is built upon trust. Would you scar the reputation of your new wife's brother? Molly," Nicholas said. "Would you willingly destroy me?"

Molly gripped an armrest, fighting down nausea.

"Kofi cannot know," she said.

John remained stoically attentive to her brother but his eyelids sagged. "The man is like my father."

"*You* are now a father," Nicholas replied. "Take another three months and carve a niche where no one knows you."

John's thigh muscles flexed as if preparing for a lunge but he stayed within his seat. Nicholas turned to Molly. He was seated near the fire and his left cheek was pinker than the right. He leaned toward her.

"You'll be showing soon," he said. "I will take you from the city. We will stay in isolation through the autumn and into winter. As soon as John is settled, I will see you to his side."

He was tearful when he said it. Molly had rarely seen him cry, and though she trusted that he loved her and believed she had wounded him, she wondered whether the light was playing tricks with her eyes.

Chapter Twenty-Three

The plan proceeded as agreed, dissatisfying all. John Summer traveled by riverboat to Kinship, there to uproot himself again and extend whatever prospects remained to distant Burn, a glorified hamlet—nearly at the border of New Rouge—that was surrounded by a palisade to fend off wolves. It was to be Molly and John's frigid, permanent home in a matter of months, and in the interim Nicholas took her out of Grayport to a cabin in the north to await John's summons.

The isolated dwelling, rented from one of Nicholas's contacts in the city, was situated in the wilderness east of Kinship, accessible only by a pitiful road and, for the last ten miles, a fur trappers' path through the untamed forest. It stood in a leaf-strewn clearing near a gorge with a creek. Thirty feet long and fifteen wide, the log cabin was a single story with a peaked roof, a door and window at the front, a stone chimney, and a crude puncheon floor. The room around the hearth comprised most of the interior. A loft along the back held Nicholas's bedding, and a dividing wall afforded Molly her own chilly space with a proper bed and—though the room's doorway had no door—a modicum of privacy. Still it seemed severe, even punitively spartan.

"Could we not have simply hidden in a well-furnished house?" Molly asked.

"We have everything we need," Nicholas replied.

This was not strictly true. Her brother had hired a man named

Edgar to carry their meager belongings and deliver supplies through-out the season. He had a grizzly black beard and the power of a bear but was short and compact: a miniature giant. Molly had failed to engage him in conversation on their way to the cabin, and he had left without a word as soon as he was able, under orders to return in two weeks' time.

After the early days of tidying and nesting, Molly had little to do but read in front of the hearth and watch her brother studying and writing at a table.

"Practice patience," Nicholas said, teaching by example as he answered her complaints. He dipped his quill and started a letter by the sunlit window. "Recall our conversation from this morning," he continued.

Heaven help me, Molly thought. *Was it only just this morning?*

"'Occupy my mind, and the hours take wing,'" she said, quoting his advice with overearnest pomp. She flapped her arms gracefully and walked around the cabin, gliding to his side before returning to her rocking chair, her twice-read books, her unchanged view of her unchanging brother with the leaves falling softly and eternally beyond him. Her mockery and flapping hadn't ruffled him at all.

At least her baby grew active as her womb began to swell, hiccup-ping and somersaulting, wonderfully alive. She noted every kick and dreamed of little heels. She made a long list of names she encountered in her books, hummed lullabies at night, and often read aloud.

She made her brother move his table to the middle of the room so she could sit beside the window, admiring the view. The weather was peculiar, captivating her and Nicholas alike with pale green sunsets, snow that seemed to pause and reascend before it settled, and tem-perature swings the likes of which she'd never known in Grayport or Umber. Nicholas said the continent was rife with strange phenomena, especially in the mountains and the Antler River Valley—a region even lifelong Florians considered mysterious—but no belly rolls or other-worldly storms could distract her from the fact that John had left her waiting.

Edgar came and went every two weeks. He delivered fresh sup-plies and kept Nicholas in contact with Grayport and Kinship, trudging through the snow once winter had arrived and speaking only to her brother in a baritone muffled by his beard. If she talked to him directly, he would pause and turn away.

"Have you told him to ignore me?" Molly asked when he was gone.

"He is terrified of women," Nicholas said. "There was a marriage, I am told, involving Edgar and a harridan—"

"I don't trust him. Are you certain he is checking every avenue of mail?"

"Edgar is reliable. Remember it is winter and the way to Burn is treacherous. It's likely John has written and the letter is delayed."

She sensed her brother had more to say—disparaging remarks on John's fidelity and character—but was keeping himself quiet so as not to start a row.

Wind whistled through the walls, challenging the fire. Both liveliness and deathliness inhabited the sound. She could linger indoors but the day called her out. She could venture outside but the cold would drive her in again. She sat in her chair and said, "I want to go to Kinship."

Nicholas dipped his quill and started writing at his table.

"What harm could it do?" she asked.

"We are supposed to be tending your bedridden sister. You can't be seen carrying an unwanted baby."

Even the baby seemed nettled by his words, kicking twice.

"Furthermore," he said, "snow has blocked the way."

"Edgar makes the trip."

"Edgar is not with child."

"Uh!" Molly said. "And I defended you when John thought little of your nerve."

He put down the quill and set aside the letter. She couldn't read the words but saw that he had quit mid-page, having made some mistake, and she was satisfied, at least, to have gotten some reaction. She read to quiet her thoughts but couldn't concentrate and laid the open book upon her stomach. Her rocking chair's creak went from grating, to hypnotic, to a rhythmic and incessant combination of the two. She felt the woods around the cabin, leagues of pine and lonesome white, and the creek still surging underneath the ice. Just today she had visited the nearby gorge, where the cold, hidden water made her think of Mr. Fen, his body long since devoured by the fishes and the crabs.

John Summer seemed as distant as a man beneath the sea, her love for him a thing turned watery and vague. What if his memory of her had similarly faded? But she didn't let him go; he was often in her thoughts, and she believed—as she believed in magic weather—he would summon her.

Molly felt a chill, turned to Nicholas again, and asked him to add a log to the fire. He stared at her and finally seemed to view her as a sister, not a person asking questions, not a burden at his side. He studied her belly with equal care and looked toward the hearth. The wood rack was empty near the feebly burning fire.

Nicholas retrieved a blanket from her bed and wrapped it around her shoulders. He walked outside without a coat, passed the window like a shadow in the wince-white snow, and returned with an armload of wood from the sheltered supply beside the cabin. The cold had shocked his lungs, and although he had remained healthy thus far, he trembled when he added a log and coughed with terrible force. He poured a cup of water from the kettle at the hearth, added a spoonful of tea, and placed it in her hands. It was merryweather tea, which she used to drink with John. The growing fire blew a shimmer of July across her cheek.

Nicholas stood above her with his back toward the window; the glare seemed to make him translucent at the edges. He knelt and put his palms very softly on her stomach. At moments like these, their life together bloomed and she remembered what a loss she would face when he was gone.

"I have sent Edgar north," he said, "to speak with John directly."

Molly's heart bumped up like a movement of the baby. "You have? Why didn't you tell me?"

"I thought it wrong to raise your hopes. You must be calm," he said. "Let me do the worrying for now."

She rocked and sipped her tea until the warmth reached her toes. The fire rose and Nicholas returned to writing letters. Molly watched the snow glitter gently past the window, regretting how distrustful she had been of Edgar and imagining his long, cruel journey in the cold. Then a draft from a chink curled around her ankles and she wondered why her brother hadn't wanted to raise her hopes.

⚓

In the final month of her pregnancy, when Molly's impatience, even unspoken, emanated such a constant vibration that Nicholas too seemed constantly distracted, Edgar returned after an absence of many weeks. He had fought through the snow with a monstrous horse and sledge, and he had only just dismounted and reached the cabin door—beard frozen stiff, cheeks flaky raw—when Molly rushed toward him and said, "Did you speak to John Summer?"

Nicholas blocked her way and raised a hand: *Give him room.*

Molly acquiesced with blustery reluctance, pacing the floor beside the doorway as Edgar, in his time, dropped a sack beside the table and returned outside to finish emptying the sledge. After the bread, meat, cheese, sugar, wine, vegetables, clothes, lamp oil, books, medicine, and sundry supplies were inside, he opened his coat and produced a sheaf of papers wrapped in oilcloth, spread it on the table, and handed Molly a wax-sealed letter addressed to her.

She snapped it from his hand and kissed his shaggy jowl. He tasted like a dog, like a dear beloved cur, and shrank away as if she might have venom on her lips.

"You saw him?" Molly said. "You spoke to him yourself?"

Edgar grunted in the negative.

"Then how did you get the letter?"

"'Twas delivered to a public house in Kinship," he said.

"Did you not go to Burn?"

He bit his gloves off and clawed the frozen mucus off his beard, and then he sniffed and cleared his throat and looked to Nicholas, ignoring her.

"Read it," Nicholas told her. "You have answers in your hand."

She did so at once, shivering from excitement and the repeatedly opened door, while Nicholas paid Edgar for his work, handed him a packet full of letters and instructions, and sent him off without a drink or even a minute by the fire. Molly was too distracted to regard Edgar leaving, and the horse and sledge were already disappearing into the woods before she thought to call him back. She was speechless and immobile.

"What news?" Nicholas asked.

The frigid winter air had met the swelter of the fire and her body felt both, as if afflicted by a fever. She might have fainted if the baby hadn't woken up inside her. The letter sagged open in her outstretched hand. She could barely hold it up. It might've weighed a hundred pounds.

Nicholas took the sheet and read it by the hearth. His shadow, long and warped, moved gently on the wall. She had memorized the letter as fast as she read it, hearing John's voice, and smelling his skin, and recognizing quirks in the style of his script: the undulating M's and overgrown I's.

> *Dear Molly,*
>
> *Forgive me. I write this heavy-hearted on the eve of my depar-ture overseas, embracing opportunities that failed, despite my efforts, to materialize in Burn. I cannot remain destitute in Flo-ria or gamble my advancement on the risk—and we would risk it all our lives—of someone recognizing you as Mrs. Smith from Grayport. I commend you to your brother's care and vow to send, when fortune allows, what money I can spare to you and your baby.*
>
> *I console myself believing that we never truly loved. A summer's dream, lost in fall. We were not meant to be.*
>
> > *Sincerely,*
> > *John*

She felt him moving off as if his hand had left her breast. Again the baby moved and John was with her, in her body. Was he right? Had she fooled herself in loving and believing? She had loved him as he'd been and yet the letter proved him other: not the kind John Sum-mer, not her own John Summer, but the real John Summer, who had panicked and betrayed her. She was pregnant from a figment—from a commonplace lie.

"I'll ruin him," Nicholas said, crumpling up the page.

He tossed it into the fire. Molly wanted to retrieve it—even now it seemed precious, like the petal of a dream—but her weight wouldn't let her and she settled in her chair. She watched the paper flare and curl. It feathered into ash. She wished she could have read it one last time and seen the angles of the words, the evidence of ink. There was something of the sender's own body in a letter. She had learned it when their father used to write them from the war, when the letters seemed a physical extension of his presence. Something in the memory would not leave her mind.

"Can he think we care a jot for his advancement?" Nicholas said.

He looked at her, apparently amazed at John's gall, but whatever he discovered in her face dulled his edges, and he came to her and held her, pulling her cheek against his shoulder, knowing not to speak or offer consolation. Molly stared across the room until a film blurred her eyes. She hugged her brother from the chair but he didn't feel solid. He was no more present in the room than John's words, as if by burning them he'd burned her last connections to the world.

She didn't speak the rest of the day. Nicholas kept the silence. He organized their newly arrived supplies and studied his own many letters. Molly neither read nor ate but sat in her chair, and looked out the window, and daydreamed and napped until dozing and waking scarcely seemed distinguishable. Snow fell, evening fell. Sun lit the woods in oranges and purples till the drifts turned gray, then pearly from the moon.

"We must agree on what to do," Nicholas said across the room.

Molly's skin felt glued to her unchanged clothes. "He's gone," she said, her voice like a disembodied whisper.

"The babe is half Aquarian, of caramel complexion. We cannot claim the child as our own," Nicholas said.

Molly stood. She locked her knees but her feet were numb and prickly. It seemed that all her blood had settled in her legs and now her heart, like a bilge pump, was struggling to move it. "We'll say that we adopted it."

"You wish to raise a child in a false marriage?"

"I wouldn't live at all in a false marriage!" Molly stomped across the room, grown heavy in her pregnancy and cradling her womb as she approached him in his chair. "You said it wouldn't last and we would move when we were ready. Surely we have means to live somewhere else. We'll try another city, another country—"

"Molly."

"We'll be brother and sister with a baby we adopted. Nobody will question us. Nobody will find us."

"No," he said firmly, standing up to meet her. "It is abominable the way John Summer has abandoned you, but I will not bear the burden, much as I adore you, and compromise our lives for the sake of an unnecessary weakness."

She cried to see him harden so but didn't wipe her eyes. "You call my baby an unnecessary weakness?"

"Is there any vulnerability greater than a child? A living, growing secret, one that might be turned against us. We would struggle for control and ultimately lose, just as I lost you when you and John set against me."

Dense snow creaked the roof, bearing down above them, and another gusty snowfall blacked out the moon. There would be no getting out for at least another week—maybe longer, given the drifts and Molly's low, heavy carriage. Simply standing hurt her back. Self-support made her wobble.

"I'll go alone," she said.

"A new mother with a bastard at your breast. How would you live? You could not hold employment with your days so encumbered. Even if you could, would you call yourself free? Would it not be far worse than what we had in Grayport, a life you couldn't tolerate—a life you called a prison? We are young and have the whole map of years spread before us. We are all we have left and no one else will help us. Remember when I gave you this," he said, raising a pinky to his chipped front tooth. "Father tried dividing us. So did John Summer. The baby is a wedge driving us apart. But together," Nicholas said, "we're the strongest people in the world."

He held her hands and finished with a sentimental sigh but the words felt old, like the fragment of tooth in her locket—something from the past that didn't link them anymore.

"But we haven't been together," Molly said, dead cold. "You've told me what to do and held me at a distance, ignoring all my questions and denying me a voice. Were you really so astonished when I finally defied you?"

"Precisely," Nicholas said. "Our disunity has hurt us. Now I wish to start again, repairing what is broken."

Molly shook her head.

He pleaded with his eyes. "We'll find the child a home. A loving family."

"No."

"We must."

"We won't be parted," Molly said, pulling away to hold her womb and showing him the meaning of the newborn *we*.

⌘

Their relations in the final weeks were taciturn and hostile, an intolerable situation in the snowbound cabin. She knew her labor was approaching—the baby had dropped extraordinarily low—and had asked her brother more than once to fetch a doctor. The way to Kinship had started to clear in a rush of warmer air, which had melted much of the snow and turned the nearby creek into a torrent, and although the muddy forest would be perilous for Molly, Nicholas could surely brave the trail to summon help.

He refused with little explanation, maybe fearing she would flee to save her baby once he left, or maybe intending—more cruelly than she had ever thought possible—to use her desperation as a final form of leverage.

"You would endanger me and the baby?"

"I wouldn't risk your safety on the trail," Nicholas said, "or leave you here alone in such a delicate condition. If the route becomes reliable, we may attempt to travel."

"And if not?" Molly asked.

"I prepared for all contingencies."

"How?"

"I read a book," he said.

We should have kept a horse, she thought, *or left the cabin sooner.*

Where was Edgar with his sledge? Why had Nicholas insisted on a place so remote? Was he really so prepared, and was she willing to believe it? *I will help if you surrender,* his demeanor seemed to say, *and then I will think of a solution. Otherwise, we stay.* But Molly would sooner give birth alone than sacrifice her baby, so they waited, far from aid, each hoping that the other would eventually relent.

Her nights felt surrounded by a wide, cold void. She would wake from fitful sleep, convinced the baby had died, and lie in mounting panic till the child moved within her. Nature seemed a threat: the downpouring rain, branches cracking in the wind. The creek filled the gorge; Nicholas checked it hourly to monitor the swell, fearing it would inundate the clearing and the cabin.

Molly was unprepared for labor but refused to ask questions, hoping to appear less helpless than she was. The act had killed her mother with an outpour of blood. She knew that many infants died—she herself, Frances had told her, had almost been strangled by the cord—and even if the two of them survived, what then?

The following week, her water broke. At first she thought it was urine. She was about to change her clothing in the cabin's private room when a powerful contraction made her brace against the wall. A cramp seized her back. She stooped but didn't sit. It was morning, but her bedroom didn't have a window and she turned toward the doorway, looking for the light.

"Nicholas," she said.

He walked to her at once, spotless in a boiled white shirt and black breeches, looking doctorly and sharp, prepared to see it through. When the contraction passed, he laid out her sleeping gown and left her in the room, allowing her to change before returning with a candle and a clasped leather bag.

"That hurt," Molly said. "Does it get much worse?"

"Yes. Don't be scared."

He opened the bag and arranged forceps, medical shears, and several unfamiliar instruments on a small table at the foot of the bed.

"Did you really read a book?"

"Twice," Nicholas said.

"Nnn," she said, moaning from a second, worse contraction. She lay across the bed, head dangling off the side, while the muscles in her back and lower belly twisted fiercely.

"Another so soon?" he asked. "Impetuous as ever."

The ceiling blurred and bowed until the tightening relaxed. Nicholas had a mortar and a pair of tiny bottles. He measured seven drops of blue and five of crimson into a glass of boiling water, set the violet mixture to the side, and pulverized a shriveled gray leaf with a pestle. To this he added a pinch of white powder from an envelope, stirred it into the water, and strained the finished liquid into a cup.

"What is it?" Molly asked, slowly sitting up.

"For the pain," Nicholas said and placed it in her hands.

The smell alone was soothing, like the first air of spring. It wasn't the first concoction he had given her over the years and yet she hesitated, looking at his face—the fine black whiskers on his jaw, his blank expression—so intensely that he seemed both familiar and unknown. Steam wet her chin. Rain beat the roof.

"It stormed when I was born," she said.

"I won't let you die."

"How can you be so comforting and frightening together?"

"Love," Nicholas said.

She trusted him and drank. He took the cup when she was finished, held her hand, and smiled sadly. Molly listened to the rain until the sound of it engulfed her.

⚜

What did she remember of the delirium that followed? Nicholas's potion didn't quell the pain. It divided her in halves, one feeling, one observing, neither part entirely in tune with what was happening. She spoke to him and cried but she didn't hear the sound. At other times her voice seemed to echo in the cabin and she wondered who had spoken, wondered who had screamed. Her contractions deepened and quickened, the ebb and flow rising to a long, full tide, as constant as a weight bearing down upon her. Then the weight swelled out instead of pressing in.

The room fell dark. She saw a lantern overhead, or maybe she was sideways and looking at a table. Nicholas was near; Nicholas was gone.

For a while she herself disappeared, mind and body, and she only felt the baby growing larger on the bed. It seemed as if her navel had been tugged through her back and she was inside out with the child all around her. Then a vision of her knees, raised and parted far below, and Nicholas's face in the gap between her thighs. She had the horrible impression she was giving birth to *him* until her eyes dropped back and rolled around the dark.

She slept when it was over, paralyzed and cold. Under the rumble in her heart was the rumble of the creek. She was certain that the cabin had been taken by the flood. Molly felt the bed sway quietly beneath her and her body felt buoyant, hollow as a bubble. Deeper than the water and her thoughts, there was loss. It made her want to sink and let it swallow her forever.

☘

Molly woke in bed. The night was soft and windless. Her sleeping gown and blanket smelled fresh—newly aired—and an inkling of moonlight clarified her door. All that made sound was the creek beyond the clearing, brooding and continuous and felt as much as heard. Warmer air beyond the room brought a fragrance of renewal: vegetation, healthy mud. She was sore through her bones but her body felt smooth.

She couldn't tell how many days and nights had passed, how many memories were genuine or totally imagined. When she moved her hands instinctively to feel her round belly, it was as flat as if her whole lower half had been removed.

Worse. She was empty. She was boundlessly alone. She jolted up with sickening ease and pulled her gown above her hips, examining her waist, where the skin felt loose and her navel had retreated. Her breasts remained swollen and were leaking through her gown. Her baby wasn't there, in the room or in the cabin. She could feel the loss as surely as she felt it in her body.

Molly slid her feet off the corner of the bed. The floor was colder than the air, still chilled by the winter-long shade beneath the boards. She took her time getting up and gathering her balance. It was odd to see the room from an ordinary height. She had lost so much weight, such a terrible amount, she moved as if afloat into the cabin's central room.

A fire burned low, mostly embers left aflutter. Their belongings were arranged in crates and bags along the wall. Nicholas's table had been moved beside the window. On its surface lay a quill, sheets of paper, and a gun.

It was the pistol she and Nicholas had brought when they escaped. No ammunition bag or powder, only the ramrod beside it. The moon drew a thin, glinting line along the barrel.

When she went to the table and looked out the window, Nicholas was standing at the edge of the clearing. He was fifty yards away with his back toward the cabin, gazing at the gorge where the creek was so high that it surrounded him with puffs of illuminated mist.

Maybe the gun was empty. Molly picked it up. She fit the ramrod inside, just as Nicholas had taught her, and determined that the gun was loaded with a ball. She twisted in and listened for the faint grind of powder, put the ramrod down, and took the pistol outside.

Nicholas wore a white silk shirt and black waistcoat. He didn't move as Molly approached, though he must have heard the suction of her steps in the mud. Gray-green pines ringed the borders of the clearing with the cabin far behind her and the torrent dead ahead. Grass had yet to grow but there was sodden, bubbling moss. The night felt luxuriously warm through her gown, at least until the creek mist wafted up around her. It had wet her brother's hair and now it wet her face. She stopped and stood behind him, terribly awake.

"You had a daughter," Nicholas said.

He turned and looked calmly at the muzzle of the gun. His skin was pearly in the moonlight. It lent his face the beauty of a nocturnal flower, one designed for poisoning whatever it could lure.

"My baby—"

"You were hemorrhaging," he said. "You don't remember."

Molly gripped the gun to fight the tremor in her hand.

"I kept you both alive," he said. "You held her and you nursed her."

"No."

"You called her Cora."

She had considered the name for weeks but Nicholas hadn't known.

It must be true, Molly thought—he must have heard her speak it—but she had no memory of looking at her daughter. Was it possible she'd held her and entirely forgotten?

"Where—"

"I did my utmost." He pivoted his heel and scrutinized her face. "A doctor would have been as powerless to help."

Molly kept her distance, stepping sideways as Nicholas moved around her in a circle, and reversed their two positions till the creek was at her back. She raised the gun deliberately and aimed through her tears.

"Nature may be swayed or briefly hindered," Nicholas said. "In the end it has its way, resolute as God."

"Where is she?"

"Molly."

"What did you do?"

Nicholas moved toward her. She retreated with surprise in the cool slick mud until her feet reached the limit of the ground beside the gorge. Vapor swirled around her from the water just below.

"Where's my daughter?"

Nicholas answered but she couldn't hear the word.

"Where's my baby?" Molly yelled.

"Gone," he said again.

The roar filled her ears, the spray obscured the cabin, and the trees on either side made the clearing like a chasm. She was plunging in the dark. Dark plunged within her. Nicholas continued moving closer to the gun.

"You planned it," Molly said. "You forged the letter and you trapped me here. What did you do to John?"

"Molly, stop."

"You killed my baby."

"Don't move," Nicholas said.

He slowly reached toward her and she fully cocked the gun. For a moment, Molly wondered if her thoughts were mere delirium, if everything he'd told her of his efforts, and her bleeding, and the baby at her breast was the truth and not a lie. But the pistol and the bullet couldn't be denied.

"Was this for me?" she asked. "You'd take me back to Grayport or shoot me?"

"Molly, please. Don't—"

She fired.

Through the billow, as the kickback knocked her off the edge, she saw the bullet make a ripple in his shirt, near his heart. He was dead before his face ever registered the shot.

Molly fell and hit the water. Night exploded in the splash. She swatted at the surface but the creek rolled her under and the noise, the sound of everything alive, disappeared. Cold crushed her, and her skin shrank tight around her bones.

She didn't know if she was sinking. She was moving. She was gone. She didn't try to breathe but let the agony embrace her. Dizzy and alone, she waited for the end.

Cora, Molly thought, seeing colors in the dark.

The colors terrified her, causing her to kick and try to swim. The water dipped and corkscrewed, twisting up her gown. She did her best to right herself and fought the urge to gasp until at last she cleared the surface, coughing but alive. The air sent vivifying tingles through her veins, but she was tired and the cold drained the spirit from her arms. The current was increasing as it barreled down a slope. She caught a branch half-mired in the mud along the shore, but her weight tugged it free. She held it for support.

The creek opened wide and seemed to spill across a plain. The current pulled her sideways. The branch kept her up. She briefly felt the ground, firm enough to stand upon, but suddenly the water churned downward like a mudslide and Molly and the branch flowed toward a river. It was calmer in appearance, oddly white beneath the moon, massive and engorged and strewn with tiny flowers.

Molly held tight. The river took control. She imagined it would take her to the sea unopposed, and parts of her desired that, and others stayed afloat.

Chapter Twenty-Four

*A*nd then *I found her,* Tom thought, *unbelievably alive.*

He'd distrusted her for months, but this was something new. The story she'd related and the plainness of the telling, all the facts lining up with terrible precision—she was either being honest and entrusting him with everything, or lying so atrociously he couldn't bear to think it. She was General Bell's daughter. She had shot her own brother. He believed it, every word, in spite of every reason not to.

The vision of her clinging to the branch wouldn't leave him so he followed it back, reversing course up the Antler, trying to think of where a creek might have merged with the river. She must have floated for hours, if she had started near Kinship, in water so cold it had weakened him in minutes. But if anything was surer than her talent for disaster, it was her lightning-proof, powder-charged talent for escape.

She'd told the story start to finish with enough vivid detail that Tom was left to focus most keenly on the gaps. She had described John Summer and their private conversations but had naturally withheld specifics of their intimacy. He pictured them together: Molly's mouth pressed to John's, Molly's breasts, Molly's hips. Once he started, it was difficult to stop. Molly's knees.

She'd described her brother's looks but not their physical resemblance. She had General's Bell's nose—did Nicholas, as well? Tom was led against his will to visualize the child, little Cora, like a newborn

Molly, light as fleece. What had taken her? The potion, or the waters of the creek?

He thought of the gun in Molly's hand and wished he could have fired it.

"You're sure your brother is dead?" he asked.

"Yes."

"He might have lived. I was shot—"

"I didn't miss," Molly said. "I shot him in the heart."

She focused on a mouse hole opposite the bed, a crevice at the bottom of the wall near the corner. She'd been looking at the hole when there was light enough to see it. Now the twilight hues had hidden it from sight and still Molly stared, disconcertingly immobile. He could just see her face outlined beside him. If she breathed, he couldn't hear it.

"What of John Summer?"

Molly shook her head in weary resignation. "Nicholas drowned a man for threatening us. He must have killed John."

"Your baby," Tom said, catching on the words. He blotted out the thought of tiny feet, tiny fingers.

"He knew that I would never let her go," Molly said. "There was only one way. He thought I might believe him."

Tom considered other questions, other challenges and hopes, but what would truly help her now that everything was final? Still he wanted, for himself, to cut the blackest parts away.

"Cora," Molly said. "I don't remember touching her. I loved her more than anyone and never even saw her."

Tom held her as she cried, curling her toward him with an arm around her waist and his other hand soft upon her hair. He felt her ear. Her face was at his chest, dampening his shirt. She hugged him forcefully and painfully, her fingertips digging at the ribs around his back. He lost his balance, pulled her down, and lay with her beside him while her teeth, bared to sob, pressed against his collarbone.

She clawed at him and seemed afraid of slipping from his side, and not since the morning he had caught her in the river did it seem so imperative to keep her in his grasp. He wished that he could quiet her by swallowing her sounds and worried that her crying could be heard throughout the tavern.

Molly's forehead and nose smudged around his lips. He tasted salt and felt her mouth gasping open on his cheek. He hoped she wouldn't roll and notice his arousal. He did everything to weaken it, remembering her story's bleakest moments as he hugged her, but her voice came through, pink and sweet within her sobs, and she was emanating heat and pressing with her bosom. They clung with sweaty clothes, and loss and reassurance, and the dark made the ceiling and the bed disappear. They were rhythmically together and he held her till she calmed.

When she finally collapsed and he believed she was sleeping, Tom listened to her breathe. Her nose whistled faintly and her chest fell and rose. He thought about her lungs and all the hidden parts within her. His skin was so moist and his muscles so drained it felt as if he, instead of Molly, had survived a bout of weeping. After thinking through her story many times out of order, he was vibrantly awake and felt the night sprawl around him. She had curled up fetal in the dark, very small, and when he tried to kiss her forehead, he missed and got her eye. She stirred but didn't wake. He could have lain with her for hours.

Instead he went to the door and left her in the room. The air was fresher downstairs, surprisingly so until he remembered the gaping hole in the storeroom wall. Ichabod had blocked it up with crates, more or less, but Tom had never left the tavern so exposed after dark. Otherwise the place was tight and everything was still.

Bess and Ichabod had closed up early in his absence and retired upstairs. Nabby opened her door.

"Me," Tom whispered.

She retreated into her room like a spider to its cranny.

Tom unlocked the bar, poured a generous cup of rum, and wondered whether anyone—Nabby, Bess, the others—knew that he and Molly had been secretly together on his bed. What would Abigail think? What would Pitt really learn, riding out tomorrow for the traveler from Liberty? He'd learn she had a husband and believe it to be true. Plus the traveler had seen her and would likely tell others. People might come looking after the curious disappearance of the Smiths and John Summer, and no amount of reasoned explanation would suffice. Molly was a liar and a runaway. The daughter of General Bell. Pregnant out of wedlock, her baby dead and missing. Someone must have come upon Nicholas's body and it was likely she was wanted by authorities already. Now that Tom knew, he was harboring a fugitive.

He quaffed his rum and locked the bar. He didn't know what to do.

Boards creaked above him: Molly coming down. She had her own distinct sound as she moved through the tavern, more gingerly than Bess and less blundering than Ichabod. A slice of moon had risen, lighting her faintly when she entered. She was badly disarrayed: skirts crumpled, shoulders narrowing, hair on one side flattened to her head while the other side moved, staticky and mussed.

He went to her—he didn't know a soul he needed more—and kissed her so hard the force hurt his chin. Molly arched back, mumbling in his mouth. He caught her round the waist and took her struggles for excitement till she bit him on the tongue, shoved him off, and gasped for air. His rum was on her breath. He felt it in his blood and her refusal left him reeling off balance like a drunk.

She seemed about to speak. Tom turned and walked away, through the kitchen to the yard, seeing items he had cared about as long as he remembered: chairs, cups, an ancient piece of antler on the wall.

He hurried out back and stood beside the garden. Hummingbats fluttered, sipping nectar from the crescent-shaped flowers of the moon tree. The river flowed gently past the town and out of sight, and Tom imagined how it started in the mountains up north—just a trickle from a peak beyond Kinship and Burn, growing wider as it snaked down the Antler River Valley, bringing flowers in the spring and pickfish in winter, flowing past the smoakwood and Dunderakwa Falls and finally spilling open into the broad Eccentric Ocean.

Something in the air reminded him of deadfall. Benjamin was right. It was coming any day—first the killing cold, then a week or two of quicksummer, leading to another long, abominable winter. He wasn't yet prepared with firewood or brewing, and the Orange wasn't ready, and he didn't even care. He missed his mother and the doldrums of the last three years, and the warm, pressed darkness in his room upstairs.

Molly followed him out. He turned around to meet her and she hugged him on the spin. His ankles tripped and down they went together, face-to-face. He landed on his back and Molly was astride him, and she kissed him with ferocity and fervor and saliva. He couldn't talk her off because he couldn't draw a breath, and so he lay and let her maul him, stunned with suffocation. When he finally got some air, he kissed her back and hiked her skirts. He heard a rip and pawed her thighs, grabbed her bottom, spread it open. Molly's hair was in their mouths. Their noses squished and bent. She forced her hands between their hips and opened up his breeches. When she tugged them down his legs, she knuckled one of his balls, and though it hurt him like a punch, he didn't mind—he almost liked it. She surprised him when she slipped him in, settling her weight. He had grit beneath his head and roots along his spine.

Tom slid his hands up her back, beneath her shift. Molly concentrated, seeming uncertain of her balance till she planted both knees and hooked her feet inside his calves. He helped her with the motion and she found a steady rhythm. Goddamn it if he didn't get a glimpse of John Summer, but he put it from his mind, far as it would go. She had twiggy little legs and childlike fingers but her strength overpowered him, her willfulness disabled him. Her moans had the sound if not the melody of mourning doves, soothing and adorable and anything but sad. He had missed this, too, more than he had realized or wanted to admit. Good God, he'd thought her *hands* were warm.

Molly closed her eyes, raised her head, and didn't breathe, face covered by her hair, palms pressing on his lungs. She was moving with intention and he watched her, full of wonder, hoping—almost praying—Nabby was asleep.

Molly rippled and contracted, panting out and going still. Tom was close, any second now. *Don't*, he thought. *Do.*

She opened her eyes and spotted something in the distance that alarmed her. Tom arched back and craned his neck to see. Even upside down, the figure was familiar: Lem Carver clomping off and disappearing into the trees.

⚘

Molly dreamt of the frigid river and woke at dawn, alone in her bed, to air so cold she leapt up straight, afraid that she was pregnant in the snowbound cabin. The windowpanes and rafters creaked, suffering contraction. Her breath was white. She looked around, goosefleshed and sore, and tried to make sense of the extraordinary change.

Deadfall had come: the brutal end of summer. People had spoken of it often but the talk had not prepared her, and her spirit, like the tavern, shrank inside the cold. Molly went downstairs, where the air was even crueler. Her muscles hurt. Her stomach griped. She hadn't eaten since the previous afternoon, and everything—the cannon, her confession, Tom and Lem—made her jittery and queasy, unfit to meet the day.

There were candles in the windows—a ritual of deadfall, believed to keep the cold-weather evil from a home. The practice had charmed her when she learned of it, in summer. Now it didn't. Molly watched the flames and looked beyond them out the window, chilled to think of forces pressing on the glass.

The central hearth was feebly lit and didn't heat the taproom. She hurried to the kitchen, where the cooking fire blazed and the smell of fresh bread, boiled smoak, and bacon soothed her appetite for comfort, then increased it. Nabby went about her work, undaunted by the weather. She was livelier than normal, quicker with a knife, her wrinkled face glowing like a well-blown coal. The season of endurance and confinement seemed to suit her.

Bess came out of the pantry with a huge sack of flour. She was breathy from the strain and powdered from the sack, and she looked at Molly with a bright-lit, curious expression.

"I wondered when the cold would finally wake you up."

She laid the flour on the table next to Nabby, wiped her hands, and tucked a loose lock of hair behind her ear. Nabby hummed. It was almost like a song; it was very nearly cheerful. Bulbous vegetables and berries, chickens, herbs, and cheeses covered the tables in profusion:

they would feast against the freeze. The color and variety were painful to behold. Molly longed to spend the day with Bess and Nabby in
the kitchen, safe beside the fire, cozying the home.

"Where's Tom?" she asked Bess.

"Boarding up the storeroom wall, mad as guns. The inner door's
blocked with crates he had to move. Oh, but take a coat!" she said
when Molly crossed the room, opened the kitchen door, and walked
outside.

The air rushed her lungs and made her stop and cough. She'd
thought the tavern felt cold but this was shocking. This hurt.

"If you're going out back, fetch wood," Nabby said.

Molly shut the door, looked around, and blinked her eyes, which
were instantly alive with cold-struck tears. The temperature had
plunged well below freezing but there wasn't any breeze. Cold was
literally falling. She could feel it as a downpour, pooling on the ground.
Plants were dead but green, perfectly preserved, and a glitter made of
very fine ice filled the air. It moved in swirls and eddies and was gentle as a mist, but it prickled like pins into Molly's skin. She rubbed
her cheeks and hands and walked around the tavern, where the river
looked sluggish, flowing but subdued. The sky was low and bright, a
hard plate of cloud. Below, the world was dim as if the light were
trapped above it, and the shadows on the ground were subtle and translucent.

The cannon hole was grim, a maw with jagged edges that compelled her to approach. She walked toward it at an angle and was about
to look inside when Tom popped his head out. She swatted him reflex-
ively.

"Sorry!" Molly said.

He checked his nose for blood. "You say that a lot," Tom answered
through his hand.

She held herself and shivered, wishing she could hug him. Broken wall barred the way.

"Are you hurt?" she asked.

"I'm frozen to the ruddy fucking joints," Tom said, "and I'm a day
away from following my brother into the navy." He turned and laid
a board on wooden horses in the storeroom, picked up a saw, and faded

into the shade. "You get a hole at sea, at least your house has the decency to sink straightaway."

The rasping of the saw sounded personal and grave, more like cutting bone than ordinary wood. Another swirl of glitter frost-burned her cheek. Molly leaned into the hole and saw the wreckage from the blast—splinters, broken crates, the barrel of the cannon. Sawdust sprinkled like snow upon the floor where a puddle from an overturned jar had frozen black.

Tom finished with the board. The end clattered down and in the newfound lull, he looked at her and said, "What are you doing here?"

She didn't rightly know.

He tucked a hammer under his arm, clamped nails between his lips, and mumbled out of the corner of his mouth, "Give me a hand with this." He placed the cut board horizontally at the hole. Molly held it there as Tom nailed it up from inside. Many more were needed for a temporary fix, and yet the single board functioned as a barricade between them.

"Did Pitt ride out to look for Mr. Bole?" she asked.

"First thing this morning," Tom said. "Serves him right. His balls'll freeze hard as lead bullets on the saddle."

"What are we going to do?"

"Everyone's preoccupied with deadfall," he said. "Maybe Pitt will turn back. We'll have to wait and see."

He softened his expression, held her hand and gave it a squeeze, and then he turned to cut another length of board to cover the hole.

They spent the morning and much of midday securing the tavern, going about their work as ordinarily as possible while Nabby, Bess, and Ichabod pondered and observed, knowing there was something unusual between them. Molly stayed at Tom's side as much as she was able. They spoke but didn't laugh, traded weary glances, and behaved like a couple who'd been married so long that everything they did had a private implication.

In the late afternoon, they were putting away glasses in the taproom when Benjamin and a stranger walked through the door.

Benjamin wore a beaver cap and lightly frosted glasses, his slender frame lost inside a fur-collared coat. Behind him was a tall, slender man of roughly thirty who was handsome but for nostrils that were permanently flared.

"Tom," the man said, shaking hands and smiling broadly. He was as spirited and loose as Benjamin was grave.

Tom smiled back. "Davey Mun. It's been a year."

"Last September." Davey entered with an exaggerated sigh, no less genuine for being done with flair. He tugged off his gloves, approached the hearth, and looked at Molly. She was flattered—it was that kind of look. He said, "You're new."

"I'm Molly Smith," she said and shook his hand. His skin was snowy cold.

"The Orange's latest attraction," Tom said. "You should hear the way I found her. Davey here's a horse trader, one of the best in Floria. He tried to buy Bones last summer."

"Fairly offered."

"That's what Pitt keeps saying when he tries to buy the Orange."

Davey smiled once more except his heart wasn't in it. He turned to warm his hands, standing next to Molly. "Pitt's the man I came for. I'm told he's ridden off. Figures he would do it in the wrong damn direction."

"What's the need?" Tom asked.

"A man has been shot," Benjamin told him.

It was the first that he and Tom had acknowledged each other. Molly had been told about the prior day's tension—tension over her and finding Mr. Bole—and she had never known Benjamin to speak with such frigidity, nor Tom to view his friend with so little warmth.

"Who?" Tom said.

"We left Shepherd's Inn this morning," Davey said. "Me and four other men who rode together out of Grayport the day before. We didn't fear the Maimers, 'cause to hell with them, and all of us together gave us better odds. A little ways along, we heard a shot up the road and galloped off to see. We came around a bend and there were four of them on horseback. They'd shot a man and one of them was searching through his bags. We missed our own shots but chased the bastards off, and then the man they'd tried to kill was in the road, still alive. Two of our party took him back to Shepherd's Inn while me and the others rode here to get the doctor. They'll be coming along soon. I rode ahead the last few miles, straight for Benjamin."

"You're sure it was Maimers?" Tom asked.

"Black cloaks and masks."

"They've never shot a man before."

"The fellow they shot was frantic," Davey said. "Said he knew them. Said they chased him out of Grayport to kill him. Then he clammed up tight and wouldn't say more."

Molly watched Tom make fists at his sides. She suspected he was picturing a rifle in his hands. It made her ill, and made the cold seem deadlier and darker.

"I'm riding back to Shepherd's with the doctor," Davey told him.

"What about your friends?"

"Craven louts," Davey said. "The two who went back spoke of tucking tail for Grayport. The ones who came with me are heading straight for Liberty. They claim it's too cold, riding back and forth, and that the fellow must be dead by now. Scared to stick their necks out."

Benjamin removed his cap. He hadn't left the door and looked at Tom across the room. "I said that you would come."

"You said wrong," Tom replied.

The doctor opened his mouth and shriveled in his coat. Davey laughed and looked at Benjamin to understand the joke, then studied both men with questioning sincerity.

"I got a hole in my wall needs proper mending," Tom said, "a storeroom blown to smithereens, and firewood to cut before Nabby has my head. You'll have to find someone else."

"Everyone else is fastening their homes against deadfall," Benjamin said.

"So am I. We'd have a sheriff on hand, ready to assist, if you and Abigail hadn't sent him off chasing rumors."

Benjamin's eyebrow twitched three times in quick succession. He put his cap back on slightly cocked above his ear and looked at Molly, who was flustered by the shame that lit his cheeks. They'd shared a garden, and a home, and pieces by Gorelli. Benjamin fumbled for a handkerchief and cleaned his blurry glasses.

Davey knew something unspoken was afoot and looked relieved, or else intrigued, when Molly grabbed Tom's arm and tugged him into the rear of the taproom to speak with him in private. Tom allowed it, seeming eager to explain. She didn't let him.

"You're going to let your best friend risk his life?"

"He won't—"

"He *had* to side with Abigail. I can't believe he meant me any harm."

Tom tried to speak.

"Either way," Molly said, "they need you if they're riding out with the Maimers on the road. Someone's dying; he's a doctor. Can't you see he has to go?"

"The Maimers won't be there," Tom said. "They never stay in place after an attack."

"They never shoot people, either."

Tom hesitated, sneaking a look at Benjamin and Davey. Molly pinched her wrist to strengthen her resolve, wishing all of them could stay and share a pot of smoak.

"I can't go," Tom said.

"Ichabod can chop the wood, and Bess and I—"

"I won't leave *you*, not with Abigail and Lem vulturing about and Pitt riding back knowing God knows what."

"We have to leave," Benjamin said across the room. He opened the door. "A man is dying."

"I can go, too," Molly told Tom. "I'm not afraid."

Except she was and couldn't hide it when he frowned, and cupped her cheek, and said, "We have enough danger right here, you and me. I didn't get a man shot or make Benjamin a doctor. This ain't my concern and it ain't yours, either."

She was his concern. What was hers? Molly wondered.

☙

A busy day, a dying day. Davey Mun's two companions arrived shortly after he and Benjamin departed for Shepherd's Inn. Tom told her to be civil—they couldn't be blamed for not riding back—but he said it with contempt and didn't greet them when they entered. Molly seated them at the table farthest from the fire. They were portly, gray, and loud, unremarkably identical. They ate and left quickly, eager to reach the next cozy inn and get away.

Very few townspeople visited the tavern: most were busy at home, feeding hearths, tending livestock, and cooking until the air, despite the windless chill, smelled of woodsmoke and meat and hard, defiant cheer. It frightened Molly—all the desperate ritual and defense only seemed to emphasize the depth of their beleaguerment. Leaves fell lifeless in the sunset red. She watched candles disappear as people locked their shutters. When the sky bruised purple and the tables had been cleared, Nabby and Bess cleaned the kitchen, Tom went to work in the stables, and Molly swept the taproom floor, pausing frequently to marvel at the smoakwood fire. Such little black logs, such consoling orange flames. She hoped that Benjamin and Davey had reached a fire of their own.

The front door opened and the cold rushed in. It was Pitt, his face as scarlet as his customary clothes, which were covered by a coat snugly buttoned to his chin. He'd tied a scarf around his ears, underneath his hat. He came inside and closed the door and walked up to Molly, giving her a look of untold doom.

She had an impulse to hit him with a poker from the hearth. Then he sniffled at the fire and appeared to lose his confidence. She saw in him the boy whose father had been hanged; there was more to him tonight—a neediness or doubt.

"Go get Tom."

"Sheriff Pitt—"

"Please," Pitt said.

He tucked his gloves under his arm and held his fingers to the hearth. Molly backed away, hesitant to turn and walk through the kitchen, thinking about the cold dark distance to the barn. But Tom had heard the horse and come directly in. He walked through the kitchen, met them in the taproom, and stood at Molly's side with an ice-cut scowl.

Pitt spoke first. "Benjamin was maimed."

Molly slumped against Tom. They propped each other up.

Ichabod entered through the front looking winded, presumably to warn them that the sheriff had returned. Pitt surprised them once again and said, "Ethel's home safe?"

Ichabod nodded, looked at Tom without a sign, and then retreated outside to care for Pitt's horse.

"I stepped off the ferry and Ethel Kale was running up the street," Pitt explained, referring to a girl who lived near the Knoxes. "Abigail sent her up here to bring word. I sent her home with Ichabod, said to keep it quiet."

Pitt crossed the room and went to the unlocked bar, where he poured himself a gin and drank it down quick. Molly took a chair, changed her mind, and wobbled up again.

"They let him keep his clothes but the bleeding almost killed him," Pitt said. "They took his right hand. That's his operating hand."

Tom joined him at the bar and raised the bottle for a drink, but it slipped from his hand and shattered on the floor. Molly flinched. Pitt didn't.

"Davey Mun went, too," Tom said.

"He isn't back."

Molly vomited in the corner. What came up was minimal and thin—she hadn't eaten since the morning—but she felt as if her stomach had been wrenched to her tonsils. Tom explained to Pitt about the man the Maimers had shot and how Benjamin and Davey had ridden back to Shepherd's Inn.

"Hell and death," Pitt said and slapped a glove against his thigh. "No one else went along?"

Tom crunched fragments of the bottle with his shoe. Molly smelled the gin, juniper-sweet and toxic, as the pulverized glass ground between the boards.

"They've never stayed put after an attack," Tom said. "It's why we've never caught 'em."

"They stayed put today," Pitt said, thinking hard. "Why the sudden change, and at deadfall to boot?"

"To find the man they shot. They didn't want a doctor riding out to save him. I'd like to know the reason."

"So would I. Shepherd's Inn. Couple hours at a gallop."

"Less," Tom said. "Davey and his friends saw four of them together. They ran from greater numbers but they didn't run from two."

Molly's gut sank low like the opposite of sickness, leadening her stance and lightening her head. Tom and Pitt scrutinized each other up close, not with animosity, it seemed, but resolution.

"You and me," Pitt decided.

"Aye," Tom said. "We can't have a crowd riding out with guns and lanterns."

"No," Molly said, stepping forward in the glass. "It can't be just the two of you. They're waiting in the woods."

Tom ignored her, seeming desperate not to look her in the eye.

"Have another drink before we go," he said to Pitt, "and stand near the fire. You've been riding all day."

He went to the closet for his rifle. Molly followed him over, rubbing her wrist bones and trying not to picture Benjamin's hand, Davey bleeding in the dark, or, worst of all, Tom disfigured. *What would they remove?* she couldn't help thinking. *Which part of him is best?* She feared to make a list.

They stood before the closet in the hallway off the taproom, where the colder air had cracked a frozen panel in a window. Night looked in, opening its jaw.

Molly told him not to go.

"They took his hand."

"It's not your fault," she said. "You stayed here for me."

He moved around her, took his ammunition bag and rifle out, and faced her. "I've run bloodier gauntlets. These are cowards wearing masks. They won't expect two of us alone on such a night."

She hugged around his arms and squeezed with all her might, hoping to make the bullet in his shoulder hit a nerve—hoping to remind him what he really stood to lose. But Tom was already gone, down the forest road without her, and she let her hands drop and felt the draft between their bodies.

"Stay with Bess," Tom said. "You'll have Ichabod and Nabby. Keep the door locked until I'm back."

Molly nodded.

"Promise me," he said.

"I promise. Don't get killed. And don't get maimed."

"When this is done, whatever is left of me is yours."

Chapter Twenty-Five

Shepherd's Inn was a small public house, one of several along the road from Grayport to Root, where travelers could spend the night or stop to rest their horses. Tom was midway there and hadn't seen a single living creature in the forest. Pitt was out of sight—he had yet to make a sound—and Tom whistled like a man in need of consolation. The song was "Jack o' March," a tune he knew from childhood. The melody reminded him of Benjamin's frequent humming, of the doctor's failed attempts to learn the violin . . . of how he'd struggle now to dress himself and work without his hand.

They had visited the Knoxes' house before riding out and Abigail had met them in a damp, gory smock. She fought for self-control, standing firmly at the door, but her high-strung voice and unbound hair gave her the appearance of a very young girl. An extraordinary girl, one of unfeigned grit, and yet afraid and overwrought and willing to be hugged. Tom held her in the cold but the hug didn't last. She quickly pushed him off to keep herself from needing it.

"So much blood," Abigail said. "He's frostbit and feverish. I've sewn and dressed the wound but he's delirious and pale."

She paused while her thoughts rushed up and overran her, and they waited at the door—Tom in front, Pitt behind him. The street was dark and empty. She would not invite them in.

"He walked for two hours, bleeding all the way, and might have died except he tied his own tourniquet with vine."

"Did he tell you how it happened?" Pitt said. "How exactly?"

"There were four of them," she said. "It wasn't thievery today. They blocked the way toward the inn. They knew him for a doctor when they opened up his bag and took his hand . . . " She gulped a sob. "They took his operating hand."

"Davey Mun?" Tom asked.

"Showed his manhood and fought. They took his manhood to quell him," Abigail said.

Tom removed his hat and almost tore it with his fists. The cold was like a razor slicing through his breeches.

"He walked with Benjamin a ways but finally lost his will," she said. "Benjamin tried to save him, wouldn't leave him there alone. Then he died and there was no good staying anymore."

Tom backed up until he was arm to arm with Pitt.

"All to help a stranger," Abigail said, taller than the two of them below her in the road. "I think of everyone in town Benjamin has healed. Nobody would join him. No one else would go."

Tom swelled his chest, not defiantly but stoutly, swallowing the blame and holding it within him. Warmth escaped the door at Abigail's back, candlefruit sweet until the night drove it in. Pitt bowed his head to hide beneath his hat.

"But it was me," she said to Tom, "that put a wedge between you." Then to Pitt, "And I'm the reason you were gone instead of here."

She seemed to shiver deep inside, without a tremor on the surface. She was crystallized, breakable, and dangerously still.

"You're riding out," she said to Tom.

He answered with a stare.

"When you find them . . . ," she began, dispassionately voiced, and let her wish grow apparent, wrathfully severe.

Now he smoked until his tongue burned, remembering her words, and wondered how he'd bring himself to ride back home, to stand before Abigail and Benjamin again, if they didn't find the Maimers and returned empty-handed. Each passing minute in the cold-clamped quiet made him angrier and lonelier. Knowing Pitt was near offered little comfort, so he smoked his pipe, and whistled again, and tried to blot his thoughts.

Hoarfur settled on his shoulders and his hat. Periodically he brushed it off Bones with his gloves, trying to keep the frost from stiffening his mane. The filaments gave the woods a moldering appearance, like a spiderwebbed crypt far below the earth. Masses of it drifted on the leaf-strewn ground. It draped off branches, delicate and pale, and now and then he parted it directly with his face and it clung, dead cold, to his stubble and his lashes.

Bones walked on, tirelessly patient even with the extra weight draped behind the saddle. They had passed Davey Mun ten miles out of Root, his body sitting up and stiff against a tree. Blood between his legs had frozen in the leaves. He hadn't looked pained, only tired, only sad. Tom had studied him—the man he knew, able and courageous, whittled to a corpse and frozen like a warning.

No plan goes to plan, Tom caught himself thinking.

He rejected any doubts. It had to work. They couldn't fail.

He thought of Molly, how her clothes made her seem more petite, how exposing her had somehow made her more substantial. He could smell her even now, in spite of the pipe and cold, from when she'd hugged him in the stairwell and begged him not to go. The fire in the taproom, hot-brewed smoak—he would have it all again. He would find a way to keep it.

Bones shook his mane, lowered his head, and slowed, swishing out his tail and halting unbidden.

Tom's boots strained the stirrups and he sat there, firm. The road was straight and narrow, covered by the interwoven wreathwood trees, and the longest wisps of hoarfur dangling from the branches didn't drift, didn't ripple when the Maimers first appeared.

There were two of them ahead, blocking Tom's way. Their horses crunched softly on the leaves as they emerged, but otherwise the silence was remarkably intact, enough to give credence to their phantom reputation.

"Evening," Tom said.

The Maimers kept their distance. It was too dark to see if either wore a mask.

"Hard night to ride," the first Maimer said, sounding like his jaw had frozen at the hinges. "What's your name and business?"

Tom puffed his pipe until it glowed: *Stay alive.*

"My name is Tom Orange. I'm a tavern keep in Root."

"A shit hole," the Maimer answered, maybe about the tavern, maybe about the town. "What are you doing here?"

"I thought William Shepherd might need a hand," Tom said. "We had news of an attack—a traveler shot and dying, taken to the inn."

The second Maimer walked up closer on his horse, leaning forward with a slow, leathery creaking from his saddle. Bones held his ground, stamped twice, and flicked his ears.

The first Maimer asked, "What are you hiding there behind you, underneath the blanket?"

"A body from the road."

"What is he to you?"

"A fellow man," Tom said. "It seemed a sin to leave him."

"How far did he get?"

"Say again?"

"Where did you find him?"

Tom drew upon the pipe and said, "Two leagues back."

"Long way with such a wound," the first Maimer said. "I applaud the man's will. 'Twas his heart worth taking. And the doctor?"

"How's that," Tom said, low and taut.

"I wager he survived and told you we was here. It's you I can't figure, coming out alone." He stepped his horse forward, next to his companion. He was angular and bearded, masked around the eyes, with the hoarfur grizzly in the whiskers on his chin. "Not a posse full gallop, but a tavern keep whistling. Don't seem right, one against four."

Tom sensed another two riders move behind him, coming from the trees and quiet as the others. He had passed them in the dark— even Bones hadn't noticed—and despite having known they would block him fore and aft, it didn't make the trap any more appealing.

The Maimer with the beard nonchalantly showed a pistol. Tom dropped the reins and put his arms overhead. "I haven't come for trouble."

"Didn't expect us here tonight? Hope to fool us?" said the Maimer.

"No. Like I said, I'm riding to the inn."

"That wouldn't be an armed companion under the blanket now, would it?"

Tom's hands seemed to freeze. Hoarfur gathered on his knuckles and his pipe, the latter still warm but slowly dying out. His gun was in his coat. All he needed was a second.

"I told you," Tom said. "I found a body in the road."

"And picked it up and took it with you, like a good Lumenous neighbor. Pull the blanket off."

"My hands are in the air."

"Do it now."

"Not until you put away your gun," Tom said.

"I'll have your arms for that," the second Maimer said. He pulled a knife. It was long and made a whisper-chime coming from its sheath, so sharp that even Nabby would have grudgingly respected it.

The bearded Maimer spoke to one of the rearward riders. "Get down and check the body."

Here it is, Tom thought. They were coming to it now, predictably and plainly, and he didn't breathe once in the inevitable pause. A rider behind him cocked a gun and thumped off his horse. Tom faced ahead and listened to him walk: seven crisp steps in the ice-chip leaves.

"Get up," the rider said, right at Bones's tail and speaking to the body underneath the blanket.

No one spoke or moved.

The rider pulled the blanket off. Tom shut his eyes. There was silence for a moment when the rider stepped close, leaned forward, and declared, "This ain't a body. It's a scarecrow."

Tom dropped the pipe over his back, behind the saddle. It landed where he hoped, near the rider's puzzled face, on the scarecrow loaded up with smoak dust and gunpowder.

Even with his eyes closed, Tom saw the flash. It wasn't an explosion but a huge, blooming flare, and the white-gold flames lit the forest like a sun. The Maimer at his back screamed and fell away. Heat billowed through the cold, singeing Tom's ponytail and blowing off his hat. Bones reared and whinnied, frightened by the fire.

Tom spread his eyelids wide enough to see, drew the pistol from his coat, and shot the bearded Maimer.

Pitt was in the woods, having followed on foot. He shot the Maimer holding the knife, who was blinded from the glare: an illuminated target for a rifle in the dark. Tom trampled over the Maimer who'd been standing near the scarecrow, and Bones began to panic from the noises underfoot. The man rolled and groaned. Hooves cracked his ribs. A stamp broke his skull like a pumpkin in a bag.

The final Maimer, still ahorse, recovered his sight and fled. Tom spurred Bones and drew a second pistol. The powder in the scarecrow had mostly burned away but now the clothes were on fire, heating up the padding that protected Bones's croup. Tom's coat was burning, too, and flapped behind him as he rode. He felt the fire through his shirt, rippling to his shoulders while his face pressed forward in the pinprick cold.

Bones raced frantically to outrun the flames; if he wasn't yet burned, he would be soon. Tom couldn't shed his coat without hazarding a fall and wouldn't stop, wouldn't hesitate for anything at all. Bones's panic had its use—they were catching up fast. The Maimer looked back and teetered on his mount, seemingly astonished by the fiery horse behind him. Tom cocked his gun, aimed hard, and took the shot. The flint didn't spark. He tried again. It wouldn't shoot.

The Maimer beat his horse but couldn't pull ahead. Tom was at his flank, feeling fire at his neck. He flipped the pistol, held the barrel, steadied himself, and threw. The cherrywood stock hit the Maimer in the back, high between the shoulder blades, and knocked him off the horse.

Tom fought to halt Bones and rapidly dismounted. He singed his leather gloves pulling off his coat and quickly cut the mess of fiery padding from the saddle. The Maimer on the ground scrambled up and rushed forward. He was addled, he was wild. Tom drew his knife and caught him in a hug. The blade plunged deep into the man's soft belly and his eyes stayed open, full of wonder, through the mask. There was a dimple in his chin. His breath smelled of licorice. The blood on Tom's glove was comfortingly warm and the man didn't struggle, only sighed and hugged back. Tom shoved the knife until it almost poked through, not sadistically but firmly, with respect for what was happening.

The Maimer slumped dead and Tom held him up. He laid him over the saddle of the man's own horse, no small job with a body that limp. Tom and Bones had lost some hair and suffered minor burns, but they were mostly unharmed; they stood together, cheek to cheek, jittery and steaming in the bleak, smoky road. Once Bones began to calm, Tom remounted him and gathered up both sets of reins, and then he rode back to Pitt. There were things left to finish.

⚓

Pitt was standing with the bodies at the site of the attack, seeming more like an ordinary man than a sheriff. Was it affection Tom felt to see him trembling but alive? Did James Pitt smile when he recognized Tom, or were they both that desperate for a well-known face?

"Are you hurt?" Tom asked.

"No. You?"

"No."

Pitt's legs looked spindly and exposed beneath his coat when he hunched up tight, blowing on his hands. Hoarfur had already formed a veil upon the bodies. Tom dumped the final Maimer off and into the road and then they lay together, frosted, oddly beautiful and still. Tom's first shot had killed the Maimer with the beard. The rider they had trampled hadn't survived the hooves. Pitt had winged the third—the Maimer with the knife. Tom didn't ask how the man had finally died, and Pitt did not explain the numerous cuts that marked the body. There were things you didn't judge, things you might have done yourself, unforgivable but better left to conscience than discussion.

The trampled man's coat showed the least blood. Tom put it on in place of his own burned coat. The Maimer's warmth was in the sleeves and Tom was troubled by its source, by the intimacy of soaking in the dead man's life. *I stole your heat,* Tom thought—*all you really needed.*

He removed the Maimers' masks and studied all their faces. One was handsome in a roguish way. One had freckles. The bearded man was oldest, with a grandfather's eyes. The Maimer Tom had chased and gutted was a boy, no more than sixteen, with a once-broken nose that had not been properly set. What had possessed such a boy, such ordinary men?

Tom turned away. "We should have tried this months ago," he said, remembering the limbs they might have saved if they had done so.

"Why didn't we?" Pitt asked.

"It might not have worked."

"Then why now?"

"Because of Benjamin and Davey."

"Why really?"

Pitt was right. It hadn't been guilt, not entirely at least, and it hadn't been a spur as slippery as justice.

"Threats to me and mine got too close. They made it personal. I had to threaten back," Tom said. "What did you come for?"

"It's my job," Pitt said. "I know you don't respect that."

"Tonight, I truly do."

Tom began untying the Maimers' horses from the trees, roping them together for the ride to Shepherd's Inn. Pitt had walked the whole way to follow along in stealth. He mounted a Maimer's stallion now, a beast too enormous for a man of Pitt's height, and refused to reconsider though he struggled to reach the stirrups.

"That was a good first shot," Tom said. "What was the distance?"

"Thirty yards."

Meaning twenty. Still a long way from danger. "It occurred to me you might have let 'em have me," Tom said.

"It occurred to me, too. But I'm a sheriff, not a scoundrel."

"Was it a sheriff or a scoundrel chasing after that traveler this morning?"

Pitt's horse was still jumpy from the earlier attack, his agitation heightened by an unfamiliar rider. He swished his tail and snorted, stamping on the ground. Pitt calmed him down with gently spoken words. He took his glove off and laid his hand softly on the withers.

Tom mounted Bones. "Did you find him, then?"

"Aye."

"And got your facts about Molly?"

"That can wait."

"Not forever."

"Not forever," Pitt agreed.

They left the bodies in the road to carry back later and continued on to Shepherd's Inn to see what they could learn.

Chapter Twenty-Six

Tom and Pitt amazed William Shepherd and his guests with news of the Maimers' demise, but when they asked to see the survivor of the day's first attack, they were told the man was dead.

"I expected him to live," William Shepherd said. "The shot went through, clean as you could ask, and he was comfortable enough. Left him sleeping 'round one and he was dead at one thirty. Must've bled worse than any of us realized."

The victim hadn't spoken since arriving at the inn, and so their last remaining hope was to send his body back to Grayport, where someone might identify him and have some answers. Tom and Pitt doubted it. The trail had gone cold, and if any Maimers remained, losing four of their number would likely scare them off until the spring. Shortly after dawn, Tom and Pitt rode back with the horses and collected the frozen bodies from the road; they made it home just as Root was fully abuzz with news of Davey Mun and Benjamin's severed hand.

Tom dismounted Bones and walked toward the Orange, where he was almost knocked down by Molly's running hug. A group of townspeople watched but he held her back tight, absorbing her warmth and smell and feeling he could cry if he were not so hardened and benumbed from the cold. Bess stood close and looked relieved to see him home again. Ichabod waved from just inside the door, opening his mouth and drawing in a breath as if to summon up his long-lost voice and say hello.

"Your hair!" Molly said, fingering the place where his ponytail had burned.

Tom sensed the nearest man considering a joke—*Never knew your hair was fine enough to steal*—but felt it dissipate quickly when the Maimers' bodies were laid on the ground. They had stiffened into arcs, having spent the cold night propped against trees. Now the corpses sat together near the tavern's outer wall in a grim, frozen row for everyone to see.

Tom had seen them plenty and looked instead at Molly, feeling that he knew her, inside and out, as well as he knew the tavern's secret nooks and scars. She studied the corpses with a deep-cut crease between her eyes, then with softness at their faces—at their dead, common faces.

Some of the crowd began to speak.

"Hope they suffered."

"Fucking vermin."

"May the devil have his way and cut 'em into bits."

But a hush came upon them when Davey Mun's body was carried into the tavern, the nature of his wound impossible to hide with so much blood frozen into his breeches.

Many more people were converging on the tavern, bundled up tight but seeming not to recognize the cold in their excitement. A farmer noticed Abigail Knox and said her name. Tom and Molly turned to look. Sheriff Pitt did, too. She walked up the road and underneath the sycamore, icicle straight and spectral from the sunlight glaring off the Antler. She was gravely underslept and raccooned around the eyes, but her stride showed the balanced self-possession of a pastor.

She had come to see the bodies. She had called for the Maimers' deaths, and she was not afraid to witness what her vengefulness had wrought. People stood aside so she could walk directly up, and she examined the row of corpses, pausing over each. Tom and Pitt approached her.

"This is all of them?" she asked.

"We think so," Tom said. "How's Benjamin?"

"Feverish and weak. Did you recover his hand?"

The men exchanged a sidelong glance above her head. Pitt faltered. Tom replied, "We haven't checked their bags."

"He wants it if you find it," Abigail said.

She held Tom for support and he escorted her inside, where he entrusted her to Bess as townspeople flooded through the taproom door. Tom and Pitt were soon surrounded and besieged with endless questions. Why had they ridden out alone? How had each Maimer died? What would happen to the bodies and the dead men's belongings?

Abigail was equally beset but she appeared, for once in her life, appreciative of so much unsolicited attention. Bess had led her to a chair and brought her a glass of sherry, and she accepted many hesitant but heartfelt assurances. Benjamin would live, she repeated several times, bolstered by the fortified wine. She had left him in the care of her neighbor, Mrs. Kale, and in spite of her insistence that she must hurry back, she drank another sherry in her seat beside the fire.

Tom could not escape the crowd, which thickened every minute—was it possible that all of Root had crammed inside the tavern? There were others here, too—men from Shepherd's Inn, late-season travelers, everyone united by the fall of common foes. Tom told versions of the story to the crowd, each iteration shorter than the last, until he ultimately snapped at a well-meaning farmer:

"They're ruddy fucking dead. Go outside and have a look."

All he wanted was to get away and sit alone with Molly, preferably upstairs with a fire and a drink, but when he looked around the room, she was nowhere in sight. Bess had vanished, too, leaving Ichabod alone to work behind the bar. Tom lingered for a minute, avoiding additional questions by feigning interest in Pitt, who had warmed himself up with free drinks and started telling his own versions of events—each one longer than the last—to a captivated group so tightly massed together that Pitt was standing on a chair in order to be seen.

Tom squeezed away and made it to the kitchen. Nabby faced him from the hearth with a wrought-iron flesh fork and approached him so directly, he expected her to hug him.

"The storeroom hams are out of reach behind crates," she said, as if he had merely just returned from a stroll around town. "Ichabod has tried a quarter hour to retrieve them."

"Any trouble while I was gone?"

"Someone hexed my right hand—I haven't determined who—and I could not make a fist until I finally guessed the healing word and scrawled it down with ash. Otherwise, no. It's good you lived," Nabby said, returning to the fire. "As for those out front, their belongings must be burned. All they carried has a blood curse, especially the coins."

"I'm glad I was missed," Tom said, nonetheless soothed by his cook's familiarity. "Where are Molly and Bess?"

"I haven't seen Molly. She's as hard to pin as Scratch. Bess is in the parlor, speaking to her father."

Tom slouched against the wall, too raw and worn out for yet another fight. He didn't resist the vision of his uncle as a corpse, rigid as the bodies of the Maimers outside, nor the wish—the near prayer— that Lem would drink himself to death. Before he had a chance to cross the kitchen into the parlor, his uncle started shouting from the tavern's front door. Molly and Bess were there, too, and all the crowd turned to listen. Tom's powder burns stung as if his body were aflame again. He shoved into the taproom and forced his way to Lem.

"And what of the hams?" Nabby said.

He was mad enough to kill.

<p>

Molly had been standing in the front of the taproom, listening as Tom and Pitt talked about the Maimers, when she spotted Bess and her father. Lem had arrived through the kitchen, and would surely have been jabbed by Nabby's iron fork if Bess hadn't immediately dragged him into the parlor, a rarely used room on the opposite side of the tavern. It was smaller than the taproom, long but very narrow, with sharp gray light coming from the windows. Molly moved fast, entering through the front just as Lem and Bess entered from the back.

Lem was oddly dapper in a waistcoat and unstained sleeves. He'd combed his greasy hair, or slapped it down flat, and he had bathed and trimmed his beard and didn't look drunk. In spite of his enormousness, he shrank in front of Bess, although he hardened some and frowned when Molly stood beside her.

"Are you going to be nice?" Molly asked.

"If I'm given leave to talk," he said, speaking with a voice more righteous than abusive.

"Talk," Bess said. "I have things to say, too."

"I come to say the tannery's been doing good without you. I hired the Button boys for extra help. We have skins in all the pits and enough hides to keep busy through the winter. And I ain't had more than two drinks a meal for half a fortnight."

Bess took a breath and shook her hair behind her, looking spirited and young and vigorously flushed. Molly fought a nervous and irrational urge to laugh.

"I ain't been myself since the pox took your mother," Lem said. "She had a softness and a easiness, a look full of comfort. We was sick and she was dying but she quieted the fear. I haven't felt that since, 'cept with you. You're all I got."

He was teary, Molly thought, or else perspiring into his eyes. Was it love that made him cry, or something else that made him sweat so profusely in the cold? Molly looked at Bess and sensed beneath her confidence a pint-sized girl who wished she had a parent. She remembered how it felt to embrace her own father and to feel, through his bones, how he faltered underneath.

"I regret the way I left," Bess told Lem. "You should have known about it first. I wanted to hurt you and I shouldn't have, however much you earned it. You're my father and I don't want us fighting anymore."

Lem smiled with relief and raised his arms to hug her.

"I'm staying at the Orange," Bess said. Lem dropped his arms. "I won't change my mind, not if you drag me off, or beg and plead, or storm around the tavern breaking fiddles with your head."

Lem's smile grew deformed, tangling in his beard. "We can make it like it was, clean the vats come spring—"

"But you won't!" Bess yelled with a sudden step forward. "You'll drink and blame luck and freeze to death by Lumen Night. I want you to fix the house and work for more than a month. I saved my earnings all summer—you could have it, every pound, if you showed real effort and convinced me I was wrong."

Lem scrunched his face and seemed to honestly consider it, the way a man of doubt might regard a glimpse of God. "And then you'd come home?"

Bess shut her eyes. "I want to choose my own way. I want you to respect that."

"And where is your respect for your own bloody father? Coming home cold to nobody and nothing, not a friend or kind relation caring I'm alone. I'll be buried in a hide pit, moldering in shit, without a soul upon the earth noticing I'm gone. Poor and pocked, cruelly widowed—so I drink, aye, and rant, and curse what I've become. But here I am, in spite of hardship, with rights to what is mine."

"Doesn't Tom have a right to live without your foolery?"

"Tom," Lem said, hunching at the name. "He disrespects his own blood. People listen and believe him. I only ever asked for respect."

"You haven't earned it!"

"Neither's he," Lem said, turning now to Molly as a stand-in for Tom. "He ain't above rolling in the dirt, now, is he?"

Molly answered in a single, unhesitating outburst and felt a rush of clarity and dizziness together. "Say whatever you like. Tell the whole town. Nobody will listen to a tar-hearted brute who doesn't fix his house, or comb his raggedy beard, and acts a menace in the tavern and a scoundrel in his home until his daughter offers money just to let her be."

Bess gawked, either startled or confused by Molly's vehemence.

Lem quivered like a beast newly branded, at the instant when the sizzle hasn't yet burned. He swung his forearm and shoved Molly hard against the wall, and then he left the front of the parlor and continued to the taproom. Molly and Bess pursued him, squeezing around his bulk and blocking his way in front of the crowd, just as Lem began to shout at everybody present.

"My nephew's done it again!" he said. "Made himself a hero! Now he's back, safe and cozy in his ready-made home, with a pair of young women cleaning up his messes. I'll tell you why I don't want my daughter in his house." He looked at Abigail and pointed, causing her to redden. "You were right," he said. "Abigail was right with her suspicions!"

Tom entered from the kitchen and began shoving through. Molly stopped him in the middle of the room as people watched. Her lungs were in her gullet. Tom was solid as a bomb.

"I seen 'em!" Lem said. "Tom and Molly like bog toads flopping on the ground, right out back where anyone could watch. So I did. I stood and watched while she rode him in a sweat."

Bess's mortified tears were scalding and aggressive. "Get out!" she said and pushed him, hard enough to stagger Lem halfway out the room. His bloodpox scars turned scarlet on his brow.

"There's your hero," Lem said. "Left his mother on her own—left her here to die. Then he came back home and took what wasn't his and now he's master of the house! Captain of the troops! I wish the cannon would have done more than broke his fucking wall. I wish I made it blow the whole tavern into bits."

Lem stomped out and slammed the door behind him, letting in a momentary gust of frigid air. Bess watched him go and then refused to turn around, but everybody else looked at Tom and Molly. No one spoke, no one sniffed. Hardly anybody shuffled.

Tom approached Pitt, leaving Molly on her own, and said, "I didn't instigate that. I didn't fight or drag him out. Forget you and me and think about Bess. He isn't going to stop. You have to understand that."

Pitt took it in, aware of being watched. His head looked as solidly preserved as Nabby's hams.

"Please," Tom said. "I'm coming to you for help."

Respect was not the angle Pitt had seen coming and it dumbed him for a second. He sighed and pinched his eyes. "I haven't slept in two days. I'll talk to Lem tomorrow."

"Talk," Tom said.

"Family squabbles aren't a matter for the law," Pitt said. "I'd think a man like you, with all your storied history, would rather keep the public and the private cut clean."

"He sabotaged the cannon."

"Said he *wished* he had. It's not the same thing."

Molly's concentrated vision gave Tom a rippling aura. She couldn't see his face and wanted to approach him but she didn't dare move, not with everybody watching—not when any quick touch might trigger an explosion.

"Lock him up or quell him or I will make it private."

"Take it easy," Pitt replied.

"I mean it," Tom said. "I won't be held accountable if things go bad."

He walked toward the stairs and people cleared a lane. Bess let him pass and Molly watched him go, and then he climbed until the shadows swallowed up his head and said, "I'm going up to sleep," to no one in particular. "Anybody knocks, I'm shooting at the door."

<p>

Tom remained upstairs and no one approached his room, not when a scuffle broke out in the afternoon, nor when the bodies were moved to the yard behind the tavern, nor when Ichabod discovered Benjamin's hand in one of the saddlebags and ran the frozen prize directly to the Knoxes.

Molly spent the day in a small, stifling bubble. She didn't know what Pitt had learned from Mr. Bole or how he meant to use it. Now Tom had gone to bed without a word of reassurance, and she hated him for doing so and leaving her alone. Still she craved him in his injury and surliness and sleep. It was almost worth the risk of opening his door. She had earned it. Had she earned it? He had promised he was hers.

Bess focused on her work, preoccupied and shamed by her father's behavior. Nabby grumbled in the kitchen and was better off avoided, especially after Scratch mauled the ham she'd cooked for dinner. Ichabod confined himself to swift, efficient signs, as if his gestures were reminding him of Benjamin's severed hand.

Once the taproom cleared and night shrank the tavern, the day's heavy pall wrapped itself around them. No one spoke. They tidied up and swept the floor, and Tom did not appear. Davey Mun's body had been carried to the barn—tomorrow they would send him home to Liberty, to family—but the Maimers sat exposed against the tavern's back wall. The town had not decided whether to bury them or burn them; if winterbears or wolves dragged them off, all the better.

Molly passed them when she walked outside to gather wood. She felt the need to touch one—the youngest—on the face. Her fingertips were moist and fastened to his cheek. It was cold, fully cold, and death was everywhere around her in the dark black river and the glitter-white grass. She tried imagining quicksummer, the transitory season that was said to follow deadfall and offer some reprieve before the full brunt of winter, but the freeze seemed far too permanent to thaw.

Molly pulled her finger off the Maimer's white cheek. Suddenly a strong, warm fragrance pulsed around her, like the sweetness of a nose-gay blooming in the sun. The child ghost was with her. Molly breathed her in. She remembered being pregnant in the summertime in Gray-port, the fullness and contentedness of carrying her baby. Then without knowing how, she perceived the ghost's name and wished that she could hug the little girl and give her comfort.

Molly went inside and rubbed the shivers from her arms.

"Her name is Gwendolyn," she said.

"She trusts you," Nabby said. "You must have told a special bit of truth when she was listening."

The fire seemed dangerously hot inside the hearth and yet approachable and smooth: the special glow of smoakwood. She took a warm stuffed apple from a platter on the table and the sugary meringue put the fear of night behind her. Bess entered from the front with a tray full of cups. Her honey-brown hair was lovely in the light. She hadn't said a word about her father's revelation, seeming to expect that Molly would confide in her and obviously peeved that it had taken all day.

"You have a letter out front," she said, putting down the tray. "The postman hasn't been. Someone else must've left it."

"A letter?" Molly asked, starting into the taproom.

"It wasn't there this morning when I cleaned," Bess said.

They went together to the broad maple table near the bar where the uncollected mail and newspapers gathered. Lying on top was a tri-folded letter. It was on cream-colored paper with a green wax seal and a single word—"Molly"—in a clear, familiar hand.

She crushed the apple she was holding, squishing custard through her fingers. "It's from Abigail," she said. "I recognize the *M*."

"Why would Abigail write—"

"To stay at Benjamin's side."

"But why would she write to you?"

Molly snatched the letter up and stuffed it into her pocket.

"Aren't you going to read it?"

"Later," Molly said. "I'm going upstairs."

"It hurts me that you still won't trust me," Bess said, blocking Molly's way and noticing the apple squashed in her fist.

"Your father knows plenty. Go and ask him. Or are you hoping my embarrassment will cover up your own?"

Had she mashed the ruined apple into the depth of Bess's ear, she would not have left her friend any more astonished. Molly shook her hand, splattering the cream, and stomped upstairs before Bess recovered her voice.

On the lightless second floor, with the stairway behind her and the hallway ahead, Molly stopped at Tom's room and listened through the door. There was no trace of movement, no snore or subtle breathing.

She was crying in the dark and couldn't see the blur, but felt the tears warm her cheeks and quickly dribble cold. She raised her hand to knock, but no—she had to wait. She tiptoed away and lit a candle in her room, and then she settled on the bed and took the letter from her pocket, fearing what was in it, dreading it was true.

☙

Abigail dimmed the lantern to its lowest possible flame, a small gold feather glowing on the wick. Benjamin had stirred; all afternoon he'd mumbled in delirium. His scientific mind had fallen to incoherent rambling and his talk of moons and stars, of meteors and tides had sounded mystical to Abigail: words of revelation. He had sipped a little broth but taken nothing else. His injury had bled again, more than she expected when she swapped the old bandage, but the stump looked clean. She prayed it wouldn't fester, forcing her to tie him down and amputate the arm. Abigail had often seen it done and heard the screams but she had never held the knife, never sawed bone. She would do it if she had to. No one else would help. He was hers, she meant to keep him, and she wouldn't succumb to fear.

She flipped the cloth upon his forehead, troubled by its heat. It was a beneficial fever that would burn away the bad—unless it ran too red and started burning out the good.

When he had first staggered home he'd been cold beyond belief, bloody and depleted and collapsing at the door. Frostbitten ears, crystallized coat—stiff as winter wood when she dragged him into the parlor. She had stripped off his clothes and salved his frozen skin, rubbing beesmyrrh and spirits onto his chest until he colored. She had not seen him naked in a good many seasons and he'd looked like a child, like an underfed boy. Delicate and trembling. Wholly in her care.

She'd found the strength to haul him up the stairs, where she dressed him in a nightshift and bundled him in blankets. While she worked, he revived enough to tell her what had happened. It distracted him from suffering and let her take control. She found his spare tenaculum, drew the arteries out to tie, trimmed the ragged flesh, and sewed up the flaps. Following his superstitious faith in extra cleanliness, she bandaged him with purified lint and boiled linen. He approved of all she did and seemed relieved when she was done.

She ran to the Kales, and young Esther sprinted to the Orange. Tom and Pitt arrived later and she sent them into the woods; then she sat beside Benjamin and prayed for his survival. Then this morning Mrs. Kale had arrived shortly after dawn, bringing news that Tom and Pitt had killed the Maimers and returned.

Abigail had hurried off to see if it was true. The bodies had neither gladdened her nor weighed upon her conscience. Possibly fatigue had stifled her reaction. But the townspeople's sympathy had buoyed her profoundly. How the wine had eased her shoulders, how unguardedly she'd spoken! Oh the shame of it, the *taverness* of spilling out her thoughts. She had gossiped with an unfamiliar man—a common traveler—who had asked about the Maimers, Tom and Pitt, Bess and Molly.

"That one," she had said. "Tom pulled her from the river. Lies and trouble ever since."

Now she couldn't put Lem's revelation from her mind—not what he had said, but that he'd said it to her. "Abigail was right with her suspicions," he had yelled, as if the two of them were equals in the dirty work of rumor. It was rumor that had sent Pitt riding off to

Liberty, suspicion that had angered Tom and kept him at the tavern. Otherwise they might have gone with Benjamin and Davey, four instead of two riding out against the Maimers.

She clasped her husband's living hand and wished he weren't sleeping. His face seemed lacking in the absence of his glasses and his larynx looked swollen in his beanpole neck. She had never known the house to feel so still, and she knelt down close and hummed beside his ear. It was a melody she'd learned from his irritating habit, one she couldn't name but recalled note for note. She hummed instead of praying, wishing that her own frigid hands could draw his fever down, and fell asleep crying in the low-lit room.

She woke before dawn, when the sun was still a blush. Leafwings sang. A smell of smoke was in the air. It might have been the hearth except the odor was impure, as when a thing you shouldn't burn is thrown upon a fire. She had nuzzled up to Benjamin during the night, and now she felt his forehead. His fever had decreased. He was sweaty, he was cool, and when she relit the room and changed the dressing on his stump, she found the wound had oozed but still looked clean. She felt refreshed, having slept, and Benjamin was better—only what about the morning felt so wrong?

There were voices outside, people in the street. When she listened more intently, she perceived the sounds of hoofbeats and shouts too distant for the words to come clear. She stood before the window and pressed against the glass. Neighbors walked briskly to the river or the tavern. Men leaned forward in their strides, full of purpose, with their hats tipped low to counteract the cold. Women hurried past, some with open cloaks, as if they'd barely thought to bundle when they walked outdoors.

She saw the blacksmith's wife, her friend Mrs. Bolt. She had her skirts in her fists and hiked above her ankles, trying not to stumble in the icy, rutted road. Abigail ran downstairs and out the door, where the wind blew sharp against her neck and through her clothes. Here the smoke was more intense: something sizable had burned.

"What's happened?" she called to Mrs. Bolt.

"Abigail Knox! Have you slept through it all?"

Mrs. Bolt came toward her, kept moving, didn't slow. "Lemuel is dead. His house is all afire!"

Abigail crossed herself, buckling in the cold.

"And that is not the half," Mrs. Bolt continued. "He was dragged from the flames but the fire didn't kill him. He was bludgeoned on the head—his skull was driven in. Now the sheriff has arrested Tom Orange in the tavern. He was found this morning drunk and there was evidence upon him."

Abigail staggered, almost tripping on her heels. She wheeled her arms and caught herself, seeing for a moment, as her head tipped back, a haze of dirty smoke in a nauseating smear.

Mrs. Bolt hurried on, craning backward as she said, "And the young woman Molly up and disappeared. The sheriff wants to find her. Give my best to Benjamin, I'll call upon you later!"

"No, I don't believe it," Abigail said.

But she was talking to herself. She was frozen to the heart.

Chapter Twenty-Seven

After Molly had gone upstairs and read the letter in her room, she sat for several minutes, wondering what to do. So much heat had risen to her skin that her eyesight rippled and her bones felt cold. It was ten o'clock at night but felt much later, and she had to act fast before Bess came up for bed.

When she stood and stuffed the letter back inside her pocket, the movement and the feeling happened out of sync. She saw herself rise and walk across the room but the actual sensation came a second later. It was as if she had an echo or a slow, ghostly twin. She dressed in layers for the cold, donned her cloak and gloves, and took her unspent earnings from the box beneath her bed. She couldn't risk the stairs and so she opened up the window. The sash scraped loudly and her weight squeaked the floor.

Listen, Molly thought. *Hear it, come and catch me.*

No one came when she ducked outside and straddled the sill, half in and half out, breathing vapor at the stars. Nobody noticed when she climbed out and hung by her hands, nor when she dangled with her cheek against the frost-sparkled wall, nor even when the sash dropped down upon her fingers and she fell to the frozen ground and almost broke her ankle.

She looked toward the barn until she was certain—as certain as she could be—that Ichabod had finished his work and gone into the tavern. She crept to the rear of the Orange, stooping extra low when she reached the pantry windows but afraid, all the same, that Nabby might see.

Around the back beside the garden, Molly crossed the place where she had thrown herself at Tom. It was dirt and dead grass: an ordinary spot. She touched it moving past, leaning down to prize a small frozen pebble from the ground. It warmed inside her hand until it felt like clay. She thought to keep it in her pocket but instead she let it fall.

The barn door's creak made her insides curl. Night was darker in the stables but she felt more exposed. She smelled the cold manure, the animal warmth of breath and hair. Bones knew her well and snuffled gladly when she passed. She had ridden him and often fed him apples in the summer but tonight she wouldn't look at him. She wondered if it hurt him.

Ichabod had stabled the Maimers' horses in the back. She sized them up and settled on a lean roan mare who greeted her with peaceable but spirited comportment.

"Hello," Molly said, slightly bowing out of instinct.

The mare tossed her head and snorted at her greeting, but it seemed more show than genuine aggression.

Molly stroked the mare's nose and whispered gently as she bridled her. She saddled the mare and guided her out, again ignoring Bones, who wounded Molly back with his own indifferent silence.

Back in the open night, she resecured the barn, and then she took the mare slowly from the Orange on foot, keeping near the tree line and staying out of sight until she was far enough away to turn onto the road. She mounted up, riding at a softly paced walk, expecting to be noticed—it was not so very late—but spotting no one at the windows, no one out of doors. The town shut its eyes and simply let her pass.

Her toes were already aching through her stockings and her shoes. She had considered taking Bess's boots—they had similar feet, similar everything, had worn each other's clothes all summer long—but while the mare's disappearance wouldn't be marked until the morning, missing boots might be noticed when her friend went to bed. As it was, she had to hope that when her absence was discovered, Bess would simply assume she had gone to sleep with Tom.

She reached the forest's mouth, where the road led to Grayport, a full day's journey in the unforgiving cold. The mare was hesitant and stiff, possibly remembering the horrors she had seen. Molly trotted between a pair of close, brambly thickets with a feeling that the woods would interweave behind her. She took a final look back and glimpsed the windows of the Orange. Then the trees blocked the view, Root disappeared, and the fireside aroma of the town thinned away.

Nothing moved: not a leaf, not a creature, not a breeze. She had heard about hoarfur and hated its appearance, how it gathered on her cloak like a pale, killing mold. She felt that any moment an impediment would stop her—broken branches on the road, a rider at her back—but the way remained clear, she hadn't been pursued, and the mare took heart and carried on with growing verve. She quickened to a canter and the cold became excruciating, rushing at her face like a nonstop slap. She was terribly awake, as if she'd slept for half a year. All ahead of her was dark, all behind her too distinct. She didn't dare imagine what would become of her in Grayport, only what would certainly become of her in Root.

The writing had not been Abigail's. She'd known the hand at once and she had lied, and wounded Bess, to face the shock of it alone. She had memorized it quickly:

Dear Molly,
    Come to Liberty and meet me at the Black Fish Inn. Tell no one you are leaving. Ride without delay. Do not return to Grayport.
    I never wished to hurt you.

                                                                With love,
                                                                N

She could still feel the jolt from the pistol she had fired. She could smell it; she could see his shirt billow from the impact. Any explanation strained believability. Nevertheless, she sensed her brother's presence in the words, same as in the letter he had forged from John Summer. It was Nicholas. He'd found her and she had to get away.

The mare tried to slow but Molly rode faster, hard against the cold until the animal's breath labored, mile after mile in the petrified woods. The trees' barren sameness and the looping of her thoughts made her progress virtually impossible to gauge. She remembered Tom's warmth when she had hugged him that morning, and the smoakwood fire, and the apple in her hand. She didn't dwell upon them, or upon the growing threat of frostbite—her skin felt brittle, like a fine white shell—nor especially on the hollow in the middle of her body, one that she had struggled all summer to replenish.

She had lived without Frances, and her father, and her brother. She had lived without Cora. She would live without the rest. Tears dribbled from her eyes and streamed along her temples, summoned by the wind and freezing in her hair. Every limb and blur Molly passed was a danger. Every shadow was her brother.

Then she saw something real.

Molly stopped the horse but her heart leaped forward. It was a winterbear, straight ahead and massive in the road, familiar from a picture she had studied as a child. Terrible and strange—how the drawing used to thrill her! She remembered telling Frances that she wouldn't be afraid.

Dark gray fur grew thickly on its shoulder hump. The rest of its coat was shaggy, like a mass of frayed rope, the color of snow and ash and dangling off its back. The bear was bulky and contracted down on all fours. It would tower if it stood. Molly hoped it wouldn't. There was no discernible tail but the ears were tall and sharp, and the long, lupine muzzle tapered to a point. A wolf-bear, a creature both gargantuan and lean. Its hind legs were lanky but its paws were big as rakes, and the broad-splayed daggers of its claws scraped the ground.

The mare flicked her ears, raised her head, and quaked. The winterbear sniffed and cocked its head but didn't charge. She thought it might be groggy after sleeping all summer. It would certainly be hungry. There was no way around it. She considered leaving the road, but the trees were tightly packed, a maze on either side, impossible to navigate. They stood a while, studying each other in the dark. The only sounds were Molly's breath and the creaking of the saddle till the winterbear woofed, growled low, and stepped toward her.

When it pivoted, the roadway opened to the right. The space was slender but they might slip through if they were lucky—if the winterbear was sluggish and the mare didn't falter. She would feint left and buy herself one or two seconds. She had ridden all her life and knew that she could do it, but the mare sensed her nervousness and started backing up. The bear stepped again, widening the gap.

Turn around, Molly thought. *Gallop back to Root. Throw yourself on Abigail's mercy. Go to Pitt.*

Cross the river, ride to Nicholas in Liberty.

Submit.

Molly tugged the reins and made a motion to the left. The bear moved to meet her, rippling with a snarl. Molly turned right and spurred the mare forward. They were tight against the trees, racing hard toward the gap, when the winterbear straightened with a roar and swung its paw.

The mare reared in terror and the claws caught her neck, partly severing the horse's head and knocking Molly off the saddle.

She landed on her side near the bear's hind legs. Blood splashed hot, covering her cloak and slickening the leaves when the horse toppled over. Molly slipped and just avoided being crushed underneath. The horse's eyes were open—how they glared at her and rolled! The winterbear fell upon the carcass with a grunt. It forgot that Molly was there, or simply didn't care, and slashed the mare's stomach so its entrails spilled.

Molly crawled, trying desperately to stand and get away, and then she stumbled into a run and didn't stop, didn't turn. She sprinted up the road until the bear, the horse, and any chance of fleeing home to Root were far behind her, out of sight, and even then she hurried on. Her lungs were so inflamed from gasping in the cold, she opened her cloak to see if she'd been clawed without feeling it. The mare's heavy blood weighed her down. She could smell it. Soon the blood froze solid in the wrinkles of her gown. The odor sickened her, the sound of the intestines wouldn't leave her, and she staggered on for miles, jogging when she could, haunted less by the bear than by the horse's glaring eyes.

At great bitter length, with her joints beyond stiffness and her muscles turned to wood knots, she finally saw a window light glowing through the trees. The sight warmed her spirit as a fire would have thawed her, but the promise of relief exhausted her completely.

She came to the house and read the weathered sign above the door:

SHEPHERD'S INN
Travlers Welcom

The inn was two stories high but smaller than the Orange, standing in a half-acre clearing by a creek. Its walls were so dark and packed with ancient moss, it appeared to have grown with its own set of roots, like a house-shaped tree from a strange, magic fable. A barn stood behind it, and a miniature garden, and a sty packed with pigs that appeared to have horns. The lighted window she had seen was one of the upper rooms, and though the downstairs windows had been shuttered for the night, the house felt awake.

It was one or two o'clock. In a few more hours, Root would notice she was gone. She had to get away—there was no time to lose—but she couldn't press on in such cold without a horse. She was just about to knock, wondering if anyone would answer so late, when the bolts unlocked and the door opened wide.

Heat rushed out, heavenly and soft. She was greeted by a musket leveled at her chest, wielded by a man who looked astonished to behold her. He was sixty and decrepit with a piebald beard and a long, blue nightcap trailed behind his back.

He gaped at her and said, "World's evil, what has happened?"

Molly's jaw was so tight, she almost couldn't speak. "I need to warm myself."

"Of course, of course. Come in!" he said and pulled her by the arm, checking the road a final time before he closed up behind them, dropped a crossbar, and guided her into a parlor.

Molly went to the hearth, disregarding her surroundings. She was much too cold to stand directly at the fire, which was painful to her cheeks from several steps away.

"You're hurt," he said.

"My horse was killed. A winterbear—"

"A winterbear! You're lucky to have lived. Have you walked very far?"

"Miles," Molly said.

He took her cloak off and hung it up to dry beside the fire.

"But you must have a drink. Forgive me, aye a drink. My name is William Shepherd," he said, pouring her a cider in a tall pewter tankard. He mulled it at the hearth and placed it in her hands.

The first warm sip was medicine and magic, midsummer sweet and flowing softly to her stomach. Her toes didn't thaw but her fingers started prickling, and she finally felt relaxed enough to look around the room. It was dank, as if the inn had not been aired in many weeks. The floor was swept but grimy and the walls were drably papered. There were chairs around a table, several of them crooked, and the touches of décor—minor antlers, wilted herbs—were so devoid of charm they left no impression.

"Come from Root?" Shepherd asked.

"Yes," she said, regretting it at once. "I live in Grayport. My name is Mary Wright."

"Wright, you say?" He looked at her with doubt, leaning forward at her side and craning his neck to see her, like a footman well trained to stay in place behind his master. "Mary. I had thought . . . But what am I saying? Never you mind. Here you are, safe and sound. Don't you worry any longer."

"Have you a horse that I can buy? I have money."

"Not tonight! Such a ride and you alone. Mary, did you say? But you must stay the night. I cannot let you go, not in proper conscience. I will send you off warm and well fed, aye and horsed, but you must stay the night."

He took her by the arm and Molly shook him off.

He cowered as if she'd hit him. She hadn't meant to frighten him but liked that he was scared. She'd had enough of curiosity, enough of conversation. Still and all, he was right—she had to wait for morning. It was difficult to keep herself from crumpling to the floor.

"I'm sorry," she said. "You're only being kind. I'll stay and buy a horse and leave at first light. May I please see the room?"

He nodded and led the way, still cringing in submissiveness. She wondered how the poor man survived here, defenseless, with the Maimers and the bears and the countless traveling strangers.

"Have you ever been robbed?" she asked him in the awkward, rickety staircase.

"What? Count my stars, never once," Shepherd said. "I offer bed and board and folks appreciate that. I have little worth stealing." This was proven when he took her through an upstairs door. "Here is my very best room. You may have it free of charge."

The room contained a stool, a bed, and a tiny iron stove that was close enough to set the mattress on fire. A four-pane window overlooked the road. Molly almost had to duck so as not to bump the rafters.

"Is anyone else staying here tonight?" she asked.

"Not a soul," Shepherd said, setting a candle on the stool. "Travel slows with deadfall."

"Why is the stove lit?"

"The stove," he said, pondering its flame, as if the thing had a tendency to light itself in secret. "My rooms are always warm and welcome when they're needed."

Any other night, she'd have questioned such an answer, but she didn't have the will and felt grateful for the warmth. "Thank you," she said.

"Would you like a bite to eat? Another drink to help you sleep?"

"No."

Shepherd sighed, disappointed or relieved. His nightcap had slipped down sideways on his head and the candlelight shifting on his face made him older. Sad, Molly thought, with his poor scraggly beard. Lonely in the wilderness. A man without a family. Molly clasped his hand and felt him shiver at the touch. He patted her knuckles with his palm and then he left and closed her in.

She sat on the lumpy mattress, cozy with the stove, and fell asleep before she could fret, or cry, or wonder what would happen when she rode away tomorrow.

She woke before light. The room was still warm. She hadn't slept deeply and her mind felt clear, but the angle of her shadow on the wall looked wrong, as if the candle had been lowered and was glowing from the floor. Her limbs lay heavy and her tear ducts leaked, but she felt the need to turn without knowing why.

She gasped and tried to stand, tipping sideways and reaching out to counteract the fall. Her palm touched the stove. She was almost too alarmed to recognize the burn, and made a fist and raised it up to hit the figure on the stool.

"Stop," Nicholas said, "for the sake of Tom Orange."

Chapter Twenty-Eight

Molly sat on the bed. The sinking mattress made her tilt and when she righted herself to face him, they were touching at the knees. His clothes were plain as ever—black coat and breeches, white shirt and stockings—and the lack of ornamentation made him fashionably grave. He was much as she remembered, though he did look older. Several years might have passed, to judge by the finely wrought lines around his eyes and the new kind of weight—a density or depth—that gave his wiry frame both elegance and strength. He was smoak instead of ordinary wood. He had hardened.

Molly leapt and hit him, covering his face and ears with hot, furious slaps. She kicked the candle out. He ducked but didn't attempt to catch her hands; she pounded with her fists on his shoulders and his crown. His hair was smacked askew. She was hurting him, she knew it, and she would have kept going, maybe till he tumbled off the stool and she could kick him, but a quick sharp pain above her knee backed her up.

He had cut her with a knife. She landed on the bed again, huffing through the hair that had fallen around her mouth. She hiked her skirt, bared her knee, and touched the wound through her stocking. It was short and horizontal, just deep enough to bleed.

Nicholas hadn't stood and Molly hadn't heard a flint, but he had managed in the pause to reignite the candle—yet another of his mysteries and likely meant to vex her. Perhaps he'd hidden a living ember in a tin. She refused to look amazed, at least about the flame.

Nicholas fixed his hair and straightened out his coat. Red welts marked his face and he was swelling at the ear, and yet he didn't touch the places she had struck or seem surprised. He looked at her with love and held the knife where she could see it.

"My happiness at finding you alive is unrequited." Nicholas smiled weakly, like a child feigning courage. Molly stared to let him know that she could batter him again, even if it meant jumping toward the blade.

"You have questions," he began.

"How are you alive? What have you done to Tom?"

"I'll tell you. Please be patient."

"No!" she said and tensed as if to stand again, defiant.

Nicholas flicked the knife above his knee to catch her eye. He cut his own leg, mirroring her wound. He didn't wince. He didn't explain. The gesture's chilling strangeness made her watch very hard.

"I could tell you nothing at all," he said, "and still your reappearance in the city would destroy me. But once you know the facts, you won't tell a soul and you will choose, of your own free will, to leave forever."

He handkerchiefed his cut with calm, delicate fingers and the candle flame stilled, growing steady in its light.

"I knew that you would come as soon as you read the letter," he said.

"You said to ride for Liberty."

"I banked on your rebellion. I prepared either way—unpredictability was ever in your nature—but your flight toward Grayport was vastly more likely."

"You said my reappearance—"

"Listen, Molly. Listen. I have answers by the bushel. I watched you leave Root. You were a little less than graceful, jumping from the window, but you left in good time. I'm sorry about your horse. At least you saw a winterbear in all its fearsome glory."

She pressed the wound above her knee. Blood slithered through her fingers, mingling with the blood from the mare's severed neck, and then the memory and the smell made her cut sting worse.

"I paid William Shepherd to keep you here until I finished my work in Root," Nicholas said.

Feeble old Shepherd. Oh, she'd been a fool!

"He is an honorable man," Nicholas assured her. "I told the truth, as it happens: that my sister was running from trouble, and that for her sake, as well as for my own, it was imperative to keep her safe until I arrived. He was eager to assist. If not for my persuasion, he would not have taken payment."

Words and words—what was he saying? Truth, William Shepherd, payment and persuasion. What did it matter? He was here and he was talking like her brother, like her too familiar, undead, infuriating brother, and the one thing she needed him to clarify was how.

"I killed you," Molly said.

He raised the blade like a finger to his lips and said, "Shush. I will tell you how we came from Grayport to this. Whatever your emotions, I encourage you to rein them. Tom Orange has a much sharper blade to his throat."

"Tell me what you've done."

Nicholas laughed and wiped his face, amused by her contrariness but grimacing—in anger?—when his hand touched a spot above his eye where she had struck him. The knife was on his thigh now, close enough to snatch.

"In Grayport," he said, "we were desperate. We were poor. Would you believe that I was terrified? I did my best to hide it, from the onset of the sickness I endured aboard the *Cleaver* to the first cold night we hid inside the church. We were victims in a city full of predators and strangers. You remember the pickpocket."

Molly watched him closely. Did he know the man was dead?

"I found him easily," Nicholas said, "the night he stole your locket. He was a coward, easily pinched, and I was struck to think the two of us had seemed an easy target. Never in our lives had we been so common, marked by common criminals and bent to common work. We belonged in higher spheres, and I resolved to make it happen. I knew of Kofi Baa from the Customs House. I knew his business and his wealth—they were no great secret—and I knew that he could lift us if his will were so inclined. I paid to have him attacked and played the selfless hero. My injuries were bought: a sensible investment."

"How could you?" Molly said, recalling Kofi's smile and his deep, melodious laugh. "After what he did for us!"

"*Before* what he did for us. I chose not to tell you—did you really not suspect?—because I knew you wouldn't approve, however great the gain."

"It's terrible," she said.

"How?" Nicholas asked. "I never did the man a single stroke of harm. He rewarded me with trust and benefited vastly. Then his colleagues and friends were benefiting, too. I dealt with business woes to start, mostly trade laws and customs, but soon their needs diversified. With every problem solved, my reputation grew. People asked for arbitration. For avoidance of scandal. For extrication from legal, marital, and ethical dilemmas. I helped them as I could and they were satisfied to pay. But everything was built upon my ironclad success. There were problems, now and then, that even I could not resolve, and one can never let the rabble question the magician. So what does the magician do? He makes his own illusions."

The candle guttered out, sending up a fine, smoky ribbon in the moonlight. Molly's thoughts weren't in rhythm with the words he was speaking. She would start to comprehend but then her memory would stutter—back to Grayport, to sitting in the office while he worked, then to waking up tonight and finding him beside her.

"How do you control a blackmailer?" Nicholas continued. "Create one. How do you safeguard a secret? Know it. Whatever is required may be summoned or invented. Put simply, I devised my own worth among my clients. The truest self-reliance generates itself. My work was not so different from the tactics and deceptions we devised for Mrs. Wickware."

"It's criminal," she blurted, feeling stupid as she said it.

"Criminal." He laughed, sounding casual and warm. "I built the cages, in they went, and I provided them the key. All they lost was money. Each of them could spare it. I hope you aren't aghast that I meddled with the law. These are men's laws, malleable and thin: made to bend. They are not the laws of nature. Not the laws of life."

There was just enough moonlight to see him on the stool. She focused on his leg, first the blood and then the knife.

"We didn't sail three thousand miles to shiver, and starve, and be the browbeaten victims of the bright new world. We came to be strong. We came to be more. And what other option did we have?" Nicholas asked, leaning forward so his eye, only one, caught the moon. "Think of the bread riot in Umber. Did you not support the wretches who demanded something more? You and I stole apples on the morning we arrived. Then we needed something better, so I took that, too."

"But then we had enough," she said. "A home and means to live."

"Had you known what I was doing—and I wonder how much voluntary blindness dimmed your sight—what would you have done? Confessed to Kofi Baa? Consigned us to a destitute existence or to jail?"

Molly leaned forward, closer to his knee. The moonlight fell upon her own cheek now—cold, white light reminding her of winter, of the Grayport snow she'd eventually adored, of the chocolate she used to sip after shopping in the market. She remembered being happy that she made Kofi happy, and she couldn't bear the thought of causing him to glower.

Nicholas paused to think, comfortable but stern. He let his question dissipate. She played the timid listener.

"I had such a wealth of work," he said, "I had to hire help: desperate men and women who were squandering their gifts. You could say I had a staff of hand-picked talent. I gave them work by proxy— very few knew my name—and any caught or compromised were freed, again by proxy, or compelled to hold their tongues. One of my earliest and most reliable employees was the pickpocket. His name was Mr. Crutch: a middling thief who lacked direction when I found him and persuaded him to broaden his ambition. Marry threats of danger to the promise of reward, and any man alive will listen very closely. It was he who attacked Kofi Baa and wounded me, with great care, according to my instructions. I used him often that year."

"And do you know what you created?" Molly yelled to crack his calm. "Your friend became a Maimer!"

"Molly, you amaze me. I had thought you more astute. Did you think it a coincidence, an accident of fate, that your Maimer was a man who used to visit me in Grayport?"

Molly shrank back, out of the moonlight into the dark. She seemed to spiral and descend, as on the night she'd given birth after swallowing the potion, and she understood that yes, she had known for several minutes now—had sensed it in the slush coldly rolling in her center.

"I learned of it in Grayport, but not the full truth," he said. "The second Maimer that night—the man whose nose you smashed before escaping up the road—was apparently ashamed to tell me what had happened. He told me they were ambushed by the sheriff and a posse, and that Mr. Crutch was dead before he reached Root. Had I learned a young woman had bested them, ridden off blind, and captured Mr. Crutch singlehanded, I would have known at once my sister was alive."

Molly whispered with a quarter of her breath, "Tell me why."

"I'm afraid the Maimers' origin is lusterless," he said. "An enterprise that blossomed more than I expected. Many individuals who came to me for help used private couriers to deliver important letters. They were a treasure trove of secrets—personal, professional, and highly confidential. I resolved to offer the city's only safe delivery. All I had to do was thin the competition. As you know," he said, "the shortest route between Grayport and Liberty is the road through the forest, and messages were sent despite the perils. If well-paid couriers were not dissuaded by wildcats, bears, and ordinary brigands, what would prompt terror? Shadow men with knives. It is one thing to risk money or belongings, quite another risking the most cherished parts of ourselves. I wish I knew whoever first called them Maimers. They became an instant legend. It was more than I had hoped.

"Once news of the earliest victims reached Grayport, only the bravest couriers would travel on the road. Naturally they charged exorbitant rates, and I targeted the first such man who ventured out. The Maimers blinded him, preventing him from any future rides, and with the information gleaned from one of the letters he'd been carrying, I ruined a prominent trader with evidence of smuggling. People in Grayport grew nervous in the extreme about sending confidential messages. Soon they came to me, the man who solved their problems.

"I offered the swiftest, craftiest couriers: men in my employ. People paid handsomely for guaranteed delivery. I couldn't freely use the information in the letters—any evidence that I had read them would destroy my reputation—but I learned a great deal of cumulative value. The Maimers were instructed to attack random travelers to remove all suspicion that their motive was the mail. I owned the road and no one knew it."

The mattress was a sinkhole, cavernously deep. Molly touched her face and patterned it with blood. It smelled of old fear, sickly as a leech. The room was slick with gore, stuffed with tongues and ears and organs, and her head began to swim.

"You're a fiend," she said. "Evil."

"I have intellect and will and opportunities to thrive. Should I not embrace my powers? Flourish in the wild?"

"Do you not have a heart for everyone you've hurt?"

"I do not," Nicholas said, as if he'd thought about the question many times, many ways. "If I once had sympathy for others, I don't remember losing it. I know I loved our mother—I was shattered when she died, but even then I had the instinct to partially conceal it. And I love you and Frances from a time, long ago, before the openhearted part of me withdrew and disappeared. Why it left me is a mystery. I cannot say I miss it. My love for you and Frances brought only pain."

He shrank as if the whole of him had atrophied and closed. His shoulders hunched forward and his spine seemed to slacken. When he spoke again, his voice was neither confident nor wise, but neither was it feeble. It was open. It was young.

"All my life," he said, "I have been beaten down by sickness, and circumstance, and the brutishness of those who deemed themselves stronger. Our father was determined to enfeeble and control me. When we broke Mrs. Wickware, I saw another way. When we finally left home, the world spread before us. And when we first arrived in Grayport—when sickness, circumstance, and commonplace brutes threatened us again—I refused to buckle under. I might have given in to terror and despair. Instead, I took control to shield myself from harm. I'd have shielded you, too—how emphatically I tried!—had you not struggled free and wounded me yourself."

Molly wobbled to her feet, making Nicholas raise the knife and look at her severely, but all she did was cross the room and stand before the stove. It was three small steps but she was desperate for the distance.

He stood and said, "Have you never done harm to satisfy your needs? Have you never cut a path over someone else's life?"

"What have I done?" Molly asked, turning around to face him. "How can you suggest—"

"Your refusal to behave led to Frances's expulsion. We defied Mrs. Wickware and ground her to a pulp, but then you wavered and suggested it was I who lacked compassion. Did you not choose freely when we sailed away from Umber, knowing full well the dangers that awaited? Yet you pouted and complained while I fought to make it work, until at last you opposed me, openly and cruelly. Did you hesitate in trusting John Summer with our secrets? We had safety and prosperity. We finally had a home. What if someone had learned precisely who we were? Think of how a cunning individual could pin us. John Summer understood our delicate position and he used it—did you know?—when he came to me and forced me to consent to your engagement. How could I be certain that he wouldn't press for more? I sent him north and made sure he never reached Burn. Still your pregnancy remained," he said, swallowing to overcome a frailty in his voice. "Unmarried, unemployed—you were wholly unprepared. I offered a solution and beseeched you to accept it. You defied me and rejected it, forcing me to carry out the necessary acts."

She lunged for his knife. Nicholas stepped aside, much faster than she would have thought him capable of moving. He tripped her as she passed and held her face against the window.

"You killed her," Molly said, her tears a moony blur, "and meant to kill me."

"No," Nicholas said.

He grabbed the hair behind her head and forced her backward to the stove, and then he kept her there and faced her with the knife below her chin.

"I left the pistol on the table, knowing you would see it. I hoped that you would find the gun loaded and refuse it, even if you blamed me, even if you hated me. If only we could pass that night without a shot, the worst would be behind us and we might return to Grayport—broken but together, possibly to heal. Perhaps, given time—"

"I know I didn't miss."

"A ball of wax," Nicholas said, "that vaporized when fired. Not that your attempt didn't pierce me to the core. Still, I would have saved you if you hadn't washed away. I searched the creek for miles looking for your body, and eventually despaired. How did you come to Root?"

She sniffed the blubbery mess escaping from her nose and said, "The waters flowed together."

"Ah," Nicholas said. "It's remarkable you floated so far and yet survived. There is more life in you, dear sister, than even I believed." He lowered the knife and returned to the stool, choosing not to sit and speaking, with the moonlight haloing his ears, like a person who had memorized a noteworthy dream. "I returned to Grayport, holding to the tale that you had gone to live with relatives. I embellished the lie by saying I had sent you off for safety, that my efforts in the city—in particular my well-known defiance of the Maimers—had opened us to threats. How quickly people praised my extraordinary sacrifice. How little they suspected what my sacrifice had been."

Molly knelt beside the bed, unable to stand or answer. Nicholas turned his back to her and looked out the window at the forest, talking so his words made frost upon the glass.

He said, "This week a man in my employ tried to blackmail me. When his plan was uncovered, he attempted to escape. He was followed and shot, only to be saved by a sudden band of travelers. I hastened here to the inn to silence him myself. He appeared to die of his gunshot wound, an end that might have been questioned if the doctor coming from Root had been allowed to examine the body. The doctor was deterred. I was spending the night in this very room—a simple traveler, paying for his bed—when Sheriff Pitt and Tom Orange arrived with their remarkable news. It was grievous, losing all four Maimers in one swoop. If your town grew courageous, I could also lose the road. I followed Tom and Pitt the following day to take their measure—to discover what boldness might develop in the future.

"Imagine my astoundment! I was so shocked with joy at finding you alive, I nearly cried your name on entering the tavern. I blended with the crowd to see what I could learn. Eventually I spoke to Abigail Knox. She was very forthcoming, even with a stranger, on the subject of the woman who'd embraced Tom Orange. 'Her,' she said. She spoke to me at length with little prompting. Your past remained a mystery to everyone in Root—to everyone, she said, except Tom Orange.

"I was just about to leave, but what a spectacle ensued! Tom's uncle shouting insults for everyone to hear, and Tom and Sheriff Pitt publicly at odds. The sheriff seemed of small concern, satisfied to bluster. Oh, but Tom. Fiery Tom, full of tempest and conviction. How to draw you off from such a formidable companion? Once I learned more, it was easier than fate.

"I paid a boy to deliver your letter, waited for you to leave, and visited Lemuel Carver at his house. Again I told the truth. 'I am Molly's brother,' I said. 'I mean to steal her from the Orange.' He let me in at once—I might have been John Lumen himself, such a thrill was in his face—and when I asked him for a drink, he turned to find a bottle. I struck him on the skull with a smoakwood stick. I cannot think the world will weep at his demise. He was far enough along before I ever came to Root. One could smell the putrefaction of a man approaching death.

"But a man without friends might have lain there for days. I needed him found," Nicholas said. "I broke a lantern in his home, waited near the woods until the flames began to spread, and then departed while the neighbors hurried out to find him and arrest the man most likely to have killed him."

Molly had passed through heat, like a seething of her blood, and shriveled now within, mummified with horror. The stove had almost cooled, the last log depleted to a black, withered husk. Molly wobbled on her knees and bumped her head against the iron, thinking of the stick that had cracked Lem's skull. She remembered Lem's tears when he spoke about his wife. She smelled the ashes and imagined Root pulsing from the flames.

"The murder will occupy the town until I see you on your way," Nicholas said. "I could have killed Tom and blamed it on Lem, but keeping Tom alive gives me power over you. Unless I'm very much mistaken and you don't care a whit—"

Molly stood in Tom's defense on cold, deadened feet, choked by dual urges to confirm it or deny it.

"As I hoped," Nicholas said. "Understand, throughout it all, I have never aimed to hurt you. That was the effect, not the motive of my actions. I did everything I could to shelter you from harm. Now I offer you a choice I should have offered during your pregnancy—a choice I failed to give because I didn't want to lose you. Come with me to Grayport, board a ship to Bruntland, and sail away from Floria to live again with Frances. She is living independently with money I have sent and will continue to provide. Our father will not find you."

The dark leapt alive at the sound of Frances's name, brightening the stark gray sea in Molly's mind. Oh! but even lighted, how it flooded around her head, terrible and vast. Back to Bruntland—it would drown her.

"I offer you the freedom and the life you always craved," he said. "Do whatever you will. Marry whomever you choose. Ask for anything you wish and I will happily provide it. But you must board the ship. You must not defy me. I have given Tom Orange word of your departure and will see that he is freed and restored to good standing. But if either of you speaks or works against me, now or later, Tom's life, as well as yours, is immediately forfeit."

"You would kill me after all?"

"I hope to see you live. As I said, returning you to Frances was a choice I should have offered you before. I have learned from my mistake. Have you learned from your own?"

"I never made a mistake!" she cried. "I never asked for any of this! I would have stayed with Tom and had a home, if you had let me!"

"Tell me truthfully, Molly—how have you fared in Root? More importantly," he said, "how has Root fared with you? Has the tavern benefited from your presence? Has Tom Orange? Or have you rained complication onto everyone you've met? How sincerely do you care about your home, or Tom, or anyone in Root if your immediate impulse was to abandon them all to keep yourself from danger?"

"I never meant to hurt them," Molly said, and clutched her chest.

"Sail away. Start fresh. Revel in your freedom. You have done so before with wonderful success. It is a quality of yours: a marvelous facility to wriggle out, adapt, and bloom without light. You have never been the smartest or the strongest," Nicholas said, "but there is a Mollyness in you that nothing stunts or changes. You are as thoroughly yourself as in the hour you were born, and that is beautiful and rare. Take it with you. Take it home."

His knife had vanished into his sleeve. He opened his arms, defenseless, daring her to push him out the window or embrace him.

"Everything I've done in Root was meant to save us both. I offer you escape, the very treasure you pursued tonight. Accepting it," he said, "is merely following your nature."

Chapter Twenty-Nine

Pitt did not consider himself unflappable or prudish, but Bess's violent tears, combined with the careless state of her nightclothes, distressed him to the point where he began to doubt his character. He rarely saw crying so emphatic from adults and might have viewed her as a child—she was, after all, barely into womanhood—if not for how her breasts kept swaying in her shift. She hugged herself and rocked, leaning forward on her bed, and when he pulled out a handkerchief to wipe his own brow, she thought he was being gentlemanly and plucked the cloth away. She blew her nose strongly, like a bugle underwater. Pitt reclaimed the kerchief, disconcerted by its soddenness, and laid it on the smoakwood chair beside the bed.

She had stomped around her room, she had clutched her head and wept, and now she blinked and cleared her eyes and looked at him in anger. Pitt retreated half a step, trying to focus on her face and wishing she would tie the open laces at her bosom. He took a blanket from the bed and draped her back, and Bess cocooned herself within it, just as he had hoped. Once again he backed away and hazarded a question.

"Can you remember anything he said or did after he left the taproom?"

"I already told you," Bess said. "The last I saw Tom was when he stormed upstairs."

"He slept all day?"

"And through the night, far as I know. He told us not to knock. We let him be, all but Molly."

"When—"

"I couldn't say, I wasn't mindful of the time. It was dark. I gave her a letter from the table and she clomped upstairs, and when I came to bed she wasn't in the room and I was glad of it. She'd spoken awful mean to me and didn't seem herself."

Bess focused on the bunched-up blanket in her fists, then glowered up at Pitt as if he'd tricked her into wearing it.

He cleared his throat. The effort made him genuinely cough. He could have used a handkerchief but didn't have a spare, and so he swallowed his phlegm and asked her, "Do you know who sent the letter?"

"Abigail," she said. "Molly recognized the hand but wouldn't open it in front of me."

"And why did you assume she went to Tom at such an hour?"

Bess scowled at his chest and seemed bitterly resentful—not of the questions he was asking, but of the whole dreadful morning. He couldn't rightly fault her if she didn't want to talk, but Bess was all he had aside from Ichabod and Nabby, one mute, the other scolding him for locking up Tom.

"Where else would Molly have gone, if not to Tom?" Pitt said.

"I don't know!" Bess cried.

She stood and threw the blanket off and hugged him with a thump, pillowy and warm and dampening his waistcoat. He held her close with fatherly intent and manly panic. How she cried and wet his collar, squeezing out his air—he swore that he would care for her however he was able, forcing down the thought that she would make a lovely wife.

She shoved him off. He feared his thoughts had been apparent through his hug but she was only growing frantic from the horror of it all.

"It wasn't Tom! I don't believe it! Not until he says it!"

Bess's volume, too hysterical, belied her growing doubt. She faced him, standing upright and gorgeous in her fury, in her fear and her confusion, while her world collapsed around her.

Pitt could see in her the brokenness he'd felt long ago, when devotion to his father smudged into loathing. He had beaten on the hangman's tree until his knuckles bled. He'd kicked his own dog the day of the execution, then regretted it and wept when the dog cringed away. He still blamed his father—first for giving away the tavern, then for shooting Mr. Orange, then for dying in disgrace.

Blaming Tom was something else: irrational, ingrained. Was it simply that their fathers hadn't lived to bear the guilt? All he knew was that the Oranges were equally at fault and Tom had gone years without acknowledging the stain.

"I want to see him," Bess said.

"I can't allow that now."

"Why not?"

"I haven't questioned him yet," Pitt said.

"Then what are you doing here? Ask him! Go and ask him!" Bess said, and pushed him on the chest. "It might have been Tom, it might have been anyone. I'm the one with reason, but you haven't even asked me if I killed my own father."

"Did you?" Pitt croaked, scared to hear the answer.

Bess punched him on the shoulder—twice—very hard.

"No!" she said. "I didn't! But instead of asking me or asking Tom or finding Molly, you've been here doing nothing! I want to talk to Tom. I need to know, I need to ask him."

Yet she didn't leave the bedroom and march up the hall, but rather threw herself backward on the bed and closed her eyes. She looked too dramatic, like a child playing dead, except she had the special wildness that often comes with grief and made him think, once again, of throwing punches at a tree. But he couldn't let emotion weaken his advantage. He had doubts enough already, holes he couldn't fill, an opportunity at last to set things right.

⚜

"It wasn't Tom! I don't believe it! Not until he says it!"

Tom could hear his cousin clearly as he sat inside the holding room, but desperate as he was to call back and reassure her, shouting would be fruitless. He had no self-defense; insistence wouldn't help. If even a sliver of Bess believed he was guilty, the sliver would infect her, and the same went for Pitt and everyone else in town.

Each time he peeked out the window through the bars, another group of neighbors had appeared just below, defying the cold to gossip in the dirty silver daylight. He felt the news spreading through the town like a spill, impossible to stop and freezing into shapes. He knew that first impressions would be difficult to shake. Once it crossed people's minds that he might have killed his uncle, they would always think him capable of murdering his kin.

He himself wasn't certain of his innocence or guilt.

He had woken in a stupor, only listening at first, unable to open his eyes when Pitt and two men—he couldn't tell who—appeared in his room and jostled him in bed. He couldn't understand the depth of his paralysis. "Murder" and "arrest," he heard. "Lemuel" and "fire." When they hauled him out of bed, his head dangled back and there were fists holding lanterns, smeary in his vision. He couldn't walk or speak and everything was fogged. They lugged him into the holding room and locked him in alone, and there he moaned in his confusion, in the darkness and the daze until the dawn light came, roseate and thin, and he discovered his bloodied hands and smelled the acrid smoke. They had searched him, he remembered. He had bruises on his ribs.

Eventually his mind cleared well enough to think and he could hear Pitt interrogating Ichabod and Nabby. His uncle had been murdered and the tannery had burned. He had planned on visiting Lem today to threaten him and break him, only how could he have killed his own uncle and forgotten? God knew he had wished it—never proudly, no, but vividly—but still it seemed impossible, in spite of all his bruises, and he hugged himself and wondered what had actually happened.

His mother felt near. He thought of her watching him and grieving for the family and the home. On the day they buried his father, she had pampered him and dressed him, having entered his room and found him out of his shift, thin and naked. His brother was already dressed. Win was older, Win was strong, and yet it wasn't until their mother appeared, beautiful and sere and wearing a plain black gown, that Tom felt childish and utterly exposed. With his overlarge feet and small, shriveled penis, he could not keep tears from springing to his eyes—tears that only intensified his mother's ministrations as she helped him into his stockings, and his breeches, and his shoes. When he finally pushed her off, she looked at him and cried. He was sorry to have hurt her but he never did apologize.

His father used to say, "Rely upon yourself. Ask for help, you ask for stronger men to come and take advantage." Mr. Pitt had asked for help and lost the family tavern. After his father had been shot and Mr. Pitt was set to hang, Tom had wondered: Who was right? Which of the men was really stronger? He reflected on it now, the man that he'd become, one who rarely asked for help but often tried to give it. He might have called it wisdom if he weren't locked up, fearing he had done no better than his father.

He felt a tiny itch just above his ankle. Such a minuscule thing and yet it overrode his thoughts, and when he scratched his calf he found something hidden in his stocking. He rolled it down, peeled a scrap of paper off his leg, and blinked until his eyesight cleared enough to read.

> *Leave Root and Molly dies. Send others, Molly dies.*
> *Stay put and keep quiet, Molly lives.*
> *You are watched.*

Whatever lift had briefly fluttered from discovering his innocence immediately plunged. He read the note again. No wonder he had not heard Molly in the hall. It was the first dawn in months she hadn't made a ruckus with an accident or laugh. He hadn't even noticed.

Think, think, think. There was spindrift floating at the edges of his vision and his head felt stuffed, ear to ear, with swollen wool. He rubbed his knuckles in distraction, hard enough to peel the jellied scabs and make them bleed again.

Unger Bolt the blacksmith was stationed in the hall. Pitt had pressed him into service—Tom had recognized their voices—and in spite of Unger's faltering reluctance to assist, he had finally agreed to guard the room. Tom had known Unger since the two of them were boys and now he went to the door, determined to exonerate himself and speak to Pitt. Then he hesitated. What if Unger *did* let him out?

His insides ached but not from the bruises. The ache was deeper, in the tension that was holding him together. He hid the message in his stocking again, crossed the room, and stood at the window, unafraid to meet the gazes of the gathering crowd below. He gripped the bars and tried to concentrate the vigor in his arms. He couldn't dwell on Molly and succumb to his fear, so he focused on the cold, black iron in his hands and tried to understand how his uncle had been murdered.

There was someone on the stairs: sharp steps, coming up. Tom left the bars and listened at the door, knowing from the sound it wasn't Ichabod or Nabby. Unger moved his feet like a giant in the hall.

"No one is to see him, Mrs. Knox," Unger stated. "Sheriff Pitt said—"

"The need is gravely urgent," she replied. "Stand aside and open the door. You cannot think I've come to aid in his escape."

"Be that as it may"—Unger's voice was thick and plodding—"he is not to speak with anyone. My job is to deny—"

"Let me in or I will tell Mrs. Bolt about the time . . . "

Abigail whispered too low for Tom to hear. The door abruptly opened.

Unger faced Tom with evident distress and said to Abigail, "You won't tell Mary?"

"Not today."

She looked at Tom, giving him a lightning-bolt assessment—hot, many-branched, bright without a sound—and then retreated to the stairs, where someone else was coming up. Tom backed away to lessen Unger's worry; he would not get the poor man in trouble by escaping. The hidden piece of paper shifted in his stocking, but before he could ensure that it was properly concealed, Abigail returned, stepped inside the room, and waited for Ichabod to guide her wounded husband from the hall.

Benjamin hung upon his arm until they made it through the door. "Many thanks," he said to Ichabod, and stood without support.

Ichabod looked toward Tom—*I'm your man*—then exited the room and walked downstairs.

"Lock us in now, Unger," Abigail said.

The frowning blacksmith complied, seeming unsure if he was worsening or improving his predicament by doing so.

Benjamin's feebleness and slushy white complexion were alarming, but his eyes were bright as ever—bayonet sharp—and for the first time in all their many seasons of acquaintance, Tom felt weaker, much weaker than his friend.

"Benjamin," he said, stricken with remorse.

"I need to examine you," he rasped. Benjamin raised his stump to straighten the glasses on his face, still favoring the arm out of life-long habit—and noted his mistake with studious attention, like a scientist compiling observations for a treatise. "Extend your hands, palms down. Nearer to the window, please—we should have brought a light. Fist them . . . and relax. Curl your fingers. And again. I'm told you have contusions on your abdomen, as well? Bruises, Tom, bruises. Lift your shirt so I may see them."

Benjamin poked and palpated each of Tom's wounds, and then he slumped and wiped his neck and offered no opinion. He had begun to sweat profusely; the beads were thick as milk. He leaned against the wall, giving Abigail the floor. It was her turn now to scrutinize the prisoner—a woman hard to lie to, who seemed to know the answers. Tom dropped his shirt to cover up his stomach, feeling in the pause as if he'd also dropped his breeches.

Then they all heard Pitt confronting Unger in the hall.

"Damn it, what did I tell you? Is your brain a bloody anvil?" This was followed by the rumbling drone of Unger's explanation. "Give me the key," Pitt said. "I ought to lock you up, too."

He swung the door inward, hiding Abigail from view. The shadow-eyed sleepiness that lurked below his zeal made him seem less official, more dangerously common. Abigail emerged and shut the door behind him. Pitt spasmed in surprise, spun around, and raised his fists.

"For pity's sake," Abigail said. "You look like a bear cub learning how to box."

Pitt dropped his hands but kept his shoulders in a bunch. "You aren't supposed to be here. That dunderhead Bolt was ordered not to let—Benjamin, go home. You ought to be in bed. This doesn't concern you. I have everything in hand." Pitt winced, seeming stricken by his poor choice of words.

"Have you already questioned Tom?" Abigail asked.

"I had to talk to Bess. She's understandably distraught about—"

Abigail stepped in front of Pitt and said to Tom, "Yesterday morning, you argued with the sheriff about Lem and walked upstairs. What happened after that?"

Tom recounted what he remembered: having a rum, going to bed, waking up to his arrest. "I didn't drink enough to sleep as long as I did."

"You sound like every drunk I ever met," Pitt scoffed. "Explain your knuckles and your ribs."

"Somebody must have done it while I slept," Tom said.

Pitt looked to Abigail and Benjamin and laughed, only to be dumbstruck by finding them attentive. "Hell and death, he wasn't tickled! Have you seen his cuts and bruises? I'm expected to believe he wasn't awake when he received them?"

Benjamin reached for Abigail, requiring her support, but neither made a show of his deteriorating strength. He coughed and said to Tom, "Describe the stupor when you woke."

Tom's grogginess had faded, making it hard to recollect, the way a half-lit dream is soon forgotten in the sun. "More than tired," Tom said. "More than waking up thick. My limbs didn't answer. Everything was smeared, like a room looks blurry through a grease-paper window. They dragged me in here before I thought to say a word and then I couldn't, not at first."

"Was there any taste or odor?" Benjamin inquired.

Tom had noticed it for hours, scarcely giving it a thought. "Cherry."

"Sweet or sour?"

"Salty," Tom said.

Benjamin's eyes flickered wider and his pupils grew sharp. He was holding on to Abigail's arm to keep his balance but he yanked it down hard with sudden, vital force.

"There is a singular native berry called the blood drop," he said, "frequently mistaken for the drupe of common holly. It is similar in size but distinguishably redder. I learned of it from Hook Feet, the

Elkinaki boy whose ankles I corrected. It is known as a relaxant, given to children suffering nightmares. In minor amounts, the berry's effects are negligible, and yet the juice, boiled to a concentrate and carefully fermented, is said to possess soporific qualities, inducing in its user a profound weight of sleep. A characteristic, I am told, is the flavor you described."

"You think a *natural* did this?" Pitt said.

Benjamin closed his eyes as if inanity had stung them. "Any individual can utilize a potion."

"Humbug and nonsense. He got himself drunk."

"Furthermore," Benjamin said, "the abrasions on Tom's knuckles are inconsistent with the oft-seen injuries of fisticuffs, unless perhaps he fought against a rough piece of granite. I believe"—here he coughed again, brandishing his stump—"Tom was physicked with a sedative and wounded in his bed."

"What on earth for?"

"To make him look guilty," Abigail said, as if the sheriff might have sipped a little blood drop himself. "Do you not find it strange that no one saw Tom leaving or returning? That Lemuel's body was halfway out the door of his house, his head wound plainly visible, as if the fire's only purpose was to draw the town's attention? Someone wanted Tom arrested right away."

"Who?" Pitt said.

Abigail turned, speaking pointedly to Tom. "Someone who came for Molly and perceived you as a threat. She hasn't been seen since yesterday evening."

"I know," Tom said, then remembered no one had told him. "I heard people talking outside below the window."

Pitt squinted at the lie, piercing through the gloom with sharper intuition than he typically displayed. Then he bungled it and said, "Who's to say *she* didn't play a part in Lem's murder?"

"There's something else," Abigail said. "I spoke to a young man here at the tavern yesterday morning. The two of you had just returned with the Maimers. So many people were inquiring after Benjamin, I was relieved when the young man asked about Molly. He didn't identify himself but he was charming, I was heady from a third glass of wine, and I confess to answering a good many questions, very uncharitably," she said with a noble blush, "about Molly's provenance and place here in Root. In retrospect, his interest was peculiarly direct."

"What did he look like?" Pitt said.

"Delicate, of slight build and milk-white complexion. He had black hair tinged with gray. One of his upper teeth was prominently chipped."

Benjamin turned to Tom, luminously keen, and said to Abigail and Pitt, "Molly's locket held a tooth."

Abigail regarded him with evident surprise, seeming piqued that she hadn't learned the information sooner. "When did you discover this?"

But Benjamin waved her off, using the stump as if to call upon her patience and her sympathy. She stiffened and relented; her expression stayed tart.

Tom looked down to gather his composure and the paper felt all the more abrasive in his stocking. Was it possible that Molly hadn't shot her brother? Had she lied, or only missed? Either way, he'd survived. The fact was like a bullet in his own bruised chest, and Tom was desperate to contain his worry and amazement.

"Did you send Molly a letter?" Pitt said to Abigail.

"No," she replied, frowning at the question.

"Bess said Molly had a letter in the taproom. She recognized the hand and said it came from you."

"What did it say?"

"Bess didn't know. I suppose you have a simple explanation for it all," Pitt said to Tom.

Tom shook his head. They seemed to grow aware that he was hesitant to speak—indifferent to the evidence that pointed to his innocence.

"Ichabod told us one of the Maimers' horses has been stolen," Abigail said. "Something in the letter must have scared her off."

"Where would she have gone?" Benjamin asked Tom.

"Her husband lives in Grayport," Pitt declared. "His name is Jacob Smith. I'm told that he's a man of influence and means."

He wouldn't have looked more victorious if Molly had appeared, summoned by his words, in a great plume of smoke. His statement left the Knoxes visibly astonished.

"The man I followed was a banker named Alexander Bole. He clammed up tight on learning I was sheriff—he's a man of crooked business, unquestionably crooked. I threatened to investigate his dealings and he talked. Her name is Molly Smith. Her husband," Pitt said, giving the word extra relish and directing it at Tom, "is a translator, arbitrator, man of private counsel—quite the jack of all trades. A fishy character, I think."

"Then of course it must be him," Abigail said. "He comes to Root and finds his wife living here with Tom. You might have told us sooner!"

Pitt's smirk disappeared. He seemed to recognize he'd given Tom a plausible defense, one that he himself was starting to believe. Benjamin, however, knew his friend too well and scrutinized Tom, sensing there was more—hidden facts that left the rest of them in ignorance and doubt.

"We have to find Molly," Abigail decided. "Send a rider in each direction on the road and bring her back."

"No," Tom said, so emphatically that Abigail's mouth snapped shut.

The blood-drop flavor had returned to his tongue, fainter than before but more perceptibly a poison. His body felt depleted and his heart felt cold, but the haze had burned away and left his mind clear as air.

"I need to talk to you alone," Tom said to Pitt.

He looked at Abigail hard, willing her to go and putting so much significance and firmness in his gaze, he overcame her poise and made her nervous, almost fearful. Benjamin nodded to his wife and turned around to leave, having come as a physician in possession of his strength but now succumbing to the weakness of a patient out of bed. With a sniff of disapproval and a quick, sharp sigh, Abigail knocked and Unger opened the door.

"Thank you," Tom said, "for coming here to help. Get yourselves home or wait downstairs. Unger—you, too. Empty out the hall and let us talk in private."

Abigail hardened at the implication of eavesdropping, but after a final look at Tom she led her husband down the stairs.

Unger hesitated, waiting for the sheriff to instruct him. Pitt paused, too, until it seemed his curiosity outweighed his reservations and he said, "I'll be fine. Lock us in and wait in the taproom."

Unger eagerly obeyed, his cannonball shoulders sagging in relief. He shut the door and left the hall, using his musket as a walking stick. They listened to it clacking as he tromped downstairs, and then the room fell silent and the men stood alone.

Pitt took a pistol from the pocket of his coat.

"There's a paper in my stocking," Tom said. "I'm going to get it."

He stooped to roll his stocking down before he had permission, stood back up, and held the message out between them. Pitt stretched his arm and took it with his fingertips, apparently afraid the paper was a trick and Tom would try to jump him if he took a step forward. He read the note in three quick glances with a frown.

"The man with the chipped tooth who talked to Abigail," Tom said. "His name is Nicholas. He isn't Molly's husband. He's her brother."

He told Pitt everything that Molly had divulged. The siblings new to Grayport. Nicholas's office. John Summer, Molly's pregnancy, the cabin, and the shot. He didn't mention Molly's real last name or General Bell, which were secrets, even now, Pitt could do without.

The room was bright and frigid, giving Pitt a fierce intensity—a glint like the nickel of the pistol he was holding.

"Her brother killed her baby and she shot him," Pitt said. "She floated down the river, started over here in Root, and now he's risen from the dead, stolen her away, and gotten you arrested so you wouldn't interfere."

"Aye."

"And you expect me to believe it," Pitt said.

"You already do."

Pitt held the paper near the barrel of his gun. "The note says you're supposed to stay put and keep quiet. You're telling me to save your own skin."

"He doesn't want her dead," Tom said. "He wants her gone. If no one took the ferry then they must have gone to Grayport."

He took a step forward. Pitt cocked the pistol. Tom reached out and grabbed the barrel in his fist, moving up close until the gun was at his chest.

"Let me stop him," Tom said.

"How?"

"Sneak me out of Root. If I'm really being watched, no one else can know until I'm well away to Grayport."

"And let me explain tomorrow how I let you get away?"

Pitt ground the muzzle into one of Tom's buttons, pressing on a bruise underneath the shirt.

"You can't do nothing," Tom said.

"I can hold you till the circuit judge comes to hold trial. With Molly gone and no real evidence to clear you"—Pitt crushed the note and shoved it into his pocket—"you're neck deep in horse shit, right where you belong. If a jury finds you guilty, I shouldn't have trouble buying back the tavern."

"God damn it," Tom said. "That isn't right."

"But it's legal. Your father didn't mind making that distinction."

"You'd let a killer take Molly just to burn me," Tom said.

"Even if your story is true, you're putting her in danger if you don't stay here." Pitt smiled so wickedly it wasn't like a smile; it was more like an ax cut opening his face. "So tell me," he said, lowering the pistol. "Where's the benefit to anybody else if you're free?"

Chapter Thirty

Molly and Nicholas reached Grayport in late afternoon. They entered through the palisade gate, taking the long way around—the outermost road beside the meadows, farms, and marshes—to the harbor with the city just beside them. They had left Shepherd's Inn shortly after dawn and traveled all day, rarely speaking in the cold. Nicholas had ridden with a pistol in his hand. Molly had considered galloping off and daring him to shoot, but her limbs had lacked the energy for darting into action.

Now the journey had exhausted him, and Molly grew alert. Nicholas's cough was grain-dust dry. He'd been forced to hide his pistol once they exited the forest and was quite a ways behind her now, lowering his guard.

A lamplighter passed, rather early with the daylight lingering around them, and the lamps began to glow in preparation for the dark. Fear of night touched the city. Deadfall, like much of Root's extraordinary weather, had stayed within the Antler River Valley far behind them, but the temperature was cold enough for nighttime frost. Molly saw a side street open on her right, stretching three or four blocks into the city's inner maze—one of many they had passed where Nicholas would lose her if she bolted. She turned: he was shivering and slumping in his saddle. Wind billowed through his coat.

Then they rode around the corner of the rope makers' storehouse and finally saw the harbor. It defeated her completely.

She had diverted herself for hours, staying focused on the present—on the weather, on the birds, on her brother's diminishing strength. Now the present was the fact she had struggled to deny. The falling sun plunged the quarter-mile of docks into cold, heavy shadow. The temperature immediately dropped. Molly sagged. Nicholas rode beside her now, enlivened by the breeze and by the tumult, grim but vigorous, of seamen hard at work to catch the evening tide.

Molly looked for anyone she knew along the way. She spied an apple cart but didn't see the vendor they had robbed, and although she had frequented the docks last summer, none of the merchants or the sailors or the yardsmen looked familiar. Molly turned toward the harbor, which had not yet slipped altogether into shade. The water lay black beneath the sun-glittered waves, and while the ships sailing off were brilliant white and gold, those closer to the shore were shadow-bound and stained. The smell of fish was morbid. Filth pervaded the docks and the salt upon the ground was like a rime of dirty frost.

Molly recognized a ship and read *Cleaver* on its hull. She stood in her stirrups for a glimpse of Captain Veer or Mr. Knacker, but the deck had been abandoned and the ship looked lifeless. The crew had come to port and flooded into the city. She could only hope that some of them had lingered on the docks.

They rode for several more minutes before Nicholas dismounted. He tied their horses to a post and offered a hand to guide her down. Molly barely noticed she had gotten off the saddle. She saw another vessel looming up before her. It was a double-masted merchant ship of moderate proportions, smaller than the *Cleaver* and far more decrepit. Its name, *Dick's Fortune,* was nearly illegible under many seasons' grime. The deck swarmed with sailors who were shouting, swearing, and laughing, a raggedy crew of several dozen souls, tightly packed. She smelled them on the breeze, waxy-eared and sweaty, even now with the unwashed voyage still ahead. Pleasant memories of the *Cleaver,* of adventure and camaraderie and sailing into life, sank beneath the memory of vile Mr. Fen. She stood as if in waterbreath, laboring for air.

"You cut it close," said a man, walking up to meet them.

He was short, roughly Molly's height, and muscularly dense. He wore a tarred straw hat and a thick, buttoned coat and she discovered it was he, not the sailors, she had smelled. Nicholas met the man indifferently but Molly backed away. He was eerily familiar—not his tan round face, nor his posture, nor his clothes. His voice, she thought: the phlegmatic rolling of his words.

"This is Grigory," Nicholas said. "He will escort you back to Bruntland."

"He's a Maimer," Molly said. "He wanted to break my teeth!"

She said it loud enough that people on the dock glanced around. Nicholas took her arm and led her between their horses.

"I'm sorry it must be him but I am short on reliable men. Grigory will treat you with the utmost care. On my orders," Nicholas said. "On threat of painful death. He will take you overseas to Frances's embrace."

She looked beyond him to the ship again, its rigging a complexity of coils, nets, and knots, carefully prepared but chaotic from afar.

"Remember," Nicholas said. "Frances cannot learn the truth of our estrangement. Tom Orange's protection depends on your silence. And do not think his freedom will enable him to act, or that your traveling to Bruntland puts you safely out of reach."

Molly's eyes fought tears, as a jaw fights yawns. "I could scream right now."

"And Tom would hang for murder."

"How will you prove he's innocent?" she asked. "You won't confess."

"There's always someone to blame. Failing that, I have the circuit judge—a man who sent a letter that was grievously misplaced. It contained certain facts he would not wish exposed."

"How can I believe you?" Molly said.

"Because you must."

Her aches had grown far too familiar to acknowledge. She was weary from the ride and sore through and through. Someone's laughter on the dock made her think of Davey Mun. He must have felt this, too: wounded past recovery, acknowledging his fate and sitting down to freeze. Her brother's explanations flooded over her again, muddied by the many accusations he had made.

"I love you," Nicholas said. "I understand if you despise me."

He studied her and paused to see what she would say. The child in him showed, along with traces of their father. Molly felt a heart-deep frothing in her blood, a wild blaze of heat consuming everything around her. The glimpse of what he had been—her family and her friend—rippled in her thoughts as if her mind were truly fevered, but her pain went deeper to a vision of herself.

She didn't say a word. She didn't blink or cry. Nicholas lowered his head and Molly walked away, having beaten him at least in the contest of eyes, and took the gangplank to leave her life in Floria behind.

⚜

The ship left at dusk with the boisterous sailors hauling lines and spreading sails until they cleared the docks, tacked south-southwest, and made a steady four knots to the middle of the harbor. Molly stood at the taffrail. She had watched her brother shrink as they departed, his dark clothes blending with the shadows onshore until his face became a dot, a tiny fleck of white.

The sun was dead-fire orange. Molly watched it set and streak the clouds lavender-red. Grayport was lovely in the onset of night, vast and indiscernible aside from all the window lights, each of them distinct but forming, in array, a constellation more beautiful than any in the sky. She thought of the Orange lit at night as she had seen it from the barn, and she could almost taste the warm stuffed apple she had savored—cinnamon and cream, a sweet ball of autumn. Nabby kneading bread dough. Smoakwood fire. The pipe-tobacco sting that seasoned Tom's tongue.

But the Orange must have closed: Tom arrested; Bess in tatters from the murder of her father. She herself had disappeared and nobody had followed. Nicholas had dealt with Tom, preventing him from chasing her, and all the rest of Root had blithely let her go. Why had she expected any different? Yet she had. After so much attention had been lavished on her coming, she'd expected more ripples when she finally went away.

She had left more than ripples in her wake, heaven knew, running off from trouble over and over again. Following her nature, Nicholas had said—but what had been her sin, except escaping from her bonds?

Mrs. Wickware and Jeremy, her father and her brother—how could anybody fault her for resisting their control? She had tried to marry John, be a mother, live in Root. She had tried! Or had all of it been different kinds of flight?

The sky was molten iron, cooling down to black. Somewhere in the dark lay the bodies she was leaving—John, Lem, Davey, maybe even Tom. She held her stomach, felt a movement like a small, soft heel, and vomited over the rail.

Grigory chuckled at her back and said, "Seasick already."

He had hovered all the while, never too close but never too far. His pipe failed to cloak his omnipresent stink—the reek of old beef caught between his teeth, a privy smell that issued like a vapor from his underclothes.

Wind thumped the sails. They would soon clear the harbor. She walked away and stood beside a monstrous coil of rope, looking past the prow to where the ocean spread wide. The air was so pure it made her thoughts effervesce. The ship wouldn't stop and she couldn't swim back, and so she looked ahead to Bruntland, past the continent of waves, imagining a trim white cottage in the country. When her breaths tightened up, she clutched her chest and pricked her finger on a straight pin fastening her gown. It made her think of Frances sewing buttons in a rocking chair, sitting near the hearth with Molly at her side. They would soon be reunited, cozy in the winter: Molly crunching through the snow with a fresh pail of milk, admiring the hills and smiling at the flurries. Home. A proper home, free of scrutiny and secrets.

Nicholas was right. She adapted. She survived. "You are you, purely you," her brother had insisted. But her Mollyness was gone, abandoned in the Orange. How could she have trusted him to liberate Tom? The whole of Root erupted into life within her mind but Tom was all she cared about, the only one she focused on, and picturing him dead sucked the color from her life and made a sinkhole, pulling all her memories inside.

Grigory approached. He grinned at her with something less than idle curiosity: a sensual appraisal and a newborn ease, now that he was free of her brother's watchful eye. He had hacked people's limbs and relished the employment. There were others just like him on the continent behind her: Nicholas's roaches, thriving in his care. They would scurry back to Root and feed however they pleased.

"I'm going to the head," she said.

"Happy to assist."

"Did my brother tell you what happened to the last man who troubled me at sea?"

"Ain't no trouble if you're willing," Grigory said, but then he stood aside and let her go without impediment.

The main facilities were unenclosed holes along the bowsprit, visible to anybody standing on deck. Molly approached Captain Lark, a wide-mouthed giant with a heartbroken manner, and he granted her permission to relieve herself below. A friendly midshipman led her into the quarter gallery, hung a lantern from a ceiling hook, and left her there alone.

The room was dankly cold and solid oak, floor to ceiling. Paneled windows canted outward at the stern, a bench with cushioned seating spanned the rear wall, and a scarred, heavy table with a brass candelabrum stood fastened into place on a mildewed rug. Molly felt ill, much worse than at the taffrail, but instead of using the head she sat on the bench below the windows, removed her cloak, and rolled her sleeves as high as they would go.

She took the pin she'd pricked her finger on and touched it to her forearm. The point was rather dull; she would need to use pressure. The first quick puncture brought water to her eyes. A perfect bead of blood issued with the sting, smearing when she moved the pin's tip just beside it. The second and the third pricks were closer to her veins. She thought of Lem's scars, numerous as freckles. Then she thought of Bess, parentless and sobbing, and she pricked herself again.

Each new stab raised awareness of the others. She continued down her arm from her elbow to her wrist, two for every inch—half a dozen, then a dozen, every pinhole a choice, every choice another vision. Frances with her handkerchief, crying in the hansom. Wickware shivering with terror in the garret. Mr. Fen underwater. Prick, prick, prick. The pin grew slippery from the blood she was drawing, and she pinched the metal harder till her fingertips paled. She remembered

John Summer riding off to Burn. She couldn't bear the memories of the cabin in the snow, so she turned her mind to Root. There the blood really flowed.

Tom's broken nose and battered ribs from having saved her. The boy she'd almost killed, glowing in the storm. Abigail's kitchen splashed with candlefruit wax.

Faster, Molly thought.

She moved the pin up and down until the skin was fully speckled, then began her second arm.

The broken fiddle and the cannon. Tom refusing to accompany his friends to Shepherd's Inn. The pricks were deeper now and quicker, and the pain was like a burn, and Molly concentrated hard and watched the bloody pin. She thought of her hurtfulness to Bess. Benjamin's hand. Lem's skull. The winterbear crunching on the dead mare's bones.

Nicholas, Nicholas, Nicholas. Leaving home. Leaving home.

Blood dribbled to her hands and gathered in her palms. She cleaned them on her skirt, wiped her eyes, put away the pin, and concealed both arms underneath her cloak. The pain was like a noise she had almost ceased to hear, blaring everywhere inside her and enveloping her thoughts. She stood before the windows but she couldn't see the water, only her reflection with the cabin light behind her. The ship was gaining speed. Had they already cleared the harbor?

She took the lantern from its hook and hurried on deck, where she handed off the light and thanked the midshipman and the captain, both of whom—especially Captain Lark—eyed her closely. Molly passed Grigory at the stern with extra haste, worried that the blood was visible upon her.

"Better now, love?" he asked.

She continued to the rail and looked toward the city. Either side of them, the land still cupped around the harbor. They were not in the open sea but there was no time to lose. It was difficult to see by the mist-shrouded moonlight; Molly scanned the water for the whitecaps and lulls, the texture and the skein of all the water far below.

"There!" she said, pointing slightly starboard into the dark.

"What?" Grigory said.

"My rescue is at hand."

He scoffed but took a step, squinting more at her than at the place where she was pointing. She had escaped from him before and he was wary of a trick; surely Nicholas had warned him that she wasn't to be trusted. But her smile held strong and had the hoped-for effect. His doubt began to waver. Molly focused on the wake. She needed him beside her, right against the rail.

"What are you on about?" he asked, standing at her shoulder, squinting at the harbor for whatever she had seen.

Molly's feet were anchors. She had strength but couldn't move. A fall would not be fatal but it was still a long way down; she wondered how fast the ship could mount a rescue. Could she do it after all? She thought of Tom, of how their limbs had interwoven in the dark. She thought of pregnancy and swelled. She was light enough to float.

She bent her knees and jumped, using her hands for extra lift and vaulting over the rail. Her skirts ballooned, her heavy cloak fluttered as she fell, and with a long cry of "Help!" she hit the water like a bomb.

The slap was agonizing, hard across the bottoms of her thighs. The salt rinsed her arms and made the punctures sting anew, and she was tossed about, blind, tumbling over underwater. She wrestled with her heavy cloak, regretting that she hadn't taken it off before she jumped, and when her mouth broke the surface and she finally drew a breath, the ship was farther, much farther out of reach than she had expected.

Shouts of sailors overlapped in the chaos on the deck. Waves flopped her under, bobbed her up and pulled her down, coming from all directions in the dark, choppy harbor. Had a minute passed? More? She was tired from her journey, having barely slept or eaten, and her strokes became desperate and increasingly inept.

At last a sailor found her. Molly hadn't seen him jump or noticed his approach before he caught her under the arm—a young man, handsome with a cheek-wide scar—and vigorously swam her to the stern of the halting ship. He looped her with a rope and she was hauled up the side. Lantern-lit faces watched her from the taffrail: worried, stern, angry. Only Grigory looked perplexed.

Many hands helped her up and she collapsed on deck, lying on her back and gazing at the rigging. Her rescuer returned, barely winded from the swim.

Captain Lark made her stand.

"Merman's hell," he said, his heartworn air turned to savage irritation. "How in all the fucking world did you tumble over the rail?"

"He threw me," Molly said.

She raised a shivery finger and extended it at Grigory. The sailors' darkened faces found a new thing to watch.

"I didn't touch her," Grigory said. "She tried to drown herself."

"Liar!" Molly answered, with an angry flow of tears. "You've been a coward and a fiend since the morning we were married."

He laughed in nervous shock. "I ain't her bloody husband."

"You'd deny even that? Oh, it's you who should have drowned!"

Molly lunged as if to hit him. A sailor held her back. Another man strong-armed Grigory beside her at the rail and Captain Lark looked at them together with his spitfire eyes, so much taller than the two of them that they had to tip their heads.

"Why'd he throw you over?"

"On account of my sickness!" Molly said. "He said it was a rash, a common sort of rash, and that I shouldn't let it hinder us from traveling overseas. But he knew! He meant to drown me and be rid of me for good. He would have waited for the wide-open sea to throw me in, except my wounds started weeping and I showed him straightaway. I said we have to tell the captain, said it's evil not to tell. But no, he said, he wouldn't spend a month locked in quarantine. And then he picked me up—"

Captain Lark had backed away. So had everyone on deck, all with pale, troubled faces.

"Show your wounds," the captain said.

A sailor raised a lantern. Molly rolled her sleeves up, exposing both arms, as roughly as she could so the friction made her bleed again. Many of the crew retreated to the masts. Some escaped altogether to the bow or into the berth. Even Grigory stepped away, bewildered and aghast.

Captain Lark regarded her with terrible rigidity. "You brought bloodpox onto my ship."

"I'm sorry!" Molly said. "Please, I didn't know!"

"But *you* did," he said, hulking over Grigory. "I'd flay you raw and flog you with your own ragged skin if there weren't fucking judges that would label it excessive."

"It ain't true," Grigory said, dry-mouthed and panting with his back against the rail. "I didn't know. I didn't touch her, never seen her in my life except—"

He faltered—he could not admit he'd known her as a Maimer—and was simply too confused to conjure up a lie, especially one that might explain the state of Molly's arms.

Captain Lark acted swiftly. A sullen, fumbling sailor was ordered to bind Grigory's arms. Afraid to touch a man whose wife had the pox, he tied a complicated knot, a kind of double double bowline, draped the loops around Grigory's wrists without touching his hands, and tightened it by backing up and tugging on the rope. The man who'd rescued Molly doused himself with vinegar—he wasn't alone in doing so—but the crew was already avoiding him, and Captain Lark ordered him, along with the half-dozen sailors who had helped Molly up, to pack whatever they owned and ride the jolly boat to shore.

Molly and Grigory were seated in the little vessel's stern. The miserable rowers sat with their oars, deathly silent, while the boat was quickly lowered off the ship and into the water. They rowed for dear life as soon as they detached. *Dick's Fortune* spread its sails and hastened on its way; they would scour, burn, or boil everything Molly had touched, but they'd be damned if they allowed themselves to spend a month in quarantine.

The rowers crossed the harbor to the dreaded Scabbard Island, where they would stay in isolation till a doctor could examine them. They would all be free to leave once the ruse had been exposed, but Molly and Grigory would not—they'd be held to answer questions. Rumors of the incident would soon ignite the docks: bloodpox, a woman nearly murdered in the harbor. Nicholas would hear of it by morning at the latest.

Molly squeezed her arms but failed to dull the pain. If she couldn't escape the island, if she couldn't get to Tom, she'd have guaranteed the end. There would be nothing left to save.

Chapter Thirty-One

Molly paced a stone-walled room in Scabbard Island's quarantine hospital, a long, gray building with a straight central corridor, which owing to its bolted doors and iron-barred windows might have been mistaken for a derelict prison. The island itself appeared pestilential. It was three square miles of craggy land and wind-twisted trees, situated in the north of Grayport Harbor and inhabited by enough rats and fleas to sicken all of Floria. Half a decade had passed since Grayport had suffered a serious outbreak of contagious disease; the hospital was poorly funded even during emergencies, and virtually abandoned in prolonged seasons of health. Physicians stayed on the mainland, and the caretaker and his assistants were quick to lock Molly and Grigory in isolated quarters—both to be examined, the latter to be arrested. They had failed to keep the jolly boat's sailors on the island: a disastrous breach of protocol in the case of actual disease, now disastrous to Molly if the story reached her brother. A doctor wouldn't be summoned till the morning, she believed, and she needed those hours. She had gone from trap to trap.

But although her solitude seemed to last a great deal longer, she had been in the room for less than three hours when a door banged open up the hall and she heard a familiar, belligerent baritone say:

"It isn't pox, you good-for-nothing clod, although I'll see you sacked and whipped for letting those sailors row away. What if they'd been sick? And they were witnesses, to boot, against the man who tried to kill her. Where the blazes have you put her?"

"Here, sir," the caretaker said.

"God's sake, quit trembling," Pitt told him at the door. "I said it isn't pox. Open up. She won't infect you."

Molly retreated to the inmost corner of the room, anxiously amazed by the unexpected rescue, if rescue it could properly be called. They opened the door. The caretaker shrank to the side too quickly to be seen, and then instead of Sheriff Pitt, whose voice had filled the hall, in walked Tom with an expression of relief—urgent, high-colored, ravenous relief.

Molly rushed to him with a gasp and hugged him like a wife. Tom squeezed back; they didn't come apart. She turned her head as she was holding him and looked to Sheriff Pitt, his wind-burned face wonderful to see, and she was startled when he winked at her and smiled with affection.

He was followed by a priestly-looking man of middle age, his shoulders lightly dusted from an overpowdered wig. His cheeks were clearly mottled with the lingering marks of bloodpox. He introduced himself as Dr. Antickson and rolled up Molly's sleeves, examining her arms as Pitt raised a lantern and allowing her, throughout, to keep holding Tom.

"It is not the disease," he said, nevertheless concerned and squinting at the punctures.

"I did it with a pin," Molly said.

The doctor frowned.

Tom stepped back—how it ached to lose his warmth!—and licked his thumb to clean a portion of the blood from Molly's wrist. She kissed him to apologize for leaving him behind, and he forgave her with a nod and a drawn-out sigh.

"You can marry up later," Pitt said, sending the doctor away with the caretaker to wait at the end of the hall and closing the door for privacy.

Tom and Pitt had slipped away from Root, ridden all day, and found a constable in Grayport shortly after dark. They had only hoped to learn the address of James Smith and instead had heard a story of the ship *Dick's Fortune*. Bloodpox panic had indeed reached the docks. One of the rowers from the jolly boat had drowned his fear in rum and spoken, in his drunkenness, of everything he'd witnessed. The rumor spread quickly, authorities were summoned, and the sailors were arrested and returned to Scabbard Island. Sheriff Pitt volunteered to accompany the prisoners; the pox-dreading constable was happy to allow it.

"Pitt knows about your brother," Tom said to Molly, "but we haven't told anybody else what we know."

"Strictly secret," Pitt said. "What the deuce happened?"

Molly told about the note, her flight from Root, and Shepherd's Inn; how her brother had killed Lem to compromise Tom; how he had forced her onto the ship; and how she had managed to escape. It chimed with what they knew and already suspected, but she stunned them by revealing that her brother led the Maimers.

"This Grigory up the hall," Pitt said. "He's a Maimer?"

Molly nodded. Pitt responded with a dark-lit grin: to have caught one alive was more than he had hoped.

"He's all yours," Tom said. "Get your name in the *Grayport Gazette*."

"And Nicholas?" Molly asked.

Tom's heat had left her body and the cold felt deathly, worse than dampness and depletion, worse than ordinary fear. The warm cooperation that had unified the men was suddenly replaced by an unforeseen chill.

Pitt massaged his hands and said to Tom, "You didn't tell me he was heading up the Maimers."

"I didn't know."

"That's a new cast of light. I might consider our agreement null and void, to catch the leader. Might be worth it if you let me take him in."

Tom inhaled so fully that he seemed about to levitate. He turned away from Molly, failing to conceal his unexplained euphoria, and searched Pitt's face as if he couldn't quite believe the overture his lifelong enemy had made. Molly stood alone and didn't understand. She was picturing her brother's neck snapping at the gallows.

"Nothing's changed," Tom said. "It's still for Molly to decide."

Pitt addressed her softly with a hand upon her shoulder, reminding her how thoroughly he fathomed what was coming. "He's your brother. It's a damned hard thing either way."

"Don't arrest him," Molly said, unsure if that was even what the two of them were offering. "Tom and I will go."

Tom suppressed whatever emotion he had felt and squeezed her hand, joining them together for the task that lay ahead. Molly turned to Pitt and kissed him on the cheek, much to his uncomfortable delight, Tom's pique, and her own bright sense of putting things right.

⅌

Nicholas slept in his spartan room over the Grayport office and woke before light the next morning, initially convinced, owing to exhaustion and the nighttime cold, that he was still in the winter cabin, that Molly had tried to shoot him the previous day, and that he had lost her in the onrushing waters of the creek.

The present returned in a flash. She was alive. He had found her. He had sent her back to Bruntland.

Yet the gnawing, tightening grief did not relax but rather sharpened as he thought of her at sea, suffering and hating him. A burden to be borne, he thought. Another chronic illness. What could he have done, aside from sending her away? Nevertheless he clamped his mouth and wept against his pillow—half a minute, maybe less, of pressurized rue. It was all that he allowed himself, all that he could hazard if he meant to carry on. He rose from bed and dressed in the dark, ignoring his cough, his chill, his hunger and fatigue, and straightened his clothes by feel, resigned to solving the myriad complications of the day with the same force of will he might have used to ice a fever.

He felt a premonition: something wrong about the morning. The mind, he knew, was capable of clandestine perceptions—of learning in the night, of discovering clues and patterns under the noise of conscious thought. Revelations bubbled up, masquerading as emotions, like the subtle voice of God or nature's finer instincts.

He left the room in dread and lingered in the staircase leading to the parlor, fearing an informant would be waiting outside to bring him news of trouble.

If only Molly could see beyond the things he had taken. He had given her more, much more than she had earned, and although he couldn't expect to win her gratitude or love, he prayed that she would keep her word of secrecy with Frances. Dear Frances, now the only soul alive left to love him. He admitted it was foolish, or at any rate a weakness, to let himself dwell on such a sentimental hope. Frances knew what he had told her—complicated lies—and she believed him to be upright, delicate, and pure. Had he ever been an innocent? He truly couldn't say. Still, he cherished such a vision of himself through her eyes and wouldn't have it slashed, maudlin as it was, any more than he would slash a real, living child.

But the fact was already clear: Molly would expose him, maybe inadvertently but certainly, inevitably. Bewailing it was meaningless. In time she'd write to Root—how could he prevent it?—and discover Tom had been hanged. There was no one watching Root to see that Tom complied. Nicholas had trusted that a bluff would do the trick; but eventually, he knew, the man would come to Grayport. Tom had to die. He would see to that today; judges could be swayed in more than one direction.

Nonetheless, he suspected that the worst was still to come. He had bought them a reprieve and forced his sister to accept it, but reprieves, like everything else, were destined to expire.

He continued downstairs and opened the parlor door. A candle lit the room. Molly stood before him. Nicholas's heart surged up and then collapsed, and for the first time in months, he doubted his resolve. She was flicker-lit and beautiful, a small bedraggled imp. Both her clothing and her hair had the haphazard look of having swirled undersea and dried however they fell. Nicholas wondered, reaching subtly for the knife inside his coat, if she had swum the harbor's length without being seen.

She didn't speak. Her eyes were terrible and dark as little onyxes.

Never had he entertained a suicidal urge and yet he felt one now, entwined with her appearance. If he drew the blade and killed her—intimately, swiftly—his succeeding act would surely be to turn it on himself.

"Give me the ruddy fucking knife before I shoot you in the knee."

Tom Orange aimed a pistol from a shadow at his side.

Nicholas handed him the knife, sagging with relief. The feeling didn't last. He calcified and burned.

"Sit," Molly said.

Nicholas didn't move. Tom grabbed his neck and crammed him into a chair. The force hurt his clavicle and throbbed down his arm. Molly stood calmly in the center of the room while Tom stayed beside him with the pistol to his knee. A fine deterrent, he admitted, more reliable than aiming willy-nilly at his chest, and yet it told him they were not beyond a measure of restraint.

He met Tom's face and there it was—that marvelous temper again—but now it looked contained: a cannon packed and primed. Nicholas smiled at his knuckles, just enough for Tom to notice. Then he emptied his expression, knitted his fingers in his lap, raised his chin toward the candlelight, and asked his sister, "How?"

⚓

"You said it last night. I'm good at wriggling out."

The parlor, by and large, was just as Molly remembered. It was small, somewhat narrower in width than in length, with a ceiling she could touch by reaching overhead, bone-colored wainscot, and dark red walls. Nicholas had added ferns and books, which added richness, but had kept the same chairs and round mahogany table. The table bore a candle near the unlit hearth. Nicholas's chair was in the middle of the rug. They had sat right here when she'd agreed to marry John, and it was strange, and reassuring, and inevitably chilling to be standing here with Tom for another confrontation.

Molly had warned Tom that Nicholas was good at spotting weaknesses and turning them, abruptly, into precious opportunities. She'd asked him not to speak unless necessity compelled him.

"You love her," said her brother. "That was instantly apparent."

Tom neither blinked nor contradicted the assessment. Molly's heart became an orange, nourishing and bright, and she was eager to be done before her brother got to squeeze it.

"I warned you not to come," Nicholas continued. "What if she had died because you tried to interfere?"

"She was managing without me," Tom said.

"All her life."

"I'm a harder man to hurt when I'm standing here awake."

"The same cannot be said about your uncle," Nicholas answered. "Did your cousin take it badly? Did she blame you, even briefly? What a wound: to be severed from the graces of your family."

"I wonder how a bullet in the knee measures up."

"Tom," Molly said.

"Dead matter," said her brother, having toyed and grown bored. He looked at her instead and then the light was in his eyes. The flutter in his irises reminded her of wasps. "You were stronger after all and now you have me in your power. Let me clarify your options. One: let me go, and both of you are dead within the hour. Two: have me arrested for my crimes and see me hanged. Three: kill me now. The third choice is cleanest."

"You seem content that one of us should die," Molly said.

"Resignation," he replied, "differs from contentment."

"Were you equally resigned the night you killed my daughter?"

She walked toward Tom and grabbed the pistol in his hand. Tom was in her shadow with the candlelight behind her but she felt his rising temperature, the tension in his arm, his panic that the gun had left her brother's knee. He wouldn't let go and wouldn't turn from Nicholas, who watched them with an eggsnake's tireless attention. They had agreed upon the plan—Tom restrained him, Molly talked— but now her move had overturned it, leaving both of them uncertain. Tom released the gun and quickly raised the knife.

Molly backed away and aimed the pistol at the floor.

"Explain to me again the necessity you felt," she said. "Tell me all the reasons you devised. Do you dare?"

She calmed her trembling hand by tightening her grip. First the gun shook more. Then she raised it and it steadied. Nicholas seemed to follow her example with his features, tautening his brow and narrowing his mouth, though what he meant to govern—his defiance or his fear—was impossible to tell.

"Given the chance," Nicholas said, "I will steal, and maim, and hurt your loved ones again. You would be right to kill me now. Even God wouldn't blame you."

She glimpsed his broken tooth and thought of the locket she was wearing. Tom raised a cautionary hand but didn't speak.

"Tell me where your instinct leans," Nicholas said.

"Kill you," Molly answered.

"Trust it."

"Let you live."

"Choose," Nicholas told her, creaking forward in the chair.

The emptiness inside her bloomed and filled the parlor, blotting out her memory, and certainty, and hope until the pistol in her hand and Nicholas in the chair became the only two things that were holding her together.

Tom had seen her indecision and begun to drop his guard. He seemed prepared to block the shot—a shot she might regret—and stepped toward her with an outstretched arm to take the gun. Nicholas faced the candle. It was close enough, she realized, that he might blow it out and plunge them into darkness.

Nicholas inhaled and focused on the flame. "Consider the possibility that Cora is alive."

Molly's vision flared. She almost pulled the trigger in surprise. Nicholas exhaled and made the candlelight wobble, and the furniture and walls swayed with bending shadows.

"Where?" she asked, choked.

"If she were," Nicholas said, neither venomous nor kind, "telling you would cost me my advantage."

"Then I'll shoot you."

"Yet there may come a time, assuming I'm alive, when I have no need of my advantage anymore."

Visions filled her mind—wispy hair, dimpled elbows. Caramel skin. She'd have given up her tongue or any of her limbs, anything, to hold her. Anything but this. Was she out there now in the city or beyond, parentless and wholly undefended with a stranger? Had another mother nursed her? Would she ever know the difference?

"Molly," Tom said. He interposed himself, forcing her to look at him instead. "Will he tell you if I hurt him?"

"No," Molly whispered.

Tom put the knife away and turned around to Nicholas. "Shoot you, don't shoot you. Bargaining and bluffs. My head was hammer and tongs *before* you started talking."

Tom punched him in the nose: a good, damp thump. Nicholas bled and held his face, too surprised to offer resistance when Tom yanked him up by his hair, produced a rope from under his coat, and tied his wrists behind his back. Molly used a second length of rope to bind his ankles. Tom bumped the backs of Nicholas's knees, bending both legs and causing him to kneel, and then he joined the wrist and ankle knots together into a hogtie and stood beside Molly, nodding at their handiwork. Nicholas's nose dribbled down his shirt.

Tom took a three-inch bottle from his pocket, uncorked the top, and said, "Dr. Benjamin Knox sends his regards."

"It's to be ironic punishment, then," Nicholas said. "Will you chop my hand, as well?"

"No," Molly said. "You're sailing off whole."

"Where am I going?"

"New employment," Tom said. "It'll suit you."

"Wherever it is," Nicholas told Molly, speaking through the blood flowing over his lips, "I will see you again."

"But you won't kill me."

"How do you know?"

"It isn't in your nature," Molly said.

Nicholas smiled.

Tom handed her the bottle, pinched her brother's nose, and moved to open his jaw.

"Stop," Nicholas said with nasal irritation.

Molly touched Tom's arm and he released her brother's face. Nicholas looked at her with bottomless, profoundly earnest eyes and tipped his head back. She placed the bottle's rim upon his lip and poured the fluid into his mouth. It had a dream-heavy scent. He let it trickle in and swallowed with a blink.

There was a long and awkward silence, not a word for several minutes, while they waited for the potion to deliver its effect.

"I might kill *you*," Nicholas said to Tom.

"Ruddy hell," Tom said. "You told me he was stoical."

Molly stuck her pinky into the freshly drained bottle. She removed it with a pop and sucked the moisture off her fingertip, savoring the hint of salty-sweet cherry.

Nicholas tried to say, "Are you sure the doctor's formula was properly prepared?" Instead he slurred, "Formula prepared the doctor proper?"

"Aye," Tom said.

Nicholas drooled and gibbered. In another half minute, he collapsed upon the floor.

Sleeping like a baby, Molly thought. She didn't cry. Instead she used a handkerchief to clean his bloody face, wondered whether he had lied, and prayed that he had not.

⚗

Four hours later, Molly and Tom stood on the dock in the overcast, pewter-lit morning and watched the *Lady's Way* spread her sails and cut across Grayport Harbor. She carried an unmarked crate deep within her hold, delivered and received shortly after dawn, and once she was safely in the open sea, certain members of the crew planned to discover a man packed inside, overlook the ropes that bound his feet and hands, and arrest him as a stowaway on their voyage to the prison colony of Exanica, which lay across the ocean to the distant south of Bruntland and always had a place for fresh criminal laborers. The captain knew Tom's brother Winward—they had served together in the navy—and had asked few questions while agreeing to assist. He had been warned, nonetheless, to overestimate the prisoner.

The docks were crowded but subdued, owing to the bloodpox rumor from the night. Molly kept her hood up, fearing that one of the passing sailors or merchants might recognize her face from her

Grayport days. She watched the *Lady's Way* becoming smaller in the harbor till it looked like a toy she could carry in her palm.

Tom held her waist as if expecting her to fall. He wore his tricorne and had the bearing of a general who had ridden all night but couldn't afford to rest. Molly held him, too, sensing it was he who needed the support.

"How are your arms?" Tom asked.

"They hurt. You look good in that hat. I fancy one myself."

He smiled at the sea but seemed to be preoccupied. Molly couldn't read him and was too fatigued to try.

Pitt approached them from the far end of the dockyard, where he had just stepped off a cutter from Scabbard Island. His authoritative swagger was belied by his shortness, and by the cavalier seamen who refused to clear a path. They made him step around or bumped him moving past, until at very long last he reached Tom and Molly with little more authority than a messenger boy.

He sniffed to stop a trickle, then again with more intention.

"Grigory is dead," he said. "The caretaker left him unguarded while I interrogated the jolly boat sailors. He swears that nobody else came to the island, but how would he know? The bastard was hiding in his room, still afraid of pox."

Tom removed his hat as if its weight had grown oppressive. "How did he die?"

"Someone cut his throat. The room was locked and there was no sign of struggle. He was lying on the floor like his neck just opened on its own."

Pitt said it thickly with a marble-eyed stare, turning his gaze from Tom to Molly without seeming to recognize the difference. Molly held her neck and felt herself swallow. Was it odd to pity Grigory, a Maimer and a fiend, for failing in his mission to convey her overseas?

"Your brother . . . ," Pitt said, blinking in the wind.

Molly swung her arm, rigid as a weathervane, and pointed at the vessel far across the harbor.

"He's nailed inside a crate," Tom said.

They fell into grim silence, looking at the ship and huddled, all three with Molly in the middle, while the overcrowded dock made their worries more anonymous but left them more exposed, in the wake of Grigory's death, to whatever secret forces had achieved his execution. Life went on around them, full of hidden threats. They watched the barrels being loaded, ropes being tied, a thousand machinations following their courses.

"How do we explain this?" Pitt eventually asked.

"We can't tell the truth," Tom said to Molly. "Your own brother, the leader of the Maimers, sent away without a trial—people will think the worst."

"We have to tell them something," Pitt said. "At the very least, we need to explain Lem's murder."

Molly dropped her hood and scruffed her matted hair.

"We blame Grigory for everything," she said. "He was the one with murderers and thieves at his disposal. My well-respected brother, Jacob Smith, sent me away for safety while he worked against Grigory's network in Grayport. Last spring, Grigory kidnapped me for advantage. I escaped by jumping into the flooded creek, and then I stayed in Root—and kept my past a secret—so Grigory wouldn't find me. But he did. He came to Root when you and Tom stopped the Maimers. He murdered Lem and framed Tom to keep the two of you occupied while he tried to steal me off again. I fled to Grayport and hoped to find my brother for protection, but Grigory caught me on the road. You and Tom," she said, "worked enough of it out in Root and followed me to Grayport, where you rescued me and had Grigory arrested. He killed himself in jail. My brother disappeared, probably murdered by Grigory's supporters."

It was a lie that might suffice, being very close to the truth, with no one to oppose it now that Grigory was dead.

"But people here thought you and Nicholas—you and *Jacob*," Tom said, "were married."

"We had enemies abroad and changed our identities to hide."

"What did you really fake a marriage for?" Pitt asked.

"That's my secret to keep. So is my daughter," Molly said.

The eastern clouds began to fracture and the *Lady's Way* passed through a clear band of sun. It lit the sails with splendor, giving the distant ship a gold-spangled light before it sank back to shadow, gone toward the sea, with Nicholas and everything he knew inside its hold.

"People will think your brother died fighting the Maimers," Tom said. "If he ever makes it back, he'll be a hero."

"Makes it back!" Pitt said, scorching at the thought. His reputation—and the lie they meant to foist upon the town—depended on the fact that Nicholas was gone. "You said the two of you would handle— It's the only reason I didn't arrest the son of a bitch myself!"

"Not the only reason," Tom said. "But no one comes back from Exanica anyway."

The blood-drop potion might have killed him already. Benjamin had failed to tell Tom the proper dosage; they had decided they were better off emptying the bottle, guaranteeing that he slept as long as they required. Molly had seen him almost die of seasickness alone. She thought of how debilitated he had grown doing Mrs. Wickware's chores; even if he reached the prison colony alive, it seemed impossible that he would survive a year, a month, a solitary week of hard physical labor.

The *Lady's Way* dipped and vanished out of sight.

"He isn't coming back," she said, knowing he would come.

Chapter Thirty-Two

The Orange remained closed. Molly, Tom, and Pitt had returned the previous day to flabbergast Root with the tale of Grigory's crimes and the final events in Grayport, then retreated to the quiet isolation of their homes, leaving the town to talk and wonder and embroider on its own. The trio had reemerged this morning for Lem's burial, and afterward Molly walked Bess home to the tavern, guided her into their room, and closed the door behind them. They settled on a bed and Molly held her hand. It was a hand with bitten fingernails, a child's smooth knuckles, and lifelong calluses below them on the palm.

Bess had heard the story same as everyone in Root. That her father had been murdered seemed to matter less than that he'd died while he and Bess remained bitterly at odds. Lem had gained the pitiable glow of many dead brutes and now his silence, so different from the bluster of his life, allowed the finer whispers of her memory to rise. Molly understood. She felt the same about her brother now that he was gone, and she remembered all the ways he once protected her from harm.

But the time had come for Bess to know the truth in all its ugliness, and Molly told her everything as clearly as she could—her childhood, her father, John Summer, and her baby. Nicholas and the Maimers. Nicholas and Lem. She rushed it out efficiently and tried to get it done before the pressure in her chest prevented her from speaking.

"I'm sorry," Molly said. "It was him. I let him go. I couldn't see him hanged, oh I'm sorry . . . Bess, I'm sorry."

Bess had dug her fingers like talons into the mattress and had listened, rarely blinking, never once interrupting. Her astonishment at learning General Bell was Molly's father had diminished when she learned that Nicholas had murdered Lem. They were sitting hip to hip and Molly hugged her from the side, if only to hide her own face and keep herself from rambling. Bess's stomach grumbled softly and she didn't hug back. The hearth fire hadn't yet heated up the room and the warmth between their bodies grew thin.

"You're bleeding," Bess said.

Molly let go. Her left-arm bandage had begun to seep through. Bess unraveled it and scowled at the irritated skin. She dabbed the blood with a cloth and studied the deepest wounds, each of which Molly could remember having made, as if the memories she'd called upon were labeled on her arm.

Bess applied a tingly mint salve with her fingers, took a fresh strip of linen, and began to wrap the arm again.

"I'm sorry about your father," Molly said. "Do you hate me?"

"No," Bess said. "I'm sorry about your baby."

She proceeded with the second wrap, and Molly let her do it, sensing that her friend's insistent ministrations were as comforting to Bess as to her own throbbing arms. Sun filled the room and tricked the iciness away. The finished bandage spiraled neatly from her elbow to her wrist, and Bess secured it with a pin and pulled down the sleeve. She looked at Molly up close and kissed her on the lips. It was sisterly and sweet and pleasantly insouciant, raising shivers like the salve she'd applied to Molly's wounds.

"You're staying now for good?"

"Yes," Molly said.

"Do you love him?"

Molly smiled.

"We'll be family if you marry him."

But something hadn't been right about Tom since they returned.

It was more than Lem's burial and worry over Bess, more than the exertion of the last few days. Molly hadn't found a chance to speak with him alone. She had spent the night with Bess, dreaming of ships and Grigory's death and little Cora on her own, and she had woken up scared and hadn't felt at home. Every minute was a footstep leading to the next but she had no clear sense of which direction they would go.

⚘

Tom stood with his back to the window in the Knoxes' kitchen, taking the twilight draft directly into his spine. Abigail added an extra log to the fire, an uncharacteristic extravagance—she thought of deadfall as God's good reminder of the grave—but one she willingly bestowed for the comfort of the guests. Benjamin sat at the table, genial and talkative but shiveringly frail. Molly sat beside him like a well-loved niece. Tom admired his friend's acuity in sensing her discomfort. It would never have crossed Benjamin's mind that Molly might blame herself for costing him a hand, but once he'd read it in her manner, he behaved with more fragility, allowing her to help him into his chair, cover his shoulders with a blanket, and remain by his side in heartfelt penance.

"It's time to change your bandage," Abigail said.

"May I help?" Molly asked, standing up and walking forward.

Abigail paused without at first replying. She went to a cabinet for an earthenware jar and fresh supplies, laid them on the table in front of Benjamin, and summoned Molly over to a basin near the window, where she washed Molly's hands and scrubbed beneath her fingernails. Molly looked pleased, familiar with Benjamin's fixity on cleanliness and seeming to believe, through the careful preparation, that Abigail was showing her a great deal of trust.

Benjamin removed his sullied bandage, which Abigail deposited into a boiling pot of water. It was an ugly wound. The flesh had shriveled since the cut and gradually retracted. Now the forearm bones protruded slightly from the muscles and would probably result, once the stump was fully healed, in noticeable bumps instead of the smoother, neater surface of a proper amputation.

Molly stood there, expressionless, long enough for Abigail to question her resolve, but then she sat and got to work as calmly as a surgeon.

Benjamin watched her over his glasses. He smiled reassuringly and said, "First a gentle cleansing. Dab lightly. Do not rub."

Molly did as she was told and asked him, "Does it hurt?"

"I am reasonably dosed to tolerate the pain. Next the unguent," Benjamin said, pointing with his chin toward the earthenware jar.

Molly applied the unguent and continued to follow instructions, next by covering the muscles and the bones with lint pledgets, then applying strips of linen that extended up his arm. She secured these with a winding roll and finally with a cap, like a baby's knit hat, that was placed upon the stump for added warmth and padding.

Abigail nodded as she gathered the supplies.

"Thank you," Benjamin said.

Molly smiled with relief.

"Can I talk to you alone?" Tom said to Benjamin.

Benjamin stood without assistance, his legs prepared to move before the question had been finished. He had expected this, it seemed, and he and Tom walked together into the hall toward the parlor, leaving Abigail and Molly uncomfortably alone.

"Her resilience continues to amaze me," Benjamin said to Tom. "Attacked by a winterbear, slashed above the knee, pricked upon the arms several dozen times, nearly drowned, and then imprisoned—to say nothing of the frigid journey and emotional toll—and yet she still appears healthier than half the souls in Root. A quicksummer spirit," he declared with satisfaction.

He crossed the book-lined parlor and sat in a rocking chair, resting his newly capped stump on a side table covered with sheet music.

"She has a talent for dressing wounds. I must consider an assistant given my impairment. Abby is adroit, as you know, but lacks the temperament of inquiry so vital to the medical pursuits. Do you suppose Molly would consider an education in basic surgery?"

"As long as she doesn't practice on me," Tom said.

He saw the jar with Benjamin's hand displayed upon a shelf, the glass softly tinted by the dusk-light blues. The hand was horribly mundane—whitened by the spirits, perfectly intact, and vertically positioned in the semblance of a wave. The gulf between the jar and Benjamin's wrist was too unnatural to dwell upon, so Tom focused on his friend's weatherworn face and on the wisps of gray hair that rose above his ears.

"I should have ridden out with you," Tom said. "We'd fought the day before and I had worries at the tavern, but it wasn't an excuse to let you go alone. We all knew the danger and it didn't stop Davey. It didn't stop you." His stomach clenched tight and bent him forward in the chair, and though he didn't bow his head or kneel upon the floor, the whole of him was prostrate. "Forgive me," Tom said. "I wish I'd acted different."

Benjamin took his glasses off and placed them on the table.

"Your first concern was Molly."

"Aye," Tom said.

"We were foolish to ride out, only two and unprepared. I blame myself for Davey," Benjamin said. "I couldn't save him."

"If three of us had gone—"

"But who can really say?"

The parlor seemed to shrink and they were close enough to whisper. Shadows in the room solidified and deepened, growing ever more substantial than the objects that cast them.

"My loss is grievous," Benjamin said. "I forgive you all the same. Decapitation—nothing less—would sever our connection."

He offered up the stump to shake Tom's hand.

"Remarkable," he said, noting his mistake. "Considering its absence dominates my thoughts, withholding it would seem the natural inclination. Yet the opposite is true. I constantly present it. Perhaps it's similar to the intellect acknowledging some ignorance, displaying curiosity in order to advance itself. We must expose our weaknesses before we overcome them."

"Might be habit," Tom said.

He touched the woolen cap, feeling some of the relief of Benjamin's forgiveness—glad, at least, the friendship had outlived the maiming—but reminded of the trials they had witnessed and endured. What had any of them gained in the balance of surviving? What would he himself present to counteract the loss?

⚜

Molly stood in the barn and smelled the quicksummer breeze. The sweet, capricious weather would last for several weeks and everyone had told her to enjoy it while it lasted. But the dead stayed dead. Plants that had fallen to the frost would not awaken, and the cold still lingered in the barn's deepest nooks, in the hard-packed ground, and most of all inside her.

Bones ate a pair of bulbous apples from her hand. The crunching sound was pleasant, like a walk in heavy snow, and Molly liked the way his mouth took the fruit, spicing the enclosure with a cidery aroma. She could smell something else beneath the apples and the musk. The tavern ghost was with her.

"Gwendolyn," she said.

Molly breathed a fragrance she remembered from the cabin: warm spring rain softening the cold. She leaned against Bones, glad of his support, until the memory of Cora seemed less another ache and more a glimmer of the quicksummer night that swirled around her. The ghost stayed beside her like a ripple in the dark, like a child needing comfort.

"Hush," Molly said. "You can stay with me tonight."

A gust brought a goose seed floating through the barn. Molly caught it with her fingertips—a black-and-white puff, feathery and light around a small gray seed. Ichabod was working near the barn's front door and Molly showed him, raised the seed, and let it go upon the wind. They watched it flutter up and join with many others, sailing to the east above the moonlit trees. Molly hugged him very hard— the truest sign she knew—and left him smiling when she crossed the yard and went inside the kitchen.

Nabby rolled dough beside a row of buttered dishes.

"What are you baking?" Molly asked.

"Quicksummer pies. The ember gourds will ripen overnight in this weather."

"What's an ember gourd?"

Nabby gave her a hex eye for asking such a question. She often seemed convinced it had to be a joke, all the commonplace things Molly didn't know. "You've seen the vines creeping on the barn's west wall?"

"Yes," Molly lied.

"Ember gourds," she said. "We need to pick the fruits before they redden and combust."

She sprinkled flour down and rolled another circle from the dough. Nabby must have made a thousand such pies during her life, and yet she didn't look old tonight; the oversized mobcap crammed onto her head gave a transitory glimpse of Nabby as a girl.

Molly laughed. "I'll help you pick ember gourds tomorrow."

"Then the barn will burn to ashes."

"Give me an hour," Molly said. "I'll help you then, I promise."

She left Nabby muttering at the row of buttered dishes, walked beneath the wishbones and up the front stairs, and hesitated briefly at the door of Tom's room.

"Come in," he said before she knocked.

Molly went inside and closed the door behind her. Light pulsed softly from a near-dead fire, and the room smelled cold, as if the sun never touched it. Tom faced her from the middle of his threadbare rug. His hair was newly trimmed—Nabby had neatened up the back, where the flames had burned the locks—but the stubble on his jaw was two days heavy and his face looked haggard, more tired than a full night's sleep could truly remedy. She hugged him but he didn't hug back, not in earnest.

Beyond him out the window, goose seeds flurried in the warm dark wind, but he hadn't raised the sash to let the quicksummer in. Molly let him go and wished she understood him—what was troubling his mind now that everything was safe?

"This used to be my parents' room," he said, looking around. "When I was young, six or seven, my mother let me sleep in here whenever I was scared. I used to stare at a knot in the wall. That one over there." He pointed at the spot. "I pretended it was the world and wished that I could hold it. One morning I took a knife and tried to pry it out. My father caught me gouging at the wall. He whipped my legs for that."

She looked to where he'd pointed, searching for the knot, but the wall was too dark for any details to show.

He sat on the bed and both of them, the bed and Tom together, sagged from overuse. Scratch, who had been hiding in a shadow near the pillow, leapt at Tom's leg. Tom seized him by the scruff and tore him off his thigh. He held Scratch at arm's length, murderously grim while the cat flailed and growled, and he seemed about to throw the creature into the fire when he softened, almost grinned, and placed him on the rug. Molly opened the door. Scratch bolted into the hall. She closed the door behind him and examined Tom's leg, which was bleeding through his breeches. Tom ignored the scratches but his spirit seemed torn.

"Why did Pitt let you go?" Molly said abruptly.

Tom hesitated, blinking at the words before he said, "He's a decent sheriff, believe it or not. He didn't want Nicholas to take you."

"He could have come for me himself."

"I said decent, not competent. The man is never subtle. He'd have blundered after Nicholas and got himself shot, or let him get away, or God knows what. I trusted him to try. I didn't trust him to succeed."

"But you haven't told me why—"

"In the spring," Tom said, "once I've made arrangements, I'm selling him the Orange."

He settled on the bed again. The hearth log crumbled.

"No," Molly said. "No, you can't. You didn't need to!"

"It broke my heart to do it, but I did," he said. "I needed to."

He reached to take her hand and pull her down beside him but she walked across the room and stood before the window. The clouds were sailing lower. Wind pushed against the sash. She tried to warm her palms by putting them on the glass.

"I'm sorry," Molly said, collapsing on the inside, afraid that if she looked at him, she might collapse entirely.

"If anyone's to blame," he said, "it's Nicholas and Pitt."

"If I hadn't run away, you wouldn't have had to choose."

"My father made a choice to keep the tavern when he shouldn't have. I always used to wonder if I would have done the same. Now I know," Tom said. "I'd like to think my mother would agree with the decision."

"But what will you do?" Molly asked. "Where will you live? What about Bess and Ichabod and Nabby?"

"I haven't told them yet," he said. "It was part of the agreement that the three of them could stay, provided they decide to. There's no forcing Nabby out, even if Pitt wanted her gone. I'd guess that Ichabod'll stay. Bess might, too. As for me"—he drew a breath, like a long backward sigh—"I plan to build a house and maybe be a smoak-cutter. I'd like the outdoor work and there's a fortune to be made. There's talk of opening a route past Dunderakwa Falls, shipping logs downriver to the sea at Claw Harbor. In the winter I would stay at home, keep brewing beer. There'll be ruddy high demand if Pitt brews his own."

She visualized a house near the smoakwood trees with their cin-namony fragrance, and the heavy black leaves, and the snows so enor-mous Tom would have to tunnel out or simply hunker down tight in the long winter's grip.

"What about me?"

"Pitt would keep you on if you decided to stay," Tom said. "He likes you."

"I want a home of my own."

"Alone?"

"No."

She opened the sash and propped it with a cherrywood stick.

"The seeds are getting in," he said.

"It's warmer outside."

She dropped her cloak onto the floor, along with her gown and apron, and stood in her skirts and stays in front of the inblown air, lowering her head and watching through her lashes as the seeds rushed around her, clinging to her hair. They tickled her nose and smelled like maple-sugared oatmeal. She brushed them off and crossed the room and stood in front of Tom.

"What are you doing?" he asked.

"I'm untying my stays."

"They look tight."

"They are. We were talking about my prospects."

She dropped her stays and tugged her shift off her shoulders, pulling it down around her waist so it bunched below her navel.

"There are plenty of hardworking bachelors in Root," Tom said, avoiding her eyes in favor of the more engaging view. "Men who would be eager for a spirited companion."

"The main concern," Molly said—she raised her skirts and straddled his lap—"is how much spirit such a man would willingly endure."

He held her under the blooming cloud of petticoats and sighed, convincing her at last he would never let her go.

"And what would you do," Tom asked, "with a good, durable husband?"

"I would trouble him forever."

"Trouble I can handle."

Molly hugged him for the heat—the breeze was not entirely warm—and buried him in hair. His stubble scraped her nipple.

"You're smothering me," he said, but then he hummed between her breasts and held her even tighter with a hand upon her back. Molly breathed the smoakwood aroma of the fire, which had boldly reignited with the fresh night air.

She held him by the ears. "You'll have to push me off."

"I'm stronger than you," he said, muffled by her bosom.

Seeds whirled around them like feathers from a cannon.

Molly freed his face and whispered in his mouth, "We're the strongest people in the world," and then she put him on his back and didn't feel cold and kissed him in the quicksummer wind, glad of home.

Acknowledgments

More than ever, love and thanks to my wife, Nicole, and our son, Jack, both of whom supported this multiyear trip to an imaginary eighteenth century. They encouraged me from the start and spent many a patient hour listening to baroque music, visiting old taverns, and hearing me talk about Molly, Tom, and Nicholas.

This book's roots extend back to my childhood, when my parents exposed me to stories that thrilled me. Those early experiences eventually blended with my own son's love of story, and gave me—in middle age—a jolt of youthful energy. I fear I would have shriveled up, writing increasingly anemic books, if not for the blood transfusion of fatherhood.

I wrote the first part of *Bell Weather* in the company of our cat, Max, now deceased, and the second part with our dog, Bones. I love them both. Arlen Johnson helped me road test the plot. Nathan Kotecki helped me refine an early draft. C. J. Lais gave me humbling amounts of input and opportunities to ramble, and has been the best literary wingman imaginable.

My aunt Catherine remains a paragon of aunty greatness and has more terrific anecdotes than a frontier tavern keeper.

Richard Pine believed in this book well before I finished it. Several of his clients referred to him as "kind" before I signed with him, and it's true—he's a gentleman of the old school and a pleasure to know. Thanks also to Eliza Rothstein, Alexis Hurley, Nathaniel Jacks, and everyone at InkWell Management.

Michael Signorelli brought gusto and vision to the editing and publishing of *Bell Weather*. His suggestions made the story leaner and stronger, and I've always felt the book had his heartiest devotion. I'm glad to call him a friend. Thanks also to Stella Tan, Kenn Russell, Will Staehle, Stephen Rubin, Emily Kobel, Maggie Richards, Jason Liebman, Ebony LaDelle, Carolyn O'Keefe, and everyone at Henry Holt and Company. Ellen Pyle: I salute you.

Thanks to my friends Kurtis Albright and Melissa Batalin. Kurt's my right-hand man in lots of regular adventures and home-improvement high jinks. Melissa illustrated the astonishing maps included in this book, which are based on terribly drawn outlines I gave her. The lady is an artist.

Special thanks to all the readers and booksellers—especially Market Block Books in Troy, New York—who supported my previous novel.

Thanks to Corelli, Muffat, Handel, and Neil Gow's dead second wife. Cheers to Pratt & Pratt Archaeological Consultants, Inc., for providing info on Hartwell Tavern in Massachusetts, which served as the basis for the Orange. Additional thanks to the anonymous author of the old sea lyric, "Oh, 'twas in the Broad Atlantic," which I warped into Molly's mermaid song.

If anyone wishes to blend smoak-inspired coffee, I would very much like to hear about it. You can find me online at AuthorDennisMahoney.com and @Giganticide. I'll do my best to answer all emails.

About the Author

DENNIS MAHONEY is the author of *Fellow Mortals*, a
Booklist Top Ten Debut in 2013. He lives in upstate New
York with his wife, son, and dog. He can be found online
at AuthorDennisMahoney.com and @Giganticide.